Rivalry in Riding Boots

By
Annie Le Voguer

Copyright © 2020 Annie Le Voguer
All rights reserved.
ISBN: 9798570753020

DEDICATION

For my family and all the horses we've known and loved

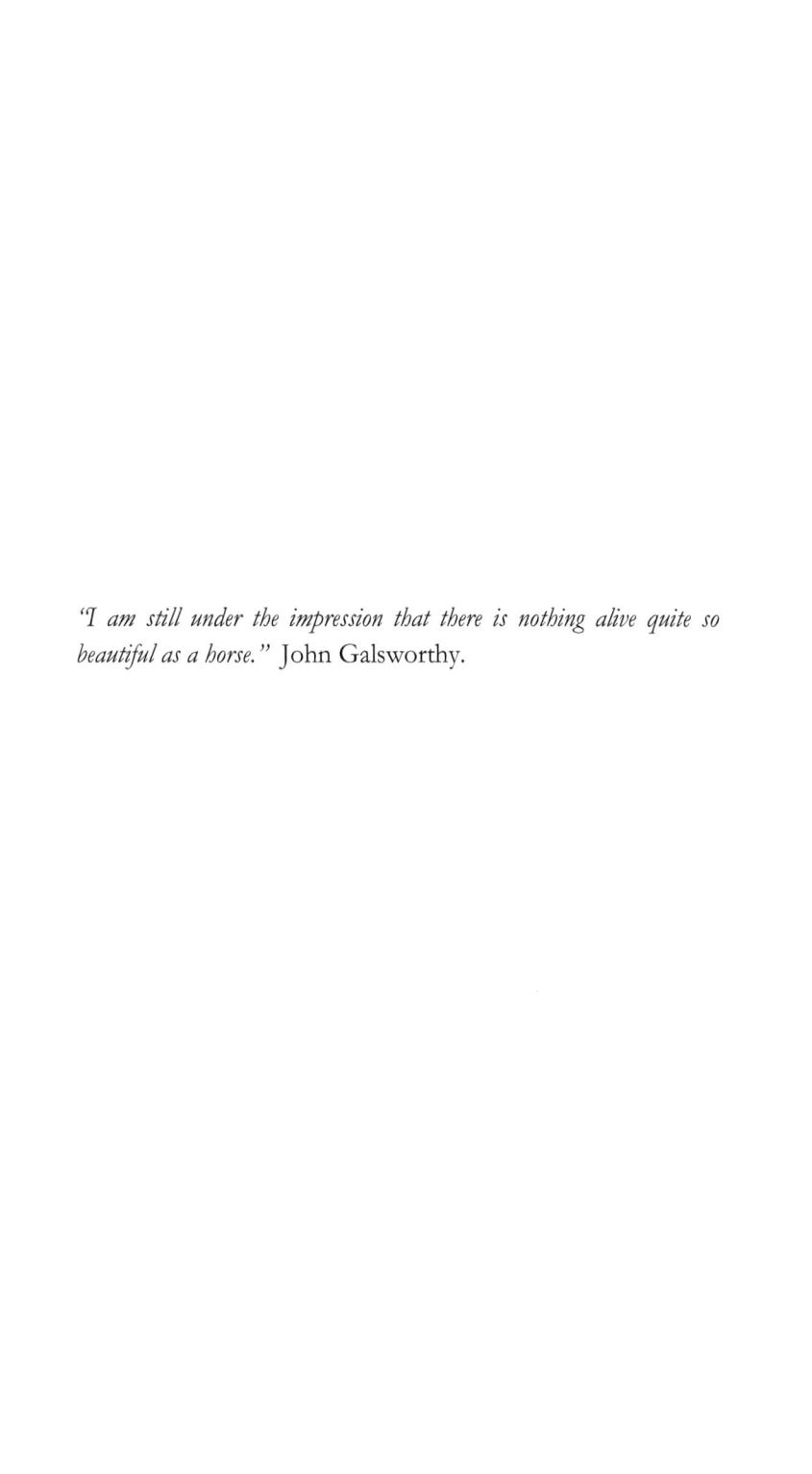

"I am still under the impression that there is nothing alive quite so beautiful as a horse." John Galsworthy.

CHAPTER ONE

Lilly hesitated, fiddling nervously with the car keys in her lap. Exhaled, tried to remain focused. This was it. This was the now or never moment she had been waiting for.

Another car crunched through the snow, made her jump out of her daze as it pulled up next to her. The driver looked at her through the window, grinned and gave her a wave. Karl Lister, the accountant.

With four other cars already parked up, it was a sign the team were all there. The pitch was on.

Her opportunity to create a fresh life, time to move on from the daily chaos of the livery yard. Currently her life was all about being the poker face of diplomacy when faced with an owner who asked the impossible for their horse. Or scouting for a freelance to cover when a groom texted her five minutes before duties to say they were sick. The horses, she loved. It was people that bothered her.

Glancing into the rear-view mirror, she tucked a stray auburn lock behind her ear, hoping the rest would remain in her scrunchy for the next couple of hours. It usually didn't.

"Karl, thanks for coming at short notice" Lilly called boldly as they both got out of their cars.

Hers, an ancient Fiesta she called Red Rocket. His, a black S Type Jaguar. Probably called curvylicious, in keeping with the sleek design. A bit like having a gleaming thoroughbred racehorse stood next to a shaggy Shetland pony.

She turned back to push the driver seat down, leant in to pull at the strap of the rucksack on the back seat. It had snagged on the saddle she'd slung in two days previous. She really needed to try it on Sage today, his owner was after a seventeen-inch black dressage fit, she could make fifty quid on the deal.

With one leg bent in, one stretched out behind her, she fiddled to free the buckle from the stirrup it was attached to.

Lilly could feel herself grow hot. Her face reddened up like an embarrassed school kid being called out by a teacher for forgetting her homework.

Of all days, today she wanted to look sleek and smooth. Like that Jag. Why had she left in such a rush? Why had she not just put the frickin' saddle in the tack room?

A firm tug of the rucksack whilst holding the saddle by the pommel, the neon pink and white bag finally gave way.

Lilly slammed the door shut in triumph, slung the bag over her shoulder, weighted down with A4 folders. One for each member of this coddled together Committee. She turned back to Karl, blew upwards to remove that stray wisp of hair now covering her left eye. The scrunchy was failing miserably in its job to keep the curls at bay.

Karl stood by his car with a lopsided grin on his face. A slim black leather briefcase with KL in gold neatly inscribed in the top corner held firmly in his right hand.

The pink flushed crimson on her face. Realisation dawned that he'd just had a view of her backside as she'd leaned in. In haste, she'd thrown on the red lacy knickers that she found on the floor. The same ones that she had been all too eager to allow Jay to remove the night before. Bugger. Now, through her stretched cream jodhpurs, she'd given this guy a glimpse too.

"Lilly." He pushed back his oversized glasses with a long, suntanned middle finger. The tortoiseshell rings made him look like an owl. A brown owl dressed in a pinstripe grey suit with a blue tie, covered in little yellow horseshoes.

"Always a pleasure to, um, see you."

"Are you wearing that for my luck or yours?" Lilly pointed to his tie, trying to distract from the ungainly scuffling, the underwear reveal. She was certain she could melt the snow settling at her feet if she got any hotter.

"Ah, matching socks too," he grinned. He brought his right leg up to his left knee, pulled at his trouser bottom with a flourish.

"I love it!" she declared, her eyes widening in exaggerated amazement. Great, bring the conversation back in touch, she thought.

"More important, where have you been to get a tan like that? Not your garden in this weather," she asked.

"Bermuda. I got home last Friday. A glorious thirty-two degrees, sun, sea, no triangle though," he replied merrily.

"You just masquerade as a boring chief accountant, don't you? I bet you were on the beach drinking margaritas with the senoritas, shmoozing the good life," she teased. "Now I know where that slight smell of coconut is from."

He winked at her, an eyebrow shooting up, reminiscent of Dwayne Johnson.

"Good, shall we? If I stay out any longer, my tan might fade," he joked.

Despite the pants on parade moment, he was a welcome reprieve. Ahead lay hard work to convince a formidable group to give her the green light. Right this minute, she wanted to throw up.

She sensed Karl was a genuine man, with his ready humour and open face. One you could depend on to do the right thing. Lilly hoped she could today.

Both pressed their key fobs. An ungainly clonk sounded heavy over the smooth higher pitched beep beep of the Jaguar. Just to add further humiliation. Well, her car may not be worth stealing, but that rogue saddle was valued at over a thousand pounds.

Brick pillars stood either side of the steps as they stepped up to the door.

Butterflies somersaulted in her stomach as she tried to fight back the nauseous feeling. Actually no. More a crescendo of bats flying into each other to escape the cave and go feed on the gnats that hung about the water troughs in May.

A flurry of snow had fallen that morning. Feeding all the horses on the yard, she'd had to break the ice on several water buckets as she went. A plastic bottle covered the lagging on the tap pipe, a trick to keep fresh water available. It was working. For now.

Lilly had thirty horses in her care. Alison, her head groom, had prepared feeds the previous day but it was always Lilly that distributed them. Stacked up in the big wheelbarrow, wobbling as if they'd tip over at any moment as she pushed it along the rows.

Despite the blackness and the cold, she loved that time of day. No one else about, just the sound of the horses waking, snorting, their breath like smokers in the cold. Whickers in anticipation of breakfast, the odd one kicking the door impatiently. This was her bliss.

She had slept little last night. Sleep was for nights when she was alone, not when sharing a bed, and his visit had been a very welcome one after two weeks apart. Country and status divided their lives. Great big chunky divisions that gave her doubts anything could come of it.

Was he really telling the truth when he said he was a one-woman man and she was his one woman? Could she dare believe he wasn't in fact saying that to all the babes in his bed?

He promised that she was the only one, claimed any sexual frustration was taken out in the hour-long gym workouts each evening. He also promised to get over more, suggested she could visit him?

Yeah, like that was so easy when you had responsibility of a yard full of horses and their daily care. Assurances aplenty that he wasn't a player, that he wanted a commitment.

Words. Words she wanted to believe. Dare she open her heart and let him in?

Oh yeah, she remembered with relish. She had been very keen to open her body and let him in last night, that's why she was so late. An early morning quickie when the alarm had shrilled the five a.m. wake up. Her body reacted at the memory.

Jay looked like he was being truthful as he said goodbye, caressing her cheek, his hand curled into her hair as he drew her back in for one last delicious kiss.

His thick dark eyebrows shot downwards to his nose like two diagonals, piercingly sky-blue eyes bore into her soul. He had gazed at her with such urgent desire; it was tough to pull away from the smouldering smooch.

Lilly could almost taste him now as the enormous door swung open, breaking her thoughts. Mrs C, the housekeeper, welcomed them both into the manor.

"Come in, both of you. I've left out hot coffee and croissant, and your green tea, Lilly." The little woman with a soft voice, severe blue grey bun and plump cheeks motioned them inside, closing the protective barrier of heavy wooden oak door behind them from the swirl of frozen air attempting to invade the inner warmth.

Lilly welcomed the heat of the hallway as she removed her coat and boots, slipping on the fleecy white slippers laid out underneath the coat rail.

She knew Mrs C was a stickler in keeping the outdoors outside and away from her clean floor. It offered less housework, something Lilly approved of. She had enough to do cleaning up after horses.

With an involuntary shiver she folded her arms about her. Skin friction worked to warm up. Last night, skin friction….. oh snap out of it, she muttered under her breath.

"Everyone's in the dining room, this way". Mrs C walked them across the shiny black and white chequerboard floor to the far end of the hall, second door on the right.

This is the big lifetime goal moment. Stop with the flashbacks, it was only sex. Unbelievable sex, accepted, but this, this today, this is the future. Lilly crossed the hall, mind-punching herself to focus.

As she stepped, she smoothed sweaty palms down her thighs, her heart boomed in her chest. The bong of the grandfather clock made her jump as it struck the hour.

Nerves jingled; doubt picked away at the steely determination previously so strong on the drive up. A resolve that had gripped her as the flakes fell and the car slipped along the farm track already covered in a fine white coat, the wipers furiously keeping her screen clear as she tore along.

Lilly now wondered if she'd done the right thing wearing her equestrian clothing. She'd argued the point with herself, smart suit versus horse gear.

Admittedly, she didn't have a smart suit, or any suit come to that, but the swing-o-meter had been that she wanted to project what she represented. That she was in the business of horses, plain and simple.

She patted down the pocket insert across the front of her forest green jumper. The last thing she needed was for something to clonk out onto the table by mistake mid-flow, like a hoof pick or a curry comb.

It was top of the range horse gear, made by Marengo, the number one fashion in equestrian wear. One of her full-time liveries owned the company and the top had been a Christmas present.

She must make sure it was pulled down over her arse though, or they'd all have the flash of red lace.

"Do I look ok?" she asked Karl before they entered.

"It's not what you wear but how you wear it, my dear," he clarified. That elongated finger pushed his glasses up his nose again, more than just reassurance on his face.

She cursed loudly in her head. Did she actually appear presentable or was he talking about her underwear?

Either way, it was too late to change. They were all in the room waiting.

At their entrance, Piers rose to his feet, strode over to shake Karl by the hand, kiss Lilly on each cheek.

Piers Wingfield Brown. Owner of this manor, the estate, her yard, and a multi-million-pound business. Albeit largely retired, he retained a token seat on the Board, along with a few Directorships of charities and trusts. His opinion was valuable, it would certainly sway the vote.

She was glad they had a good rapport. That she continued to encourage him to visit the yard when he felt low. Following the loss of his wife two years ago, he had spiralled into a state of despair. With gentle persuasion from the Board, he stepped down from running his empire.

On those visits, Lilly offered coffee and time. Often, they sat together in her lounge as he re-countered memories of his youth. The swashbuckling days, as he called them, a time when he mixed with Duran Duran in Rio, partied like Jagger in New York, drank cocktails in Juans Les Pins. Many a polo tournament too, often with Prince Charles, in Argentina. Golden years.

She would laugh with him at the stories. As his face became animated a twinkle would appear. This twinkle could develop into a mist of laughter or tears as his recollections spilt out over a cheese and pickle sandwich.

Janette had walked into his life at the international Hockmead show. His eyes lit up bright each time he recounted the story. How he'd been enchanted by her eyes, the blue of the brightest summer day. He had never left her side until the day she died.

It would be at this point he'd get his hankie out and dab at his eyes, melancholy etched on his still relatively handsome yet weary face.

Today, however, Lilly saw him animated, back in the game, eyes alert. His thinning white hair tumbled over his forehead with purpose as he pumped hands with everyone, joking and smiling.

A Committee gathered to decide whether to give the go ahead for a project she first raised with him months back.

How many hours must she have spent? From a spark she built a bonfire, poured over google maps of the fields on the estate, pieced together a route, researched costs, sponsorship, even the tiniest of detail such as the design of the rosette.

The final folder was placed on each of the seven settings. She plugged the laptop into the overhead projector. As the lamp flickered into life, so did her plan. A background image of the manor grounds, thick black typeface over the middle:

'WINGFIELD THREE DAY TRIALS – THE PROPOSAL'

CHAPTER TWO

As everyone made their way to their seats, she scrutinised them. With a cup in one hand, a hot pastry or biscuit juggled on the edge of the saucer, she imagined how they felt. Hoped the joviality was positive and not reactionary to the snacks. A thoughtful touch. Note to self, send Mrs C flowers for the effort made on her behalf.

With a scrape of his chair, Piers stood. Drew himself up to his full six feet, clapped to announce silence. The room fell quiet.

Lilly noticed that Karl had opened the folder and was studying the contents, nibbling on a digestive.

Sat motionless, staring at the screen was Mark Larch, Director of Wingfield Aggregates. A figure trusted by Piers, not by Lilly. She wondered if he was silently willing that the projector's bulb would blow and along with it, her break.

Steel grey hair moulded to his head with a good dollop of gel. He had taken off his jacket, placed it over the back of the chair. His shirt appeared starched rigid, creases down each arm that might cut through wood. She wondered now if his pyjamas had creases on the sleeves too.

Pam Cook. PR guru for Wingfield Group plc. No doubt primed to pull apart her attempt at event marketing. Pam sat to Mark's left, her highlighted blonde hair a perfect bob, full face make-up with bright red lipstick. A navy-blue military style dress fitted like a glove.

She must be about the same age as me, Lilly assumed, yet different world. Make up? She couldn't remember the last time she'd worn anything other than mascara, maybe a bit of lippy.

Just how long would she need to create a face as perfect? Too long, she suspected. Likely as not, she'd be able to get four stables mucked out, and a dozen haynets made up in the same time.

At the far end of the table sat Dean Mullins. He shot her a conspiratorial glance as he bit into his croissant, flakes spilling down his red pullover. Some landed in his hipster beard which he brushed away surreptitiously to the floor.

Manager of the local Council events team, they'd been after opening the Estate to the public for years. Guaranteed to vote yes. Preliminary meetings with his team had helped with some crucial facts and figures.

Next was Joe. Farmer of the two-thousand-acre estate. He too had worked with her in terms of footprint, or hoofprint. Although, he had made it clear he would go with `whatever Mr. Wingfield decides'.

At twenty-eight, he was the youngest in the room. Being the size and shape of a bear, she amazed how he blended into the background. No doubt due to his quiet demeanour and choice of seat at the far end by the projector.

Not to be underestimated as only last year he introduced revolutionary technology to the estate and was being touted as an industry motivator. Lilly recalled the description in Farmers World, an economic and environmental saviour. Piers looked on him like a second son.

Lilly moved on around the table, analysing each one gathered to decide on her dream.

Karl. Could go either way.

The man himself, Piers. Well, who knew how he'd be persuaded? Aware his moods could swing dependent on his choice of breakfast, let alone a board discussion.

Last but no means least, on the far end of the table, someone one hundred percent team Lilly. Carole Beattie, from Horse & Hound magazine. She agreed to attend to help emphasise the importance of such an event.

Both for the equine industry and the local economy. Scarf wrapped around her neck as if she were about to walk the Matterhorn. She turned the pages of her folder with keen interest.

"Good morning and thank you all for being here," Piers began.

"Quick introductions so everyone knows who you all are. I'll start by asking you to say your name and why you're here, Lilly, you go first."

She stood up, a little shaky, smiling as boldly as she could.

"Hi, my name is Lilly Marshall. I run the Wingfield Equestrian Livery yard and I'm asking you all here today to approve the formation of the three-day horse trials set amongst these lovely grounds."

"Thank you, Lilly, I'll go next. Piers Wingfield Brown, and these are my lovely grounds the proposal is based upon." He chuckled as he sat back down.

Once the room knew name and job title, Lilly clicked the clicker that started the power point presentation. The one she'd reworked a hundred times. Anxious it be slick and professional. No turning back.

All her life she'd been around horses. First as a child, then gaining an equine diploma at college. A further two years teaching children and adults the art of sitting on a horse and staying on.

It always went ok until she summoned the dreaded words 'trot on'. Then she'd watch the rider bounce helplessly, or fall, or be unable to even get the unhelpful steed to trot more than five paces before returning to a walk.

She had enjoyed getting them over this and into a unified 'up, down' to the horse's gait.

The line goes that you need to fall off fifty times to be a good rider. In her eyes, to be a rider at all, you needed to pass the trotting stage.

A few other jobs in-between. Now this.

The livery yard had been home for the last two years. Whilst Lilly loved her business, it was hard work, physically and mentally, the days endless.

Always an incident; fencing would break; someone would complain the wrong rug had been put on their horse; a shoe would be thrown on the morning of a show. Or, as she was prayed would not happen again, the pipes froze and there was no running water.

She'd lost count of the times she'd been kicked, knocked over or squashed by horses vying to get in or out of their fields. Trapped between them, dangling by a lead rope, being ignored as she shouted 'whoa there'.

Not to mention money was tight. Just when she thought she had enough to invest in new equipment, something happened that took that spare cash. She hardly ever took a wage and the fourteen-hour days were taking their toll.

If this event proved a success, Lilly planned to hire more staff, take a backseat and spend her time developing the trials to make them better each year.

Less of the daily chores, more time with Jay, remain involved with horses without the constant smell of wee soaked straw on her clothes. Not so much Amen to that, but Ammonia.

She'd approached Piers with the idea just before Christmas. He knew several people on whose estate such sporting events took place.

His response was positive, the thought of so much activity took him back to the old days when the manor was party central. There was a but, he needed to make sure it was watertight. Every aspect checked. He didn't want his grounds ruined in a free for all. Or his reputation.

So here they were today. In summing up, Lilly knew Dean and Dawn were on side. Mark was the sticking point, which meant Pam, Karl, Piers and Joe might be too.

Mark was not a fan of horses, viewing the proposal as a half-baked horse gymkhana filled with Thelwell style children falling off and screaming, not a vision he felt matched the company profile. His position being that the potential failure would reflect on the reputation of Wingfield Aggregates. It would be a no from him.

Lilly pressed the clicker for the next slide, pinched herself for luck. Exhaled the air held tight within her that altered her voice several notches higher than usual.

"I'll run through my presentation with you. I'll be happy to answer any questions you may have after that."

She scanned the room to see that she had their attention. A quick sip of water and away.

"A little background." She faced the screen which displayed a line of cavalrymen, all ready for battle.

"Where did eventing start and why? Well, its roots go back to the days of comprehensive cavalry tests. Those required the rider and horse to master several disciplines.

Steadiness in parade, being able to cross-country at speed in battle, plus the fitness and agility. These offered the rider a better chance of survival."

Click. Next slide.

"Ever wondered where the word management comes from? Lord Cavendish, first Duke of Newcastle." She used the laser on her clicker to beam a red light onto his face.

"Back in the 1600s, he established the manege. An indoor arena where he could practice his skills. Prowess in this art demonstrated an accomplished horseman.

"Today, when you manage your team well, you offer a stable environment. See how our language, even in business, involves horses." She paused a moment to take in the acknowledgement about the table, in particular Mark, who remained stony faced.

"I've got the bit between my cheeks on this," she added. A couple of chuckles.

Click. New slide. One in which a horse leapt a fallen tree against the backdrop of Burghley estate.

"Burghley. One of only six events in the world at five-star stage. The best of the best. Burghley started out in 1961 with just nineteen competitors and twelve thousand spectators. Today, four hundred and fifty horses take part, eighty are the best in the world. One hundred and seventy thousand spectators. Some six hundred exhibitors and food stalls."

Give them facts and figures, Jay had said. Money. Makes the impact in a Boardroom. Deliver up the potential for making money.

She relaxed into her stride. Nerves faded; her passion fired up as she continued the presentation. She proposed three main classes and to follow guidelines, she had poured over the British Evening rules and regs right at the start of this journey. Checked and double checked every element of the course.

So far, so good.

"Now, the financial projections." Lilly noted that even Mark was checking her spreadsheet as she spoke. Head bent, pencil running down the page. At least he was listening.

"Yes. This is not your everyday pony club event. This is high end, high spend, high quality sport," she pitched.

"I've detailed every aspect of projected income and outgoing. You'll find it all in your packs. Though, to avoid a protracted presentation, I'm happy to explain any of it later.

Lilly wanted to establish a first-class national equestrian event. Maybe take it to international level.

"To conclude. My vision is for The Wingfield Horse trials to become an established name on the circuit. Thank you for listening."

Lilly sat down to a round of applause.

Mark was straight in. Chose not to clap, or even wait until the clapping stopped.

"All very slick, Lilly, but is the world ready for yet another horse event? I refer to page seventeen in your folder, a calendar from last year's eventing activities. I count twenty-five. Accepted, I may have seen clips of Badminton on TV. But to be honest, I'd rather go to Silverstone for the cars, a premier league football match even. I suspect others will agree. It's elite, old fashioned, just like your Lord Cavendish." With a smirk, he looked about, searching for approval.

As the conversation battled between for and against, Lilly noticed the snow was falling heavier, a blur of white through the windows that made her think about the horses, that the water troughs would be iced over in the far pasture.

Some didn't mind the snow, but access to fresh water would be essential. She'd drive past on the way back and check.

Karl brought her back to the session. "I see this as potential revenue for the estate. We've looked at detaching running costs from the company for a while.

With the right-wing roof in need of urgent repair, would this not be a prospect worth considering? Net profit figures along with year-in growth could offer a solution."

"Where is our Vice President today?" asked Pam. "Do we have his opinion, maybe it would help everyone vote?"

"I had hoped my son would be here today too." Piers replied. "He flew in overnight but had to drive up to Sheffield first thing on a call out from Wingfield quarry." He looked across at Mark. "Didn't Julian call you?"

"No. I tried first thing this morning, but his phone went to answer."

"I caught him." Joe spoke in his deep Hampshire burr. It suited him, an earthy quality that stood out amongst the well-spoken Londoners. "Last night, he's been helping me with a funding proposal."

A mop of black hair fell out around his cap, three-day-old stubble covered his chin. Lack of time, not designer. Lambing was in full swing.

"Said it would give his dad something to do. Something not business related."

Mark spluttered loudly.

"Hardly the seal of approval," he muttered.

"Maybe not, but he also said I were to add his yes to the vote." Joe added, eyes full of mischief.

"He said yes?" Mark questioned, rolling his eyes with an audible sigh.

"Aye, he did. Sent me the text to confirm it too. Said I was to show you as you may question my word."

Joe searched about in the large pocket of his baggy fleece for his iPhone. The room alive with drawn breath, whispers.

"Here you go." He thrust the phone towards Mark, who sat three people down. Mark squinted, refocused his eyes on the screen. A scowl of disgust and inevitability appeared.

Lilly returned to the room with a jerk as Joe made his revelation. Her heart was in her mouth, surely this was going to persuade Piers to push for a yes?

"I'd like to record my strong objections; I refuse to be held account further down the line when it's goes pear-shaped." Mark stated, annoyance written over his face. He shifted on his chair, irritated by the fait accompli.

"Acknowledged. Thank you, Mark." Piers glanced at his watch, clapped his hands together.

"Ok, shall we wrap this up? I expect you are keen to return to your jobs. A show of hands please, all in favour of the Wingfield Horse trials?"

He looked around the room. All hands up, except Mark.

"Splendid. Lilly, you have the go ahead." He gave her a broad smile.

Out of the corner of her eye, she caught Mark about to say something. Probably that his hand had not been raised. He shuffled the folder and papers into his briefcase, snapping it shut. His chair almost fell as he jumped up, grabbed his jacket then strode out of the room, radiating disapproval.

"Lunch?" Piers whispered to Lilly hopefully.

"What do you have to offer?" she whispered back, continuing to nod and thank people as they filed out.

"No meat, I assure you, I've been told by the doctor to cut down. Likelihood it'll be something green, I seem to be turning into a rabbit these days." His eyes turned down; mouth formed a fake pout. "No chance of being an old rebel, I'm afraid. Mrs C's cleared the freezer of the hidden sausages behind the peas." He let out a dramatic sigh.

"Go on, Piers, lunch it is," she accepted. High on the adrenaline surging through her body, she owed him another hour of her time.

CHAPTER THREE

The ice had already been broken in every field as she checked on her way back. Lilly stopped for a moment to take some photos on her phone, the sky had cleared and a weak sun had appeared.

The land lay in front of her a deep white, several horses kicking up the snow with their hooves as they cantered about.

The boughs of the oak trees on the left bowed with the weight, droplets of water falling as the snow melted. She'd post the photos onto the yard facebook page, a fun moment of horse play.

Back at the yard, Lilly stopped in on Alison to see if there was anything urgent. Reassured, she agreed to be back in time for the afternoon shift. Part of the day when horses needed to be brought in, hooves picked out, mud hosed off legs.

Once in the stable turnout rugs had to be taken off, stable rugs on, horses feeds, hay, top up water. The daily winter routine.

Ruby, her little brown Staffie, was waiting in the hallway. She flung herself at Lilly's legs as she bounced about with the joy of a dog.

"Miss me, did you, sweetie? Sorry, this time I couldn't take you. How's about a treat as you've been such a good girl?" She fussed over her companion, reached for a biscuit from the jar she kept by the front door.

Ruby gave a little woof in delight, scoffed down her bone shaped delicacy in two crunches, wagged her tail, eyes eager for another.

Lilly's kitchen and lounge shouted horse. Walls adorned with various photos and paintings of horses she had known and loved. At one point she wondered if it she over-cluttered. Then she reminded herself, you can never have enough pictures of horses. The collection continued to grow.

Rosettes, trophies and plaques decorated the pale blue walls. Most were from her moments of success in the ring. A turquoise and pink rosette, her first and most special, had pride of place, framed with a photo. A clear round, aged nine, on a pony borrowed from the riding school where she helped out.

In exchange for the work, she'd received a weekly lesson. Even though the rosette was faded, it represented the beginning. From first small success to present day. A much larger win. She gave a little shudder of excitement at this reflection.

The lounge doubled as a meet for the team every Monday morning. Over coffee they would chat about upcoming events, both on site and the shows liveries wanted to attend that involved preparation.

A relaxed and comfortable setting, the drawback being that the floor was usually covered in bits of shaving, hay and general muck from the yard. No matter how much she hoovered. In all honesty, hoovering was low down on the list of objectives after a full day outside.

Occasionally, she just about managed to eat her dinner before falling asleep, never mind being Queen of clean indoors.

Upstairs lay her sanctuary, a haven in which to unwind. Only one other saw this inner sanctum. And Ruby. Her little pink bed and blanket set out at the foot of the bed.

Blood still pumping, she needed to remain active. With a glance around at the clutter she began to grab items to tidy. Leg bandages spilt over the coffee table she threw in the washing machine along with brushing boots, a couple of towels and a hoodie, ready to switch on later.

Next, she turned to the tack. Lilly kept a large bucket in the corner for body parts. Already half full with bits, cheek pieces, reins, the odd browband, a couple of stirrups and a riding boot. Who was walking around with just the one? The boot had been there for at least two weeks now.

Some pieces needed a stitch, some a clean. Others were things that people brought with them and forgot as they left.

Eventually, they would root them back out when they remembered.

Tidy complete, she picked up the mugs that lay about. Filled the kitchen sink with hot soapy water, placed them in to soak.

The window above the basin looked out to the yard to the right. To the left, fields reached down as far as the main road, a drive split down the middle. Near the bottom of that drive, tucked away from view, was the DIY area. She could just see the start of the car park from here, but not the stables.

Lilly settled at the kitchen table, picked a numnah that had been left on the chair to wash, under which lay her laptop, the latest issue of Horse and Hound on top.

Before she could dance about the floor doing her winner winner chicken dinner dance, she focused. Ever the professional.

She had to check emails, texts and look on Facebook, put the photos up. The account was used by all for posting information, several used it to ask her for last minute extra services.

Being 'friends' with many of her clients on their personal sites also meant that she knew what they were up to. If they'd been out late, had an argument, upcoming holiday plans, and moods.

Feeling 'meh' or an angry emoji could upset the atmosphere on the yard from pleasant to hysterical. 'In a relationship' might tip into anarchy.

She also wanted to update the spreadsheets with the services from yesterday. This information was all in the big diary she took earlier after seeing Alison.

The yard Bible, the most important document of all. Filled with the life of the yard, purporting to the daily schedule. From the neat inputted duties written up each Sunday to scrawled notes. 'Tov had an extra haynet'. 'On a course, please can you ride Noddy'. Or 'Bo needs one sachet of bute in his night feed for the next week'.

If she didn't input these changes every day, she worried things might go astray, become mixed up, missed out, which may cause accounts going out wrong.

Only last week, at the start of the month, she'd had one client complain about additional costs that she was able to show had, in fact, been requested. It all worked because she was such a stickler for detail.

Lilly usually covered this job after morning feeds. Time when she had a quiet hour to herself. Today, it was past two o'clock. If she didn't get the book back out before bring-in time, the grooms may forget the add-ons.

That or write them on a scrap of paper that they might then lose. With winter tasks such as washing down muddy legs, the one pound fifty might not appear much. But it added up with twenty odd horses seven days a week.

By sitting down and concentrating, Lilly hoped it would calm her down. Stop the shaking of excitement that gripped her. It made her jump about like a madwoman with little whoops of delight.

Her mind was on full gallop. She needed to calm, prepare how to tell the team the good news.

Methodically, she worked through to find each owner, the additional fee input against the horse. Next, she scored out the diary note in green highlighter to acknowledge its entry.

How would she start?

"Guys, I'm going to be less hands on for a few months." No, that was not a good opening bid. They'd immediately see extra stables lined up for them.

"Guys, I need your help." Better. Get them on side, be sympathetic.

As she fumbled about for words her phone beeped. A message from Jay.

"Great news, my red-hot entrepreneur. Sorry for late reply, it's been a long drive. Catch up later xx."

She smiled. She'd sent him a text as the Committee said their goodbyes, desperate to call him but knowing it would go to answerphone. His six-figure salary didn't offer time in the day for frivolities like personal calls, he'd stated from the outset. Often it didn't offer time in the evening either. But she wouldn't focus on that right now.

Lilly replied, with lots of kisses and a naughty gif. She hoped catch up meant he'd be able to make another overnight stop.

He seemed so different to the last man she'd fallen in love with. But that one had seemed so right to start with too. She shuddered. She *never* wanted to encounter one like him again. Ever.

A fleeting memory flashed in her mind. Wayne, the ranch hand. Or should that be randy hand? She'd worked with him on a ranch close to Carson City, Nevada, the ranch where she'd gone to train mustangs just weeks after her twenty-first birthday.

Fact. Her real-life cowboy turned out to be more Crystal meth than Rhinestone. His star-spangled rodeos were drug splatted romps, and he would NEVER get cards and letters from her.

Fuckaroo was, in fact, how she had described him to his face. It was the day she'd had enough and fled to Reno to pick up a flight home.

One lucky night at a casino and he'd spent the next month snorting the money up his nose whilst cavorting with prostitutes in the nearby brothels. Not her type of guy after all.

Jay was the first man Lilly had allowed back into her life since having her heart broken. The previous ten years she'd chosen to focus on horses.

They met at a summer ball for the local pony club. Her best friend, Rico, persuaded her to go along as his plus one. She expected to make polite conversation, watch as others drank too much, danced until they threw up, or stagger into bushes with a willing partner for a casual sexual encounter.

But as Rico led her to their table, there he sat. To the left of her place setting, sporting a tan that looked like he'd just walked off the beach in St Tropez. His dark eyebrows drawing her into intense blue eyes. Blue like a Greek coastline on a summer day. She knew that because it had been her one and only holiday destination.

He jumped up to pull out her chair as she stood dazzled by his Hollywood smile. When his fingers touched her, a shudder shot through her, one she'd thought dead and buried.

Handsome, charming, witty and extremely attentive. He could have his pick of women and there were plenty that flirted and flaunted before him that night, desperate to get his attention.

They had clicked instantly, talked the night away. Followed up by more nights whenever he was in the country. Six months in, Lilly stalled at making it public. She was determined to get this event up and running before making such a commitment, wanted to make sure she was actually ready for the next step.

"I promise, I will even change my Facebook page to 'in a relationship', please wait," she'd pleaded just the night before.

Love had not been on her agenda. She reminded herself that career came first. If he really was the one, he'd give her that. If not, well, she didn't want to consider it.

To halt further dissection of her love life, Lilly closed the laptop with a snap. She grabbed her coat, called to Ruby, and went back out to bring in the horses.

The process was never smooth. In the snow, mud and freezing cold conditions, horses tended to play up more, eager to get to their stables where a haynet would be waiting, a dry floor, a warm fleece instead of the wet rug.

They jostled each other at the gate, paced up and down, threw their necks high, whinnying with expectation, adding to the already churned up mud.

You would think it be a simple enough task to hook a head-collar over the head. Not when they all wanted in at the same time. They pushed against the field gate, an ominous creak as the weight of several horses vied for prime position. With a high-pitched squeal, a pair of hooves would fly out with a splatter of mud flying in several directions.

A successful capture of one. But they took the horses in pairs.

Now the game would hot up. With her left hand gripped to the lead rope of one, she had to push several horses aside to step towards the other pair. Her boot may be sucked down into the mire, leave her rooted in position.

Or worse, dangled at the end of the lead rope. One boot on, one boot firmly in the mud, one socked leg bent at the knee so as not to make contact with the ground.

The process was similar to making it through the legs of a rugby scrum whilst spinning plates.

This winter, Lilly had fenced off fields to reduce the herds into smaller groups in an attempt to avoid riots, it gave the grooms a fighting chance in the Gladiatorial battle. She didn't want an injury; a flying kick could be lethal.

In the summer months it was the total opposite. Horses weren't interested in leaving behind their lush grass. A walk through a field towards the horse you wanted to catch, its head down, casually grazing. Until you were within touching distance. Head would come up. A withering gaze. A turn to swish its tail in your face, to trot away to the furthest corner of the field.

Today, with minimal fuss, all horses and grooms made it back in one piece. Legs washed, hooves picked out, stable rugs in place. Finally left to merrily munch on their evening meal with contented noises, an occasional kick against feed bucket as the team completed their day.

Lilly elected to make her announcement at the team meet next morning. She figured it gave her time to gather up ideas, prepare a rota, include them in the organisation. She bid them goodnight, headed inside to make herself some food and begin her notes.

Half way through eating, there was a furious knocking at the door. Lilly glanced at the time on her phone. Seven fifteen. Panic spread over her. Had someone taken a fall in the sandschool? She knew several owners were outside. The staff may have finished at five, but people showed up after their own work to ride in her floodlit sandschool.

"Whoa with the banging, I'm on my way," she shouted as she got up.

Taylor, the teenager from the DIY yard, stood on the doorstep looking pale and worried.

"Robin has got out of his stable again. Eaten all the feeds left out for the morning. I don't know which horse has what, so I can't make more up. They're going mad, kicking their doors like they're going to break them down. And I'm worried Robin now looks like he may have given himself colic," she wailed.

"That little bugger, I suppose she forgot the kick bolt on the bottom of the door. For the hundredth time. I've warned her, if that bloody horse gets out one day, he'll kill himself." Lilly muttered more to herself than the girl before her.

Picking up a coat, she pulled on her boots, told Ruby to stay put. With a shiver as the icy night air hit her, she ran with Taylor as fast as she could down the track to view the damage.

No one else was at the DIY yard, they had all been up already. Ridden, well maybe, their horse put away for the night. She knew Taylor was always first up in the morning and last at night. Dedicated to her little grey showjumper, Mystic. Come spring, it would be a different matter, with warmer and lighter evenings. Then, all the owners would stay til late, drink coffee, even make dinner in the compact kitchen. It offered a chance to be social and talk horse.

But now, pitch black and with a light drizzle hitting the snow that remained from the morning's fall, the car park was empty.

Lilly felt sure the sludge would be compacted ice by the morning. She made a mental note to send out a text message to warn her team to take care tomorrow.

The routine with owners on this section would be to leave out their bucket of feed by the stable door for the morning, covered with a waterproof stretched fabric, often with the name of their beloved horse machine-sewn across the top. Or with the obvious 'morning feed' stated in pre-prepared lettering.

Whoever was up first would do the round, throw the bucket over the door. Some might even have left hay alongside a note, asking to check the water.

They all knew that it would be Taylor. Although she didn't seem to complain. She needed to feed her horse before returning home to change and catch the school bus. Her view being, why leave the others go hungry whilst hers tucked into his breakfast?

This yard had been the original stable block close to the back exit of the estate. Built over fifty years ago, the increase in horses led to the larger yard being created further up, the main livery. These buildings remained empty until Lilly came along.

She had seen value on an initial outlay of her own money to have them tidied up. Wood replaced as needed, plus a good coat of paint to brighten the faded doors.

She reasoned that not all horse lovers had the means to pay for livery. After all, she had never been able to afford to buy a horse. Over the years her journey had been to offer free labour in exchange for rides.

A lack of funds, or the owner preferred direct involvement in every aspect of their horses' life. Just two examples for being DIY.

To enjoy every spare moment of their life to care for their horse. She got that. There was something very satisfying in the daily routine of horse ownership. Lilly wouldn't be in the industry otherwise.

However, was there an excuse for not getting up to feed your horse? Well, yes, she considered on reflection. If someone else says they will do it for you. Just tip a bucket over the door, then yes, a temptation anyone would bite at.

How many times had she wished she could pull the blankets up a bit higher, give herself another half hour? As a student at Pinnington, taking her two-year diploma in equine studies, she'd had no choice but to get up before dawn. In order to get a course discount, the deal was to be a working pupil. To look after the college horses and those on livery.

Time and again she had been tempted to not look at the weather app. To avoid the realisation of another cold long day ahead. Though, when you rugged up horses ready for turnout, you had to have an idea of the weather to decide which rug. Or two.

The DIY stable block came with its own setup. A wash area, muck heap, tack room, toilet. It also had a kitchen big enough for a few chairs. They shared four acres among the ten horses. Fields that reached down to the road at the back entrance to the estate.

As a result of the limited grazing, there were strict rules on time out. The current one allowed only two hours.

In the summer, it reached up to seven hours as the grass grew quicker. In the midst of winter, to avoid a mud hole, two hours was enough.

A pocket of time to offer a bit of exercise for the horse, to enable them to at least stretch legs. Usually, the horse would wonder about for a few minutes before returning to the gate. Then it would hang its head over the metal bar for the remaining one hour fifty.

Lilly had asked Piers for the extra four acres that he owned across the road. The land led down into a beautiful valley with a small wood where hares would run from in the spring and bluebells could be found in abundance.

There was even a stream that ran through in a snake like way into a little waterfall at the furthest end of the copse. It would save lugging water containers back and forth.

An ideal problem solver, she could fence off into squares, even offer individual turnout. It had been a firm no. He claimed the whole area was allocated for a project, one yet to materialise.

She didn't push further, but determined to raise the subject again shortly. She had plans to provide better facilities for this section. It was important to have the whole yard running smoothly before the summer. After that she'd have no spare time to manage the usual moans on the issue of grazing.

Piers had suggested the DIY horses be mixed into the livery fields. No way was that even a possibility. All too aware of the snobbery amongst the equine owners at the main yard. Several did not want to share with what they termed the riff raff of DIY.

To add to the case would be the problem of bites or kicks. Imagine the insurance claims. The pointed fingers. Cross words. All ugly scenarios to avoid. This was the main reason she kept the DIY down on the lower yard. She did not need the clash of personalities or the risk of argument. There was enough of it already without additional reasons for a gripe.

"So, where's Robin now?" Lilly looked over to Taylor as they jogged across the car park.

A clever ex polo pony, run into the ground by an unscrupulous owner. He struggled to keep weight on, always looked malnourished. Vicky bought him for two hundred pounds to save him from the container headed for the Parisian abattoir.

Whilst fairly successful at local shows in her teens for a few years, that was before she fell pregnant. Now a single mother, living with her mum, she struggled to find time to do anything with him. Despite the lack of time, she refused to sell him.

"I put him back in his stable, but he looked a bit rough." Taylor replied.

"And the others?"

"As mad as hell."

On cue, they could hear the commotion of nine outraged animals.

"Any of them on meds?"

"Bess has half a sachet of bute for her leg. I think Terry said he was giving Austen supplements, not sure which. Otherwise, it's mostly chaff, nuts and a few helpings of beet."

"And the beet has been soaked?"

"Yes, as far as I'm aware. But at least five take it in their feed, so he's eaten a large amount."

"Did he eat all the feeds?" Lilly continued to quiz Taylor for information. It would help her assess Robin quickly. An overdose of medication could be serious. Too much beet, even well soaked, would still bloat his stomach and result in an impacted gut.

"As good as. He must have been out for a while. I came back from a lesson at Ivy's. I took Mystic out of the horsebox, round to the stables to find Robin wondering about. He's taken the covers of all the buckets. Five are clean, the rest are eaten to varying degree."

They arrived at the block. Set in an open square with five stables on the left, five in the middle, the storage and kitchen area to the right.

The night spotlight came on above the far end. It offered a yellow glow to the central yard, dark shadows stretched towards the stables like the setting of a whodunnit.

But it was clear who the culprit was in this crime scene. He was back behind bars awaiting sentence.

Lilly paused at the entrance.

"Ok, Taylor. Is there a list anywhere in the feed room of who has what?"

"Some, not all."

"Best we put the buckets away for now. I'll work through that once we have the sick boy under control. Which one is he in?" She remembered the horse, but not which stable.

Taylor took her over. Looking over the bottom half of the door, it was clear Robin was feeling the effect of over-eating. He stood at the back of his stable, faced the wall, his head down, ears back.

"Thanks, Taylor, leave him to me, you carry on untacking Mystic. Where's your mum?"

"She was driving the box back home, then coming back with the car to pick me up."

"Good, so you're under control at least!" Lilly teased.

The girl smiled with relief.

Taking the headcollar and lead rope from the hook by the door, Lilly entered. In a soft voice, she spoke soothingly to the horse, the headcollar at her side. Robin looked round at her. Fidgeted on his legs. Remained still.

"You stupid boy. You don't learn do you, third or fourth time now isn't it?" she soothed. She reached the horse, stroked his cheek as she murmured to him. With a fluid motion, slipped the headcollar over his head, hooked the clip at the side of his right cheek to secure it in place.

"Come on, let's check you over."

Lilly led him out with a tug on the rope to encourage him to move. His reluctance offered her further evidence that he was not well. Once outside, she tied him up on the ring with a treble release knot, to be on the safe side.

With her fingers she pressed about his belly, felt how tight it was. If she had a pin, it would probably pop.

Half a bute wouldn't cause him any issue, but the beet had doubtless been too much. All that extra sugar that he wasn't used to. He managed a couple of farts as she pressed in, her head near his tail.

"Thanks mate," she muttered.

"Have you phoned Vicky?" Lilly called over to Taylor who headed towards the tack room. She hurried, saddle over her right arm, bridle slung over left shoulder. A bright green woolly hat sat firm on her head as the temperature continued to plummet. A drizzle of sleet fell, highlighted in the spotlight's yellow glow.

"Yes. Said she couldn't get up as she had no-one to look after Jessie. She's asked if I'd keep an eye on him till her mum gets home from work to give her a lift up." Tay called back.

"Absolutely not!" Lilly snapped. She saw Taylor's eyes open wide, startled, stopped in her tracks, unsure how to take the change in tone.

"Sorry, not aimed at you. What's her number?" Lilly asked, removing a glove with her teeth to search for her phone in the pocket of her coat. Knew it was on her contact list, but quicker to ask Tay and tap it out.

Vicky answered on the ninth ring, which didn't help Lilly's mood.

"Vicky, it's Lilly from Wingfield Equestrian. It would appear your horse has eaten himself into colic yet again. I think I've already mentioned the bloody kick bar, to check it before you leave at night. You need to call your vet and get yourself round here, now?" Lilly's voice rose at the last sentence, angry that the horse was suffering.

"Er, yeah, er, right. Well, thing is, I ain't got nobody for Jessie as me mum is out," Vicky spluttered.

"Well I suggest you ask your vet to pick you up on the way then. Wake up, Vicky, Robin is really sick. I'll see you here shortly." Lilly ended the call.

Why oh bloody why, did that girl still have Robin? Life as a single mum was hard enough. With Vicky out of work she had to rely on benefits. Money and time for a hobby were more than tight. Absolutely, the kid had to come first. Though this meant the horse came last. When did you draw a line, sell on?

Robin's rescue had been a good deed. Vicky had been devoted to him. She took him from skin and bone to a fit, healthy show jumper. Time with him made Vicky feel positive, helped her cope better, boosted her mental health. But owning a horse was expensive, time-consuming, with all the responsibility an animal entailed.

Lilly had a pang of guilt for being sharp on the phone. A reaction to how sorry the horse looked. Who was she to take the moral high ground? She resigned herself to change the top bolt. One Robin could not open. Being a Houdini didn't help the situation. If he would just stay in his box, he could avoid these repetitions.

The vet was up within half an hour, Vicky in the passenger seat. As Lilly approached the van, she noticed the little girl, dressed in pyjamas, tucked up in her mother's arms. Wrapped in a blanket, her teddy bear in one hand. She appeared to be asleep.

They sedated Robin to allow for the vet to perform a rectal examination. This followed with an injection of buscopan to relax his gut, and finadyne for the pain. With instructions to keep him monitored, he handed Vicky a few packets of bute should they be required. Absolutely right in Lilly's suspicions, it was colic.

"You know the drill, avoid him lying down, don't let him roll. Call me if he doesn't improve in the next couple of hours." he stated the obvious.

With Lilly's assurance she would drop Vicky back home, he headed for his car.

Vicky, visibly shaken, began to cry.

"It's ok, he'll be fine soon enough. Keep him up, keep him relaxed. I'll hang about a bit. You can't keep an eye on both horse and child." Lilly had been short tempered before. She put her arm around the girl's shoulders, drew her into her with a squeeze.

"It's not just Robin that I'm worried about. I now have an emergency call out to add to my overdue bill with the vets. I don't know how I'm going to manage." Vicky choked out. Her shoulders heaved in an attempt to stem the sobs. Her face screwed up as the tears ran down her cheeks. Cold and wet, her skin a shade of grey, despair was clear in her sad brown eyes.

Lilly walked with her as she led the horse around the yard. Vicky shivered in a reaction to the worry and the cold. Robin was hesitant, stopping every over stride to bite his tummy and kick out. Vicky kept him going with a tug on the rope. Encouraged him to step forward again.

"If I were you, I'd find him a new home," Lilly ventured. Immediately, Vicky tensed up, drew in a breath. Lilly continued quickly.

"I understand, believe me I do. Once you let a horse into your life, there is no way back. However, we do need to do what's right for both of you. Robin needs care and so do you. It's clear you're making yourself ill, struggling with it all."

Vicky looked at Lilly. Her pretty, freckled face, streaked with rivulets of tears, smudged with dirt and mascara, crumpled. It was hollow, empty, a reflection of her own perception of a failed life.

"First things, I'm going to give you a new lock that will be Robin proof. But what about a loaner? Someone that could take the strain off you financially and help ride him?"

A flicker of relief illuminated Vicky's angular features as she blinked away tears and sleet. Then a wave of despair descended back over face.

"You could suggest, but who would want to loan him? He's as stressed out as I am most of the time. Nor is he an easy ride. A neurotic bucker is not a quality most look to take on, is it?"

Lilly felt wretched. There she was, having just had the most amazing day. Reached a milestone in her ambitions. Only half an hour ago been ready to read the riot act on the bedraggled girl now standing, cold and frightened, in front of her.

"Let me think on it, we'll sort something out. For now, it's beginning to freeze big time. What about we get him back in the stable for a bit, then I'll walk him around for fifteen minutes? We can alternate until he's safe. You need to wrap a stable rug around Jessie before she catches a chill. You don't want a doctor's bill on top of the vets," she winked, attempting to make Vicky laugh.

It was gone nine by the time Lilly considered Robin to be over the crisis. By now, Jessie was fast asleep in the straw and Vicky was blue with cold.

Bolting the stable door firmly in place, Lilly drove them both home before a final check on all the horses. Finally, she could turn in herself.

On her own. A crisis up north had kept Jay from being able to drive back to her, and tomorrow he was on a plane to Europe.

Standing under a hot shower, letting her body thaw out and the sweat and dirt of the day wash away, she considered her current predicament.

Life in riding boots. Like a circus. Swings and roundabouts, with her yard being the carousel.

CHAPTER FOUR

Saturday, the last day of February. Show day! Preparation had taken much of Friday. Horses in the hot wash, shampoo and set, whiskers shaved. Manes pulled, hooves oiled and rugged up to the nines against the freezing air overnight.

Rico Ortiz arrived early Saturday morning to plait up Serendipity ready for the kids. The unruly mane now a neat row of plaited bumps as he gave him a final wipe down with a damp sponge.

Despite the stable rug, lycra neck and hood, bandages up to his knees, Seren, predictably, had lain in his own poo overnight. On his right bum cheek, streaks of dark yellow ran down towards his hock.

Rico moved around steadily, taking his time, not wanting to mess up a plait or upset the other horses still sleepy in their nearby stables.

He'd assured Lilly he'd do the early shift. Living only ten minutes away by car, he was an early bird, always awake before five.

"It's what best friends do, Lilly, payback for all the times you saved my skin." He'd told her after the tenth time she'd objected.

He'd met Lilly when on the European show jumping circuit. She worked for Yves and Charles Moreau as a groom. Initially it was lust at first sight.

He had been blown away as he took in the delicate alabaster skin and teardrop green eyes, a mane of dark chestnut hair, as rich and shiny as the body of a bay horse. It dropped around her head in tendrils of curls that escaped her riding hat. He watched her keenly as she walked La Tonnerre around the warm up arena.

Thunder proved a good name for the dark grey stallion. He sounded like the growling of Greek Gods when he was wound up. It would take all of Yves' strength and experience to get him around the ring.

It impressed Rico that such a wisp of a girl was able to contain this hulk of warmblood x, high on testosterone as he pranced around, fighting for his head. What impressed him even more was her beauty.

Lilly resisted Rico's sexual advances no matter how hard he tried. And try he had. Every trick in his extensive book of tricks. Once he'd realised the chase was futile, they ended up best of friends. His fall guy, even.

He had a habit of getting into scrapes. Not for him exclusivity, often not even for one night, if the temptation was there. When Hilda was swopped for Harry or Olly became Ali in his hotel bedroom exploits, it was Lilly to the rescue. She hid him in her room. Calmed the injured parties. Allowed his manhood to remain attached to his body. Si importante.

He had fallen over himself at the opportunity to remain close to her. After the accident, she had been his salvation. He became her freelance instructor, a contract that suited them both. Available to her clients, he could also work elsewhere with a small list of private clients.

Today, frost was still thick and slippery under foot as he walked from the stable to the tack room to boil a kettle. He shuffled from one foot to the other, blowing warm air into his hands as he waited, breath appearing as if he'd dragged deeply on a cigarette.

He emptied a packet of bright white into hot water to make a chalky thick paste to spread over the stains on the little pony's backside and legs. Once at the showground, he'd brush out the dried paste to reveal a clean backside and legs once more.

He was to ride Cam today in the one metre ten show jumping event. A warm-up for the season. A bonus first was Paul Greenwood's palomino, Viking.

Rowena, Camelot's owner, would be there, somewhere, most probably in the VIP section. Mingling with whoever looked worth a mingle with.

That woman is bonkers, he told Lilly, the first time they met her.

She had turned up in the yard about a year ago. Strode towards him with a determined air about her. Honey blonde hair teased into clouds held tight by sweet-smelling sandalwood and jasmine hairspray. Scents he recognised from childhood in Southern Spain. It made several horses snort as she wafted past.

Tottered unsteady in pink boots with six-inch heels, tight white pants covered slim legs. She completed the ensemble with a powder pink bomber jacket. Dressed like that, he wondered if she should audition for a part in Grease. Not quite the usual yard attire.

"Hello. I'm Rowena. Rowena White. I am here about your facilities. I'd like to house my horse here?" she inquired, hand thrust outwards towards him. Perfectly manicured, vivid pink nails that looked dangerously shovel like. A large blue stone sat on her middle finger surrounded by diamonds. It caught the sun at every step she took.

Lilly took her to the house for a chat. To discuss the details and no doubt have her sign a contract. He smiled as he thought about it. Lilly was so organised. Nothing was left to chance with her liveries, even he, her best mate, signed an agreement.

The following day Lilly confided to him that Rowena was a Euro millions winner. The lucky bitch. He did a row every Tuesday without fail. Hardly ever did he match two numbers, let alone the jackpot.

With this bounty she purchased a five bedroomed country home. Decided to try horse riding to become part of the country life. She wanted her new life to be the very essence of her dreams.

"Why this horse?" he first asked when Camelot arrived on the yard a week later. A sixteen one dapple grey he'd seen on the circuit the year before, under a different name.

The horse was a prolific showjumper, though by no means an easy ride. He'd thrown the rider, then proceeded to career about, fizzing like a shaken can of soda, as he descended into a frenzy of bucks between fences.

"I just fell in love with him. Isn't he a pretty colour?" she whispered breathlessly. A voice he since noticed she used for any man under the age of forty. Channelling her inner Marilyn.

Initially she tried to ride. She even had lessons. It became all too apparent that she liked to look, rather than sit, on a horse. As a result, Rico was offered the ride on this amazing gelding.

He had accepted on the spot, an opportunity to increase his reputation. And his riding prowess. He'd learnt to sit into the bucks and squeeze hard. There was no way he was going to be eating sand in front of a crowd.

Viking was added to today's list as a last-minute addition. Paul, his owner, was abroad on his journalistic world travels.

Rico rode the horse a few times during the week, worked on his approach to fences, kept him on a shorter rein, reduced the stride. Viking had a habit of dropping a pole just when you thought you were home and clear.

Moving back to the stable, he pasted the chalk onto Seren's bum. Rubbed it in thickly to make sure it took hold. It would draw out any dirt. His mind drifted back to its wonderings. To the current woman in his life.

To the affair with Sam, married mother to the two children that rode this pony. It had been going on since last November.

Charlie and Sophie, how old were they? He couldn't remember. Around ten or twelve perhaps, Charlie being the elder. Both pony mad. She had approached him about giving the kids lessons when they moved to the yard months before.

From the outset she watched from the sidelines, sat on the bench to the side of school's entrance, huddled up, phone clasped in her hand, staring at it distractedly. An air of misery hung about her.

Once the lesson finished, she would walk off to wait in the car, a silver Mercedes Benz. In truth, he barely gave her a second glance. Her jet-black hair hung limp over her face, like a curtain, body clothed in an assault of mixed colours and layers, hiding flesh and personality. He had more interest in the car than the mum.

As the lessons continued, she admitted later that the glance over to him turned to a full-on ogle, mesmerised by his tight cream breeches, stretched over a sexy pert backside. How he'd turn the lapel of his bomber jacket up against the wind.

Or, in the sun, a tight plain tee stretched over his pecs. Rain or shine, a trademark baseball cap firmly in place, shoulder length hair, tied up in a ponytail, stuck out the back. Sam would listen as he spoke into his microphone that linked to the earpiece her child wore.

From her vantage point she caught his deep sensual voice. The lilt of his Spanish accent. Strained to hear his every word as he explained the required action to his student.

When he looked her way, his intense brown eyes had caused her heart to flutter. He was all too aware of their potency. He had used them on many an occasion. A highlight on his repertoire of charm offensive. Surrounded by thick long lashes he could bat as good as a girl.

Each time he glanced over; he made her feel as if she were the most desirable woman in the world. It made her feel good. No, more than good. Sexy, desirable, *wanted*. It had been a long time since she had felt wanted.

Unaware his eyes had offered so much information, of her increasing pulse rate, he stuck to his instruction. Sure, he checked out everyone he met as habit. But initial introductions had revealed nothing more than a mother asking him to teach her children. To give them confidence in their riding ability, push them further.

The little pony had more going for it. Nice deep chest, powerful hindquarters, intelligent head. Plenty of potential. He would be pleased to work with them. But no, she had lit no flame for him.

Sam had slowly transformed over the weeks. As the summer warmed up, she shed the brown oversized coat, the layers of knitwear, the bright assortment of colours. Realisation that under her coat, just like a woolly horse losing its winter fur, was a sleek body.

Now she piqued his interest. His eyes were glued to her body as she strode along. A pair of tight jeans, a fitted single colour jumper, a black gilet, a pair of Lariat boots.

Her hair, previously pulled back in a bun like an old housewife, now hung lose, flowing down her back almost to her waist. He noticed how thick it was, how the light caught it, turning the black a shiny blue. He mostly noticed her boobs. With mounting interest, he imagined his hands on them, soft and warm between his fingers. Now she gazed at him boldly, almost daring him into action.

Opportunity took over for him one morning. The yard was quiet as she returned from taking Seren to the field.

As she walked down the slope, head collar slung over her shoulder, she hummed to herself. Denim jeans, a loose blouse, a dark green gilet to keep out the chill from the November air, hair swinging about her body, she was a vision he could not resist.

On impulse he darted out around the back of The Colonel, tied up by his stable door as he untacked from a hack. He took her by surprise, grabbed her hand, led her into the adjacent feed room.

With his free hand he pushed the door closed. Moved in to kiss her passionately. She'd melted into his arms, her body going limp as she gave herself to him without a murmur.

He smiled to himself as he remembered that first encounter. He'd used one of his standard chat up lines, smouldered his eyes and pouted his lips.

"Oh babe, I want to see you naked." Corny but effective. His hands snaked up her top as they kissed. Too soon, he'd heard someone approach. Dropped her instantly. Spoke in a loud voice about the right diet for Seren, how important for the pony to maintain his physical peak. He whispered 'like you' as he brushed his hand over her blouse. A broad smile shone across her face.

It inevitably happened one lunch time, when the grooms were on their break and Lilly was out meeting a potential client. For once the yard was super quiet. No one was about. He had wasted no time, sought her out in Seren's stable, shavings fork in her hand, mucking out.

Without a word, he laid her on the clean shavings of the pony's bed. Master of seduction, Rico showed her what she'd been missing for so long.

Without hesitation she melted to his touch, her hands fumbled at his clothes as fast as he shed hers. She told him that as she came a dozen champagne corks popped in her head. A few party poppers too.

He wondered how rich he would be if he had a pound for every time a woman had said that to him. He gave a good masterclass in lovemaking as well as horse instruction.

Partly because he found pleasure in unleashing her sexual awareness, partly because she was such a willing conquest, he continued to take her at every available opportunity. In the stable. The hay barn. A corner of the field behind the giant oak. In his car. He'd even been to her house under the pretext of discussing Seren's show season.

Sexy Sam, the lonely housewife. Her dick of a husband had quit the commute down from London, bought a flat up there where he stayed put. Made an appearance over the weekends, or not as the case may be. He'd lost interest in her. Usual excuses, too stressed from work, too tired.

Rico was not so easily fooled. Tom must be in his early thirties. He suspected a mistress in London. Rico couldn't imagine not having sex for a week, let alone months.

Sam said she'd given up trying, accepted that he had fallen out of love with her. Refused to discuss the alternative.

Who was he to interfere? All he wanted was a regular lay with a beautiful body. Which is what bothered him now as he worked on the little grey.

He could tell she was becoming too involved with him. The questions sneaked in. Subtly asking if she was the only one? Wondering out loud if she left Tom, what would happen? He had changed the subject each time. The answers, had he voiced them, were a firm no to the first.

He had only ever been faithful once, and that had not worked out well. To the second, that she would be a single mother. Alarm bells echoed in his ears; walk away you fool.

He loved women, all shapes and sizes. He also loved men. No particular sway, whichever turned him on the most at a particular time. He was not about to become limited edition.

Rico switched back to the present as he heard Lilly call out to him. It stopped all thought on his sexual preoccupation as she appeared.

"Hola!" He smiled in delight as he opened the stable door. Rubbed the head of the little dog as Ruby bounced up at him.

"Hola Rico. You ready for the first outing of the year?" Lilly asked as she kissed him on each cheek. She ruffled his hair, hung loose about his shoulders in shaggy dog fashion. He'd tie it up before they left.

"You look like you've dragged yourself from someone's bed?" She scrutinised him, her eyes searched his face.

"Lilly, what can I say, you know me too well." He shrugged, a wry smile parted his lips as he ducked his head sideways from her. No point lying. She read him like a book.

"Rico?" she grabbed his left arm to stop him walking away.

"No, not her, a guy I met at a bar on Wednesday, ok?"

"Rogue bastard," she replied, giving him a small punch.

"What about Jay, has he been over to service you recently?"

Rico was the only one who knew the truth about her love affair. After all, as he liked to remind her, it was thanks to him that they even met.

"No. Not for a couple of weeks." Lilly bristled.

"I'm doing feeds then we're good to go. Would you mind starting the lorry so it's warmed up a bit, I'm freezing." she asked, pointedly ignoring his question, instead wrapping her arms about her coat as if to confirm her statement.

"Muy bien, of course," he agreed. Happy to alter the conversation before she dug too deep. He knew better than to push her when talking about her own sex life. The hackles would rise and she'd be more likely to bite him than Ruby would.

But it worried him. That gorgeous man could not be a saint. If they didn't meet up between now and September, he was definitely getting it elsewhere. And that would knock the delicate trust that teetered on the edge into the burning abyss. Leave her a spinster for life.

He gave a shudder. For his friend and for his own view of a sexless world.

CHAPTER FIVE

Lilly walked off with mixed emotions.

She adored Rico, but couldn't help feeling a teeny-weeny bit jealous. Ok, quite a lot jealous in fact. That man would sleep with anything on two legs with a pulse.

Yet there she was, in love with just one man, going without sight or sex for weeks at a time. She wasn't into casual flings, but she did miss Jay's touch.

The sensations that pinged through her as his hands caressed her naked body. Just thinking about him made her flush, a warm feeling flood her groin.

Soon. She scolded herself for being lovesick. Remember, time for love once the trials were established. She'd take a bit of time out, ask if Rico or Alison would cover whilst she had her own marathon. She must check out where would still be warm in October.

Lilly knew about Sam, had already asked Rico to end it. She had literally stumbled on them, going at it in the barn as she'd gone to pick up fresh straw for a new horse arriving that afternoon.

"Whoa. Rico, not the place please." Her face flushed then, and now, at the image.

They'd tucked themselves around the corner behind the bags of shavings. Though she couldn't see them, she could hear the sighs and the grunts. Lilly almost turned around and walked out. She had no choice. She needed to see who it was.

There, bent over, breeches around his knees, riding boots still on, shirt undone. Rhythmically pushing himself into a woman underneath him, her naked legs wrapped around his back. Lilly knew that arse too well, but not the legs of the willing partner.

It wasn't the first time she'd caught the lothario out on her premises. For real, he must have bedded a good half dozen people on her yard. Along with her groom, Kerry. And Matt, the farrier.

Who was it this time?

Bugger! As she walked closer, she realised it was Sam. The woman was attempting to cover herself up, without success. Her breasts fell out of the blouse he'd unbuttoned.

In the past, she possibly may have smacked his butt cheeks. Even thrown a wad of straw between his legs. Whereas, today, this was her business. She had to be professional.

"Hey, Lilly, you know how it is, no harm is being done." He assured her with a lopsided grin.

"Maybe not, Rico, but you're here to ride horses, not, well not to…"

"Ride their owners?" he laughed, glanced at Sam as he spoke. The woman struggled not to laugh, overwhelmed with nervous giggles and total embarrassment. She lay half naked on her back on a bale of straw. Rico inside her. The woman she paid to care for her children's pony stood over them. Mortified, she continued to tug at her top, using a sleeve to at least cover her nipples.

"Exactly. You want to carry on, do it in the comfort of your own beds, please. I don't need to see it here. Sam, you have straw in your hair. I've a brush in the kitchen, you're welcome to go in and tidy up. Save the entire world knowing about your roll in the barn." And with that, Lilly had walked back out, forgetting the straw.

She'd waited fifteen minutes before venturing back for the straw. Wanted to make sure they had dressed and gone. Glimpsed Rico headed towards the tack room ready for his next 'ride'.

This time, a horse he was working in for a show. He waved. She shook her head at him, tried hard not to smile at the same time.

She wanted to laugh at the crazy life of the yard. She'd seen enough during the years on tour around Europe. Knew that people had sex when and where they felt the urge, lorry parties were notorious. Half the children that accompanied the riders were likely as not consummated in a stable or a lorry toilet.

However, she needed to calm him down. What if it had been Charlie or Sophie that discovered the tryst? They'd be gutted, both being crazy about Rico and his equestrian abilities. The last thing they needed to see was Rico humping their mum in the hay.

Despite his wandering willy, she would be lost without him. Not only someone she classed as fam, but when it came to horses, so reliable, ever happy to go the extra mile. Like turn up at stupid o'clock on a chilly February morning in the pitch black just to help her.

Sure, Rowena and Paul would pay him for the ride on their horses. Whereas, the rest he did because he loved her. She knew she would always love him. No matter how many times she found him in bed with the wrong person.

We'll stick together through sick and sin they'd once declared one drunken night, celebrating a major victory for La Tonnerre. Sin being an appropriate word in his case.

As the dawn flickered awake another day, streaks of pink soaked through the grey fuzz of the early morning mist. Rico drove Lilly, Ruby on her lap. Alison sat on the far side having arrived in time to help put on travel boots and walk the horses into the lorry. It was a short journey, a mere thirty miles up the motorway to the showground, ready to kick the season off.

Rico barely spoke to Sam all day. He had two rides, Camelot in the one metre ten affiliated and Viking in the one metre. The Spaniard had fences, not females on his mind.

Paul Greenwood normally took Viking himself. He'd been sent on assignment to Kentucky, to cover a race meet.

Everyone loved Paul. A freelance equine journalist, with a keen eye for a story. Late twenties, he'd rock up to the yard, often unshaven, a little rumpled, but always down to earth, with more energy than the national grid.

He bounced around like a Tigger on speed, greeting everyone with a bear hug or a kiss, happy to help anyone out. His presence at the stables could lighten the darkest of moods.

To Lilly's alarm, Tom turned up with Sam, though both seemed distant with each other. Distracted. Walked together but minds miles apart, as if neither saw the other as a partner any longer.

He was wrapped up in a pair of blue cords, a Burberry coat and matching scarf. The ensemble finished off with a peaked green hat. His wellies, Hunter she noticed, looked like the only mud they'd seen was from this morning.

Sam was in an old pair of jeans, rainproof anorak, wearing a pair of well-worn riding boots. The type perfect for long country walks, covered with a well engrained layer of dirt. She topped her outfit off with a beanie hat, long dark locks cascaded down her back like the mane of a Friesian mare. Cherry red lipstick highlighted her full lips against the pale winter skin.

One in perceived country gear. The other in country gear people wore. Two different worlds. Lilly gasped inwardly as a sudden image crossed her mind. What if that was how she would be seen in relation to her own man?

With a lurch, she pictured the horror. Both at a dinner party, amongst his friends. He dressed in an exquisitely tailored dinner suit, polished shoes, an antique tie pin clasped over his silk tie.

The pin no doubt re-worked from what had once been part of an earring from a Maharajah in the early 1400s.

Whereas she would be clad in something she found in a charity shop. A dress, long and floaty, slightly tatty around the edges. A pair of old strappy sandals and dangly earrings that had once been on the rack at Primark.

She made a mental note. Never to look so out of sync with him as these two now did.

What everyone was in agreement on was ensuring the children enjoy their day. To kick off their first show of the season with a bang. In that, it was a success, despite the ominous black clouds that offered the odd downpour.

Charlie, to his great annoyance, fell in the jump off. Seren tripped, turned too fast to the last fence, stumbled to his knees as the adults gasped. Whilst the pony righted itself, the boy was thrown sideways, landing with a thud, face down in the sand.

For several moments he lay still, winded from the fall. Lilly and Rico both leapt into the ring just as he rolled into a sitting position. With a nod to the announcer that yes, he was OK, he stood back up, walked out, leading the pony behind him. Rico walked him to the lorry as Lilly was left to reassure both parents that no harm was done. Just knocked pride.

With five others all also in the jump-off, he missed being placed, no rosette. He blamed himself for the disqualification. For being an idiot rider.

To add to the boy's frustration, Sophie won her show class. With a whoop, her father came alive. The stern expression on his face, creased with years of city life, melted away.

It revealed the Tom who may have once been. Eyes shone with pride; he whirled his daughter around in his arms with delight. Lilly took Seren's reins to lead him back to the lorry and a welcome haynet.

"Lilly, thank you for all the trouble you took in helping to achieve this success today." Tom shook her hand, pumped it enthusiastically. With his left arm, he held Sophie close to his chest. Her arms wrapped around her dad's neck, she grinned wildly. Part in flush of success. Part in being daddy's girl for this fleeting of moments.

"Oh, it was a pleasure," Lilly replied. Her body felt like it may spasm into a Mexican wave if he didn't let go of her hand soon.

"Rico has been doing all the hard graft teaching Charlie and Sophie. He was up early this morning to prep Seren for me, too," she added, without thinking.

The triumphant look flickered. His eyes narrowed, a dark glaze hastened across his face, before the smile returned.

"Well, I'll be sure to ask my wife to thank him for me next time she sees him. I understand she values him as an excellent instructor," he replied. A comment laced with a bucket of sarcasm.

In that moment Lilly knew that he knew. She glanced hesitantly at Sam. Sam looked away into the distance, a fixed smile that spoke louder than words. It said there had been an argument. Lilly just nodded and smiled weakly.

Tom put Sophie back on the ground, stood up with a stretch of his arms. Turned to both his children.

"A victory lunch for you guys?" he suggested.

"Cheesy chips at the café!" Sophie jumped up and down with excitement, clapping.

"Not what I had in mind, but if that's what my Princess wants, she gets," he said.

The quartet walked away. Tom clasped both children to him, talking loudly. His wife two steps behind, dragging herself along as if her legs were made of stone.

Lilly would have to tread delicately around Rico on the subject, but tread she needed to do. If this blew up, it could create an unpleasant situation for her. Even force her to make choices she was unwilling to make.

Back at the lorry, she tied Seren up then untacked him, sponged him down where his saddle and girth had been, his neck and his rear, taking off the sweat.

Finally, a firm rub down with a towel, she threw a fleece over his back, then walked him up the ramp, threading a lead rope through the ring where a haynet was hung ready for him to feast on.

Alison had already taken Viking out to saddle him up. Rico was getting changed into his show breeches and shirt inside the living quarters.

Viking was up first. Lilly walked the course with Rico whilst Alison warmed the horse up in the practice ring. Once she'd covered a few rounds of the ring at walk, trot, canter she took turns with the other competitors to jump the two fences in the middle of the sandschool. First one way, then in the opposite direction. After a few leaps she walked him around to keep him supple and his muscles warm.

It was a simple figure of eight course with one double and a small water fence. Held indoors, the water jump was in a blue tray which could spook a horse into a refusal.

Rico felt the biggest problem wouldn't be the water, it would be the gate two fences before the end. White and narrow, a classic trick by the course builder to avoid too many clear first rounds.

Lilly felt confident Viking would fly it without skipping a beat. As easy-going as his owner, they jumped for fun, not prestige. The aim of the day being to have him ready for the season which Paul fully embraced.

She knew how he loved the whole buzz of show days. The clamour of horses whinnying. The loudspeaker announcing classes. The dull thud as a pole would fall, the crowd all ooh'ing at the same time. The smell of horses, saddle soap, leather, hoof oil. And the atmosphere of people enjoying the day.

All this and more appeared in the many articles he'd written over his ten-year career. She agreed with every sentiment of his words. There was nothing quite so exciting or unpredictable than a horse show.

Viking, true to Lilly's belief, jumped clear in the first round without hesitation. Sadly, despite Rico's work that week, he knocked a pole in the jump off.

Rico was gutted. Blamed it on a stupid error of his own doing. He'd given the horse a squeeze to take off a stride too late. Caught too close to the fence, Viking had tapped the top red and white pole with his front hoof.

The one metre ten class wasn't scheduled to begin until two thirty that afternoon. So far, no one had yet seen Rowena. Lilly, nevertheless, had heard her, knew exactly where she was. In the VIP room talking to judges gathered for a sandwich and a drink. Rowena didn't drink herself, it was a pretence to walk around with a gin in her hand when it was in fact just water.

"How on earth would I be able to drive my Disco if I'd been on the gin, darling?" She'd informed Lilly the first time she had tracked Rowena to the VIP tent. She'd seen the tumbler and pointed at it with a quizzical eye.

Rowena admitted that winning the lottery had been a total game changer for her. A makeover of monumental gain. All her dreams came true with a little over sixteen million pounds landing in her bank.

She'd had her body upholstered and sculpted, her mouse brown hair highlighted; extensions topped up by the London hairdresser to the celebrities. A spray tan every six weeks kept the bronzed St Tropez just-off-the-beach look. And the shopping. So juicy walking into a shop in Chelsea or Kensington High street, picking out one in every colour from the latest designers, she'd regailed Lilly.

"It's a long way from the small Yorkshire town I used to live, working as a shop assistant in Boots. Though don't you dare spill the tea on me," she'd laughed, her twenty-thousand-pound dental makeover dazzling whiter than white.

Lilly had tried to help her with her riding ability. She even agreed to teach mid-morning when there was less likelihood of lots of eyes watching. She'd borrowed Jeremy's little grey Connie, Timmy, who was perfectly schooled and would offer every confidence to a nervous newcomer.

"Trot on."

Yet again those two short words the kiss of death to Rowena's fate. No matter how she tried. Because Lilly wondered if try was all she had done. The woman just bounced about, holding on to the safety strap. Even running next to her, holding her right leg to encourage her to push down in the stirrup, raise herself up off the saddle.

That had only ended up with Rowena standing for the entire length of the school. No attempt to come back down again.

"I give up, I really don't get it," Rowena had wailed the last time she'd fallen. This time over the mane, head first. A nail snapped as the strap caught up in her hand.

"You know, Lilly, to be honest, I can't take the smell or the fur on my clothes. I have to go back to the hairdresser the next day to fix my waves as the hat crushes it all," she had declared. She had looked as if her finger had fallen off rather than the shellac falsie.

"Thank you for your help, but I'm happier, and safer, watching."

Inside, Lilly agreed. Despite all efforts, if the surefooted Timmy couldn't keep her on board, nothing would.

Rowena focused on the social side of the horse world. Her horse offered up an ice breaker. Something to start the conversation as she tottered up to men in show jackets. Those whom she felt were influential in this equine society.

Lilly found her in animated flow with Robert Chapman, today's showing judge. How she would love him come to dinner sometime soon. Maybe with Mrs Chapman?

Lilly couldn't help but chuckle. Robert was a confirmed bachelor, a significant partner would not be a she. Poor Rowena was barking up the wrong tree by flirting with this one.

"Ah yes, love to, must arrange it soon. Oh, hello Lilly, good to see you, must be off deary, think I'm judging shortly." He muttered as he excused himself with a sigh of relief. He extracted the pink talons clutched to his left hand. With a polite nod, he disappeared.

Lilly led Rowena to the fixed seating at the edge of the ring. She tried to explain to her what Rico would do throughout the course.

"We've already walked it, you know, checked the strides to each fence. The double is a bounce and go. Some might try to fit one stride in, but we think it's too tight for Cam. Next, it's the water tray, four strides to the gate which is fence number seven."

"Whoa, I'm lost already, which number is the water did you say?"

"Ok, let me point them out in order." Lilly detailed the name of the fence along with the colour as she pointed towards each, checked at each one to confirm that Rowena understood.

"Many are finding the run to clear the water, followed by so few strides to the straight white gate, too much. They have no time to pull the horse back into check. As Rico predicted, it's been falling."

Rowena nodded.

"One day I may understand all this. But horses' paces, the number of strides they need, the fence names, just confuses me," she admitted. Gazed at Lilly with pure emotion.

"I just love watching my Cammie, I get all the feels with him. That tail of his is almost black, whereas, his white stockings go up past his knees. See? I remember what you call those." She gave a triumphant grin.

"Rowena, if you get enjoyment from him this way, then that's all that matters. You picked a superstar, he's an ace jumper, Rico will get the best out of him." Lilly touched Rowena's hand in a gesture of understanding.

The woman was one of her favourite liveries, despite her dizziness. Perhaps because of it. Certainly, there was nothing fake about her heart. That was firmly in the right place. Neither did she quibble over any extras added to her bill to keep Camelot in top condition. The monthly invoice was paid the same day Lilly sent it. Rowena may be ditzy, but she was a good client.

Camelot didn't consider the pace to the gate a problem as he cleared it at speed, giving him first place.

Rowena whooped with delight, trotted into the ring. Togged to the nines in her white jodhpurs with diamante pockets, Omina label tan brown jumper and matching jacket. The ensemble finished with boots hand made by Sirelec, chocolate brown faux leather with a pink sparkly trim.

Total worth of her outfit? Close to an all-inclusive week in Majorca for a family of four.

She reached the centre of the ring where the horses stood lined up in order of placing. As she gripped the left rein she smiled up at Rico.

"Well done, you were brilliant! This is so exciting, our first win of the season, Rico, so very exciting," she gushed.

He smiled down at her. Wondered what it would be like to….. no, seriously, what was he thinking? She was as mad as a box of frogs with fake boobies. Fake body parts turned him a definite off.

He was pleased to have continued the winning streak of Camelot, aware that Rowena wanted bigger stuff now. Especially after his Hockmead success at the end of last season.

It would serve him well to keep her sweet, but never in that way, was he nuts? That would be too complicated, even for him.

"He truly is one in a million," Rico agreed, as he leant forward to give the horse a tweak on its ear.

His mind buzzed with the thrill of jumping this exceptional horse. Along with the attention he received.

He sat proudly on its back, shook hands with the various officials as they presented rosettes and trophies. His thoughts were twisted in the dilemma of how to cool it down with Sam. Now more than ever, after earlier today. An incident that had taken him by surprise and unhinged him.

He had been minding his own business, walking around the show grounds, when Tom had found him. The man had pulled him with a jerk to his shoulder from behind. Pushed him round the back of the vans that were serving a line of people hotdogs and hot drinks.

"I saw how my wife looked at you earlier. It confirmed my suspicions. I've asked myself time and again these past months, what has changed? Why does she seem so upbeat, happy even? I should punch your fricking lights out, but to be honest, you do me a favour. Keeps her from nagging me do the biz for her," Tom had whispered coarsely.

Rico could smell the pancakes as they cooked on the hot pads. Distracting him as the man ranted about his wife. As if he cared a jot what the guy thought, he was nothing but a jerk.

He was about to deny it all, but remained quiet, his mouth firm shut. Probably best not to add to the outrage, the guy had lost the plot.

Tom's eyes widened, wild, his lips puckered in a sneer as he spat out the words.

"Take this as a warning. I will not, under any circumstance, allow anything to damage my reputation. Or to embarrass my children. I warn you. If she makes any attempt to divorce me, I will have your name smeared so badly you'll be on a boat to Spain before you can say adios. Do I make myself clear?" Tom's expression twisted in a menace as he delivered his threat.

Rico felt anger rise like bile in his throat at the nerve of this cold and calculating man, but choked it down. Instead, he took a step back and returned the hard stare, his eyes black with rage. He sensed his hands curling into fists and thrust them in his coat pockets.

With a voice as steady as he could control, Rico replied.

"Tom, can I call you that? Are we on first-name terms? I see it like this. You're taking the piss mate. With you up in London all the time, it is you that embarrasses your kids by not being a real father to them. Imagine the excuses they make as to why daddy hasn't turned up to watch their sports day? Watch their mates hug their dads at school pick up? Each missed weekend makes it worse for you. You don't call the shots, your wife does."

With that, he patted Tom on the shoulder, shook his head and walked off before the man could close his mouth enough to speak.

La mierda! El nervio! To threaten him. Wives don't stray if they're happy at home.

Rico enjoyed Sam's body, the thrill of the affair, but he was not about to risk a commitment. The words *if she divorces me for you* rung like a nuclear invasion in his head. Had she said something to Tom for him to speak of this?

The last thing he needed was a married woman turning up on his doorstep, bags packed. Cramp his lifestyle? No way! He would not be a replacement. Neither did he want surrogate fatherhood.

He had kept himself busy throughout the day. By the close of show, he was ready to get back to the yard, settle the horses, then go home and get drunk.

As they led the horses up into the lorry, secured them in pace for the journey, Lilly noticed that Rico seemed decidedly wonky. She caught his face off guard, the narrow mouth, distracted eyes, disturbed and smouldering.

He brushed off her attempt to draw out of him the problem. He merely gave her an overzealous smile; told her all was well. Why should anything be wrong? He'd had an amazing day, though admitted he was dog tired from the early start. She must be too?

She agreed, not convinced he was telling her the truth, but knew he wasn't ready. Yes, she loved the excitement of show days, but as they packed up and made their way back, she yearned for bed and a solid night's sleep.

Alison drove the six-horse lorry back to the yard. Rico insisted on helping settle the animals back into their stables with a good feed, warm rugs and a dose of electrolyte in their water buckets.

It gave Lilly a few minutes to run down and check the DIY's. She had been making it a thing to do at night now since Robin's last escape, unconvinced her talk had made any difference. It hadn't. Robin's kick bar was up, along with two others. She flipped them over with a sigh. Thank goodness she'd lost no time in fixing the new top bolt that kept the keen Houdini firmly inside.

Ruby padded along with her, despite her own exhaustive day of running about. The little dog had greeted dozens of dogs that attended the horse show with their owners. She was glad when Lilly finally opened the front door. She was up the stairs and in her little bed before Lilly had locked up.

CHAPTER SIX

Lilly woke early on the Sunday, her mind full of tasks to do, on and off the yard.

The long day at the show had taken a big chunk of precious time. Well aware that she had more reason than one to keep on top of her schedule. If she got behind at all, a swift swish from Mark Larch the Starch and his crisply ironed cuff, sharp as a blade.

Why was he being a constant thorn in the hoof with terse emails in response to her updates, full of negativity? She didn't seek a pat on the back from him, but she could do with him backing off.

She sighed, stretched out as she uncurled herself, ready to shower. After the morning feeds, she would need to tackle his latest note. Even though the project remained on track, he found reason to challenge her.

Part of the joy of success will be to have the smile wiped off his face, she reminded herself. It gave her more confidence, put the fire back in her belly despite the exhaustion.

Many of her liveries were five-day assist. Although their owners came up at weekends to do their own mucking out, she did still have eight full-time livery. Not to mention several requests from people who were on holiday, skiing or Caribbean.

With just Rahima in all day and Mike for the morning, she had fifteen horses to split between the three of them. Again, she questioned her sanity. Did she really roster just the two youngsters to work with her, the day after a show? She had buttons for brains.

With no option to stay in bed, to snuggle into her pillow, she threw back the duvet and jumped out. As she stood in the shower, she tried to focus on the day ahead as the warm water hit her body, waking her up.

Lilly thanked her good fortune for the horse walker. She could have four horses in it at a time, reducing the exercise later in the sandschool, which would free up an hour at least. Next, offer Rahima the ride on Bluey. Would Mike take Kabishka? Brent was in St Moritz for the week and the mare needed the ride or she'd be nappy next time out.

A quick towel dry, Lilly pulled on a pair of long warm socks over her jods, double fleeced, then ran downstairs for her jacket and boots. Braced to start the feeding frenzy.

Lilly rubbed a velvet muzzle, tweaked an ear, spoke softly to each as she dropped a bucket over the door. Overnight the wind had picked up. She felt the sting of the cold on her face as it bit at her eyes, her lips, made her nose run.

With a shiver, she tugged her beanie hat down further over her head. Shook and wiggled her hands between doors, in an effort to keep the sensation in them.

With a final glance before the task was complete, she headed back inside to switch the kettle on.

Settled with a hot mug of tea and a bowl of porridge, Lilly wrapped a blanket around her shoulders and powered up the laptop.

At this time of year, updates to her yard spreadsheet seemed to take twice as long each morning. A wet and muddy winter day guaranteed extra requests for services, and extra time taken to do them. Once finished she turned to her event schedule.

Joe had agreed to let her use a couple of his fallow fields for the public zone. This allowed her to offer a hundred stalls, either for trade, exhibitor or catering. Also agreed was parking for two thousand cars.

Several emails were in. Mobile Munchies and Pizza Paradise confirmed attendance. Two more to cater alongside the noodle bar and chippy already booked. Five food vans in total as she had rung The Hungry Man to ask if they could come only yesterday, on the way back from the show. They did a great veggie range, Lilly being a frequent visitor to the local cafe. The variety of fare would provide an added element to the day.

St John's ambulance had been secured from the outset. A mobile crew of three and a stand by ambulance.
She noted their response along with the cost and wrote out a cheque for two hundred pounds as a deposit.

Lilly had set up a bank account to use for the trials, it provided validation of separation from her own business and allowed her to send the Committee the bank statements beside her own financial forecasts.

Also in her inbox was a draft website link from Dean at the Council, for her opinion. It reminded her she needed to send them some photos.

She scribbled on a notepad next to her. They were keen to get onto social media as soon as possible, to advertise the event in advance and encourage interest.

With the additional caterers and several stall holders confirmed, she replied. Go for it. Lilly felt a thrill go through her as she pressed send. She couldn't wait to see the site live, to read the feedback from people.

Maybe it would attract more sponsorship or bring more exhibitors in? She hoped there would be a buzz of chatter on Facebook and twitter, a powerful marketing opportunity.

To be able to show that she had an interesting shopping centre, something to watch and a pleasurable food experience was vital. Every show had them.

Carole from Horse and Hound wanted to bring a photographer up on Wednesday, to interview two of her liveries due to compete. Did she have any names yet?

She checked if Jojo had sent her a reply. No. She texted her, hoped she'd pick it up this time. Jojo was due over and would be a perfect candidate. Katie was lined up as the second one. A vet and an eventer, she was sure to give professional answers that would read well.

Lilly gathered up the printed documents into a folder, ready to take up to Piers later. Piers preferred the old-fashioned paper and person procedure. For the rest of the Committee, she pinged them over an email with attachments.

A quick glance at her kitchen clock, with a groan saw she had run over. She needed to get her yard boots back on.

Rahima and Mike had already taken the horses to their fields and were at work on their designated stables.

Despite the desire to yawn much of the morning, Lilly kept on the move. The work warmed her enough to shed a couple of layers of clothing.

It also kept her from having time to think about the desire to sleep. Being tired was all in the mind, she told herself as she turbo charged her way through the pile of wet straw and manure.

One thing guaranteed in life. Horses trashed the nice clean beds offered each day.

Although some more clean than others, every day, the team went through the same process. Take the poo out, separate the shavings or straw wee'd on.

Once clean, fluff it all up, neaten up the banks that bordered the walls. A fresh bed provided for the horse to re-enter at night.

And how did said horse thank them for this chore? They would circle about the stable, two or three circuits. Paw the ground with a front hoof, snatch a mouthful of hay.

Finally, with a tail lifted up, a sound like a deep grumble from the pit of their stomach, out came the waterfall. As if they had held onto their wee all day for this very moment.

The process would begin again the next day. And the day after. Thankless task? Yes. Essential for the horses' welfare? Yes. Eat as much chocolate as you want, you'll burn the calories doing the job? Oh yes. Well, there had to be *some* benefit.

Lilly felt lucky with all her current team, though not everyone had made the grade. She had seen potential grooms turn up to interview dressed in a tiny vest that ended just above the navel, hot pants and ballet pumps. One whose dyed hair had been teased to perfection, a face covered in heavy makeup.

Then, there were ones that turned up in correct dress, yet appeared to have never used a fork in their lives.

Those who certainly had no idea how to muck out. Even one girl who screamed like a banshee when a horse tried to rub his head on her arm.

It had been a steep learning curve in how to ask the right question in a phone interview prior to the offer of a trial.

Having shovelled shit for over fifteen years, she had the floors clean and ready in an hour. It even gave her time to shovel up the muck heap. Lilly took the hit on this, being, she admitted, a little OCD on keeping the pile tidy. Others had tried, and she'd been polite in her thanks.

The minute they had left for the day, she was over to re-do it all. No, she was not a control freak, she insisted when her team took the piss. Except that she secretly knew she was. She liked the job done a certain way.

Mike was a lanky lad with a mop of long brown hair that hung like a curtain about his head. He would tie it back with a plaiting band until it snapped under the volume.

At seventeen and in his last year of school, Mike worked most weekend mornings. Lilly liked his attitude, gentle in movement, gentle around horses, always polite.

But he would tip his wheelbarrow up and walk off, straw and poo strewn where it dropped. Rahima a little better.

Though she didn't like to wheel the barrow up a plank of rotten wood lined up as a route when the pile had grown high. She'd once lost her balance and fallen sideways into a vast pile of fermenting manure.

Lilly paid for it all to be removed every couple of months to contain it. However, it didn't take long, with daily wheelbarrow loads, for it to spill out towards the field walkway. On the plus side, it was a great upper body workout. Lilly had biceps as hard as rock.

A quick sit down with both youngsters. Fifteen minutes to ask if all was good, any problems to overcome or anything they might need.

Next, a run through of jobs that she required of them for the rest of their shift. Afterwards, Lilly checked in on the DIY yard. Taylor had warned her of unrest amongst some owners.

Lilly debated on whether to keep it as a DIY or to change it to assisted livery. She understood not everyone could afford to pay for their horse to be managed.

Buying a horse was one thing. But the maintenance could be a major slice of the monthly expenditure. To others with the means, just a way of life they enjoyed.

Spending spare time being sole carer for their horse was part of the fun. No, the problem with this part of her business was the increase of disagreements she seemed to hear.

In addition, too many loaners had begun to appear out of the blue she didn't know about. Though the biggest and most serious issue to cause her to think of change was poor animal hygiene.

On her early evening rounds she noticed near empty water buckets on more than one occasion for it to be a simple error. Clocked up over a dozen times having to replenish them to ensure the horse did not dehydrate overnight. Seen mud caked over a face left to dry in a hard lump. A forelock tangled in whorls and bits of twig that twisted like dreadlocks.

And she didn't even want to think about the fields full of horse shit no one had bothered to poo pick for over a week.

If she made these changes, she would employ someone to muck out, manage the feeds, ensure water was always available to the horse. She viewed the idea as a solid solution, one that would offer greater peace of mind. Both for her and those on site genuinely concerned that the horses were cared for.

Of course, Vicky was high on the concern list. The new bolt served its purpose, and Robin remained in place, but she struggled with time.

Lilly had a compromise for her. She knew of someone keen to help out, to ride a few times a week, an ideal loaner. Someone capable of dealing with the neurosis of both horse and owner.

If Vicky said yes, she'd leave her on DIY rate. The loaner to split the cost with Vicky. That would give Vicky money in her pocket to help pay bills and days when she didn't have to be at the yard. The horse would benefit most, and that was the ultimate goal.

Next on her hit list, Jane and mad Mel, Jane's daughter. She shuddered at the thought, a pair of know it all's.

Jane had owned horses for thirty odd years. Her dark bay gelding Larry was always lame, but no one could find the reason.

Mad Mel. A small round woman with ears that stuck out like Dobby the house elf. She strutted about with an air of snobbery; her long nose turned up at those she did not deem her equal. That would be the entire human population then.

She turned puce if anyone made a suggestion to her on equine management. With a loud harrumph she would turn her back and march off.

Her horse, Belle, was a beautiful chestnut mare. Long white stockings half way up her fine boned legs. A very thick white blaze down her face that covered most of it. As mad as her owner. When on form, she won every show she entered. But most of the time she'd buck at the mere sight of a blade of grass that waved the wrong way at her.

Lilly could put up with their idiosyncrasies. Just. But how would they take to the changes? To insist that someone else muck out their stable, turn their horse out? She didn't think they'd be too keen.

Will, early twenties, wide grey eyes that danced with mischief filled his face. He was a yard favourite, in part because he was always happy, but also because he'd bring leftovers from the bakery he worked at. Usually cake.

With irregular shift hours, to enable him to keep his chestnut mare Pippen, he had taken on a loaner. A moaner would be an understatement. One of life's glass half empty stories. If she spotted Lilly, she'd be over with a bag full of woe.

Would he stay? Probably not. But this is business, she reminded herself as she walked. One exception she could justify. Two tipped over the whole point of the reshuffle,

Lilly knew she was going in at the deep end by making changes at the same time as the trials. Though, no time like the present. What did her mum always say? In for a penny? She needed all the pennies she could make.

In contrast to the main livery section, this yard did not bring value to her enterprise. Every month saw additional expenses she had not factored in, these brought her profit margin down. Once wages and feed had been paid, bills, rates, rent, her take-home wage barely matched that of her head groom.

To make it all work required difficult decisions. No one got rich by being the nice guy, did they?

How to keep Taylor on site had been one she'd tussled with when going through the list. Assisted livery would add at least a couple of hundred pounds to the girl's invoice. Chances were her mum would want to move to a different yard.

Lilly had decided to offer Taylor the option to make up the difference with weekend work for her, similar to Mike. She enjoyed watching the teenager ride the little grey Welsh section A of an evening. On occasion, even offered a free lesson just for the pleasure of seeing the progress.

Now, as she neared the corner, voices could be heard, one louder, more agitated. Lilly stiffened, resolve sharpened. Stopped for a moment to listen to who it was that shouted the loudest.

With a sinking feeling she realised who. A mean-spirited little man who found fault in everyone else's riding and liked to point it out without embarrassment.

Sure enough, as she stepped into the yard, there he ranted. Terry Fletcher, fists tightly clenched as he squared up to Will. His grey hair spiked up like a hedgehog under a purple screwed-up face, not unlike an angry gargoyle.

"You calling me a fucking liar?" he screamed, inches from Will's face, spit flying like darts. Will flushed scarlet as he tried to step away from the snarling smaller man.

"I just pointed out that you have had more than your share of our hay. That's all, mate, and you know it. I've been gone two weeks and in that time we've doubled my normal usage. It's left me thirty quid out of pocket."

"Bullshit Will. I've used no more than usual. It's your horse that eats like a gannet, you know your horse is overweight." Terry continued to shout, took a step forward just as the taller, younger man stepped back.

"Terry, I've already spoken to Tay. She says she gave Pip the same amount as always, so I know it's not me."

Will continued to hold his ground. His hands flew up to defend his face against the tirade, his voice tight and nervous.

"Well, that fucking haynet is packed solid." Terry was not going to give an inch. Determined to scream and dominate the other into submission.

"Whoa there, stop, both of you, please!" Lilly waded in. She put a hand on Terry's shoulder, who flinched it off as if it were a fly.

She stepped around more, desperate to distract Terry from Will, who looked ready to wilt under the torrent of Terry's anger.

"Mind explaining what in hell is going on here?" she asked. "I'll ask Will first. Terry, I think you need to calm down for a moment."

She gave a cool stare at Terry to emphasise her authority. She hated raised voices in the yard. Horses were sensitive, they didn't react well to human high emotion.

Will looked at Lilly, hesitant in whether to speak. She kept her focus on him, nodded that he set out his story.

"Well ok, so we've been sharing bales of hay. First it was me and Sue. But Dawn asked if I'd go in with them." he began.

A snort came from across where the smaller man stood. His neck looked like it was fit to explode, the veins twisted and swollen.

"I didn't really want to, but I went along with it to keep everyone happy. From the start, it appeared I was going through the bale quicker than usual. It just didn't add up."

Lilly put a hand up to Terry's face as she saw from the corner of her eye his eyes bulge. She could almost feel the hot steam from his nose as he breathed like a raging bull.

"Go on" she nodded to Will.

"I've been on holiday. Tay has been looking after Pip for me on the days my loaner wasn't up. I got a text from Terry to say he'd got another big bale and I owed him for half. I couldn't understand why at first. But now I've been back three days and each morning I've clocked him taking a massive hay net into Honey's stable. Like, way more than that horse should eat. It's obvious he's been taking more than his share." Will finished, relieved to get his side of the story out to Lilly. He even threw in a bold look at Terry.

"Fucking liar! I've done nothing of the sort, you fucking trying to get me in trouble, you fucking idiot." Terry screamed with ferocity.

Lilly's hand flew up again. It almost smacked Terry in the face as he'd lunged, his arm up as if to swing a punch at Will.

"Back off, Terry!" she warned. He glared at her, his mouth opened like a goldfish, gulping for air. Lilly repeated herself with as much steel as she could muster. "You need to calm down right now."

"If it's not either of you, then we have a thief on the yard," Lilly stated. "Which is a potential risk to my property." She looked from one to the other as she thought how best to action a serious situation.

"Good news for me, I have CCTV in place. We can't be too safe, not just the horses, but you all have tack. I will take a look through it in case we need to call the police. Meantime, easiest solution all round is to change back to the original rule. From now on, you can buy the smaller bales direct from me. Individually. I'll confirm the change in your monthly newsletter, effective from April first. It sorts out any future argument over who has what.

Terry went to mutter something but choked on his words instead.

"Good. That suits me," Will said. "At least I won't have to worry about paying for someone else's consumption."

Both Will and Terry strode off in separate directions. Lilly remained to check on the others. Jane was in her stable, keeping out the way. Taylor was up in the sandschool. Whilst Sean and Lee were both at a show with their coloured pair. The rest had turned out already and gone home.

She stayed long enough for her to be satisfied tempers had calmed, said goodbye and walked back up the track. As she passed a white Suzuki jeep in the car park, she noticed the back was stuffed full of haynets. Several very large and very full haynets. With a surge of irritation, she marched back down.

"Who does that white jeep belong to?" she demanded. Though she had an idea, she knew the answer.

"Ours, why?" Dawn, Terry's wife, emerged from the kitchen with mugs of coffee in both hands.

"Want to explain the haynets in the back?"

On hearing Lilly, Will shot off to the car park area. He returned livid, but victorious.

Terry was left to splutter, grasping for excuses as he continued to deny it. The culprit was all too obvious.

"You might want to arrange a refund for Will?" Lilly suggested politely. Professionalism stopped the urge to shout 'fucking liar' at Terry.

The man kicked his boot into the ground, his face stone cold. He turned and stomped off loudly, threatening Will, threatening Lilly. He shouted for all to hear how he'd had his fill of this yard; he could find better.

Will grinned sheepishly, grateful and wildly triumphant at the same time.

Lilly walked back to the main livery yard with a deliberate slow pace. She was more than a little stunned at just what had happened.

Later that evening, she recounted to Jay via Skype the saga of haygate as she coined it.

"You know, I don't think a week goes by when it's not DIY SOS. Honestly, it's easier to deal with the biggest diva on the livery yard than walk down there," she laughed.

"Tell me, love, who is the biggest diva on the livery yard?" he enquired with a tilt of his head, his eyes wide with expectation.

"That depends on the day." Lilly smiled with a wicked grin. "Some days it might even be me!"

CHAPTER SEVEN

Early March saw a thaw in the weather. A time for horse riders to start in earnest ready for the show season. Bring their horse back into full time work with determination.

Lilly was in the top arena schooling Spartan. She had received an exciting call from his owner, Andrew, to discuss the forthcoming season with an announcement of wonderful news, a European tour.

"I've got entries for the top ones, Lilly. I just know that this will help me hit the big time, he's got it in him to go international." Andrew sounded so excited.

She understood exactly how he felt, been over the moon for him. Spartan was a one off, a lucky find. A tip off from a friend about a horse bought to pull a carriage that refused point blank to back into the shaft.

On the first attempt he bolted out of the yard to jump the six-foot gate back into his field. Andrew paid a few hundred pounds to secure him.

The owner, in his fury, threatened to send him to slaughter. Declared, that was all he was good for. Since then the horse had won every time out. Now, with a sponsor to offer financial backing, it was time to step into the top league.

The deal covered payment for transportation in a live-aboard lorry, plus stabling at each event, entry fees and costs associated. The only thing Andrew needed to find would be accommodation and food.

He told Lilly he would bed down in the lorry habitation. A microwave, kettle and running water would see him through. He'd sleep in Spartan's stable if that's what it took. Last season in the UK had been so successful, his horse a jumping machine, he felt sure they could make it as professionals.

Mr and Mrs Longford, his sponsors, owned a multi-million-pound luxury travel company built from scratch twenty-odd years previous. Now in their seventies, they took pleasure in giving others a chance to shine.

With horses as their hobby, they backed several riders already. They knew the moment they saw Spartan win his class at the Lincolnshire County show that they had found their next project.

Lilly and Andrew chatted on the phone about the shows pre-booked. Many of them she had been to during her time with Charles and Yves. She congratulated him for such an opportunity and suggested she would speak to them, arrange an introduction. It didn't hurt to have a friend or two in a foreign county.

Andrew wished to pay to keep the stable until he returned at the end of September. Eager to avoid an alternative yard. If she wanted to use it as a stopgap, he reassured her she would be welcome. He hoped his return would be a victorious one when he would rest the horse over the winter.

Before departure he was paying her to her to help prepare this magnificent horse for the journey. Spartan was big, a seventeen two hand animal, with power in his back end that gave him the edge. It's what helped propel him over everything.

Whilst a good-natured horse, he was strong, wilful even. Having agreed on a programme of daily exercise to establish maximum fitness, she was in the zone. He'd need to jump fences higher than her. Spreads as wide as they were high. Water, brush, bricks, gates, coloured, whatever the course contained, he must be trained enough not to refuse.

Not that there was much chance of that happening. Nothing stopped him so far, but she wanted to make sure Andrew felt he'd spent his money well. To allow them every chance of success.

Lilly delighted in this opportunity to be part of the journey to success. Despite her increased workload, she accepted the addition of a daily one hour of schooling and light jumping, followed by an hour hack.

A chance to gallop amongst the beautiful countryside around them, up hills to increase his stamina, muscle up his rear 'spring'. What was not to like about the deal?

Today she was in full concentration as the ride wasn't straightforward. A reminder that no horse had such power, the ability to jump at great height, without being a little crazy. She required a firm rein as he pulled her towards fences like a steam roller.

With front feet crabbing and bunny hopping, his back end throwing small bucks, his head attempted to snake free to rush the next hurdle. Every muscle in her body stretched taut in order to keep him in check, her attention keen, focused. All the while, keeping him going forward and in a straight line.

If she could bring his mind back to the job, she would have an easier hack later. On days like today, galloping was both a thrill and a dice with danger. His speed could make her face sting as he whipped up the wind. Added to that, a random buck.

More than once she'd almost tipped over his neck on an off-guard moment. She had taken her fair share of trips to Accident and Emergency over the years and could do without anymore.

He had him settled into a nice even trot when from nowhere he spooked, bolting across the arena. Lilly pulled hard on the reins, sat in, leant backwards. Her fear being that he would clear the five-foot fencing around the ring without batting a hoof and be away.

The reason for his flight, Lilly could now hear, was a whirring in the sky. At first it sounded like a large hornet. Spartan reacted to her request to slow down. Thank you Epona, she muttered to the Horse God. She gave him a pat on the neck in appreciation and reassurance as the noise became louder and vibrated.

Squinting up at the bright sky, she saw the helicopter and almost sighed with relief. Jojo was on her way.

She pictured the woman in her mind's eye. Imagined her seated in the back, blue eyes perfectly spaced above her slender nose, no doubt Vogue magazine in her hands. A tremendously high voltage person, her creativity would be splashed across the pages. Be it clothes, boots or jewellery, her latest collection would be on display.

Jojo invariably gave Lilly the used magazine before she went, like a discarded gem. Lilly never quite knew how to take the gesture. Either Jojo offered it to her for genuine interest, or it was a hint Lilly needed the guidance. More likely the latter, she reckoned.

The French designer would not be far wrong though. Lilly had not the slightest idea about fashion, unless you were talking saddles.

Josephine de Causans characterised the epitome of French aristocratic chic. Almost six feet, fine limbed, well spoken. Her expensively styled chocolate coloured hair skimmed the top of her shoulders. A face that looked like it should be on the cover of the magazine.

Piers made the original introductions. Lilly remembered how she had felt, a little dumbstruck. How did one manage to be born so perfect? All the while he recounted the story that connected them. Whereas now she had heard it over a dozen times as he reminisced. Thierry de Causans and Piers had been in the same polo team for years. Their wives became firm friends.

As children, Jojo and his son would play together, waiting for their fathers to be victorious. Of course, they invariably were, he would add with a swell of his chest. Pride in his exploits of days gone by.

Now Jojo was a grown woman with several successful businesses of her own that took her all over the world to retail and advertise.

Poppy, she explained at their initial meeting, was the horse she wished to take to Badminton. Cross-country being her thrill, she had declared. A danger that made her feel alive.

Whilst papa and Piers had been happiest on the polo pitch, knocking a puck around the field did nothing for her. Her adrenaline only kicked in as she jumped hedges into ditches, or raced down dunes towards a six-foot log.

She'd competed throughout Europe at smaller events, but Badminton was the ultimate challenge.

Jojo's horse, Poppy was a bay seventeen hand warmblood that floated like a dancer in dressage, yet jumped fences with the punch of a boxer.

But with Jojo's business commitments and home life in Paris, visits were sporadic. This meant Poppy was on full livery, ridden daily by either Lilly or Rico. Sometimes even Alison, if time was short. Every other week Lilly scheduled in a trip to Eastbank. A cross-country course you could hire out that provided the conditions necessary to keep Poppy engaged.

There was no doubting the mare's talent. Last year she placed on most outings. Dressage stopped her from the red ribbon. Bred to leap banks and bushes, Poppy behaved as if the discipline of fine movement was a chore.

The dance of a butterfly she produced was due purely to the dozens of hours worked in making her listen. It didn't guarantee she'd remember when in a ring. Sometimes she preferred the wooden leg look.

Lilly reined in Spartan, gave herself a further five minutes to cool him down. She walked him with a long rein for several circuits of the school, to stretch his neck and for his heartbeat to return to normal.

She had learnt the procedure that followed the sighting. The helicopter would land on Piers' immaculate lawn. He would race out to greet her. To offer a cup of tea, a freshen up, a few snatched minutes to chat with his favourite Goddaughter.

Lilly had at least half an hour before they appeared once he had stopped fussing over her.

She walked Spartan back to the yard in-hand. Untacked then led him over to the hot shower cubicle to remove all the sweat from his body. Left him to stand under the solarium, the heated strips overhead warming him through. This horse was too valuable to sponge down and throw in a field still wet. And heaven forbid he might then roll and cover that perfect coat of black fur with a layer of dirt.

Despite the temperature finally going up, rain showers kept the ground soggy. The heavy-duty rugs that kept horses warm and dry were now being replaced with rain sheets.

In Spartan's case he also had knee high neoprene padded leg wraps and a lycra neck hood, finished with a tail bandage. Many of the horses came in from the fields, mud up to the top of their legs, tails caked with lumps of soil, manes matted with various field plantation. Spartan needed to remain spotless.

Checking the time, she dug out the saddle and bridle from the tack room. Laid the saddle over Poppy's stable door, gave the mare a quick brush whilst she was in there, to remove any stray shavings, talking gently to her as she did.

Lilly enjoyed interaction with the horses, rare as it was nowadays. Other people might own them, pay for them to live with her, but she fed them. It gave her star status in their eyes.

A final flick of body brush, a spray of coat shine, she was ready. Timed to perfection. Moments later she heard the golf buggy puttering into the yard that announced their arrival. Piers had purchased it from his club to enable him to drive around the estate more easily.

Lilly greeted JoJo warmly, kisses on each cheek and a genuine smile. The scent of a rose garden mixed with marzipan overwhelmed her senses for a moment. Wow that woman smelt good she thought.

"Piers, Jojo, I have coffee and biscuits if you'd like to come in?" she suggested. Lilly knew Piers hankered to remain with Jojo a while longer, happy to provide him with a reason.

As they accepted, she inwardly gave a little cheer having remembered to hoover that morning in anticipation of a visit. Piers might overlook the mess, but this was a woman who was used to the most spotless of conditions.

The very thought she would appear to live in some manky mess of a pit had urged her to set a reminder on her phone. After all, nothing inspires cleanliness more than an expected guest.

Clean the bloody house! The reminder had screamed at her first thing.

Now the lounge floor no longer looked like a carbon copy of Poppy's stable. For once. It appeared tidy, no visible shavings or hay, no muddy leg bandage spilling across the coffee table, nor a bit or a stirrup iron down the side of the chair. Sure, it was by no means up for a spread in Country Homes, but today a passable eight out of ten for a quick stopover.

Ruby threw herself at the French beauty's legs like a jack in the box as she bounced her paws against the female knees. Expectant of affection. Her tail wagged with similar speed to that of the helicopter's rotor blades. Her speciality was a quick lick of a hand or exposed ankle when they weren't looking. Both humans appeared to like it as she received a good tummy rub from both.

JoJo declined the refreshments with a polite 'non merci'. However, she seemed eager to discuss the September trials, offering to help in some aspect. She assured Lilly that she would be very 'appy to ask friends to sponsor classes.

Music to my ears, mon amie, Lilly thought. This meant some big names and big money would come her way. That would benefit the show, offer the high-end style she had boasted to the Committee she would attain.

Lilly opened her laptop and worked through the spreadsheet that listed items still needed.

Bob, the drinks merchant who owned Cav, had already claimed the booze marquee. He would also supply bar staff to serve up the drinks on a sale or return basis. However, she still needed money to cover the hire of the VIP tent. It came with a raised wooden floor, crystal ceiling lights, tables and silver service. Ideally, she'd like floral displays on each table too.

In addition, she had several fences that required a sponsor. The money enabled the purchase or build, dependent on the style. A selection of fences were bespoke designs. A sponsorship of the under eighteen event and finally going begging was accommodation for the judges.

As she spoke the words Lilly saw Piers break into a broad smile. A little cough interrupted her flow.

"I have seven empty bedrooms. Well, maybe six if my elusive son actually turns up for once. He seems to prefer the gatekeeper's cottage in the wood to his old dad's company, claims he likes the chance to be alone like he was Marlene bloody Deitrich," Piers sniffed sadly. "I'd be happy to offer up rooms for the judges, I expect I will know them from somewhere. Go on, put my name down, my dear."

"And me, I should like to 'ave my name on the under eighteen class. Do you 'ave trophies for them?" Jojo inquired.

Lilly showed them images of the silver she'd sourced from a London company. A firm who had been designing trophies for various sporting events for nigh on a century.

For the second and third prizes she offered a trophy with horseshoes for handles that came in various sizes. Whereas, the first-place trophy of preference bore a horse leaping a wooden gate, behind which a narrow tubular shaped cup rose up behind diagonally.

"Fantastique! These are perfect, non?" Jojo exclaimed.

Delighted that Jojo approved, Lilly smiled with relief. When Jojo agreed to the purchase, she wanted to throw her arms around her. With the trophies now sponsored along with the class, and the offer to speak to well-connected and wealthy friends, Lilly had good reason to celebrate. Key elements to the success of her show.

Lilly had secretly hoped for the support of this warm French woman. She felt a click on first introduction. Visits became more like a friend showing up rather than a client. Jojo also knew Charles Moreau.

Lilly discovered it was his men's fashion line that had first bought Jojo's designs for equestrian wear. Now, less than ten years on, she ran a flourishing top brand in its own right, Marengo. The name of Napoleon's favourite horse offered the association of ancestry, even though it was not a dubious link, he did feature as a distant cousin in her family's genealogy.

Why not? Lilly agreed. If you have it, may as well use it. The connection stirred up further publicity and ensured rapid sales.

"Bon, now, I must see my darling Poppy. I am anxious to ride her, more than ever now that I 'ave a focus date for my big moment." Jojo smiled with satisfaction after signing a contract of agreement. Lilly was not going to let an opportunity slip by to confirm every offer whilst on the table. Never allow someone time to change their mind was her motto.

Piers kissed them both again on each cheek, an enthusiastic smack. But then, he was always ready for a bit of skin contact, she remembered. She made sure to move her face enough, so he only caught her cheek, not her lips, as he honed in.

He too wafted, too strong, of spicy overtones. Lilly caught a hint of alcohol. That explained it. He was often a little leery when he had started on the pop before noon.

With a wave of his hand, he assured them he'd be at the sandschool to watch. To go on without him as he needed to use the toilet. She wondered if he was carrying the hip flask she'd previously seen him take a swig from.

Lilly had spent a good hour the night before scrubbing it clean. Being a Domestic Goddess was not top of her list of daily jobs. An impossibility on a large yard full of horses. Situated on the steps to the entrance of her house, the downstairs loo served as the yard toilet.

She often wondered what people's own bathrooms must look like. No matter the sign above the toilet 'Please flush before you leave', or the bleach and cloth left on the shelf. It was like sanitising a cess pit.

As the women walked together to the yard, they chatted amicably. Jojo keen to learn the gossip. She could draw water from the Sahara dunes with her persuasive nature and loved to know what was going on.

Yard drama was part of life. Who had fallen out with whom, and why? With no names, Lilly recounted the hay tale, knowing it would amuse her friend.

"Mon dieu, it really is a bed of hotness" Jojo laughed gaily.

"Oh, I almost forgot, I 'ave a small gift for you. A merci for the 'ard work you do for my horse. It is part of my new collection." Jojo fished out a small box from the pocket of her riding coat.

Lilly gasped as she opened the light blue velvet lid to find two beautiful drop earrings. The stones were an off white, a fine brown vein running through in haphazard fashion.

"You are too generous, they are beautiful," Lilly gleamed, picked one up to turn it around between her fingers. "What is the stone?"

"Dry Creek white turquoise. I 'ope you like. The stone can only be found in one mine in the world, chouette non?"

Lilly carefully returned the jewellery and closed the lid, clutched now to her chest with a wide smile.

"C'est si gentille de toi, merci beacoup" she replied.

"I 'ave left you the magazin, you will be able to see the rest of my collection for this season in there."

Jojo mounted her horse that was being held by Alison. She threw her leg over Poppy's neck, lifted the saddle flap to check the girth. With a tug at the buckle she racked it up two notches with a practised hand. Leg back in place, with a squeeze the horse moved forward. Jojo gave a small wave as she gathered up the reins, her feet reaching for the stirrups.

Rico was in the sandschool, having just finished a lesson with another livery. He had plans to work Jojo hard on Poppy to get her flying changes in canter perfect, something the horse had struggled with last time.

Following, he would discuss the next couple of weeks work. Agree targets and review videos he'd previously sent her of Poppy jumping or lungeing. Jojo liked to be involved in all aspects of training even if she couldn't be around.

Once they were finished, Jojo would say goodbye, return to Piers, have a sandwich and head back out. The helicopter overhead would signal her departure, as usual about three o'clock.

Lilly knew it would take her to the Alberough airport, where all the rich seemed to use as their UK travel base. Her family jet would be there, to take her back to Paris.

Lilly was glad it was not later. Attempting to extract horses from a field whilst a loud hornet buzzed overhead was sure to provoke a stampede. They would be wired from the commotion, all a jig at the gate, hooves and teeth thrown about with indifference.

Once bring-in and feed was complete and having escaped Hugo, an awkward livery that asked irrelevant questions or complained, she perched at the kitchen table.

With a quick count, there were thirty unread texts on her phone and sixteen emails. A scroll through allowed a scan of the first line. She knew straight away those that could wait. A handful she would ignore, sales reps or spam.

Lilly spotted the magazine left for her on the kitchen table. Reached across to open it up with a degree of intrigue. She had been knocked out by the unusual earrings given to her as a gift. Even more by the story behind them.

A chance discovery in a remote mine deep in the wilderness of Nevada not far from where she once worked. A single ridge of turquoise void of the sulphate which gave the colour, it made this semi-precious gemstone unique. Jojo explained the background before she left. If Lilly thought her gift amazing, what did the rest of the collection look like?

She smiled as she spotted that Jojo had inserted small pink sticky notes on the pages to read. It was something she had a habit of doing too.

Opening the first, in finest gloss paper a top end magazine produced, sat the jewellery collection. Spread over several pages and draped over the bodies and faces of the most fashionable and beautiful models in the world.

Wow, this was pretty spectacular. What an eye the woman had for beauty. All notion of her text messages went out of the window. Caught up in the translation of the French words that described the images she poured over.

She read how Josephine, as Vogue called her, had spent months working with her team to develop this season's pieces, sketching out her ideas and sourcing the stones.

Josephine was described as a designer with an eye on trend. Her vision lay in finding unique, individual gems. Ones ethically mined that offered employment to local tribes. A product that many had never seen before.

The entire series was turquoise and silver. As the article continued, it claimed Josephine was thrilled to discover so many varieties of this beautiful stone on several trips to the US.

From the standard blue turquoise, she added White buffalo, white with thick black splashes. For this, Josephine partnered up with the Navajo to create a natural, indigenous design. Feathers were detailed into the silver.

Lime green turquoise from the Tonopah Mine, that epitomised freshness and tranquility, which worked well in the spring theme of the collection.

A sky-blue stone with no markings named Sleeping Beauty offered the obvious, the Princess range. A model was dramatically strewn on a bed under a glass dome with ivy surrounding her in a cliché that only worked due to the pose and the mood lighting.

The article finished on a description of the final item in the collection. The Hubei turquoise of the Cloudy Mountain in the Zhuxi mine of China. Described as being so intricately woven that only a spider could have designed better, the campaign noted it being an item to encourage spiritual grounding and wisdom.

As she looked over the images with admiration, Lilly noticed that one necklace was selling for over five thousand euros alone. Her friend really did have the gift of making money. To boot, the collection was all but sold out.

It made her stomach tighten. Overcome with determination that she too would find the art of making money in her own sphere. She didn't aim to be stratospheric like Jojo. But the trials could offer up a better way of life for her that didn't leave her exhausted and penniless.

Originally, she'd believed that this livery yard offered up the answer. But only today two liveries had given notice, the washing machine was on the blink and in the post, a larger than usual water bill.

The liveries she wasn't worried about, she'd fill the spaces in no time. She had a waiting list of people with horses, eager for the facilities she offered. As for the washing, she would order a new machine at the end of the month. But the water bill was something she would have to investigate. Almost double the average consumption and they weren't even into summer excess.

Lilly put the magazine down with a yawn. A check on the time made her start. Nearly ten at night and she still had to catch up with the trial work. With the extra rides she'd been asked to do along with Jojo's visit, she was in danger of falling behind in her schedule. Stretching out on the chair, she picked at the stir fry she'd cooked up half an hour ago. Ate it cold with half-hearted enthusiasm, too tired to feel hungry but knowing she needed food.

A quick look on Facebook made her wide awake and bolt upright. Jay had posted a picture from a dinner with business clients.

She dropped the fork with a clatter at the image of a very glamourous and scantily clad blonde sat next to him.

Her hand lay on his arm, a diamond bracelet dangled over her wrist. She smiled up at him with adoration as he talked to the group.

What the fuck? She zoomed in on the image, read the comment.

"A great evening with new clients, glad to have you all on board."

Choking back the green finger that was stuck in her throat, she reminded herself of his last conversation. Three nights ago, on Skype.

The comment continued, "Welcome to our team! A wonderful family from the US, looking to relocate their business to Europe. A meal out to offer them our appreciation. Well, someone's got to do it!"

Lilly breathed out through her mouth. Sure, she knew what job he had. Always surrounded by rich people investing their cash through the company.

In fact, he himself wasn't short of a bob or two. They discussed this. He didn't care she wasn't one of the jet set, that she hadn't seen a hairdresser in at least a year, or that she'd purchased her one and only designer gown from a charity shop. She'd bought it the week before she attended a ball in La Rochelle with Charles when Yves had been unable to go, delegated as his plus one.

Jay had even spoken the L word. Both declared their feelings for the other, she had no reason to be jealous. So why was her heart in her mouth? Her hand shaky? Maybe because she'd just turned the pages of Vogue, seen such beautiful models? Now this.

A young woman dripping in diamonds, her boobs squashed against his arm. They were the sort of woman on the circuit. Women in his daily world. Temptation abounded. Was he leading a double life?

She shook herself. How many times had he told her, never read into anything. He'd put it on Facebook after all, how obvious was that? He knew she'd see it. If he was a player, he'd have kept that photo well away from social media.

Lilly retrieved the fork that had fallen on the floor as she'd gasped. Rubbed it on her jods before taking another mouthful of cold vegetables. With a slam, she closed the laptop, turned to her list of things to do.

With a degree of forced concentration, she spent another hour staring at course plans. The email from Dean, noting the Wingfield Trials website had four hundred 'going', a further a hundred and fifty 'interested'. This was positive. A few scribbles on the to-do pad for morning. Check Joe's car park field. She may have to beg an overflow field. She'd also need to find more parking marshals, though if desperate she could beg volunteers from the yard.

It was near midnight when Lilly turned her bedside lamp off, settled down to attempt five hours sleep. Just as she shut her eyes, she felt a vibration from her phone, a message.

"Don't read anything into that photo. It's been a long night, speak tomorrow. Love you xxx."

She replied with a love heart and four kisses, her heart leapt with relief. She really needed to find time in her crazy schedule to meet up. If she felt like a nun, he had probably ordered a monk's outfit.

CHAPTER EIGHT

Next day, with no time to dwell on her own personal relationship, Lilly rushed from the morning routine to a meeting about Portaloos.

Who knew there was such a choice, she discovered, as Jim went through his catalogue of styles and makes? A quick decision, she was not going to waste time on, er, waste. Then the half-hour trip back to ride Spartan.

Over breakfast she'd re-edited the power point, added more detail to ensure accurate projections. Pictures of the course design gave it a welcome splash of reality.

With the likes of the top UK female eventer having paid to compete, maybe, just maybe, Mark would accept this being a quality equestrian sport.

She determined to remove the image of Thelwell ponies and pig tailed girls firmly fixed in his mind. Surely if nothing else, Jojo's sponsorship would add gravitas of the event.

With no time to fit in Kabishka or Jasper, both in the diary to school, she persuaded Rico to take the reins. Not that he needed much persuasion. Sixty pounds cash was not to be sniffed at.

She shoved away the thought of how that money could have replaced several haynets already re-threaded over a dozen times with bale twine.

Lilly powered the stable muck out, an audio book playing in her ears. One that advised how to cope with anxiety, which was on her mind right now. Anxious she was stretched too far. Anxious about her relationship with Jay. She needed every ounce of help she could get to make it through the next seven months.

She left the grooms with their tasks a little after midday. A quick change of clothes, then up to the manor where Mark and Karl would be waiting for their monthly update.

Lilly was not going to give them ammunition by turning up smelling like a muck heap.

As a ploy to gain advantage of any possible disagreement, she had arranged for Carole to be there to interview Piers. She would run it as a segment of the Horse & Hound article she was preparing.

Piers enjoyed the new found hustle and bustle that picked his lonely life up, made it exciting once more. He walked about with a straighter back, a broad smile, a whiff of expensive aftershave. She hoped the whiff of alcohol would lessen as they progressed.

She'd secured Tony Machin, a top dressage rider and judge, to be the head judge on the Friday. Tony was an old acquaintance of Piers' from the hunt circuit and he'd been straight on the phone, offering one of his seven rooms.

It gave her another strike against her detractor who seemed more determined to prove he was right than admit that she was keeping to her promise of a horse trial to be proud of.

Relief washed over her as Piers knocked Mark back at every caution he raised. Rushing through the details, he ended the meeting early and rather abruptly. His focus was in the lounge where Carole was ready with her camerawoman to get on with the interview.

Mark's face appeared to fold and pucker at every wave of Piers' hand, every tut, tut as he tried to raise an objection or pick a problem.

By the end, he looked like a steam iron had blown hot in his face. He stormed out, red and angry. Lilly would have felt sorry for him, if he were not so determined to prove he was right at every meeting. That the Wingfield name was, in fact, doomed.

Despite wanting to stay, to see how Piers dealt with the questions, she turned the offer down. Having already run through what Greg would ask, she gave Piers a few buzz cards with notes on to help him.

Her mountain of jobs lay heavy on her shoulders. Martin Morley had only this morning spoken in her ear. 'You will feel so much better even if you can scratch off just two of your tasks for the day'. She aimed for more. Ten would help.

As she parked her car, she saw Taylor waving at her. Crap. Now what? That wave looked more than just a friendly greeting.

Lilly had arranged for the girl to help on the main yard over the past couple of weeks. Part of the process of her DIY to assisted plan.

Tay ran over, a worried look on her freckled face.

"Oh, I'm so glad you're back," she gasped, both relief and anxiety etched on her face. The bearer of bad news she didn't know how to give.

"Tay, are you ok? What's wrong?"

Tay appeared anxious, her eyes wide as she wiped a hand through her fringe, stuck to her brow with sweat.

"Inside." Lilly ushered her into the kitchen, her reflex was to put the kettle on. Something was wrong and it was best heard out of earshot of others.

The teenager sat, her hands tucked under each thigh, rigid, strained.

"Ok, but I don't want to put the blast on them," she blurted, her face going pink.

Lilly put a can of soda in front of the girl, pulled up a chair next to her. Elbow on the table, her face rested in her hand, she studied Tay. Small and delicate featured. Pretty, impish even. Under which was a determination and strength that Lilly admired.

This girl was not part of the gossip gang or prone to histrionics. Whatever was on her mind was serious enough for her to feel she had to speak to her.

"Of course not, I won't tell anyone you have revealed any secret. Give me the tip off and I'll keep you out of it," she reassured the girl.

Tay babbled so quick it was over in seconds.

"Belle has a bad case of worms. Mel knows but has been putting her out in the field with the other mares. Everyone's lost the plot. Then, this morning, Sue asked her to keep Belle in. Mel went cray. Sean tried to calm them, but TBH it's all kicked off and now everyone is yelling.

Lilly felt a surge of anger as Tay spilled out what had been happening. Despite her stepping up the visits to involve them more, included them in yard news, updates on the trials.

She also felt overwhelming tired. Up at four this morning, non-stop since. Lilly now relied heavily on her grooms.

Mostly Alison and Kerry, but the younger team too, to keep the livery yard ticking over for her whilst she was out, which was becoming increasingly more frequent.

Her schedule did not stop. Due in an hour to meet Dee, a seamstress, to discuss flags. Then an interview for the local paper who were running a feature on her.

Was Mark right after all? He'd thrown her a last dig as he stomped out.

"You are biting off more than you can chew." His words.

Had she overstepped herself? Even without his dig, there were times recently she began to wonder. She didn't need more cracks like this.

Lilly was a stickler for a rigorous worming routine. It included the DIY yard. All the wormers were purchased from Katie who got them in bulk via the vet practice, thereby keeping the price down.

Lilly only invoiced the owners at cost price. No excuses for why they hadn't been able to buy themselves. A date would be fixed when the horses would be given the paste, followed by a blanket twenty-four-hour stable layover.

In addition, she sent off a soil sample to test the fields twice a year. This would determine the egg count. High would confirm they had a problem.

With a regular clearing routine to remove horse manure from fields twice a week, Lilly was proud of her record. Ever since she started, she had kept the land clear.

Sure, no one liked to poo pick. To encourage everyone to get out with wheelbarrows and pooper scoopers, she took part herself.

Well, that was until these last few weeks.

Lilly kept reminding those on the lower yard about field management. They were not so zealous in their efforts within their acreage. How she would groan every single time she drove past their fields on her way to meetings or the shop. Seeing the scattered lumps grow day in, day out. Another good reason not to mix fields with the main yard.

The last soil sample results came back only two days ago with a higher count than usual. She suspected someone hadn't wormed. In fact, it was on her list of to do this week, drawn up on Sunday night. To send out the results with a request that the fields were cleaned. If she could just find the time.

No surprise, really. She knew, deep down, had an inkling Jane would be the guilty party. Wasn't it Jane that was always spouting on about herbal remedies? How she mixed her own concoctions for her mare. Swore it made the horse calmer.

Which, coming from the person with the most highly strung horse on site, was farcical. She had even boasted about a cure for back pain. Claimed Belle no longer required the physio out once a month. In all likelihood she'd done the same for worms, rather than use a paste tried and tested by experts.

Taylor confirmed those thoughts now as she continued to spill out the information. She rattled on, full flow now that she had made the decision to offload.

Yes, Jane and Melanie had indeed taken it upon themselves not to administer the last round of wormers to either Larry or Belle.

"They said the stuff was all chemicals, that it wasn't good for horses and a more natural herbal alternative should be used." Tay revealed.

A flash of irritation spread over Lilly. She regretted the lack of a spare hour in the day to have gone down there to oversee the administration, to be sure they all kept to the rules.

Mind you, then the accusation would be that she was overly controlling. Which would have been fair comment. She couldn't just rock up and demand to watch, stand by as they fought their horse. She knew the battle. Try to hold its head down long enough to squirt the product down the throat. Horse try to hold its head up long enough for you to give up. Worm paste more on your clothes than in their gut. Emerge flustered but victorious.

"Ok, thanks Tay, I'll take it from here. I have to be somewhere now, but I will be down later, possibly around six. With luck I can catch everyone together, have this mess sorted out. And yes, I will keep it."

As they both stood, she gave the girl a hug. Tay looked relieved but nervous.

"It's fine, go on. You finish up here, go do your pony and act calm. I won't let on, promise." She reassured her.

Seeing Tay out, she checked the time as she closed the door. Damn not enough. She would have to make some quick notes.

She flipped her laptop open to print off a page. Lilly needed a helicopter herself, to fly to all these meetings. Dee's prelim call offered to provide her with all the flags required for the cross-country course at a discount rate, in return for a promotional banner.

Though, equally as important, she needed to knock this on the head. It was evident she was unable to put the reshuffle off any longer. The DIY yard had to become assisted livery.

As she drove, she let the ideas roll around her head. She would prefer Vicky sold her poor creature to someone that could afford him. Immediately vetoed the idea as a tad too dictatorial, nor a solution for all concerned.

The horse came from a background of abuse. Not only was Robin damaged goods, but she was all too aware how Vicky hung onto Robin. As much for her own mental health as anything. To say horse and owner needed each other was an understatement.

Jane and Melanie. Wow, the couple she'd most like to serve notice to. Definitely on the hit list. Though she'd have to wait until Belle was given the all clear. If their herbal remedy had worked, sure, great, she'd even buy it herself. But worms were a serious issue and they could not be reckless with the animal's welfare.

Sue, Will and Carolyn, all three, offer them assisted livery. If they said no, she had no alternative. She had to make some tough decisions.

Tay had already begun part-time work for Lilly to offset costs. The teenager had popped up to the yard to hang out and offer help for months now; the team saw her as an invaluable addition.

Lilly just needed to finalise a contract on paper for the official move to take place. With Tay still a minor, her mother was required to read it, approve, and witness.

What she needed was a Personal Assistant she sighed. Paperwork. Administration. It challenged her daily.

One easy result occurred only last week. Lee and Sean appeared one early morning, mid-stride with a pitchfork and a pile of dirty straw. Now they were a shining example of horse ownership.

With Sean being promoted to Senior Manager at his firm, it offered the extra money required to make more of their hobby. With two nice looking coloureds, they sought to work their way up the line at shows. They sought two places on the main yard on a five-day full livery package for Pan and Roo.

A perfect fit. James and Sandra were off to Wales, where they had found work and a house with two acres of land attached. Fulfilment of their dream in life to see their horses grazing from the window of their own home. They moved in three weeks, Pan and Roo in place the day after.

Lilly reminded herself of her own dream goal in life.

Once it had been the Chief Exec of Wingfield three-day trials, to be one of the top annual equestrian events in the UK calendar.

Though at this very moment in time she would happily amend that to spend a week in bed with Jay. Somewhere hot. With no horses. And no mobile phones.

Delayed as ever by a livery wanting to ask about changing their horses feeding plan, she arrived closer to seven. In time for more screaming. This time Jane shouting at the top of her head for the world to hear.

Arguments always happened on a yard. That was life. People came together not because they chose to, but it was where they kept their horse, Lilly rationalised.

Some formed lifelong friendships from it, but all too often it was a re-enactment of Lord of the Flies, rivals gathering groups of support.

But OMG, this place! Only a small yard, ten horses. Did anyone actually get on with anyone else? When had she been down here and found harmony? If they weren't bickering over who was meant to be poo picking, it may be about mugs left lying about the yard. Who was smoking, leaving butts around the corner by the water?

She could list the gripes she heard as she paused each time before rounding the corner. But the list would roll onto twenty pages.

Two women faced off in the feed room, the door open. The abuser like a rabid bat with her arms arched over in front of her, as if threatening to feed on the other. The victim, like a bug being pounced on, trying to make itself small and invisible.

Shit. Where was a dragon when you needed one?

Lilly reckoned that Carolyn must have dared to raise the worm topic up as a concern. As she approached, she saw the drama unfold in prime soap fashion.

"Jane, if we'd realised, we'd have avoided putting our horses in the same field. If BamBam is full of them, he could become sick. How would I tell the kids?" Carolyn pointed out.

"Don't fucking tell me what I should and shouldn't be saying, you fucking cow. It's none of your fucking business. Huh, you of all people. You are clueless with what you know about your pony. So ignorant it pains me. You have no right to advise me, and I don't want to fucking know."

That was Jane. Angry and very defensive. How come every time she came down to this yard, she heard more swear words than she'd hear for months elsewhere? Everyone swore, even she. But really? Every other word?

Terry and Dawn had left soon after the haygate saga. Lilly had hoped that the likes of this type of argument ended with their departure.

"I am only trying to say that you told us you had a good herbal alternative. Now we discover Larry has a severe infestation that threatens all of our horses. He needs to be separated." Carolyn maintained. She stood her ground, despite the force ten vocal gale inches from her face.

"Fuck off Carolyn, you have no idea what you're talking about. I've had horses all my life. I know what I can and can't give my horse. Bullshit, you stupid woman!" Jane barked.

Her face so red Lilly feared she may burst a blood vessel. Visions of Terry re-surfaced, his neck pumped up, going at Will. Actually, not far away from this very argument now.

"Hello, ladies." She stepped in from the other side of the square. "Time, please."

"Don't you fucking tell me when I can or can't speak." Jane turned her fog horn to blast at this newcomer. Her face froze for a moment as she realised who it was.

"Er, I believe it a reasonable request to stop screaming?" Lilly held her hands up and continued before the red-faced woman had time to draw breath.

"I understand that you are the reason people here have concerns?" Lilly suggested. "You know the rules of the yard. It's in black and white in the contract you signed when you moved here. A date is fixed, I supply the wormer, you give the wormer. Simple. I've checked, you even paid for the paste. I just don't get why you chose not to take part. You owe me an explanation, Jane. In a moment you and I are going to have that chat."

Lilly turned to the bug. She stood shrivelled but stoic in defence of her view.

"Carolyn. To reassure you all I've called my vet. She will test every horse for worms. If the result is positive, the horse gets another dosage and remains stabled until clear. Though, I'm confident it won't come to that. Why don't you go sit down? Have a cup of tea?" Lilly led her over to the kitchen.

Jane simmered with bottled rage. Lilly proposed quarantine for both Larry and Belle until further tests were carried out. Any course of action would be agreed between them. She made it clear that the horses came first in any decision going forward.

Despite muttered asides, the woman nodded agreement. War over, Lilly decided to check the fields on her way back.

Even though it was still only March, tufts of ragwort were clear to see. More visible were the mounds of manure. With a mutter to herself, she marched back, face fixed in annoyance. Without a word. For she feared if she spoke, she may explode with frustration.

Did anyone give a fuck about their horse? Field management was as important as stable and she didn't notice much of the former going on.

Scribbled a note which she pinned to the kitchen door.

"Polite Notice. Fields to be free from horse dropping and ragwort. Work to be completed by the fifteenth of this month. Failure may result in additional charges being made to cover the use of a professional removal service."

Savage? Maybe it was. But sick horses were unacceptable. Someone had to make it plain.

She stormed back up to the house to make a note on her phone's calendar. If they took action this weekend, she would offer a couple of hours to help.

With one eye on the time, she followed it up with a text to Jay.

"Help. Your body required." Adding a see no evil monkey emoji and a panting face.

Was she ever going to survive until September?

CHAPTER NINE

Rico reeled from a conversation with Sam he'd rather not have had. He needed to consider his position carefully, over a bottle of good Spanish Rioja. Drinking was a danger sign. He turned to it to blot life out.

He was exhausted, both physically and mentally, after riding three highly strung horses for over an hour a piece. To have such an intelligent creature perform the steps asked, required him to use all his knowledge in horsemanship. Ensure each movement of his body, the sleight of hand, the tone of voice, exacted in the way the horse understood.

One thing he knew for certain. You never underestimate the power of a horse's brain or the strength of its willpower.

He wouldn't call it a battle. He didn't believe you fought a horse. More a combination of two sentient beings working together to produce the fluidity required to perform the discipline. As he often told his pupils, to master the art of horsemanship first you must understand the horse. It is the horse that teaches you.

Too tired to cook, he picked up a takeaway on the way home, then rummaged around in the back of his cupboard, found the wine covered with dust behind the tinned soup.

Stripped of his riding clothes, he settled into his chair in front of the TV wearing only his boxers. Gave a deep sigh and exhaled slowly.

At thirty-two life had been full of ups and downs, and not just whilst in the quest for satisfaction.

His desire for human flesh was as great as his love of horses. And of both, he'd taken a full booty.

Whereas, he'd only ever fallen in love once.

Having travelled around Europe show jumping, both he and Lilly found their way to Olympia in London via different teams. They'd partied ruthlessly each night and worked hard each day. It was here that he'd met Ben.

At the end of this crazy week with little sleep, he realised he liked being in the UK. He liked Ben even more. An invitation to spend Christmas with him saw Rico jump into Ben's Audi Quattro with excitement. Well, he didn't party with anyone cheap.

Ben was a vet. Part of a team that covered much of Bedford and Northamptonshire. He preferred the equine side, though he had several farms on his books.

He worked long days, too often long nights.

Despite his schedule, he returned to Rico, never too tired nor too grumpy. A one in a million that Rico enjoyed being around more than anyone he had ever met. He felt complete, as if this was where his life had been leading to.

He'd given notice at the show yard in Germany and moved in with Ben. Together they lived happy for three incredible years. Until the accident.

He slugged a large mouthful of Rioja. Swallowed hard. It stung his eyes to even think about it. He blinked back the tears that felt like acid on his skin.

The police said it was instant. But how instant would a fifteen-ton lorry be, hitting you from the side?

He blinked several times more. The pain coursed through his body as raw as the first time he'd been told. The image of that solitary policeman stood at his door that morning. The flashing blue light of his car like a beacon of despair in the dark.

The words he heard in disbelief. A sick joke. Except that it had all been true, a nightmare to repeat over and over when he let his guard down.

If not for Lilly he had been tempted to turn his own light off too, his heart broken beyond repair. Lilly had rushed up to their home as soon as he had sobbed the words to her in a phone call.

She had arranged everything, the funeral, the paperwork, packed his bags. He had moved in with her, an open-ended invitation. Made him continue to get out of bed each day, work with the horses, teach, not give up. Lilly had kept him alive.

Over time, his heart healed, life had continued. Except that he swore never to love so deep and complete again. He deliberately destroyed relationships by cheating. Never again would he allow anybody the chance to chip away the ice in his veins.

So why was he here, thinking about the woman as if she meant something?

Despite his caution. Despite that, unbeknown to her, he met Andrea from the gym every Tuesday night. Not to mention Steve, the judge from the working hunter class he'd entered two weeks ago. They had been engaging in explicit text messages ever since. Or the brief encounters he took advantage of.

He definitely wasn't in love with Sam. Yes, he had to admit; she was fun, made him laugh out loud. On top of this, she offered sex on a plate. And so pretty. Hazel eyes like cats, surrounded by long sweeping lashes. An impish nose that scrunched up when she was happy. Her mouth, warm and sensual with a smile that made you feel special. Oh, and her body. He could bury himself in it, come up for air between those magnificent breasts of hers like a submarine breaking surface.

But tonight, she'd dropped a spanner in the works. They had just finished making love in the back of his jeep; her sat astride him. She rolled off onto the seat beside him with a satisfied murmur. That's when she decided to announce it.

"So, Tom left me this weekend."

"Excuse me?" he'd almost choked, immediately pulled up his boxers and jods. As if he couldn't bear to be naked, exposed, as the man's name was mentioned.

"Yeah, you never guess what happened?"

Oh, he thought he could.

"You recall he'd let me down over our holiday? Ditched our usual ski break with the kids that we take every year. Some bum excuse about an important deal he was involved in?

Then, like I've already told you, he started staying in London at weekends. More reasons, business meal, client day out, stuff I've heard before.

She had looked at him, her eyes piercing his. A command to acknowledge that he remembered. He nodded, reaching for his tee shirt. To be honest, he glazed over each time she brought the man's name up.

Sam sat, her black hair tumbling in a tousled mess almost to her waist, legs now crossed. As she became animated in the story, his eyes were unable to keep from her legs.

"Listen to me when I'm trying to tell you something important." She slapped his arm, stretched out her legs to sit upright. Rummaged in the front for her coat which she now used to cover her lap.

"So, I started getting suspicious. You know, just how many times does your boss expect you to give up your family for clients? It didn't make sense, right? Out of the blue he appears on the Friday before the show last weekend, like at four in the afternoon. Just as the kids were home from school, doing homework."

Sam had continued with her tale. How Tom acted like Mr bloody super dad right up until the Sunday night. Revealed he knew about their affair. That he couldn't care less.

Rico had lost interest, his mind wondered off. About how he might get her dressed, back in her car, make his exit. An in-depth monologue on her marriage was not on his radar.

"I dropped the envelope in his lap with the photos. You should have seen his face!" he vaguely caught.

"What envelope? Sam, what are you talking about?" he'd asked. Distracted, wanting her to shut up and go.

"Do you actually ever listen Rico?" she shot him a fierce look. A weak nod. If it got her to the end of the tale.

"The one the private investigator sent me. Oh fuck me, did he come up trumps! What do you think he has been doing?" she asked again, this time with an air of theatrical suspense.

"Fucking his secretary? Hired a rent boy? Converted to Scientology? I give up. Sam, you will tell me?"

She stared at him for an instant. Leant into the front seat again, this time to fish out her bag. Pulled out an A4 brown envelope, offered up one of the photos inside like a prize.

La merdia! That got his full attention. Tom Parker, super dad, was certainly an avid fan of dressing up, but not in cape and tights.

He was chained to a wall with a latticework of leather straps covering his torso. Two women in leather bondage outfits whipped his chest. A man in a pvc bodysuit knelt in front, his head firmly in Tom's crutch. Like a scene from a bad porn movie. He had not expected that.

"He's a regular Saturday nighter at Sadie's massage parlour. Though, of course, that's a cover name for the S&M club." Sam informed him with a flourish.

"What are you going to do then?" he asked. He'd felt saddened that her husband was a sick jerk.

"I told him straight. That he made my skin crawl. Any future trips home, he'd spend in the spare room. Stuffed if I ever want to make love to that again. I also told him, if he tried to cause trouble for me, those images would be winging their way over to his employer."

Sam looked triumphant. The jeep filled with a cacophony of sirens. It took a moment to realise they were all inside his head.

"Sam...." he'd tried to speak, but no words came.

"It's ok. I'm not about to ask you to move in or become a surrogate father to Charlie and Sophie. To be fair, they'd be pretty grossed out mum was intimate with their instructor. But it does mean we can be less secretive," she declared. Moved closer to him, snaked her hand down his boxers, his jods still unzipped.

And this is where his problem started and ended. Why he sat here now. In front of the telly, sinking red wine and forking a chicken madras down him. Wondering how the hell he was going to get out of this.

Why did he react to her hand? He should have just said no. Told her it was for the best they move on.

He knocked back another mouthful of Rioja. Emptied the last drop from the bottle into the emptied glass. He felt light headed. A bit confused on where he was with his thoughts. A total lightweight with booze. Which was why he didn't normally drink.

That's it! Sam. He resolved to explain. It was just sex, no more. A married woman with two children was fine to have sex with, but way out of his comfort zone for a life partner.
What a passion killer that would be. Being involved with the divorce battle. Charlie and Sophie in the same house. Cute as they were, no no NO!

His phone beeped. He glanced down at the screen. A message from Paul. A reply to Rico's text from two days ago after Viking went double clear to win the open stakes one metre twenty.

"The drinks will be on me! Hope you're having a good evening. Paul." Smiley face emoji, party hat and a bottle of champagne.

He smiled. Replied with two smiley faces and a thumbs up. Paul was such a great guy. Truth be told, Rico enjoyed taking the palomino out.

Viking was an honest jumper, no trouble at all. Compared to some of the high energy horses he'd taken in a ring. On more than one occasion he'd wondered if he were to come out alive by fence four.

Then on impulse, or maybe because of the Rioja, he sent Sam a text. 'Let's get down and dirty again soon.' Then he sent the same message to Andrea. Just to be on the safe side, he sent Steve a text to see if he wanted a drink sometime.

Reclining back into his chair, he drifted asleep. His half-eaten curry, full glass and empty bottle on the table next to him. Netflix continued to play through the episodes of the drama he'd switched on.

Rico knew how to create more dramas of his own than any TV could play out.

CHAPTER TEN

Early May. Lilly's stress level soared as the mountain of work piled up. She realised with growing panic how she had vastly underestimated quite how much she had taken on.

How the hell had she believed she could set up a major sporting event? From scratch. Whilst managing the day job? She lay awake at night worrying about it. Come morning, as she tried to input the diary notes into the spreadsheet, she felt scrambled. Her mind unable to concentrate.

Even with the audio book offering her advice and focus as she mucked stables out, she wondered if she was actually going totally mad.

Even with the majority of people keen to be involved, encouraging, enthusiastic, that still created work.

Look at this colour chart for show jumps, choose the style of rosettes, lunch with a sponsor to persuade them to part with money.

Then there were the phone calls, the five-hundred-word updates for the website, photos to upload from her phone. Time, time, time. How to create fifty-four hours out of twenty-four in order to get it all done.

Not to mention the daily work on the yard. Lilly had insisted, protested, that she continue to take her share of stables to minimise the impact on her team.

She helped bring horses in. She checked on those that were sick and on bed rest, updated the client to their improvement. Filled dozens of haynets, cleaned buckets, prepared feeds.

And every day spent on the yard she appeared accessible to the owners. Clients who all expected to discuss the minutest aspect of their horse with her. Should they buy this supplement? No way. Not only expensive, but it would make the horse hotter, not calmer.

Did she know if the farrier had been for their horse? No. He'd been up to shoe five. Was theirs on the list? She realised just how picky her clients could be when time was short.

Further unhelpful events on the lists, the one where her part time groom left to go travelling. Sara had been invaluable as an extra pair of hands four afternoons a week. She did the work, didn't engage in yard gossip, was efficient, reliable and easy going.

She had no alternative than to replace her. Which meant advertising, at over a hundred pounds. After sifting through the usual unqualified, those that wanted live-in positions, and any that expected more hours, she ended up with Tessa. Two hours a day. It held the team together. For now.

The equestrian show season was underway at full throttle. The shower bays were constantly in use. Twice in one week she'd had to dash out to the local garage to pick up more gas bottles to ensure hot water.

Heavier rugs were washed, packed away for winter. Now, nothing went out without a fly rug. Many also wore a fly mask to cover their face. Some wore sweet itch rugs, turned out almost head to hoof under cover of fine mesh.

The ground began to dry out, and the grass grew thick and lush. Lilly put the grooms on high alert for signs of laminitis, sweet itch, cracked hooves and loss of weight. So far, they had been lucky. All horses came in by four o'clock, it kept away the worst of the frenzied swarms of midges.

Today, Lilly was meeting up with Joe. He had agreed for many of the event jumps to be placed in the fields ahead of time. His livestock didn't bother, they grazed around them. It allowed for the fences to settle, be fixed firmly in place.

British Eventing were due up at the end of July, six weeks prior to the start. They would test them all, give approval of their safety and build. Seeing Joe was a weekly check, to ensure nothing was broken. Only last week part of a ditch had collapsed after a heavy rain shower.

The biggest problem, they discovered, was how tasty some jumps seemed. His sheep had been eating the brush in the middle of the zig zag fence and by the time they got to it, all that remained were wispy sticks. They agreed to wait until the week before to refill it.

Later, an update with the Council on the public side. How sales of entrance tickets were going, to flag up any problem areas. They seemed confident of a big turnout.

Acknowledgement of entries took another chunk of her day. The postman arrived with a wedge of mail; her email box with lines of black unread messages.

William Fox Pitt sent his apologies, away in Europe that week. Kerry had been disappointed. On the bright side, Lilly received several confirmations from other well-known names on the circuit, including overseas riders.

The big names would draw in the crowds. Some would enter to be involved in the same event, others to enjoy the challenge.

Jojo was one of these others. She continued to maintain a weekly trip over to take a lesson with Rico. She had even attended a jumping clinic, performing better than she dared expect.

It offered her more confidence that the horse had the ability, even if she needed a pep talk to herself as she approached the fences. They were designed to be scary, and she confirmed, they were! She returned from it, exhilarated, eyes bright with optimism.

One good thing was the DIY yard. It settled down after the worm incident. Katie, the vet, was forced to suggest legal proceedings for animal abuse before Jane and Mel came down off their own high horses. Finally allowing their horses to be treated.

It took box rest and another round of worming before the two horses were all clear. A thorough clean-up of the fields had also taken place before Lilly approved turn out.

During this time, Lilly sat down with each individually. Explained about the changes to the yard. That it would be assisted livery only.

She talked through options, tried to be as generous as she could. Despite the desire to go ahead with giving notice to the few troublemakers. Gave them all two weeks to make their decision.

Will was the first to get back to her only a few days later. He thanked Lilly for everything, but would move to another yard five miles away. She was sad, she liked the lad, but he didn't have the money.

On his last day he even left cake and prosecco as a thank you. It did make her feel a tad guilty. With a firm handshake, she asked him to stay in touch. To give her a shout if he got into difficulty.

Sue confirmed she would stay on, take up the offer of five-day assisted livery. She'd be up each day after work to ride. Not having to muck a stable out gave her more time for Bess. Recently qualified as a lawyer, the elevated pay meant she could afford the care.

The workload had already built to match the status. No early morning turnout meant she could go straight to the office for seven thirty. Right time all round.

Jane and Melanie informed her they had 'a better place' to go to. They were gone the same day the vet signed off the horse's bill of health. Much to Lilly's relief. They disappeared along with the rubber matting she had installed at great expense in all the stables. Still, for the five hundred or so quid it cost to replace, she would not chase them. They be sure to deny it anyway.

All local yard owners knew each other, and it wasn't long before Flick Parker emailed her, asking if Jane had been a bother to her. A cautious response, to be aware they understood the rules of the establishment and complied. Otherwise, a more jokey line that Jane liked to be a bit of a know it all, loud and proud.

Carolyn asked to stay on, her husband agreed to pay the extra. Both were keen to ensure the children continued to enjoy the opportunity of having their own pony, that included the responsibility that went with it.

He hated modern day technology, said that children spent too much time in front of computers or phones. He preferred to encourage his two to be outside. A bit of dirt to build up their immunity and lots of good healthy fresh air was his view of childhood.

Taylor worked part-time hours over the weekends. She was delighted with the trust Lilly put in her and the opportunity to earn money. She wanted to get to equestrian college. Whilst the state would pay the fees, she had in mind a college in another county. One she would board at.

A small income would give her argument the backup she needed against her mum. Not so keen for her little girl to be leaving home.

That just left Vicky. Lilly had racked her brains over this issue for too many nights. What to do for the best? Eventually she had agreed to a special deal. Only on condition Vicky found a loaner.

Vicky had finally agreed for the woman Lilly had put in touch to help. A small victory.

Those staying, she moved up to the main yard. This left her with an empty area to redesign. She envisaged stripping back the kitchen, removing the broken fridge, the grease laden microwave, and the broken chairs. Give all the stables a deep clean, disinfect, leave to dry thoroughly before painting.

Once the work was completed, she would wade through the list. Invite people up, show them around, agree terms, sign contract, job done. Easy, in theory.

She walked with Joe, distracted by this workload. In her mind she wondered whether she could start tonight. Then remembered the other tasks already requiring her attention.

With the extra money the smaller yard would generate, she would finally be able to obtain a quote for a cover on the larger of her two sand schools. Nothing grand or expensive. Some heavy-duty posts, a roof, maybe a half metre lip to attach floodlights? She drew out the design last week in preparation.

The liveries would be pleased to continue schooling in the dry. Additionally, she could arrange for clinics, teaching small groups. Even once a week would boost her finances.

Even though the yard wasn't hers, changes like this were a necessity if she were to make her name. The DIY livery made her just under a hundred and fifty pounds a month each horse. Whereas, assisted livery doubled that sum without extra services. The business had to show growth.

She smiled to herself. Who knows? She may even be able to start taking a wage herself.

Her biggest and most pressing problem at the moment was her relationship with Jay.

He was a high-earning Chief Executive, sat on several Boards, both in Europe and the UK. His days were spent on the phone, on the laptop, on a flight, on a dinner table, in a taxi and often in a hotel.

She'd seen him twice since February. The rest of the time it was all via the internet. When he was free. Lately neither of their free time clashed. Like two blue whales in an ocean.

"Why can't you get someone in to cover the yard you now, Lilly?" he kept asking her.

She knew she should. It overwhelmed her. Lists lay all over the kitchen table. Last week she'd driven half an hour to the feed merchants as she'd forgotten to make the monthly order, unable to make up evening feeds without.

She'd crammed in what she was able in her little car, paid cash for a next day delivery for the remainder of the order. But it was a costly error in time and money.

"Because...." she'd started. Rolled her eyes about the room, searched for a logical answer.

"Because you're a bloody control freak, Lilly!" he'd blazed. He'd leant forward, filled the phone screen with his face, irritated, creased up, his slanted eyebrows almost buried his eyes had they not been so blue.

"I'm not. I don't have time to sort it, that's all," she muttered.

"Find time. I want to see you more. I miss you. My body misses you. We can't keep this up," he'd warned her.

She felt the finger of accusation reach into her body and twist her stomach. A warning shot she didn't want to hear. She'd only just got past the pangs of jealousy after the photo on Facebook incident. He'd reassured her the girl, a twenty-two-year-old American, had been drunk on champagne and excited at her first European trip.

"Lilly, darling. I want you more than anything. But you have to want me the same way, too," he'd declared. His face softened, though his eyes remained dark. His mouth, usually so full and sensual, a tight thin line.

It was the closest they had come to an argument ever. Lilly had to promise him she would look at finding someone to help cover the daily work. Promise that she'd take a weekend away. Just the two of them. No talk of horses.

How easy it would be to find cover, based on the previous advert, was another thing. Unless you offered live-in accommodation, it was tough to find someone in the area she hadn't already tried.

She continued to mull over her worries whilst doing the rounds of the course. At each fence they tried to wobble every branch, post and rail. So far, it all held firm, secure. She thanked Joe for his time.

"You don't happen to know of anyone wanting summer work on a livery yard?" she asked suddenly. She shuddered at how Jay had looked last night. All this effort, this hard work, the lack of sleep. All to make a better life for herself. But at what cost? The thought he may not be a part of that better life was a bitter pill she did not want to swallow.

Joe looked surprised, stopped to rub his beard pensively as he looked up at the sky.

"I don't think the big guy up there is available." Despite herself, she laughed.

Joe grunted in reply, looked back down at her. He put his hands back in his coat pockets and shook his head.

"Don't let Mr Starch hear you," he quipped back, in reference to Mark. She had called him Larch the Starch last week in conversation to Joe and he had roared with laughter. Like a grizzly emerging from hibernation and telling the world it was hungry kind of noise.

"I know. You probably think the same. That I've bitten off more than I can chew. You'd be right. If I had someone that could help, take my share of stables, maybe even do the show runs, it would give me that extra time I really could do with. Not to mention I could avoid the clients. Not the ones I love, just those that feel the need to tell me about their hard day at work. Or ask for an in-depth account of the laminitic problems caused by eating too much grass.

He peered more closely at her. Saw the puffiness under her eyes and the weariness of her face.

"Aye, there's always a lot to do when it comes to animals. Can't say I do, but I'll keep it in mind for you." He tried to look reassuring. He'd left the beard grow. It was like being reassured by Khal Drogo before he bites off the head of a rival.

She thanked him and got back in her car. She would stop at a store on the way to her next appointment to grab an orange juice and a banana for lunch.

Lilly resolved to find a solution. She had promised she would meet Jay in London. A client was running an art exhibition and he saw it as a chance for them both to be there. She knew she had to make it, or risk him telling her to forget it.

She shuddered involuntarily at the possibility of the next image she might see on social media. That bloody American socialite snogging the face of her man.

Her mood didn't improve the next day when Rico came to see her. He wanted to gossip and tell her all about his love life. He was full of lusty talk about some judge he'd chatted up at a show.

"I texted him one night to see if he fancied a drink. When I woke, I had a date secured. Lilly, he's just what I need to sort my head out about Sam. Then I have Andrea too. She is so easy, no strings attached, same time every Tuesday night, a solid two hours. Wham bam and in the can or whatever it is you say." He divulged in a gush of rapid talk.

"Tart." Was her response.

"How's it with Jay?" he'd asked casually after recounting the tale of Tom and his salacious appetite for kinky orgies.

"It's not!" She nearly bit his head off in a sudden outburst.

He jumped, his face startled, surprised at her. She descended into sobs, tears coursed down her face unchecked as the pent-up emotions spilled out.

He held her tight as she wept for several minutes, her body heaved up and down, her arms tight around his waist. With a final deep sigh, together with a hiccup, she stepped back. Full of apology for the break down, and his tear-soaked tee shirt.

Rico immediately offered to help out. He'd stay at the house, do her shifts, he'd even work on the trials if she wanted. She was grateful. But he couldn't be in two places at the same time. That weekend he was due at a County level show up north with client horses.

They were interrupted by a knock on the door. Jojo popped her elegant head around the door, fully kitted up, hat in place. Ready to ride.

"Shit, sorry Jojo, I am on the way." Lilly jumped up, a quick glance at the clock. Realised she'd been with Rico for nigh on an hour. She went to the sink and threw water on her face, wiped it with a tea towel. Glad she didn't wear mascara or it would be streaked down her face like a bunch of spider legs.

"Is not a problem, Lilly. Alison 'as Poppy ready for me. I just wanted to say 'allo and to 'ope I see you after my lesson. And of course, to find Rico, who is giving me that lesson." She pointed her riding crop towards him with a wink.

"Oh, heads up!" Lilly called as they both headed out of the door.

"Brent arrives sometime this morning," she advised. In her misery she had clean forgotten that many of her top clients were on the yard today.

Brent Chapman. The dream machine, as women might call him. What he called himself, with his Perma tan, white blond surfer's hair, a physique honed by hours of power workouts.

A swole as he told her, a gym rat. Brent worked as a senior accountant in London, which funded his passion. Horses, in particular, dressage.

His bay mare, Kabishka, was on top form to provide him with a strong season in the arena. He had even brought in a former Olympic trainer at the start of the year to work with him.

Under normal circumstances, women chased Brent. The reversal occurred when around this graceful French woman.

"Merde!" JoJo pulled a face.

"On the plus side, both Paul and Manny will also be here," Lilly remarked.

"Ah, in that case, we are all saved!" Jojo exclaimed.

Looking over her shoulder, she suggested "we should all take the lunch."

Lilly smiled with a thumbs up.

Despite his fixation with how he looked, Lilly liked Brent. Several on the yard classed his as a bore, but she saw his commitment to his life goals and admired them.

He worked hard. At his job, his fitness, his horse. He gave them his total focus, leaving little else to interest him. Other than a beautiful French businesswoman.

Paul Greenwood, the polar opposite. The man was comedy genius with his wealth of stories. He travelled around the world to cover major equestrian events, to highlight a current hot topic, or to interview a notable equestrian. He had recently returned from attending a show jumping event in Miami with several top international names.

Sophisticated and full of charm, Manik Halim was another favourite client of hers. He worked for his family business as the PR executive, marketing their property management services.

The company had a portfolio of hotels rapidly expanded over the last five years into the US, India and Australia. His current project was the opening of a luxury beachfront hotel and spa in St Tropez.

Manny, too, show jumped. His very successful horse, Red Star, was a big attraction at shows. However, the major draw was the rider. Handsome in a Bollywood lead way, charismatic and exuberant, he had gained a fan club of girls.

They followed him about the country and made up his very large social media network. He only had to put up a photo of him, ebony hair tousled, a muscular arm or a glimpse of torso and 50,000 likes hit the site. His Instagram sponsorships paid for his sport.

He told Lilly the social media success was a bit of fun; it paid for his love of being in the ring with his horse. He was an extrovert, he needed the attention, to be flattered. Lilly had watched on the ringside as his name was called over the loudspeaker. Had seen his face scan the crowds for acknowledgement.

It would be good to take an hour with them all, it was rare to have them together on a weekday. It offered a small break from constant lists. Some light hearted banter was just the ticket.

She walked to the fields to bring in Brent's horse. She never tired of the view she had from the top pasture, with the manor rising from the tops of the trees to the right, the open acreage pocketed up in wooden fence parcels with horses grazing.

Occasionally she'd spot a fox loping from the trees, a small group of deer cautiously picking at the tufts of grass along the fence edges or a gang of hares filling their faces brazenly amongst the horses.

She led Bish along the track between the fields with a swish of her tail, stopping to yank more grass to chew as she made her way down.

Once in the stable, Lilly gave her a haynet and a light groom in readiness for this afternoon, when Brent would want to ride. As she was closing the door, she heard a cry for help. Looked over the yard to locate the cause.

In the far corner stood Tessa. She had agreed to cover for Willow, on leave this week. Next to her stood Sebastien. A large, rather daft, lovable chestnut gelding.

Sebastien was less than three feet away from his box. Immovable, solid as a rock, whilst the slip of a girl tried to encourage him to go inside. She pulled at his lead rope from the side, stood at the front and tugged, clicked her tongue, called 'come on, boy'.

In desperation she tried to push him from behind, both hands on his flank. She tried to coax him to walk, but he did not give an inch.

As she begged for help, not just Lilly came to answer the plea.

As the pantomime played out, Kerry broke into laughter, as did Alison. Lilly tried very hard to keep a straight face. But the confrontation of the poor girl in her attempt to shift the animal, as if cemented in place, became too great.

"I'm so sorry," she burst out, walking over. Tessa looked at Lilly whilst she continued to try to drag nearly a ton of immovable horse into his stable.

"What is wrong with him?" Tessa wailed. Sweat poured down her forehead from the effort.

"It's dark." Alison croaked, gasping for breath in between racks of mirth.

"Huh?" Tessa looked exasperated. "What's dark? What's she on about?" she looked at Lilly with confusion.

"He needs his light on. There may be a monster under his bed," Kerry burst out. She now held onto Alison by the arm, both near collapse with laughter.

Tessa was wide eyed, red faced with effort.

"A clue please?"

"I forgot to mention Sebastien. He's on Willow's list because she knows him so well. Seb is one of the best characters on the yard. A big boy, totally harmless. He will love you forever…. if you turn his light on, first," Lilly explained.

As she finished talking, she took a step forward to flick the switch in the stable. The light went on.

Instantly Sebastien walked in without as much as a blink.

Alison and Kerry came over, still giggling.

"He has many quirks. You'll pick them up soon enough. But he will never enter his stable, no matter what time of day, even bright daylight, unless his stable light is on. You can turn it off now, he won't mind. He just needs to know it's on when he arrives." Kerry chortled.

"Thanks for the warning." Tessa grumbled. She looked embarrassed, definitely did not see the funny side.

"Like I said, I'm so sorry, it totally slipped my mind. We're so used to him; we just know the moment he stops we have to figure out what he doesn't like. You'll get used to him too and I promise, you will laugh the more you learn about his oddities.

He may not like the colour of a bucket by his door. A cloud in the sky. The wrong lead rope. When he stops you have to look for the culprit. He won't move until the problem has been sorted for him. Oh, and the colour of the bucket? It maybe ok in blue today, tomorrow he'll prefer red." Lilly explained.

"Horses. Anyone says they have no personality are idiots. They just need to meet this boy," Alison added. She patted him on his rump as he stood in his box, taking a drink from his water bucket as if nothing was up. She wiped her eyes, wet from laughter. It would make an entertaining story for the tack room later.

"It's ok, Tessa, we have plenty more horses with their own little ways. You'll pick them up as you go along." Lilly tried to placate her new groom.

"Alison. Kerry. I'm off to lunch, I hear that's a thing to do, going to try it out myself," she announced.

"Oh, and tell Rico when he's back with Jojo that we'll meet them up at the local. Thanks."

The local being 'The Three Legged Mare' pub. Not quite as fitting as Lilly had once thought. Rather than the obvious link to horses, the name referred to a gallow. One that could hang three people at once and built on the site of the last hangman's noose of that area.

Of course, it was haunted. Well, that's what the landlord claimed. The few bedrooms available to rent upstairs were always booked up for Halloween. It's uneven exterior walls and black wood gave it the air of age to enhance the reputation.

The hanging baskets of bright red geraniums and verbena to emphasise the blood of the victims.

Once all seated in the corner of the window at the back, Lilly took food and drink requests. At the bar, the new blonde girl at the till appeared chatty. She seemed curious to know which yard they were from. Dressed as they were in a standard uniform. Jodhpurs, polo shirts, long riding boots. In a variety of styles.

Lilly hated being questioned like this. She was always a little suspicious of people. In response, she waved her hand and replied. "Just a little further up the road."

"Oh, ok, well, enjoy your meal," the barmaid had sniffed, looking a little dejected at the rebuff.

Lilly thanked her, then walked back to the table, the various drinks piled onto the tray. Each glass received eagerly by an outstretched hand as she distributed them. Jojo arrived at that moment. Still perfect, the only giveaway of having spent an hour on a horse were the bits of horsehair on her white jods.

Brent started up a conversation about his new Audi R8 Spyder.

"I had it tailored to my own specification. The roof can open and close in twenty seconds, and whilst I'm driving. It's got a top speed of just under two hundred miles an hour!"

Jojo glanced at him with a well-practised air of disinterest.

"Tell me. When will you be doing these two hundred miles per hour, Brent? I believe the speed limit is seventy on your motorways, non?"

Looking a little crestfallen he shrugged, suggested he would take it to race tracks to 'burn it off'.

Paul chirped up.

"I have a Superb. Skoda superb estate to be exact. It's a good ten years old and seen better days. But, it's economical and does me well for long journeys up and down the UK."

"And that is all a car is needed for, surely?" Jo asked, looking directly at Brent as she spoke.

Lilly was grateful when Piers interjected. She had invited him as he loitered at the sandschool to watch Poppy work. He had looked so pleased to be asked, his face creased into a wide smile of content.

"I say, Brent, what if we do a classic and sports car display on my forecourt for the public to view? I'd be happy to get my old Bentley out. The sixties' vintage. We could charge people to sit in them, raise money for charity. Road safety awareness or something? Manny, do you have a flashy car too?"

This cheered Brent up. Especially when Manny admitted that, other than the Frontera he drove to the yard, he did have an Alpine A100. None of the girls had heard of it, Manny showed them images from his Instagram account.

Two hours passed in good company. Rico had bowed out. A lame excuse she recognised as a rendezvous. Still, Lilly found herself enjoying every moment of this power lunch. Everyone spoke in support, keen to be a part of her dream.

They offered up ideas, contacts, sponsorship. Her anxiety of earlier faded as she felt reassured the trials would be a success. Elevate her even, put her on the map. She was thrilled when Piers offered the car element. After all, who didn't love looking at such a collection?

She realised with sudden certainty that it was time to find someone to give her daily stable duty to. To allow her time to take a break. To have a social weekend with her man like he'd asked. No, appealed.

To reunite them as a couple rather than text messages or face-time. Sit in a pub together. Talk about cars, holiday destinations, current affairs. Whatever came to mind.

As she was thinking happy thoughts, a commotion took place. The front door opened and someone burst in like an explosion. Rico. Distressed, panicked, his face flushed and his eyes searching.

Lilly turned as he called her name. Her immediate guess was woman trouble. Sam caught him out, was after him with a kitchen knife.

She stood as he reached her, grabbed her arm, his grip tight and urgent. He pulled her across the pub into a corridor to the toilets, out of earshot of the others.

"The most terrible news. Lilly, we need to act fast. Katie thinks Templar has brought Strangles to the yard."

Strangles! Lilly was gripped with a fear, vice like as it constricted her lungs. She felt strangled herself as she struggled to draw breath. Strangles could wreck everything.

CHAPTER ELEVEN

At the bar Ella wiped the corner top down with a cloth. Moved glasses about. Tried to appear busy. In reality, she had been eavesdropping on the group of handsome equestrians ever since they arrived.

Ella noted the slender woman with the corkscrew hair the colour of conkers as the Manager. She wore an old tee-shirt with Keep Calm and Trot on emblazoned on it, jods and boots well worn, like she used them every day.

Unlike the rest. The wealthy clients. Togged out to the teeth, hardly a fray or a scratch on their clothes.

The woman that came in later was head to toe in Marengo, the ultimate fashion word for a horse rider. She could spot designer equestrian a mile away. Just a pair of socks from that range would cost half a week's bar wage.

She was well pissed at receiving the cold shoulder, hated being snubbed. It was a perfectly valid question. Why the mystery about the yard whereabouts? Who did she think she was being so rude?

Ella recently moved down here from London with her boyfriend, following a misunderstanding on the private yard they worked at.

The memory burned inside, just the thought opened up the pain to rush through her veins like poison. The look of hatred on the faces of the other grooms as she was marched to her car, taunts of 'grifter' and 'bitch' as Ed drove away.

She had stupidly turned to look back, seen them all with their middle fingers up, some still shouting. Sure, she'd taken the fucking book and the cash tin, not to steal the money, to see what the yard made, every intention to put it back when her research was done.

She swallowed hard as Ed's face came into her mind, those kind eyes reassuring her, his arms around her, his London tones telling her it would all be tickety boo.

The accent soothed her even now as she recalled it. He believed her side of the story; had even agreed to forget her night with Jim, the owner of the yard and all ten horses, agreed that her head had been turned by his money.

Reliable Ed, her one true pairing, always there for her when it all went to pot.

They had moved county; she took this bar job to supplement the supermarket shift work. Even though it meant a total climb down her ladder of success, it kept her safe whilst the storm settled, time for people to forgot about her. Resigned to wait for the next opportunity.

As she was about to collect glasses, a tall guy burst in. All shaggy long dark hair, deep eyes, concern etched across his extremely attractive face.

Conkers jumped up quick, was whisked away to the side passage. Close to where she now wiped the same bit of polished wood over and over.

As she heard the word 'Strangles', she leaned further over to listen. Being an equestrian from birth, she knew instantly the devastation that word conjured up.

Hah! Not so keep calm now from the manner of her. Still, it was a chance not to be missed. Maybe her next opportunity?

She glanced over at the table where the others sat in silence, unsure what was happening. Where's there's muck there's money as the old saying goes, she told herself. And where there's horses there's always muck.

With a renewed optimism, she raised up the wooden latch to the bar, darted through, over to the couple.

"Hi. Sorry to butt in, but I overheard you as I was cleaning the bar counter. Do you need help? You see, I've worked on yards most of my life." Ella announced.

"Excuse me, this is a private conversation." Mr Banderas look alike didn't even glance at her as he snapped.

"No, Rico, hear her out. She knows what Strangles means, or she wouldn't have interrupted us." Conkers replied. Ella was surprised. Maybe she had misread the woman? Quite possible, she and women never seemed to get along.

"Go on. You suggested you can help. Do you have experience with an outbreak?" she questioned.

Ella nodded. Yes, she had experience with the illness. Knew how to manage an outbreak.

"My boyfriend and I can offer you assistance with a deep clean at the very least?" she suggested.

Rico. Ah. She'd called it right, definitely Spanish with those looks and that name.

Rico stared at her as if scrutinising her soul, which she sincerely hoped he wasn't.

The woman, however, appeared to already have the world on her shoulders, visibly crumpled by this news. Had she been hasty in judging her? Maybe she just needed help?

"Are you both free this afternoon?" she was being asked.

"My shift finishes in five minutes. I can ring Ed and be with you as soon as. Tell me where your yard is, other than just down the road." Ella confirmed, unable to miss the swipe at the previous snub.

"Ok, you're on. We need all the help we can to act fast. Sorry, quick introductions. I'm Lilly. My just down the road yard is in fact Wingfield Equestrian. This here is Rico, my Chief Instructor."

"I've seen it as I've passed for this pub." Ella nodded. "And I'm Ella. Ella Bailey." She shook hands briefly.

"I'll ask the Manager if I can leave now. That way I can get to the store and pick up a pile of cleaning products. Ed can bring his high-powered pressure spray, that will reduce cleaning time. She continued.

Lilly nodded in gratitude; every bit of help was vital in getting the yard prepared.

Ella ditched the bar cloth, took off her apron and sought the landlord out. She was needed at the Wingfield Estate, sure fire guarantee he'd release her.

Ella had seen the old guy who was sat at the table with the others several times before. Had asked Pete who he was. Only the owner of the massive house and grounds on the village outskirts.

More importantly, a multi-millionaire! Pete treated him like the Lord of the Manor which, apart from a title, he was. Attentive, insistent on serving him himself, on hand to take his hat and coat the moment he walked in to the bar. Pete would snap his fingers at the staff to serve up a pint of lager on the house.

Now she could introduce herself, find out more about the yard and those on it.

As they all hurried back to the yard, a five-minute walk down the road, she showed her usefulness as loudly as she could. Called Ed on her mobile, asked him to pick her up at the entrance to the yard, to take her to Andersons. The local hardware store would sell everything they needed for this emergency.

Those that had been at the meal now spoke with concern for their horses. She heard Lilly reassure them that Katie was already there, taking swabs to send for testing. Ella presumed that Katie was the vet.

She knew that Strangles was an airborne virus. Whoever had brought it to the yard would have been none the wiser. Similar to catching flu in an office.

But the fact that it was airborne meant that it could sweep through the horses in a matter of days unless action was immediate.

Rico was walking very close to Lilly, looking at her from time to time. Ella wondered on their dynamic, were they lovers?

He gazed at Lilly with such tenderness and concern. His body she would be happy to explore, she mused. She watched his muscular shoulders flex as he put an arm around Lilly, hugged her to him, whispered in her ear.

He smiled, but Lilly's face remained fixed, pained. Though she hadn't resisted this handsome Spaniard's touch, Ella reflected. Hmm. Chief Instructor, she said. Ella was going to have fun finding out the gossip on him.

She turned to watch the others as they walked along the path next to the road. Lane would be more apt, surrounded either side by banks of trees and overgrown with weeds, any traffic was mostly pub related.

The stunning woman screamed sophistication. Well-groomed was an understatement. She'd heard a foreign accent, French she decided. That turquoise necklace, like nothing she'd seen before, definitely something she'd like to own. It would look great around her neck.

Ella couldn't work out the guy with the beach hair. He looked like he belonged on a surfboard, yet he dressed expensively. His deep tan, possibly salon spray? It made his teeth shine like perfect white drops.

Ella wondered if all the men on the yard were this handsome? If so, Ed would never let her out of his sight.

Next was the bouncy man with the perfect eyebrows and just a hint of bronzer. He came across as a huge personality, full of fun, the entertainer of the group over lunch, but probably more interested in Ed. His hands waved about dramatically, emphasising each story, the others had roared with laughter, encouraged further stories.

Last not least was the striking Indian. Her heart beat slightly faster just to look at him.

Rich blue-black hair stiff in front with gel, designer stubble about the strong jawline. Confident, self-assured, hadn't she seen him on Instagram? He'd appeared a couple of times on the search button.

She knew that he was the son of a magnate with an empire not far off Byzantium in size. He looked more delicious in the flesh than in the photo.

She tingled with excitement at the prospect of this unexpected change of circumstances.

"It's very good of you to offer help. Have you experience of Strangles?" she heard someone ask as they walked along.

Ella turned, saw that Mr Wingfield Brown himself had stepped into her stride. He gazed at her with the usual admiring hunger she received from men.

With hair the colour of buttermilk, straight and long, almost to her waist, eyes like two pieces of sapphire set under Bambiesque eyelashes, she had been referred to as a Disney Princess on more than one occasion. She batted her eyes like one now as she replied.

"It's my pleasure. Yes, I have, and I know how emotional this can be for people." She breathed; seduction laced her voice.

"Piers." He stuck out his hand as they walked, as if he required an introduction.

"Ella." She smiled back, taking his hand in hers. Gave it a squeeze. Enough for him to register the gentle touch of her skin.

"I've seen you at the pub a few times. I would have introduced myself, but Pete seems to keep his lovely barmaids at arm's length. Shame."

"Pete likes to offer a personal service. I think that's what keeps his pub so busy." Ella attempted to offer a reply that was neither rude nor dismissive.

"Well Ella, he does a grand job. Now you are doing the same. To offer your help to us so readily, Lilly could use it. She's already working herself into the ground, what with the grand event we're doing in September and all the changes she's implementing on the yard. It's reassuring that you youngsters are still ready to pull together." He held her hand for a moment longer before releasing it.

For real? Her day got better by the minute. This was just the sort of thing she had hoped for.

The group arrived as Kate, the vet was packing up. She was in the midst of reassuring several people gathered around.

"No, it doesn't appear that any horse has early symptoms," she was saying.

"I'm confident we have reacted quickly. But we must put normal procedures in place. I'll expedite the swabs. In the meantime, a thorough clean must take place."

Ella stood close to Lilly. Noticed how she immediately took command of the situation. Asked Kate key questions. Watched as Lilly absorbed the information. She stood quietly; her face fixed on the vet as they talked.

"If Templar has it, we will know within a fortnight if it infects others. For now, the usual. Lockdown on the yard. Isolate. Don't share haynets, water, or utensils. And take temperatures twice a day," Katie advised.

"Everything needs to be disinfected. The lot, buckets, tack, doors, boots, wash all rugs. Oh, and I recommend a tray of disinfectant at the entrance for people to walk through." She added.

Ella stepped back from within the circle to avoid being too conspicuous. She wanted to remain under the radar for now. All too aware horse owners questioned strangers.

It gave her a moment to take a quick look at the yard set up, how everything was so clean and tidy, a couple of wheelbarrows stood haphazardly on a track next to the end stable full of used bedding the only giveaway to the work being done.

"Right, quick update guys." Lilly turned to those gathered. Ella turned back to make sure she caught the conversation.

"Whilst Strangles might be a possibility, nothing is certain. Until Katie receives back the results, we are going to undertake full precautionary measures. Regular bulletins will be posted on the yard Facebook page so keep an eye out for them."

Ella was impressed with how calm and reassuring she sounded. How four that were probably the grooms took her command without question. That's how I want to be when I have my own yard, she told herself.

Ella grew up around horses. Her parents had owned a very successful Arab stud. Bred top quality foals that sold for thousands to use in endurance races, showing, valuable hacks. Despite the slightly unpredictable temperament. The quick flare up of the nostrils. Snorting with terror at a leaf. Their beauty surpassed any other creature.

This highly strung character literally reared its ugly head when their top stallion, Amyr, had become agitated being led to a mare.

He went up on his back legs, kicked out with both front legs. One of which caught her dad on the forehead. The kick killed him instantly.

Her mum sold the stud and all the horses. Moved as far away from that lifestyle as she could. The two of them lived in a small flat on the coast in Devon.

Mum had helped out at a local café on the beachfront. Served tea and toasties in the winter, ice cream and soda spritzers in the summer. When her shift ended, she returned home and served herself gin.

Ella had been angry with the world for many years. Hated her mum, rebelled against society.

Now she channelled the rage into energy and focus. She wanted back the large house, the horses, shows, parties, the fun.

She'd missed her childhood and was going to recreate what she had lost.

So she'd messed up a few times? Fuck it, you only live one, she moved on. Kept her head down, waited for something like this. Strangles. To her, this was opportunity knocks.

Lilly asked what plans people had over the next couple of weeks.

The funny one said that he was scheduled out on Viking this Saturday. Surfer dude was prepping for a dressage class in a fortnight. Ella found it hard to associate him in elegant top hat and tails doing canter pirouettes. Surely, he should be riding waves in Newquay?

Katie told Paul, the funny one, his show was a no go. However, Brent, of dressage not beach, should continue as he was for the moment. Results would be back within the week. If positive, no-one would be leaving the yard.

Manny announced he would also cancel his show this Sunday. He flashed a dazzling white Hollywood smile. Shrugged his shoulders.

"Hey, I can issue an Instagram post today. It will keep my fan base in suspense," he remarked.

"Sad face, fingers crossed emoji," Paul joked. Everyone laughed.

Ella would have to look him up. She didn't recognise him, but by his manner and speech, he might be a popular influencer. Handy information and someone to bring over to her corner.

As her mind whirred through endless possibilities, her phone vibrated in her pocket. Ed. At the bottom of the drive ready to pick her up.

CHAPTER TWELVE

After a nervous week, the tests came back in. A negative result, Templar did not have Strangles. Even though they were in the clear, Lilly enforced a two-week curfew as a precaution.

Templar received a full examination during which Katie felt a sharp back molar in his mouth. This could have caused the loss of appetite and the lethargy symptoms.

A dental visit sorted this for him. He was eating as normal within days.

A rollercoaster two weeks for Lilly, who had barely slept or eaten. Though where there are negatives there are positives.

What a stroke of luck meeting Ella. She and Ed were blinding. Lilly felt she would never have coped without them.

Ed had arrived back that day with a whole car full of equipment, including an industrial-sized power washer.

Neither he nor Ella wasted any time in getting stuck in. He took the lead, offered out tasks for the grooms, worked as a unit.

Stable doors scrubbed, feed and water buckets soaked in hot water. Ed even found a huge old barrel from the pub that he filled with disinfectant to soak all the hay nets in. Daily wipe downs, plenty of hot water and a large dollop of disinfectant on both yards. Lilly watched as Ed went about the work.

She knew he had caused a flurry already. The grooms wanted the low down. Who was this guy with hair the colour of creamy smooth fudge, the hottest face this side of the sun and a twinkle in his hazel eyes? They stopped to watch as he powered through jobs with the force of a steam engine.

Ella was slightly more reserved. Beautiful, but remote. She was friendly enough, but seemed to remain in the shadow of her enigmatic boyfriend.

The following Friday evening Lilly was sat at home with Rico. In her lounge, drinking beer and eating a Chinese takeaway he had brought round. It gave her the chance to talk through the emotional rollercoaster of the past fortnight.

"Well that was a nightmare two weeks," she declared, sipping from the bottle, then scooping a forkful of noodles into her mouth.

"Geesh Lilly. Don't you ever learn to eat junk food delicately?" He scolded as she dribbled soy sauce and bits of spring onions down her chin.

She threw a chopstick at him, dabbed her face with a tissue.

"I'm bloody starving. I can't get it in quick enough."

"Hmm, is that what Jay says when he finally gets to see you?" Rico continued to tease his best friend. Ducked as a browband was flung at him.

"Stop! The next thing in that box may be a stirrup." He put his hands up in mock surrender.

She looked down into the tub, then back up at him. Triumphantly, having hooked out the next item she could see.

"This riding boot. It still hasn't been claimed!" she declared before replacing it with a shake of her head. "Anyway, that's a sore subject at the moment," she confided. She looked at her dinner sadly.

Rico picked up the drop in tone, realised he'd touched a nerve. Kicked himself for the comment. He had been made up for her when she confirmed the romance. So happy she may finally have met someone that made her heart sing.

He had noticed how the handsome man reacted at the table when introduced that night. Rico was too experienced in love and lust to not pick up on the vibe as the evening progressed.

After the first date, Rico picked her up, spun her round and round. Kissed her face in delight. Finally! Someone had broken the code.

In all the years touring Europe, same shows, same after parties, she never did more than dance with a man.

They discussed this. Usually after she'd rescued him from yet another near-death experience, yet another threat to his genitals. She just dismissed him with a smile. No one interested her enough.

He put his plate to one side, moved over to sit next to Lilly on the larger sofa.

"Tell Uncle Rico?" he coaxed gently. An arm around her shoulders, he hugged her towards him.

"Oh, you know, the usual. I never have time for him yet I've always time for the horses. I keep telling him, it's my career, my ambitions, plans for my future, that he has to be patient.

But the last conversation we had he was not a happy bunny." She looked her friend in the eye. A tear formed as she brushed her hair off her face.

"So, go see him. Have great sex, it's what you both need." Rico brushed the hair back over her ear, took her hand and squeezed it tight around his.

"I can't. There is too much to do. My list for the event gets longer, not shorter. Then I have the DIY yard to repaint and tidy up before I can get anyone in there. Plus, I have a groom down. I barely have time to eat these days Rico, let alone think about sex."

"You must always find time for sex, it's important in life." He reasoned.

"For you maybe!" She laughed. "Rico, if we all had sex as much as you do, we'd never have time for work."

He gave her a pretend shocked look. "If I had sex as much as you do, I'd take my vows and enter the Church," he countered.

"Ok, good comeback, you burn. But what do I do? He's told me he'll be over in London in two weeks' time and wants me there for the whole weekend or else he's calling time on us. I can't leave this place for half a day, let alone a whole forty-eight hours!"

"I can cover for you," Rico suggested.

She hugged him, buried her head in his chest for a moment.

"I love you Rico for offering. But we've had this discussion already. You have the big County show up in Yorkshire with four of our horses. And you agreed to help Manny, you can't let them down just so my boyfriend is sated.

No, I'll just have to accept it's over. My career comes first before any man, even one I love. It's for the best, I'd make a rubbish full time girlfriend for him anyway. Always covered in hay and smelling like horse shit. His upmarket friends would run for the hand sanitiser every time they met me." Lilly replied with a long sigh.

"Hey, we'll think of something. Vamos! Eat and we think of a plan. You will go to the ball, Cinderella." He rubbed her shoulder, kissed her head.

Lilly desperately wanted to keep the love alive. She had never met anyone like Jay before. Doubted she ever would again. Yes, she did take longer to give herself to a man. But when she did, it was in the honest belief that he was 'the one'.

Wayne Rivers had been 'the one' previously. For a solid six months until that moment he'd come home under the influence, smelling like a stag in mating season.

A few dates that never went anywhere had followed. She'd watched from the side as what seemed like the entire equestrian world bonked each other's brains out. Casual acquaintances were not her thing.

When she met Jay, she felt something click inside her. When she had first allowed him into her bed she'd felt, well, a lot more than a click inside her. It was like that every time they were together. He was her perfect match.

With all her heart, she wanted to say yes to him. Yes, she'd be in London. They'd make up for the weeks apart.

But she had one shot at this event. If she let anything slide for a moment the Wingfield Director would dance. Dance in his neatly creased pinstripes on her equestrian headstone. Singing "there lies the failure of Lilly Bailey. I told you so, I told you so."

She'd tried to explain it to Jay. Yes, he was aware of how important it was to her. But he wanted to be more important to her. He wanted to know that his love was worth more than being an event organiser.

He had urged and encouraged her to fight for her dream. But at the same time, he too was a top priority.

No doubt another sleepless night awaited as she tried to figure it out.

For now, she attempted to lighten up the mood of the evening. To avoid feeling jealous of her Spanish lothario. She reminded herself that he played with fire, juggled three lovers. It was only a matter of time before one would find out. She hoped it wouldn't be Sam.

"Enough of my woes. Cheer me up! How's your love life, Romeo?"

He tilted his head and gave a slight shrug of his shoulders.

"I think what you ask me is about Sam, no? I don't know, Lilly. One day I want to call time. Next day, I get a snapchat, she's draped over her bed wearing a bit of black lace. I get hot, arrange to view it for myself. Since the incident with her husband she is hungrier than ever for my body," he revealed. "She is unreserved in bed. I can't say no to such temptation." At that he gave her a sheepish grin.

"But what if she finds out about the others?" Lilly was concerned about the fallout.

"She won't. I am not in hotel bedrooms now, Lilly," he assured her.

"Well, make sure she doesn't. Her heart has been broken enough already." She chided him, wagged a chopstick his way.

Lilly knew that at some point he would move on from Sam. But he promised he had explained all this. Sam accepted it was just lust, not commitment.

"You know me. Ben took my heart with him the day he died," Rico added, a little wistfully.

Lilly took this as a signal to move away. Turn to other talk, like yard gossip. Lighten the mood before both became too melancholic.

But how to ensure her own love did not move on bothered her. Lay heavy on the noodles.

Not to mention that bloody socialite she had stalked the night before last. Curious. Jealous. There, on the bitch's Facebook page, was a photo of Jay, stood next to her at another event.

A love heart surrounded them both with a comment 'lifetime goals' to which several of her friends had commented. 'Hot as a Miami sidewalk in summer'. 'Lucky bitch'. 'Keep working on him girl, he won't be able to resist'.

She was being driven insane. Should she come clean? Risk what she'd worked so hard to achieve under her own steam? He didn't care who knew, but on reflection, after a fitful night, she realised she did. However, she was not about to give him up either.

She had an idea.

CHAPTER THIRTEEN

The next morning, Lilly was on the yard helping out with the stables. Being a groom down, she needed to help the team. She took five beds to muck out, made up haynets and washed the feed buckets for Alison to prepare later.

A good four hours labour. She couldn't offer more than this as she was due to meet Piers at eleven sharp. They were off to lunch with a potential large sponsor. One she would be mad to rain check.

Lilly had kept up a thorough cleaning programme for a further two weeks. She waved as she saw Ed changing the trays of disinfectant in the hot shower cubicles. Dipped brushes in, scrubbed forks, spades, hoofpicks, all utensils they used every day.

He stood upright, gloves dripping in soap suds, his tee shirt soaked, dirt smeared across his tanned arms. Gave her a cheery smile.

It confirmed her thoughts following her conversation last night. She'd asked Rico what he thought of the young help.

"I like Ed. Too straight for me, such a waste. But he is for sure a hard worker. No complaint, gets the job done. The Ice Queen? She make me uneasy. I can't quite state why."

Ella continued her shifts at the pub. She walked up to the yard from work, quietly helped Ed out. She seemed particularly good with the livery owners, chatted about their horses, asked the right questions.

Whereas, she kept away from the grooms. It ruled out shyness, but Lilly wondered if maybe she didn't want to tread on anyone's toes. The grooms knew each other, the daily routine. Ella and Ed were additional to this. They were there to ensure the yards remained sanitised and safe.

Lilly wondered if Ella was overshadowed by Ed's character. From the moment the car door opened, he bounded out like an enthusiastic puppy with just one gear, high.

She noticed how Ella dropped the smile when she thought no one was looking. Saw a more detached, guarded face, troubled even. She dismissed it as nothing.

None of her business. Not everyone had to have a bubbly supersonic personality to be here. She'd seen more miserable faces on a Monday morning from her staff.

There appeared no cause for concern. Ella seemed friendly enough to her whenever she stopped to chat.

She tossed straw in the air. Separated poo from stems, clean from wet. Systematically worked her way across the floor of the stable until it was clear. A huge mound by the entrance left ready to fork into the empty wheelbarrow.
Once done, she pulled straw back down off the banks, covered the floor, neatened it all up. If more bedding was needed, she'd wait till all stables were finished.

She had made a decision to ask Ed if he would stay on. Contract him to five, maybe six hours a day if he agreed. Who better to prepare the DIY stables for the new five day assisted liveries?

They all required a thorough power wash and paint. The grubby kitchen needed a clear out, add a new fridge, have the electrics tested. Last of all, fix in the new rubber matting in the stalls she'd purchased in readiness.

A thunderbolt in the night idea. How to lighten her load. Having someone else take this massive hit off her task list removed a major stress.

As for the additional groom post, would Ella take it? She mentioned she'd worked with horses before. She appeared capable of doing the job.

The niggle in her head was that Ella kept changing the subject each time Lilly asked about her previous yard job. Why? Pretty much standard. Why the diversion tactics?

Next part of the thunderbolt, if they agreed to terms. Would it be an ask too far to see if they would cover the weekend? She would want them to stay in her house to be on call, look after Ruby. If they said yes, it was game on.

She'd tried her parents as the last-ditch resort three days back. She knew that if she left them instructions, they would care for Ruby. Pay Alison to do the early shift.

As she dialled, her heart had dropped the moment the ring tone came up. It was the international one beep, rather than the double dring.

About a year or so after she left home, they had told her they were ready for their own adventures. Sold up, purchased a small flat near the coast. Travelling the world on the remainder of the proceeds.

"Darling, how lovely of you to ring," her mother answered.

"Hey mum, where are you?"

"In our lodge, about to go for dinner. What's up?"

"Mum, I meant, are you in the UK?"

"Oh no, we're still in Australia. Don't you remember? We're doing a trek through the Eastern side. Is everything ok?"

Fuck it, nope, completely forgotten. Until this second. Of course, they had told her weeks ago. Six months in the southern hemisphere like a couple of teenage backpackers. Which threw that line of thought straight out of the window.

"Yes mum, now I do. Yup, all's ace here. I was going to ask you to do a bit of dog sitting next weekend. But as it'll take you that time to fly back, I figure it's a no." She laughed, despite the frustration.

Lilly chatted with her mum for a few minutes longer. Heard all about their trip to Perth. How they drank espresso martinis on the beach at midnight.

Mum had assumed it was just a lovely coffee until her head spun. Dad carried her back to the hotel, and she slept until lunchtime. Now they were camping in an eco-retreat surrounded by parrots.

"Mum, it all sounds brilliant. Keep on with the experiences." Lilly was pleased for them. Though she wondered if she would ever have the chance to do such crazy things with the man she loved. She signed off with a request for a didgeridoo.

Plan Number 74 out the window. One last shot. As she walked to the muck heap the idea whirled about her head.

Once it resembled a neater square pile than the spilt mountain of debris, she decided it was worth a shot. With her heart pumping, she went off to look for Ed, found him in the staff room, making everyone a coffee. A mixture of yard folk sat chatting amiably.

She joined in for a few minutes, as people wanted to tell her the latest saga of their lives. Ed held up a tea bag from her packet, pointed to it. She nodded gratefully.

"Ed, are you free later on for a quick chat?" she asked as he handed her a mug. "About four o'clock ish? Nothing awful, don't look like that, honestly, nothing bad. I've got to get changed now and head off to yet another meeting. But I'd like to put a proposition to you."

"For you, Lilly, of course. Though, I have to tell you, I am already taken." He winked at the others.

"Oh, Ed, do let us know if that changes," Kerry giggled. Immediately the banter started to fly around the room on Ed's potential eligibility.

"Guys, you're making me blush," Ed protested in jest.

It was clear that everyone liked him. It cemented her decision.

"Great. I'll see you later. Ella too, if she is available. Right now, I really must go change. Mrs C won't be too happy if I walk into the manor with the warm scent of horse shit wafting about."

Lilly took a final gulp of her drink, thanked Ed for the tea, then left them to it.

Piers was in a shit mood. Lilly was warned the moment Mrs C opened the door to her. He grumbled to Lilly. His large frame not being made for such a small car. He might not be able to unbend himself when they arrived. How much bloody further was it? Who was this man? Never heard of him. Can't be anyone important. On and on.

She clenched her teeth. By the end of the day she would know if she had a chance with Jay. She kept it in her mind to focus against the endless complaints Piers made.

It was with relief she pulled into the car park. She jumped out quickly and ran round to help Piers detach himself from the seat. He stretched rather dramatically and hobbled in.

The staff went into overdrive. Took his bowler hat and blazer. Showed him to the window table upstairs. Sir this, Sir that. It did the trick. He brightened with a gin and tonic in hand as he relaxed, surveying the smooth green surface of the golf club's course visible from his position.

The entire premises had been revamped under new ownership, re-opened in May. Jed Owens, a sport merchandise tycoon and the club owner, had shown interest in becoming a major sponsor for the three-day trials.

From their window seats they could see a small lake to the right of the undulating green and, in the distance, the sea. Several golfers were hitting the iron as they watched.

The plush surroundings of this restaurant did not go unmissed by him either.

"He's done a wonderful job. Overhauled what was a rather standard course and club facility into a very impressive set up. I played here years back, nothing like this," he lamented as he looked about.

The table settings were covered with white starched cloth, silver cutlery and crystal glass. Blooms of pink and white flowers in identical green vases provided visual and scented aesthetic.

The wall to wall windows on three sides of the restaurant permitted the clientele to observe the course whilst dining.

The menu boasted lobster, twenty-eight-day matured steak, mushroom tortellini or a carpaccio of meats. The room was designed to impress. Piers took it all in with a contented smile.

"Why thank you, Mr Wingfield Brown. A compliment indeed for my vision." Jed stood at the table, a vision in white. Open-collared shirt, chinos, socks, brogues. All white. The only colour came from his forest green blazer, which he offered to the waitress as she hovered close by.

Lilly jumped up from her seat, her hand out to greet him. He ignored her hand and rested his on her shoulder, kissing her on the cheeks. A warm scent of something woody wafted over her as he leaned in. He turned, man hugged Piers with a flourish and grabbed a seat.

He shot Lilly a dazzling smile of teeth to match his outfit. Thanked them for meeting with him, started his pitch.

Jed was charming and attentive. A man in his mid-forties, the threads of grey in his short beard not yet showing in his dark comb over. Dyed, Lilly decided as she quietly studied the perfect coif.

The overall look was more photoshoot for Tatler than a business lunch.

By the end of the hour she was breathless. Jed had agreed to be the big-name sponsorship for the trials. Guaranteed up to a quarter of a million pounds in order to pay for 'the best' as he said with a lilting Brummie accent. Now it would be known as The Wingfield Jed O Sporting trials.

Just wait till Starchy hears about this, she thought. What would he have to say? Still insistent on the jumping japes gymkhana he envisaged? Now they were on the same lines as other, much larger sport events.

Everyone had heard of the Jed O sport shops across the country. The brand would be tagged with her trials. Everyone would now hear of her event. She pumped air in her head, remained the embodiment of professional cool on the outside.

In addition, Piers secured a lifetime membership of the club. A complimentary offer from Jed in recognition of the years of his of polo playing.

It was not a sport Jed knew much about, but he admired the Royal Family. He asked Piers if he had ever played the Prince of Wales.

Here we go, Lilly thought. Piers launched into the time when he had spun a corker that the Prince had tried to stop. The top spin and speed on the chuck meant the Prince had to lean right over. In doing so, he had fallen from his horse.

"We shook hands after, had a glass of bubbly in the bar. The Prince is a true sporting gentleman." Piers completed the tale. Took a sip of Chablis as he acknowledged the raptured face of Jed. Noticed several others on tables nearby that eavesdropped.

"Sir, you tell a great story. You must join me at my table more often." Jed clapped rather too enthusiastically.

Ah, got ya, Lilly thought. Contact is King and Jed is after connections! She was not going to spoil the moment and tell him it happened over thirty years ago. Who cared if the man was a social climber? Not her, not with the massive sponsorship deal he'd agreed.

Piers could not stop talking about this added benefit all the way back. The size of her car and the discomfort no longer an issue as he endorsed the club and its owner.

"I think it could become my regular, what say you Lilly? Seemed a jolly decent sort of group up there. I think I recognised a few faces, too. The travel will be a bit of a bind, what, an hour each way? Still, it gets me out of that big old empty house. Yes, I think this has been a rather good result, my dear."

At least it was better than listening to him moaning and grumping about the lack of contact he currently had with his son. She had been dumping him on a verge on the way here.

Home just after four thirty, Lilly immediately sought out Ed and Ella. They were in the tea room, drinking coffee with a few of the liveries. The women giggled like teenage girls over something he had said, a huge grin on his face.

Ella sat quietly next to him. A beautiful mannequin, Lilly observed. She recalled Rico's words from the night before. Ella seemed cold, distant. But Lilly noticed a hint of sadness about her as well. Someone broken, pitiful rather than petulant.

Lilly put her negative thoughts aside, way too high from the deal she'd just made. Imagined announcing the huge, tremendous, fantastic news to the Committee when they met next. The media release was bound to stir up more interest.

"Hi guys. So sorry I'm a bit late. Do you still have a few minutes spare?" she asked.

Now to see if she can make a difference to herself, secure her own deal and get her relationship back on track.

Those words, life goals, were haunting her. The replies of encouragement from the friends. It affected her focus, rearing back up in her head at every opportunity. She hadn't mentioned it to Jay. Hashtag stalker was not a status she would be proud to own.

Well, sorry not sorry girlfriend, she decided. She was ready to reclaim her man for good.

CHAPTER FOURTEEN

Ella watched whilst others chatted amicably with Ed about life with horses. From epic successes, to major catastrophes, even general tales of their life experiences. Such an easy-going guy, always a kind word or a ready laugh. Everybody loved him.

They'd first met when she had started work on a livery in the outskirts of London, Kings Lodge Farm. The clientele was all super rich, a few celebrities, a footballer, millionaires, even a billionaire from Dubai.

She caused total meltdown each time she arrived. Chauffeur driven Bentley, a bodyguard, a secretary and someone that just ran around shouting orders at people.

The majority wanted to own a horse, to ride when they were of the mind. Whereas they were not so keen on the maintenance. Keeping it stable clean, or a six thirty a.m. start to turn out, or even to tack their own horse up to ride.

Each groom got assigned six horses to care for as their own. Their job, to ensure the welfare at all times of these six horses. Along with regular photos to provide the owner with updates.

She learned quickly that the majority of these people didn't care about the grooms. But they were precious over the management of their beasts.

So many saw their horse as a status symbol. Something to talk about at a dinner. To show off in the VIP area of an event where the horse was competing. Others did enjoy competing, even went out on a few drag hunts during the season.

All six of her horses were valued at over fifty thousand pounds apiece. Every day she was required to provide the team leader with a signed checklist on each, to verify the wellbeing.

A small cut from where the horse may have kicked itself getting up in the morning? Noted. A scratch on its nose from a bramble in the field? A kick or a bite from another horse? A whole new recording. External signs of illness, stiffness, gunk in the eye, it was all on the forms.

The facilities were the best, white wooden picket fences divided individual turnout, each stable within the American barn was double the size of a standard, the rubber matter thicker, a system in the ceiling so allow for warm air in winter and cool in summer to breeze over the back of each horse.

The indoor sandschool had a window at one end through which owners could watch, sat in leather Chesterfield sofa's whilst having lunch.

Ed joined the team as the property maintenance man. He fixed fencing, as horses are not known for caring how nice their enclosures look like. If spooked or in a fight with a neighbour, they thought nothing of smashing through it.

He also harrowed the sandschools daily, mended stables where a horse chewed off part of a door panel, or kicked a hole in the wall, loaded heavy bales of hay into the barn that arrived every fortnight. In fact, Ed's job seemed to cover just about everything. He even helped the grooms tack up if they asked. The girls always wanted him to give them a leg up.

Six foot one and the muscles of a superhero, a face of a Romance novel character, a twinkle in his hazel eyes and a mouth she wanted to kiss the moment she saw him.

Young and fit, only twenty-two, he was an instant hit with everyone. He appeared to have been dipped in honey with the way the other grooms attached themselves to him.

He fitted all her dream qualities for a partner, bar the one she craved most. Money. He had none.

Ed's background was of a family that worked hard. Third son of six children. Fuck me, she had thought at the time, his mum definitely was a glutton for hard work with that lot. Ella could not imagine one child, let alone ruin her body knocking out half a dozen for ten years of her life.

He told her that his dad worked in construction. His mum took in whatever work she could do from home. Baked for a local café, took in ironing, even part time cleaning in the evening. They never went without a decent meal, they always sat down to a table of delicious food at the end of the day.

He was the warmth to her cool. The fire to her ice. His gregarious nature versus her bitchiness. Every time she messed up, he reassured her it would be ok, that they would start again elsewhere.

After a lifetime of holding her emotion in, little by little he'd drawn it out. All her anger, her bitterness, how unfair her life had been. He never judged. Just listened, held her, let her rage, howl, whimper.

"Babe, you cannot keep the past alive. It has to remain where it is, in the past. Move on. We can make a new life. Be happy," he'd encouraged.

Although she couldn't. Not until she was able to reclaim what should be hers.

She had suffered years of turmoil following her dad's death. The move to the coast, all references to horses, their former life, all scratched from conversation. Not even a poster from a pony magazine she'd sneaked in, hidden at the bottom of her sock drawer.

She yearned for the past like an addict yearned for drugs. It ate away at her, made it her first thought when she woke each day. The last thought at night.

To own what she grew up with. A house, land, horses.

Depression kicked in during her teens. Not helped by her mum's increasing dependency on gin. She became rebellious, destructive, the usual teen outrage, drank heavily, smoked weed, stayed out late.

She flunked school exams, hung out with a bad boy gang, stole cigarettes from the local store. Her long, straight platinum blonde hair dyed various colours. The mesmerising blue eyes she hid behind dark sunglasses. A nose stud and a dozen rings through her ears created the dark character she considered herself to be.

"You look like a bull in a china shop." Her mother had slurred the first time she came home with a chunk of metal sticking out of her nostril.

"Whatever." Her standard reply.

Eventually her teachers gave up on her. The relationship with her mum slid so badly they barely spoke. Her life was a mess.

Then one morning she woke to realise it wasn't ok. At eighteen years old and six months left at college, nothing to offer her a career to value. Only the prospect of being a benefit betty or working at the local supermarket for minimum wage.

Neither were meant to be her destiny. She had been a solid A student in private education, had lived in a beautiful five-bedroom house with a swimming pool on one side. On the other, stables with twenty of the most beautiful breed of horse on the planet. A mum and dad that were happy and who loved her.

She drank a lot of coffee and smoked a couple of packs of Marlboro lights that day. She refused to answer the calls from her boyfriend, 'Badass Billy', the leader of the Devon Devils gang.

He texted her several times asking if she was ok. That tone changed to 'what the fuck are you playing at, answer me'.

After that, a final 'we're off to get stoned, meet us at the abbey'. That being their usual haunt for smoking pot and running about the gravestones. The vicar wasn't so keen, but he accepted it. Felt he could keep an eye on them.

Early the same evening, she received one last text message 'you fucking with me or what?' With a sigh, had composed a reply. 'Need to sort my shit out, moving on, enjoy your life."

She knew his fury, so she blocked his number and that of the rest of the gang. She imagined he'd curse and shout for a day or two. Then he would shrug his shoulders and take up with Paula Pothead, who'd been making moves on him for months.

She poured yet another coffee. Dragged heavily on a cigarette. Then sat at the kitchen table. Laptop open, googling 'jobs as groom'. She found a good site, 'Grooms quest', aptly named. She steadily worked through the hundreds of opportunities in the equine industry.

That was the morph moment for her. The beginning of the return to her true calling.

Ed now collaborated with her to make this happen. Not that he knew the entire story, her true intent. But she played her part well. She adored him, gave him great sex, cooked and cleaned. The perfect gf. For now.

She had seen a potential gap the day Lilly turned up in the pub with the wealthy clients. Strangles had been a welcome word for her, though she was extremely thankful that it was a false alarm, for the sake of the horses.

Here on the yard Ella kept her distance from the grooms. Whereas, she did google the clientele. Some were local, with good jobs who paid for five-day livery. Some made her jaw drop.

Manik Halim, for starters. Further digging had shown a family with a portfolio of hotels worldwide. A fan club crazy about him. Aged twenty-five, listed as single. She wondered why.

Bob Chapman, another bingo buck horseman. A multi-millionaire owner of a drinks company that was listed on the stock-market. His clients who recommended his booze went all the way up to Royalty. At forty-one, Facebook told her he was currently 'in a relationship'.

Once she had placed them in top ten order of wealth and availability, she watched them. Eight appeared to have a good rapport with Lilly. One had not put in appearance to date. The last one avoided Lilly and she him. Finchy, a London stockbroker. He kept his hunter on the yard and came up every Sunday to ride over the downs.

Duncan Finch, of Finch, Rathbone & Young Associates. Founder. Serious spinodal. He owned a superyacht that spent the summer in the Med, the winter in the Caribbean, used it to entertain friends and forge business deals.

Aged thirty-eight, his bio was full of sporting achievements. Divorced, three children that lived with their mother in the South of France.

Somehow Lilly had pissed him off, though not enough for him to move his heavyweight chestnut off the yard. Intrigued, Ella spent extra time in his company, a little flirtation in her attempt to find out more. To date, he eluded her questions, although he appeared very interested in her.

Her mind returned to the present as Lilly ushered them into her home. They sat in her lounge, Ella's eyes on the walls of photos.

Lilly apologised for the hay on the floor, the body parts of bridles strewn across the coffee table. Then she launched straight into her proposition. It couldn't have been better.

Jobs for the pair of them.

Ed beamed, delighted at the prospect. His first task was to prepare the lower yard. Ella had seen it each day as they drove up, had wondered why it lay empty, presumed they must be in a bad state of repair. Lilly spoke about the change from DIY to five-day assist. That would provide a decent extra income, she considered as she rapidly worked out the difference in her head. Less staff costs, feed, overheads like electricity.

Ed nodded like a wagtail bird, ones that flew down in the summer to peck at stray bits of bedding about the yard. Dip, dip nodded his head, clearly up for it. Lilly passed him a folder to take back and read.

"If you take a glance through, it will provide you with details of the horse trials. All the plans are in there, the design, course layout, budgets, and a ledger. That will show where cash is for field work, fences still to be done, that sort of thing. I'm afraid it's rather a long checklist. But it will give you an idea of where you can help," she explained.

Ella let out a squeak, which she quickly turned into a cough. Hit her chest with her fist, a look of apology to Lilly for the interruption.

Once they were home, she'd rip that from him to read. To see exactly what this woman focused on.

Lily confided in them about the huge sponsor she had just secured this lunchtime. It was confidential, the Event Committee had yet to be informed. It meant money was there to prepare the course, build the bespoke fences, pay for good quality products.

"I can't tell you the name of our sponsor until all dots are dotted, but it's a major name and an enormous cash injection," was all Lilly would say on the subject.

Lilly turned to Ella.

"Ella, I'd like to ask you about your previous work with horses if I may. I'm really interested in you doing some work on the main yard. I'm at the point of no return. I need to step back from muck out, turn out, all the chores that take half my day. I have to blast this event."

Fuck. Why do people always want to know about previous work? She'd made it clear, she had grown up with horses. Worked on yards. Wasn't that enough?

"Tell you what. How about I take your shift on tomorrow? Oversee me as you wish, but I guarantee I can muck a stable out as quick as you," Ella boasted.

Lilly seemed delighted with Ella's own proposition. Held out her hand.

"Then you accept my offer? I really need help to cover all this work I've given myself. You have both shown me so much help already, I can't believe my luck. Being in the pub when our near Strangles episode, there you were.

"It's just what we were looking for, so it seems we are all winners," Ed declared. He stood, moved over to Lilly to shake on the deal, glanced at Ella. His eyes told her to do the same.

She stuck out her hand, a little surprised at the steel grip of the return.

"Right, fantastic. I'll see you both in the morning. I meet with the team at seven when they arrive, I run a checklist for the day with any extra services that have been added, we all agree the duties and get cracking. Rugs on, horses out. Wheelbarrow, fork, shit, shovel." Lilly beamed, her eyes shining with relief.

"Thank you, Lilly, you won't regret it." Ed too was smiling broadly.

"Ah, but you may," she replied with a wink.

Ella said nothing. She was busy plotting scenarios in her mind. Could she finally have found herself a step closer to the end game?

CHAPTER FIFTEEN

Even more exciting was the pair had agreed to cover for the weekend. Ella even suggested they stay in the house to look after Ruby.

After all, it would be easier for the early feeds. Lilly agreed, she'd give them the spare room and stock the fridge up.

Ella seemed keen to find out who she was meeting. Lilly brushed it aside with a wave of her hand, claimed it was a catch up with a school friend who'd emigrated. They were going to hang out in London, do the sights, go clubbing, see a show. Be two crazy ladies in town.

Ella asked her what seemed like a million questions. Why had she emigrated? Why she was back? What they were going to watch? What hotel had she booked?

"Oh gee, it's a quiz!" Lilly exclaimed with a grin, washing over the answers. "What do I win if I get them right?"

"I'm sorry, way bad," Ella replied. "It's just, you work so hard I doubt you get away much. Me and my big nose," she shrugged.

"No, it's fine. You're right, the struggle is real, I never get away. Which makes it even more exciting."

"So, definitely not some secret lover we should know of?" Ella suggested.

"I'm dead, you got me!" Lilly quipped back.

Before it went further, Lilly checked the time on her phone.

"Fuck, now I do have a date with a man, to discuss shit," she exclaimed.

Ella nodded, she too had her jobs to do at her new place of work Putting the kettle on would be first but she kept that to herself.

"And you're really, really sure you don't mind? Lilly asked one last time.

"No sweat," she insisted with the sweetest of her smiles.

Delighted that she had spun it to suit her. That's what looking like a Disney Princess does for you, she told herself. Just smile sweetly, act innocent, they fall for the face.

"You're a total star, I owe you big time." On impulse, Lilly hugged her. "Now I really have to get to this meeting. Let's discover how exciting toilet talk can be."

Lilly walked away with a spring in her step. Ella watched her go. Both with secrets yet to be exposed.

Unaware of any negative mood, Lilly planned her own secret weekend away.

At last. She could tell Jay, if he still wanted her there, she'd fixed it up. Now to meet with the portaloo guy again, he'd asked for cash payment.

Lilly skyped Jay late evening with the good news. He'd appeared on screen, tight-lipped, jaw up, eyes burning with simmering irritation from her previous rejection. As she spoke, this lightened, his face uncurled, and he grinned with delight.

"I've been worried you were going to let me down," he told her.

"To be honest, I've worried too. It's a long story I'll tell you when I see you. For now, I'm hoping for a full night's sleep for the first time in weeks." she declared.

"Good. Because you won't be getting any next weekend," he hinted.

"I can't wait. Meet me at Victoria station Friday night. I'll text when I'm on the train."

The prospect of an entire two nights with him made her squeal with pleasure. Two whole consecutive nights, with more to come if it all works out. They had managed a couple of overnights together before, but this was the first full weekend yet.

As she lay on her pillow a wave of panic surged into her head. Oh God, what would she wear? She lived in jodhpurs and tees, jeans occasionally. Did she even own a dress?

The village didn't have a clothes store. That meant a trip into town to try things on. Impossible with her workload over the next few days.

She jumped out of bed and rifled through her wardrobe. Found the one dress she did possess. It sat at the back, forlorn and faded. A pair of strappy sandals she wore last year to a summer fete, still with the mud on the heels, were her only summer shoes.

Back in bed she scrolled through her phone. By the time she finished she realised she'd gone a little wild. Her rationale being that she would send stuff back if she didn't like it on.

Once she'd pressed 'buy' on the last dress, a green velvet A line with halter neck straps, she checked out shoes, opting for two pairs with small wedge, a third with an impossibly high stiletto heel which she might manage two steps in. Because they looked fabulous.

Job done. With that little lot, she might almost look the part. The part of a sophisticated lady out on the town with her refined and handsome man.

Admitted, she'd have to work on that image big time. It had been a while since she'd dressed up feminine.

Thought back as she snuggled under the duvet. Probably three summers ago at that ball, when Charles Moreau won the Grand Prix in Bordeaux. If only she had kept that gown. Instead, she had given it to Sophie, their PR girl.

Lilly drifted off to sleep, memories of that evening and ones to come.

Friday arrived after a whirlwind week. Each morning she met with Ed to review the DIY yard clean up followed by a check in with the grooms. Satisfied she could leave them all to it, she began her jobs.

All week was a blitz of meetings, another trip to Jed to agree terms, emails, account reconciliation, writing an article for a Horse magazine and lunch with Piers. During which a livery gave notice, she taught, she schooled. She even fitted in a quick hour on Cochise across the downs, tacked up western style.

Lilly enjoyed the comfort of the larger seat; it made the canter feel like she was on a rocking chair, sent her back to her life on the ranch, the trail rides she'd enjoyed over the vast plains with the view of the mountains almost purple in the heat haze, scraps of sage and brush, watching out for rattlesnakes or coyote. Both could grab at a leg, though all the mustang were from the range and not easily startled. If not for that dick Wayne she could have happily stayed longer.

Maybe she would return one day with Jay, show him round Lyon County and all it had to offer.

For now, she made do with the one-hour hack around the woods, with the less dangerous blackbirds and an occasional squirrel to be seen.

She fixed the house up ready for Ed and Ella. Though she did get distracted by midweek as the parcels arrived. Never had she bought so many girly items and tried everything on at once. It all looked great, she'd keep the lot.

She had cleared the boxes and books in the spare room, most shoved under the bed or in the back of the wardrobe. Made the room up to provide an air of comfort and welcome.

A visit to the supermarket offered a lampshade to cover the bare bulb. Fluffy new towels, a thank-you card sitting on top of them, a bottle of prosecco and chockies. That should do it.

All her financial records, laptop and audit books, she felt it prudent to lock in her bedroom. After all, it was her only privacy and it should remain that way.

Even though she was incredibly grateful, she had only just met the pair. Lovely as they were, it gave peace of mind to her.

Finally, bending down to hug her little dog, she double checked she'd left a list of her meals, treats, emergency vet number. Was still going through last minute items as Ella drove her up to the train station entrance, her case in the boot.

"Oh shit, did I mention that when you put Star in the walker she has to go in backwards?"

"Stop it already! Yes, you have, twice already Really, Lilly, we will manage for two days. Ruby will be fine, we'll do everything that you've written on your very extensive notes, that I have read three times at your express wish. Now go!" Ella told her, giving her a quick hug in a show of goodwill.

Ella could not wait to wave this woman off and go investigate. She was desperate to have a rummage through the house.

Despite what happened the last time, the promise she made to Ed. For real, there were accounts to review, clients to check out, contracts, budgets. Anything and everything to help her achieve her own goal when the time was right.

Lilly had secrets, that she was sure of. She sat in the car anxious, excited, fiddling with her hair. It was the first time Lilly had displayed any sign of nerves, not even during the Strangles episode.

Ella had learned at a young age how to bottle emotion. It had been more than a necessity; it had been vital. Just as she learned how to read emotion. And this book told her there was a man.

As Ella drove off, Lilly turned and went to sit inside the platform for the arrival, reminded herself yet again that Ruby would be ok. That she was about to spend a whole weekend with the man she loved. Be pleased, relax.

She breathed out through her mouth, pushed the loose curls from her face. But had she remembered everything?

The train up to London was full. With only three of the five expected carriages, she stood for half the journey. At least she didn't have to make this trip every day for work.

Through the ticket barrier, she searched the enormous domed floor space full of people.

Only six in the evening and still a balmy twenty-eight degrees Celsius on what was promising to be the hottest weekend so far this June. Hundreds milled the station, ready to be somewhere other than the city.

Lilly caught sight of him stood to the right of the gates, waving like a windmill, a huge grin on his face. She stood, pulse racing. He oozed casual and cool in a pair of blue jeans and open necked lemon short-sleeved shirt.

After being cooped up like a chicken in an egg factory after the air conditioning packed in the first ten minutes, she felt like a mess of sweat and crumpled clothes.

Wow, he looked more delicious than a bowl of vanilla ice cream covered in salted caramel and chocolate.

Her body regained movement as she rushed over to him. Her holdall bounced and dragged as the wheels refused to keep up, her legs wobbled at the novelty of wearing heels.

The case dismissed, he crushed her to him, his arms wrapped around her, kissed her for what seemed like a week. He finally came up for air, gazed into her eyes, burning a hole into her soul, his hands cupped about her face.

Releasing the tight grip, he twirled her in front of him, nodded approval as he did.

"A dress, no less. How hot are you, showing those legs off," he whistled.

Lilly beamed back at him with desire and happiness. The fit and flare dress, the bright red of a first-place rosette, came to mid-thigh. And, yes, too freaking right, it showed off her legs, she knew her body was in great shape.

Mucking out several stables each day and riding kept her trim and athletic. She ate like a pig, but worked like a donkey. It kind of guaranteed no fat had any chance to stick on her bones. The long limbs she had her mum to thank for.

He pulled her in again. One hand gently caressed her hair, brushed it with his fingertips. His face grew solemn.

"I need to tell you something," he announced.

Oh God, this is it. She could feel a pain clutch her heart, her chest tightened. Elation plunged to dread. He looked like he had bad news. Here's the bit he tells me about the socialite flashed through her head. Half closed her eyes in an attempt to lessen the pain.

He wore a frown. A small crease of wrinkles formed in his otherwise smooth forehead as he held her in his gaze.

"My darling, I'm sorry……," he paused.

Her body went limp, she bowed her head. He picked up her chin with a finger, forced her to look back.

"We need to go. I'm bloody starving and there's a table with our name on it at Les Cinq Chemins. Come on, let's get a cab."

She could have throttled him there and then as he broke into a wicked grin.

"What did you think I was going to say?" he teased as he grabbed her hand in his left, her case in his right and steered her through the throngs of people towards an exit with taxi rank signs.

"I refuse to answer on the grounds of your mockery," she shouted above the noise of the traffic as they emerged onto the street.

As they entered the restaurant, the Maitre d' rushed over, greeting Jay with a small bow. She was introduced as his girlfriend and Pierre, as Jay addressed him, held her hand for a moment. She thought he might kiss it, but to her relief he gave another small bow of his head.

"Mademoiselle, enchanté. What a radiance you bring to my humble restaurant."

She thanked him, slightly awkward at the over play of their arrival. Looked over to Jay for guidance.

"Lilly has joined me for the weekend from her busy life in the equestrian world."

"Horses? Mais, bien fait. I used to do a little riding when I was younger." Pierre declared, patting the paunch that had since formed in his later years.

He clicked his fingers at another waiter as he led them to their seat. With a flourish, he offered a menu for both. The junior arrived with a carafe of water and glasses, a bowl of bread and a pat of butter.

As she sat holding his hand over the table, she was overwhelmed with joy. To be able to talk so openly in front of others. To laugh, share a kiss, the simplest of gestures for two people in love. Lilly found herself watching his every move, taking it in as if she would never see him again.

How he broke his bread. How, in European style, he mopped up the sauce on his plate. A smile as he asked the waiter for more water. The way he dabbed his mouth with his serviette.

With a pang, she realised this was standard for most, yet she forced him to keep his distance. To deny him the chance to say as he had to Pierre, this is my girlfriend.

He caught her and stopped eating. A quizzical look on his face.

"What? Have I spilt the hollandaise on my chin?" he asked.

"No. As if such a man of the world would do that!" she laughed. "I was just wondering how you put up with me and my tyrannical attitude?"

"Darling, I have to be honest. It's tough. But I'd rather take the hit than offer it out to someone else. I have to think of my fellow men, save them from such fate," he replied full of humour. He reached out for her hand, kissed it with a brush of his lips, soft and warm.

"But I act like a diva. We should be able to do this anytime we like. I tell you we can't, that you have to wait, all because I want to prove myself in a professional capacity." She took her hand away, her face serious.

"Really?" His eyes bore into her, the blue so intense, like gazing into the Caribbean Sea. Those crazy downward slant eyebrows of his almost touched the top of his nose as he focused on her.

"To be honest, I hate the time apart, I do. I want you in my life. To live with me, eat with me, meet friends together, make love. Especially that one, by the way," he winked.

"I have been so busy recently. What with the American family who drain me of spare time, I have never felt so lonely without you. It's why I got so grumpy, gave you a bit of an ultimatum. I would rather spend snatched moments with you than a lifetime with another. I love you. I am so bloody proud of you. For what you want to achieve and your reasons why. Whereas, I am lucky I can make money at a desk, you work five times as hard."

She smiled at him, the faintest of dimples in her cheeks.

"So, the daughter hasn't tempted you?" She asked as casually as she could muster.

He looked at her for a moment, his mouth slightly open, puzzled. With a roll of his eyes and a snort, he sat back with realisation. His hand slapped the table, dislodged a knife which bounced up and onto the floor with a clutter. He roared with laughter, tears fell down his face as he shoulders shook uncontrollably.

A waiter rushed to help. Jay waved him away, leant down to pick it up himself. As he emerged from under the table, he was still in fits, holding his stomach and gasping for breath.

Lilly realised she had maybe read too much into her nights of stalking.

"Oh, my goodness, I was not expecting that!" he declared between breaths. "No Lilly. Quite the opposite. Do you know how annoying it is to be someone's fantasy crush? Actually, scrap that. I imagine half the male population lust after you. No. Absolutely not. She literally bores me to death. She has zero talent, lives of daddy's money, wreaks of entitlement. Not my type." He continued, his body still convulsing.

"Anyway, I have decided its best we keep it secret. What would my work colleagues think if they knew I'm in love with a woman who enjoys cleaning horses for a living?" His mouth twitched at the sides, unable to keep the laughter in. He swallowed and began coughing.

Lilly jumped up, grabbed his glass of water, made him drink it until he stopped spluttering as she rubbed his back.

With a mischievous glint in her eye, she admonished him.

"That's what happens when you try to be funny about me and my cleaning habits. But thank you for your patience. September fifteenth the world will learn the truth. That your girlfriend is not some supermodel idolised by thousands on her Instagram account, but a poo picker that lives in a hay barn somewhere south of civilisation. Then you'll be sorry!"

He pulled her close, kissed her lips, smiled at the diners who had watched in amusement and concern at both his outburst and his choking.

With a wink to Lilly he stood, gave a little bow to the floor, a flourish of his hand to indicate the show was over. People pretended they had not been engrossed in the corner table's conversation.

"Even if my event turns out to be a monumental disaster, I'll have you in my life to make it all better," she acknowledged him.

He raised his glass.

"I hear it's all going too well to be a flop. I fear it maybe me that's left in the shadow."

They chinked glass. He lowered his, his right hand reached over to her knee, edged up her thigh.

He gazed at her intently, his eyes now a darker blue, a turbulent ocean, full of desire.

"I'm ready for dessert," he whispered.

She locked eyes with him in a mutual understanding, eager now to leave the restaurant.

They hailed a taxi to his flat. High up on the twelfth floor of an old apartment block, almost wall to wall windows that faced The Thames. As she walked in, she could see Tower Bridge lit up, and the lights of London shimmer on the river below them.

He caught her by the waist, warm lips covering hers. The weeks of denial burst into a fury of urgent hunger.

Without another word, he led her to his bedroom. Lifted the dress over her head, removed her bra before coming back to her breasts, taking them in both hands to kiss softly, teasing her with his lips.

She felt a moan slip from her mouth as the sensation of his touch sent electrical currents like wildfire roaring through her body.

With a shudder, she brushed his arms away. Began to undo the buttons of his shirt, his eyes fixed on hers as she made her way downward. With each button she brushed her fingers softly against his skin, leaving him shaking as hard as she was.

His skin smelt so clean, fresh, a subtle scent of wood filled her senses. The black chest curls sprayed in a V down his honed flesh. For a moment she paused to admire the hard muscles that confirmed his reassurances he had worked frustration out in the gym.

As she pushed the shirt from his shoulders, her hands moved up and wrapped around his neck, drawing him to her. She kissed him on his lips. His mouth parted as his tongue pushed past her teeth and took her mouth, opening the door to a fire that had been smouldering in both for weeks.

Running his tongue up her neck, he caressed her back with the most delicate of touches. Across her arms, her shoulders, then her breasts, before he removed the last of her underwear and lay her on the bed.

Little jolts of pleasure sent sparks zipping through her body as he kissed her all over before finding his way to the juncture of her thighs.

"Now," she breathed, taking his head in her hands. Urgency overwhelmed her as her body craved him, focused on the sensation mounting inside her.

"Not yet," he teased, running one fingertip down between her breasts. To her bellybutton. Then below, gently rubbing her, watching as she swelled with expectation.

Pent up emotion became too great, he lurched forward, straddling her. His mouth taking hers, kissing, licking, nipping, as he entered her in one swift motion.

Lilly let out a gasp of delight. Her hands over his firm bottom, squeezing his cheeks, pushing him deeper into her. Moving in rhythm as the intensity grew, their breath drawing in and out faster and faster.

With one hand he caressed her right breast. Teased the hard nipple, driving her wilder, her cries louder as she gave her body and soul to this man and the urgency of their lovemaking.

With one final push they both felt the juddering of their orgasms, washing over them in a crescendo of delicious waves of ecstasy, emotion and love.

Jay moved to the side, pulling her to him in an embrace of entwined bodies, catching his breath as he held her close.

"Your heart is pounding like the hooves of all your horses," he joked.

"I have just been ridden by the best stallion in town. It's no wonder," she sighed with contentment.

"Well, you can do the riding the next time. Give me ten minutes."

The sun was breaking over the buildings opposite by the time they had finally sated each other's needs. Both fell into an exhausted but satisfied slumber, curled up as one.

Lilly woke with a jolt, nearly jumped out of bed ready to do the morning feeds. Wondered why the sun was so bright in her bedroom. Before an arm came over and pulled her back.

"Where do you think you're going?" he murmured as he wrapped her once more in his arms.

"The horses," she replied.

"We're in London, babe, remember? The only animal requiring your attention today is me."

With realisation she melted back into him, as they once again explored each other's bodies. Less urgent, more focused on offering each other sensual, gentler touches, the rhythm slower, languid.

Later, showered and dressed, she took a good look around his 'pad' as he called it. The pad was larger than her house.

The entire ground floor of hers would fit in his bedroom alone. The enormous king-sized bed seemed insignificant against the expanse of wooden floor. Large, deep pile rugs lay scattered about.

There was even a two-seater sofa and swing chair next to a coffee table in the far corner. Adjacent a corridor led her through a dressing room.

She noted her his clothes hung neatly either side according to occasion and colour. Boxes of shoes filled the floor, boxes of accessories on a shelf above.

Opposite end opened into an ensuite bathroom. A white whirlpool bath she could swim a horse in. A square basin, toilet and bidet all surrounded by leaf green tiled walls. The fluffiest of green towels laid out in bundles on the wooden sideboard.

A second bedroom, decorated similarly, smaller in space. Bedroom number three he used as a study. An oak desk and bureau filled with technology and paperwork sat in front of an impressive wall of books.

She looked in admiringly, but wondered at how the digital age couldn't ever quite disperse with paper. Which lay strewn around in piles of folders.

The entire apartment opened onto a decked balcony with stainless steel railings that ran the length. The Thames lay below them. Boats flowed up and down, big and small.

The noise of a city, the smells from a thousand local café's and restaurants. Central London and its wonderful architectural buildings. She could have sat and watched it all for hours.

Jay walked over to the kitchen. Part of the open plan space divided by a trendy half wall, covered in artwork. Like the rest of the walls in the flat, full of colour and design.

"Such interesting paintings, they are all so different, are they all yours?" she asked.

"Most of them. Though, one or two are from dad's era that I like to keep. But I try to pick a piece of art up from local artists wherever I travel. Part reason as an investment, but mostly it's a memory."

"I like." She nodded as she studied them further.

He moved to stand next to her. Pointed to a particularly vivid scene of a tropical paradise, parrots, toucans, palm trees and ferns.

"Take this one, for example. I was in Brazil for a month working with a client who was developing his brand and needed our resources. He took me into the jungle, where I saw the most spectacular, colourful creatures this world has to offer. This one reminds me of that trek every time."

"A bit different to my walls." She laughed.

"We'll have to compromise. Maybe find our own place to live?"

"A wall of horse photos versus a wall of the finest paintings. That will be an odd combo." She grinned at him with amusement.

"I can't think of anything I'd prefer more. Just as long as it's you in the same bed as me each night." He drew her in, hugged her close, kissed her lightly on the lips.

"Brunch? We are way too late for breakfast now. Then we visit London." He announced, reluctantly drawing away from her.

She was glad he offered to cook. Looking at the space age kitchen she would be clueless to know where anything was. She could see a sink, and a glass-fronted fridge full of wine, but little else.

An extreme contrast to her own place, with conventional kettle, toaster and oven on display, horse paraphernalia strewn across all surfaces.

Jay tapped a wall which opened up to reveal a built-in coffee machine. One of those you put in a pod and press a button, gurgle gurgles, then produces frothy barista style coffee. Lilly had seen something similar being advertised by the Hollywood star Doug Ross but had never used one.

When he tapped another part of the wall, a full set of crockery was revealed. He took out a couple of mugs, opened another drawer. Turned with a 'ta-dah' as he waved the box of cherry green tea at her. Her favourite.

She was mesmerised, set about pressing all the segments of the wall to find what sat behind them.

He laughed, caught her in a twirl as if to dance.

"Pretty neat, huh? I had a redesign last year. Before, the place looked a bit tired. It's been in the family for years," he explained.

"Wow." Was all she could manage as she looked about. "Never would I have imagined a place like this. It's like being on a sci-fi set." She shook her head in amazement. "I'm just waiting for Robbie the robot to appear and tell me we are all Lost in Space," she added with a laugh.

"But, do you love it? I mean, I realise there is no random stirrup sat on the sideboard. Nor is there any hay on the lounge floor. Should I buy in a copy of Horse & Hound magazine to make you feel more homely?" he asked her, a mock frown on his face.

She kissed him. With a giggle turned to look at the Thames from the edge of the window.

"This place is you, isn't it? When you redesigned it last year, it was as you wanted. So, of course I love it." She paused to take a sip of her green tea as she added,

"But a few scattered horse magazines and that odd riding boot no one has ever claimed may make it more homely."

She turned her head slightly sideways towards him. The mug still held at mouth level, as she sneaked a look at his reaction. He was leaning on the rail, staring out over the water. A nonchalant face, a slight dimple in his cheek the only indication he was working on a witty reply.

"Neatly arranged magazines accepted. The lost boot? Maybe leave it outside? We could grow carrots in it for you to feed the horses." He turned to her with a question.

"Eggs benedict. With veggie bacon or without?"

"No idea who benedict is. But yes to the eggs and the veggie bacon." She felt overcome with hunger. All that sex had made her ravenous.

The rest of the day they shopped. Kings Road in Chelsea, Kensington High Street, Sloane Square, followed by afternoon tea at The Ritz. Champagne and the most perfect selection of cakes she'd seen in her life.

The art exhibition was in Mayfair, the artist a Cuban whose paintings sold for thousands. She had expected Cubanism but was surprised to find he studied movement in various forms. Movement of people, animals, even transport.

The flow of paint over canvas was so smooth, how someone could create the impression of a flamingo in flight, or a dancer twirling about the floor was magical. Art not being her usual focus she wondered around with the gaze of a child, delighted in each new discovery.

"Which do you like most from my exhibition?" Gianluca asked her, pleased at her enthusiasm.

"Yes, darling, which speaks to you most?" Jay asked, his arm wrapped firm around her waist as he stood to her side, his chin in her neck.

"How to pick one, they are all so incredible, though the chattiest one has to be the rearing horse, naturally".

"How did I know? Good job I bought it before the exhibition opened, Gianluca could have sold it five times over."

She spun around to face him.

"You've bought it?"

"Our first piece of artwork as joint collectors," he smiled back, pleasure obvious in his face at her reaction.

"It has been an honour to meet the beautiful lady I have heard spoken of," the artist took her hand, kissed it.

Having helped Gianluca to shut up once the time was up, Jay hailed a taxi to take them to a Cuban restaurant to complete the theme of the evening.

Settled, with a mojito and the food on order, he made another announcement.

"I've met with the UK partners of our firm, it's where I'd been before I met you at the station. They've agreed to my transfer from our Geneva branch to the office here in Central London. There's a bit of work still to sort out, which clients I keep, which I need to hand over. There are some Europeans that may want to remain with me. It's good, I can commute every other week for an overnight. The bosses see this as potential for me to market us more, bring in new clients."

Lilly positively beamed at him. She leant over the table, swept her arms around his neck and kissed him.

"All being well, I should be in the UK more over the next few weeks," he announced, his arms fixed about her waist as she hugged him.

"Come visit, get to know where the plates are kept in the kitchen," he suggested.

"Cheeky," she wriggled free from their embrace to wiggle her finger. "If I visit, I expect fine restaurants and art exhibitions every time," she laughed.

She hoped that she could find the spare time. She feared it unlikely with ten weeks to go. Although Ella and Ed may be good for an overnight if she could shoot up after work on a Friday, be back Saturday.

As her thoughts tumbled about, she sat back down in her chair, picked up her serviette and took a sip from her cocktail.

The glass was at her lips as she saw him reach into his jacket pocket. A small velvet box appeared in his hand that made her gasp. Lilly gently replaced the glass on the table as the room began to blur and spin. A wave of emotion flooded her body that stopped time and sense.

Jay moved to kneel next to her. His hand trembled as he opened the lid.

Raw emotion caught in his throat as he spoke her name.

An enormous emerald with two square cut diamonds either side of a platinum base was sparkling at her.

"I know, before you say it. September fifteen is still the fixed date. Where I get to shout out about unbridled love for my beautiful poo picker. But I had this designed for you, sourced the gems myself. Well, with a little help from a close friend. This moment, now, just feels kind of the right time to let you know how much you mean to me. How much I want us to spend the rest of our lives together."

She gasped, so stunned her mouth could not form words. Frozen in a time warp, Lilly nodded as tears poured down her cheeks. With one hand over her mouth, she held the other for him to place the ring on her finger.

A cheer went up around the room as others had stopped to watch the moment he had bent his knee. They both looked round, smiled.

"I think that was a yes!" he laughed to the onlookers, which attracted another round of applause.

To Lilly he whispered, "I want you to know how committed I am to you, my love." He kissed her hand, the ring, then moved in to kiss her lips.

"I love you," she stammered.

He grinned with relief for a moment before desire swept over his face.

"Drink up, you can show me just how much."

As they lay in each other's arms that night she felt complete, happy, secure. As if the yard and the intensity of work involved to fix up the event were trifles in her life. That nothing could go wrong now. She fell into a deep and dreamless sleep.

CHAPTER SIXTEEN

Rico was also on a weekend away. He took the yard lorry with Viking, Crackers, Mr Simpson, Camelot and Red onboard to the Hertfordshire County Show.

It offered big prize money in the show jumping arena and valuable points for the horses' career. An important event for the owners.

He'd explained to Rowena how a place for Cammie here would be a big deal. Just as important as her horse gaining points was for her to have her name known. She agreed readily, booked herself in at a top hotel close by.

"Wow, I was there with a friend a couple of years ago, that's some building." Rico whistled when she told him the name.

He remembered with a stabbing pain through his heart how he and Ben spent their first New Year's Eve there. A small party of friends together, drinking champagne and being happy.

He pictured the elegant reception in his head. The exquisitely designed bedrooms. So different to the usual standard of budget chain motel he'd stayed in when touring Europe.

For a moment the image of Ben clunking his glass, leaning forward for a kiss, threatened to destabilise him. If he lingered, he'd be able to smell his aftershave, taste his lips and know he would never do so again. Rico shook his head.

"Oh, you've been? What did you have, double or suite?" Rowena looked slightly disappointed.

"A double. We couldn't afford anything more. It was a group special offer as it was."

She flashed him a triumphant smile. Dazzled him as she proclaimed "Well, I have a suite booked for the three nights. After all, if it's good enough for the Royal Family, then it's good enough for me."

He nodded back at her, pleased to flick off the flashback. Rowena liked to stay in the very best of places. She loved telling everyone about it even more. Especially if she could find a link to Royalty.

In contrast, Rico was happy to bunk down in the double bed above the cab of the horse transport. He had a kitchen area, a TV, a sofa and a small bathroom. Total luxury in fact, compared to some lorries he'd stayed in.

Before now he'd hopped through grass at two in the morning to find a Portaloo in the grounds. Always they were on the farthest section of the lorry park to where he was. Such forays in pitch black, often raining, when desperate for a poo, were not highlights of his career.

A bathroom was king in a horse lorry. He'd added a little extra of the blue stuff into the tank before leaving. Just to be sure of no smells.

He agreed to take Viking along for Paul, originally booked to cover the show.

Paul had pre-arranged to write articles for an agricultural magazine, the local gazette, and to post updates and videos on the show's social media sites. Once again at the last minute he had been re-routed to Ireland for a racing rumpus. Two top jockeys had come to blows and the Racing Post wanted him to check it out. With negotiation all round, a replacement had been found.

Sam had gone mental when he told her about the trip.

As Tom turned out a better single parent than he ever had a married one, Sophie and Charlie had been enjoying weekends in the whirlwind of London. He took them on meals out, to all the attractions, expensive shopping trips, visits they looked forward to.

Rico had been pleased at first. It finally gave her time to be a young woman again. He encouraged her to find part time work, be more social, wear more makeup.

All this made her into a siren. Her sex appeal shot through the roof and every time he thought he was ready to call it a day, she hooked him back in.

The Thursday before the show had been one of these moments. She'd missed being at the yard for a few days, busy arranging summer holiday schedule for the kids. Now packed up and departed for their two weeks with Tom she'd persuaded Rico round for a sleepover of their own.

Laying spent on crumpled sheets, legs still entwined, she casually asked him what he was up to for the next few days.

"Ah, the big county show, you remember?" he replied casually.

"No, not this weekend?" she pulled up from their embrace, sat up, her face darkening, mouth downturned.

"Yes, this weekend, it's been booked for weeks. Why?" he asked, wondering several moments later what idiot asks a woman why.

Turning to her bedside table, she picked up a brochure, slapping onto his stomach, making him jump.

"Because I've been planning this as a surprise for you," she shrieked, accusingly.

He glanced down, images of a spa hotel nestled into a leafy corner of a village, wild ponies on another. As he picked it up, he saw the words New Forest across the centre.

"Sam, listen…" he began.

The first row. And the last in his opinion. Then the tears, the suggestion she might go with him.

That was not happening any time soon. He knew Manny's fan club were like oven ready ducks once they'd whipped each other up watching their man from the sidelines. Any one of them, or more, would be hot for action.

The young women were devoted supporters, followed him on social media. Manny's missies were a growing club that brought a touch of celebrity to the sport. That they had been featured in Horse & Hound only swelled the numbers.

Rico had watched Manny greet them. Chat, pose for selfies, post on his social media his thanks for their continued participation. They all longed for special attention. But to receive a kiss on the cheek, a pat on the back or a few minutes in his company? A guarantee to leave them besotted.

They were so keen they'd even created their own sweatshirts. Red, with Manny's missies on the back in silver letters. Attendance at a show became a quirky element of the day, if a little noisy at times.

Puissance was always the big attraction. The centre stage at events. Advertised in jaw dropping stage show theatrical extravaganza to encourage maximum viewers.

The spectators would hush at the approach. Sighs of 'oohs', 'ahs' and 'oh no' as they held their breath, let it out, gasped, laughed, cheered and clapped.

That Manny was doing the puissance for the first time would excite them further. Both Rico and Manny had prepared Red for this class in the sandschool for weeks.

Used a lighter touch, kept her collected up to the fence until the last few strides. Opened the reins to allow her to stretch. Her jump was bolder, higher, than ever before.

Whilst Manny kept his distance, Rico was only too happy to throw a party. To indulge in a champagne fuelled ménage à trois, quatre, cinq, the more the merrier. If Sam tagged along, it would put paid to his wild antics.

Manny had admitted at the start of the season that he didn't have time for a steady girlfriend. Though, that wasn't to say he didn't enjoy himself when out of the country.

"Between you and me," he'd revealed to Rico, "I'm seeing a European movie star who lives in St Tropez. She owns a villa above the resort, it's where I spend my spare time. Drinking cocktails around the pool, amongst other things."

Rico was relieved to hear this. He had wondered if Manny was a eunuch. Now it made sense. Overseas territory was out of sight of his strict family. He was free to pick his own girlfriend.

Rico turned to Sam swiftly to nip this crazy idea of being at the show in the bud.

"I won't have time. Once I arrive, I have the horses to get off the lorry and into their stables. I feed, I school, I prepare tack, I do all the jobs. Then, I have to walk the course, ride, return to the stables, wash the horse down. I barely have time to eat at these shows." He tried to be kinder than he felt inside.

"There you go, see. I can assist you. I've learnt loads since I started helping with Seren. I can muck stables out, cook, keep you warm at night…." She pouted, traced her finger down his chest towards his groin, whilst fixing him with wide, suggestive eyes.

It took all his will power not to react to her touch. Rico moved away, dressed quickly, turned back to the bed. She lay naked on her side, her head on the pillow, her face focused, willing him to change his mind.

"Sam, no. Listen, please don't push. It can't happen." He blurted the words out, hands on his hips. Wished he'd never started this.

"Fine. I'll find a man that wants me then," she replied sharply, covering her body with the throw as if she was embarrassed to be on display.

"Please do." He'd stormed out, slammed the bedroom door, then the front door on the way out. He thought he saw a flicker of a curtain from the house opposite. Glared with a rare show of anger. Could imagine the fingers of gossip as they tapped out a message on twitter.

He slept fitfully, a bag of nerves as he arrived at the yard the next day to load the horses. Relief washed through him as he saw, in Lilly's black book, a request for Seren to be turned out had been added.

Rico realised Sam was in too deep. He had to end it before he hurt her. After this weekend, he would tell her. For sure. No excuses this time.

He threw his holdall into the cab of the lorry. Hung his show clothes up in the small wardrobe by the steps to the living quarters. Emptied his ready meals and milk into the fridge.

Next he opened the back up to lay a bed of shavings on the floor, hang up haynets and fill a container with fresh water.

The lorry was equipped with built in metal boxes for feed and he added a few bales of hay to ensure the horses had plenty to eat.

Once he had checked the mechanics, tested the brakes and lights, he was set to go.

Kerry helped him load the horses, bathed and bandaged in their travel gear. As soon as they were in, he set off on the three-hour drive.

The puissance was scheduled as Saturday afternoon's main event in the central arena, starting at five o'clock. Rico had Friday afternoon and most of Saturday to make his own mark in the ring.

He'd worked Viking hard this summer, helped Paul with extra lessons, improved Viking's natural ability over fences.

The help he gave the horse with his take-off timing appeared to stop the leg drop. The one that knocked fences down.

To date, Paul had won more shows this season than in the previous five.

Friday afternoon, Rico walked away with first prize at the Senior Newcomers open jumping. The booty included two and half grand cash.

To cement his luck, he'd scored again with Cammie, both in the one metre thirty class and the six-fence challenge. The latter Cammie was the only horse to clear the last fence in the final round, a five-six oxer.

Fifteen hundred pounds and a gold watch were the spoils. Rowena told him to keep the watch and half the cash.

He knew for her the win was the chance to stand at the centre of the enormous open arena. Here, hundreds of spectators were at hand. A multitude of cameras popped. She would stand next to her 'darling horse' with the silver trophy clasped to her chest.

She continued to smile even when said darling dribbled his grassy saliva over her very white ruffled blouse shoulder.

Rico had been impressed with her resolve, well aware of how she felt about designer clothes and cleanliness.

He chuckled to himself as he imagined her internal screams at the stain. Heaven forbid she would be photographed less than perfect.

And still more classes to go, including the Grand Prix event Sunday. He was glad not to have remained home to dog sit Ruby after all. Though he hoped Ed and Ella were reliable. It would do Lilly the world of good to have a weekend with her man.

As he fed the horses, he contemplated the two new members of the team. Wondered how they were coping. He still couldn't pinpoint his reserve at the frozen one. She was a stunner, without a doubt.

Those long coltish legs of hers would look good wrapped around him all night long. But it was the flash of irritation in her eyes. The narrow look of anger he'd glimpsed when Lilly jumped off Bluey, handed Ella the reins and asked her to take him to be sponged down.

The girl had watched Lilly walk off to the next task with daggers for eyes. It sat uneasy on him. He had decided to dig about, see what he could unearth.

He had tracked down a woman who recalled a couple that fitted the description. They had worked at a yard next door to her in Somerset until an incident over accounts and the owner. He took a number and arranged to call back after the show.

For now, he could only speculate as he settled the horses down in their temporary stables. Fed and hayed, he filled their buckets with fresh water, added a dose of electrolytes in their water. In the blistering sun, the exertions would have lost them kilos in sweat.

As each horse drank deep, he wondered if he should take a dose himself, replenish his body. Heaven help him if he was under performing with a group of eager women.

Before the showground closed for the day, Rico had a walkabout. Enjoyed the huge variety of exhibitions, demonstrations, food, drink and craft sellers that spread over these county shows.

He picked up a punnet of discounted strawberries and a jar of chilli jam, stopped at the photography shop. On a whim he bought a picture of himself on Viking receiving the trophy, and another of Viking making the ultimate stretch over the water jump. He'd give that one to Paul. The guy had sent him such a lovely text message. Lots of emoji's too.

Paul was definitely an emoji man. Smiley face, party hat, champagne bottle was how he would best be described.

He stopped by the stables on the way back to the lorry, skipped out the droppings, chatted with the other folk doing the same. He'd return around ten-ish to check one last time for the night.

A ready meal on four minutes thirty in the microwave, he glanced at the bottle of champagne Rowena had given him.

Tempting, but no, save it for Sunday night when the party began. Make it available for the missies, get them loosened up.

Rico never partied between classes these days. He remained professional, if not for his own standards but for Lilly. If she caught him playing the fool, she'd tick him off for the bad image and for letting her down.

He could picture the scene tomorrow afternoon. A whisper into pretty little ears. The recipient would giggle coquettishly. Slip a bit of paper stating where to find the lorry into her handbag.

Or more daringly, if he received heavy vibes, maybe push the note into the crease of the cleavage. It had worked like light to the moth on many an occasion.

As the microwave turned, he switched the TV on. Reached across the couch to draw the heavy emerald green velvet curtains that kept daylight from entering.

Relaxed, he stripped down to his boxers, settled onto the sofa to watch a film and chill.

Just as he took his first mouthful of spaghetti Bolognese, there was a knock on the side door of the lorry.

He was not expecting visitors tonight, not even spoken to anyone yet, other than Manny. And he'd waved him off in his sports car two hours ago.

Shit! The blood drained into his feet leaving his body freeze over as a thought now crept into his mind.

Sam.

She had left him a soppy text earlier that he'd ignored. He'd noticed the word sorry. Something about a surprise. Surely, she hadn't driven up here?

OMG. Sam. His conundrum. Her body, her enthusiasm, her delightful smile, good in bed. Resolved as he was never to allow love back in after Ben, he had put a ring of steel around his heart. Ok, accepted, the steel may have got a little hot, melted in part. It was time he reached for the ice pack.

Rumours rumbled at the yard. He did not want to end up having to make a decision he'd regret.

He used both Andrea and Steve to help keep the resolve. To allow him to step back from the deep hole he had dug himself.

A potential leap from a lust filled encounter to attending parent evening. Or worse. A budget holiday deal for four in Costa del familia.

It was time to step away, draw the bedclothes up. Move on. He decided that he would tell her it was over on return.

Perhaps take a couple of weeks away, go visit his sister in Barcelona? It must be at least a year since he'd last been.

All these things he could prepare for. Whereas here, now, he was not ready for a show down. Didn't want the argument, or to watch heads turn as he stepped out of the lorry in the morning.

Instead, he played ignorant. Turned the TV down in the hope it was inaudible. He took another mouthful of spaghetti in the hope she would go away, think that he wasn't in, or had booked a hotel room last minute.

Before he could check the message from her, read what she had in fact written in full, a louder knock rapped at the door. She was not going away anytime soon. To his horror, the door handle began to move. Almost bringing the food back up in panic, he recalled he had locked it.

Merda! Now what? He had no option but to face her. Jumping up, he reached for his jogging pants slung on the side of the sofa he'd left ready to chuck on later.

"Give me a mo." He called out, wrestling with a top, paused to take a deep breath. Be as cool as a lettuce he told himself. Tell her she couldn't stay and that was that. If she tried anything, he'd have to let go of subtle and offer her savage.

Opening the door he was greeted not by Sam. Not even a woman. It was Paul.

"Aren't you meant to be in Ireland?" he asked as he welcomed him into the square of habitation. Almost laughed out loud at the release of the tension built up inside.

Before shutting the door, Rico scanned the darkened lorry park to check Sam really wasn't lurking in the shadows. A few people wondered about with bits of tack over their shoulder. Someone shared a joke with a competitor, two people laughed.

The warm scent of saddle soap and cooking was all that was in the air. Sam wore so much perfume nowadays, he'd have smelt her half a mile away.

"I was. But it seemed it was all over in a spat. The woman involved turned out to be the trainer's wife, so neither wanted to talk. Racing News were happy to drop the story, and I still got paid. So, there I was with a spare day. I thought I'd make my way here instead, with this." He produced a bottle of champagne and a couple of glasses from his rucksack.

"A thank you for the change you've made to my boy. A toast to further success." He smiled, his boyish face an explosion of humour and happiness.

"The pleasure has been mine. Viking is willing and eager, we've had a really good day." Rico assured him, moved cushions about to clear a space for Paul to sit.

"Just like his dad!" Paul winked, crossing to the sink. With a swift twist of the top, the cork popped, froth erupted into the glass he held, over spilling onto Lilly's pale green carpet.

"My bad, oops" he put his free hand to his mouth, but Rico waved.

"It's champagne. A lot worse has spilt over this carpet, believe me," he reassured the guest.

Rico clinked his glass with Paul's, took a sip of the fizz. Half a glass would be fine.

"It's good to hear your day has gone well too. Sit, tell me about it."

"Oh, yes, but I meant the willing and eager bit, darling." Paul took Rico's glass, placing them both on the sink. Stepped forward, inches from Rico. At around the same height, he looked directly into Rico's eyes. There was no mistaking the intention.

Rico didn't hesitate. Kissing Paul made him feel light-headed, as if he'd downed in one, not sipped the bubbly. Giddy and with a sudden deep desire, he pulled back for breath.

"I've wanted that for a long, long time, darling." Paul told him, as his hands snuck into Rico's joggers. A guttural moan found its way from Rico's mouth as he felt himself react to the touch.

"It would appear so did I." Rico replied as he looked down, then back up at Paul. A weird feeling made its way through him as Paul's hand worked on his tack.

With a swift movement, Rico dispensed of their clothes. Climbed up into the bed above the drivers' cabin. Rico reached back to take Paul's arm and bring him up to join him.

With trembling bodies, they delighted in discovery. Every touch seemed like a jolt of electricity channelling its way to every nerve ending of Rico's sweating body. Every kiss a surge of ecstasy. Every touch of Paul's fingers offered increased pleasure.

The coming together of their bodies was powerful. After as they lay in each other's arms they finally spoke. Paul admitted that he'd wanted Rico since the yard party.

His original view that Rico was a lady's man, that evening he had seen something as they talked. His gaydar told him this was someone on the swing- o-meter. He'd hoped to swing him his way ever since.

"So, me riding Viking for you was a ruse to get a ride yourself?" Rico teased.

"Moi?" Paul pretended to be offended. Though admitted it had been a helpful way for them to spend more time together. The more Paul learnt about him, studied him for signs, he knew that he was right. The early return from Ireland had been occasion to discover for himself.

"Of course, I have heard rumours about Sam. What's going on there? Are you guys an item? Like is it serious or just a fling?" Paul asked.

Rico paused from stroking Paul's thigh. Why was his heart doing cartwheels like some teen in love's first flight?

He resumed the tender caresses but looked away as he spoke.

"For a while I'd say somewhere in between. We reached a situation just these last few days. That path is over."

"You mean she wanted you to take the bins out and drop the kids off at school?" Paul joked, realised he'd touched a nerve as he saw Rico flinch.

"Si, exactly!" Rico was grateful for the humour. To lift the mood back out.

"At which talk of children and bins. I need to check on horses, including yours. You want to join me?" he offered.

"Si." Paul nodded.

Viking neighed a greeting, happily accepted a carrot as Paul rubbed his nose and told him how happy his daddy was to be there.

Leaving the sleepy horses to the remainder of their hay, they strolled back to enjoy some more time together.

With the curtains withholding the streaks of daylight that began to rise over the showground, both were still fast asleep at five a.m. Wrapped together in embrace under a thin sheet. Oblivious to the door to the cabin as it opened.

A figure crept in, silently, closing the door behind. Gathered themselves up with a sweep of the hair, unbuttoned the coat. Opened it wide as she shouted "surprise."

CHAPTER SEVENTEEN

Rico almost shot through the roof, banging his head as he sat bolt upright. He had been in a deep, exhausted sleep dreaming of Ben. Sam had entered their bedroom in the house in the Cotswolds. What was she saying?

Shaking himself out of the daze, he remembered he was in the lorry bed. He looked down to see Paul already leant over the canopy. His eyes blinked rapidly; face screwed up from the light.

A ripple of foreboding told him the voice had not been a dream. His eyes focused on a figure.

Sam stood frozen on the spot. Her hands remained fixed on her open coat. Her nakedness revealed for all its glory. Her face wide eyed in horror as she looked at Paul.

With a swift movement she closed her coat, her face flushed with embarrassment. Sam appeared to stumble, almost fall, onto the edge of the seat. One hand went to her mouth, suppressing a howl that spluttered through her fingers.

After what felt like an hour in slow motion, Rico shook himself. He wiped his face with the back of his hand. Rubbed his eyes, his curls tumbled over his forehead and past his nose, as he blinked and shook his head in disbelief.

"Sam? What the hell are you doing here?"

"I think you need to answer me that question first." Sam's silence exploded into rage. She tugged at her coat, pulled it across her tighter, grabbed at the belt to tie it into a knot with hands that trembled.

"Whoa there. I think we have to get a few things straight." Rico replied as he rooted around his feet under the sheet to find his boxers. He climbed out, down the short ladder, reached for the clothes he'd left strewn over the cabin floor. All the while remaining nonchalant, unfazed by her glare as he picked up a top and sweatpants.

"Paul, coffee?" he asked casually, switching the kettle on. He took out three mugs from the cupboard to the right, focused on keeping his hand steady.

"Sam, coffee?" he turned to look at her. His face was composed, as if it were every day his lover found him in bed with another. Once it had been the norm. Though this time there was no Lilly to rescue him from his dilemma.

Sam nodded with a scowl. She looked both humiliated and angry. Maybe he should offer her iced tea to dampen the molten lava that bubbled below the surface.

Once cups were handed out, he sat down and took Sam's hand. She tried to pull away from him, but his grip was solid. He studied her eyes, wet with tears, and attempted his most sincere voice. With his left hand he brushed imaginary sparks from her face. Placed a finger on her ashen lips and let out a deep sigh.

"You must understand, I didn't plan this, Sam, I really didn't. This is not why I told you not to come up. Honest, Paul arrived unexpected. I'd texted him about Viking's win yesterday afternoon thinking he was in Ireland and then there he was. We just, well, we, it happened, ok. I know, it's wrong, and I am sorry, but I never led you on to believe we were going places. I cannot give you what you need. Yeah for sure, I can take your body, but I can't give you my soul Sam. I just can't."

Sam nodded, her head low, blinked back tears as her shoulders sagged in defeat.

"I've been a fool." She whispered; her voice toneless.

He nodded. His mind spun with a million words. He needed to fill his mouth with the right ones. And in the right order. As long as he could avoid hysterics, possible attack, he could get through this.

"Maybe it's a good thing. You catching me with my hands in the dough. What is it you Brits say, red fingered?"

"Red handed." She corrected.

He glimpsed a hint of a grin that Sam tried to swallow.

He shrugged his shoulder in a dramatic gesture.

"Only day before I leave, we argued. I have to call it a day. Allow you to find someone to love you with all his heart, deeply, forever. Divorce Tom, make a life for yourself, be happy, it's what you deserve. But it won't be with me."

He lifted her head with both hands and met her eyes. He saw her struggle with the desire to smack him versus acceptance of his words.

"Fuck you, I was having such fun. You made me feel so good, you absolute bloody bastard." Now she did slap his face.

"Ow! I guess I deserved that." Placed his hand over his cheek, but winked at her.

"Yes, you did. Even though I've known you were bi, that this might happen." She sniffed, wiped the tears from her face with the back of her sleeve. Rico reached for a pack of tissues by the sink, handed her one. She blew hard as he waited. Surprise now on his face.

"You knew? How?"

"In your sleep, when you've stayed over. You've called out for Ben. Enough for me to know that he isn't a horse, or a dog, or even a fucking rat. He was someone you really loved, wasn't he?"

Now Rico was the one to look sad. As the name came out in the open, he jumped up, startled, paced the floor. He wanted to capture it, put it back out of sight, afraid of his emotions. As he paced, he took a sip from his coffee, placed the mug on the sink, turned back round.

He peered up to where Paul sat cross-legged. A sheet wrapped around him like a shawl. Poker-faced as he observed the scene play out below like a spectator at the theatre.

Rico sat back down next to Sam, picked up a cushion and patted it absentmindedly. He tried to compose his emotions. His heart pounded. Looking at the microwave rather than at either person, he replied.

"With my soul. And before you ask, he died."

The cabin went quiet as both current lovers let the revelation sink in.

"I didn't realise, I'm sorry." Sam understood she had touched an open wound. She reached over to him, an arm around his shoulder, as she pulled him close.

"Maybe Paul will be the one to mend your broken heart?" she offered gently.

Paul had dressed quietly and descended from his viewing platform. He placed himself on the other side of Rico, a sheepish look on his face.

"Sam, you are a darling. Sweetie, I'm so terribly sorry if I've hurt you. It's my fault and now I feel so bad. Please don't be salty." His bottom lip drooped in apology.

"Rico. Promise I can always call on you if I want to cry about something. As for you, Paul, you are to promise that you fix him."

Relief rushed over Rico as he hugged her hard. He kissed her head; his hand scrunched her thick black mane one last time. This was the best result he could have asked for.

"Whenever you need me, I'll be there. And be warned, I will be vetting every man who even looks at you with a hint of suggestion in his eye," he reassured her.

She burst out laughing.

"So, you are ok now?" Rico asked.

"No, I'm bloody not! I drove four and a half hours to get here. Nothing on but a coat and a burning desire in my lower regions. After all that, I find my fella with a fella and fat chance of satisfaction. So, make me another coffee as I'll need it for the drive home."

Rico hugged her tight again, kissed her gently on her lips.

"You will always be special in my life, if no longer in my bed," he whispered.

"I bloody hope so, it had to be worth something," she chided.

He squeezed her in reply.

Once gone, he turned to look at Paul.

"Funny, you did call out for Ben last night. I take it he was important." Paul said gently.

Rico nodded. Drained, he felt relief, sad, happy, most of all, raw. Swept away with emotions good and bad. He swatted away a tear as if it were a fly.

"More than life itself. I will tell you eventually, but now I say this." He moved to take Paul's hand, clasped it to his chest with both of his. He took a deep breath. Swept the flood back into its tank, stored for another day.

"If we don't get a move on, I won't be doing any show jumping today. Rowena will be chasing after me with her designer heels, shouting that I've lost her a photo call."

They both laughed, released the tension from the air. Returned to the focus of the day. The reason Rico was there.

With Paul to help, Rico felt a surge of happiness he'd not felt in some time. Just watching him as he made up feeds, took in the pooper scooper, removed the overnight dung. Walked each horse out to tie up and groom. It was all so easy. Paul knew what had to be done without being told.

Having looked at the schedule, Crackers was due in to the working hunter at ten thirty in the main ring. He would need to warm up first. It left a tight turn around as Mr Simpson was in the coloureds, Ring Five, scheduled for one o'clock. With sixteen booked in the workers class, it could take a good two hours dependant on the judges.

"Why don't I do the plaits? Then, if you're running late in the workers, I can jump on and warm Sim up, get him listening. If you don't already have a volunteer, I could be the groom when you're in the ring?" Paul suggested as he loaded up the wheelbarrow to take to the skip.

Rico looked at his watch. Seven thirty. They had lost nearly an hour with the unexpected night visitor. He was definitely behind time with his list of jobs to do.

"Perfect! I hate plaiting anyway; Lilly usually does those. So, yes to it all with thanks on top!" He threw his hands up in mock cheer.

"Vamos!"

Crackers took third place in the Open Working Hunter class. She cleared all four of the one metre fences with ease, as if her little chestnut legs had springs. In the show section, Rico felt her hesitate in transition from canter to gallop enough for it to be seen, which knocked points off. However, she stood well for the confirmation, trotted up in a straight line.

He believed it a fair placing and was confident she had it in her to be better. If he could persuade Jan to take her to more local shows, work on being in an open ring with people and noises. The more she did, the less likely the mare would react to her surrounds. Allow her to concentrate on the job.

Paul was a game changer. He now stood in the collecting ring with a warmed-up Mr Simpson, a change of boots and coat for Paul.

Each discipline required different kit. Paul swopped tie and jacket, offered him a leg up. It allowed Rico time to complete a couple of circuits before time to find ring five, nearly the other side of the showground.

Paul led Crackers back to her stable, washed her down, gave her a haynet, a fresh bucket of cool water. Returned ready for the next task.

Mr Simpson, stable name Homer. Obviously. A tri-coloured sixteen three gelding, part thoroughbred, which showed in his fine legs and head.

Now in his second year of showing, and at the age of eight, in his prime. Kel bought him from a breeder as a two-year-old. A bargain buy. His head believed to be out of proportion to his body, useless for what he was bred to do. Except that, as he developed, his body grew into that head. He now stood out in the ring; confirmation close to perfect.

Kel had won everything at the smaller shows but lacked confidence to take him further. She moved to Lilly's yard on recommendation that magic happened there. Rico had been her Harry Potter.

Rico studied every competitor as they walked into the arena. He took in the form of the horse, the name of the contestant. He made his entrance closer to the end of the pack. Performed an effortless walk, trot, canter.

When each took their turn to gallop the length of the ring, he held Homer back, judging the moment. A swift kick to urge the horse on, gave a burst of energy. Homer took off at pace. A wow burst out from the crowd. As he reached the far corner he reined in, a perfect collection back to canter.

With Paul having warmed him up, this horse was ready. He listened to every movement of Rico's hand or leg. Perfect manners.

As they waited for the confirmation judge to finish, he thanked Paul for being there. He had been ready with a basket of brushes, wipes and sprays to buff the horse up as he took the saddle off.

"Seldom have I enjoyed it more. We make a good team." Paul whispered back.

Everyone remounted and began walking in a circle around the judges. The grooms took their baskets and made for the exit.

Both the confirmation and the rider judges ignored them all, deep in discussion. Rico continued to walk slowly, his eye on the steward for a signal. With an indignant snort, the rider judge marched off. Strode over to a woman holding a large basket of rosettes and envelopes.

Just as he did, the steward started to point to horses. Called in from eighth place down.

At second the steward pointed at Mr Simpson. Rico urged him forward to the centre with a mutter of surprise under his breath. In first place, came a smaller but chunkier black and white horse with feathers and a long mane.

Both judges walked along, dishing out the rosettes, offering the odd word of advice or congratulations to each.

The rider judge held back, edged a little closer to Rico.

"I wanted you to win, but he prefers the cobbier look," he divulged in a whisper.

Aha. That was what the argument was about. It didn't matter. Jan would be happy with the result. But Rico would make a note to add the confirmation judge's name to his list for future reference.

It wasn't unusual for judges to have a 'type' they preferred. To know in advance permitted him to tailor which show to attend.

Blake Green would be good for the chunky type. Rico would be sure to keep an eye out for classes that Jerry Campbell was in. The heated difference of opinion meant Jerry would remember Simpson. It was a guaranteed placing.

He'd contact the owners to give them both the good news later. But as he cantered around the ring, blue ribbon flapping on the side of the bridle, he realised he'd be in the championships.

First and second placed from all coloured classes would be pitted against each other for overall best in show. He hadn't factored that into his schedule. Idiot, he admonished himself.

As he left the ring, he spotted both Paul and Manny on the side lines. More than ever he was glad Paul was there. He'd need both to prepare Cammie. Paul could take his own horse in the pick a fence class later. There was always a spare set of show clothes in the lorry.

He missed a placing in the open with Cam by a flick of the tail. At the last fence in the jump-off, someone in the crowd had cheered, clapped too loud. Too soon. Cam took his eye off the small yellow and white upright which, in Rico's mind, looked like the pole was slightly off the cup from a previous knock.

Paul chickened out of the offer, which had meant Rico took Viking. Pick a fence classes were great fun. They got the crowd involved. The commentator ran with it, suggested the next fence to pick, or urged the contestant on. As the horse got faster mistakes could occur. Rico was tired but determined to have a weekend to remember.

He picked carefully, cleanly, allowing him to take the bonus fence with ease. Second place was good enough against Rozie. A young mare being ridden by an international show jumper using the event as practice for the immensely talented six-year-old Holstein cross.

Rico kept a very clear distance from the gaggle of red tops. A mere glimmer of shimmer from the silver, he body swerved out of there. Tonight, he preferred a quiet pub dinner just for two rather than an orgy.

CHAPTER EIGHTEEN

Ella had been delighted things had moved so quickly, both securing jobs on a yard full of moneyed horse owners.

Glad she had gone out of her way to be nice to Lilly. The added request to stay over in the house, be on hand for early feeds, care of the dog, was a yes without hesitation.

Ella was not so happy with her boyfriend. She despaired of his attitude. Always the nice guy. Mr goody two shoes. He didn't understand her justification for half the things she did.

Take the first evening of their stay as a prime example. She rummaged through the lounge, the kitchen, the cupboards, in search of info. Nothing. No laptop, no notes, clean. She did find a snaffle bit down one side of the sofa, a riding boot perched on top of a bucket of tack, along with a box of rosettes for Wingfield Equestrian. But no juicy titbit.

Desperate to learn more about the trials, the running of the yard, anything of value, she tried the door to Lilly's bedroom.

That's when Ed had stepped in.

"No. Never again. You promised, Ella. I don't want you to mess up this one." He grabbed the wire from the lock as she twisted it about. Waved it in her face. His brow creased in deep furrows; eyes cold with anger.

"Oh Ed, you're no fun. What's the harm in me taking a sneaky peek? I only want to see what she makes. For when we get our own place." She batted her eyelashes at him, pouted a little.

He refused to speak to her over dinner. Pushed his fork about the plate without eating. She wasn't going to waste her meal. She tucked into the pasta she'd made, twisted her fork around the pile of penne with relish. Working with horses gave her such an appetite. If not for the workout from cleaning stables, walking miles to fields and back, she was certain she'd be three times her size.

"Are you going to be like this all weekend?" she asked petulantly.

He glared at her. Threw his fork into the bowl, pushed it into the middle of the table. He stood up, scraping the chair on the floor as he stalked over to the sink to look out of the window.

"Ella, we discussed this last time. Not even a year ago. You got away with it then by the skin of your teeth. The only reason they didn't press charges is because I said you had mental health problems. I promised I'd get you support. Fuck it, Ella, it's the only bloody reason they didn't call the police." He span around, his eyes boring into her as he continued.

"We moved two hundred miles to start over. Somewhere no one would have seen you before, as clearly, it's not like you blend into the background. But babe, you just have to stop before you go too far. When my excuses no longer work. You could get locked up. Sometimes I wonder what goes on in your head."

She carried on carelessly spinning her fork in the centre of her plate. Refused to look at him as he stood now with his back to the window, hands on the edge of the sink, his gaze fixed firmly on her.

After a few minutes like this, she stopped. Set her fork down carefully, with precision. Elbows on the table, fingers overlapped. With a sigh she finally returned his stare.

"Ok, ok, I'll stop. I won't try again this weekend. You happy now?" she promised. A bright smile lit up her face. It caused him to take a sharp intake of breath. Ella knew he was a sucker for her. She could twist him around her finger just like her pasta on the fork.

Ella let the subject drop but lay awake that night thinking about what to do next.

When the solution came to her, it was so simple. Although it would come at a cost. She looked across to her boyfriend, sleeping peacefully, his head facing her on the pillow. So handsome, the bones in his face strong, perfectly placed. The body of an athlete. Tanned, gentle, like a superhero. Her rock. She let out a sigh of sadness. Her life was so fucking unfair.

Before she knew it, dawn announced her arrival with the trill of birds from the open window. She heard the sounds of horses snorting softly, hooves scraping floors as they rose from their slumber.

Ella felt like she had only just fallen asleep. She listened peacefully to the music of the animals before the buzzer of Ed's phone alarm brought him round.

Still yawning, she settled into feeding time, enjoyed being the bringer of good tidings to each horse. She dropped each bucket over, trying to avoid the horse as each one nodded, snorted, or pawed with expectation at the door.

Once fed, they went back to the start, rugging up ready to take to the fields.

The forecast was for another warm day. Sweet itch was rife, as were the swarms of little biting flies. The majority wore a light rug of some type. Some were covered from head to toe, like a war horse going into battle. Others sported a more humorous look with various face masks and fly fringes. Several she sprayed with lotions, in accordance to owners wishes.

The little grey mare, Wishes, had to be washed once a week in a sweet itch solution designed to stop the scratching.

Once Ella had bathed her, she rugged her up along with a hood that covered the neck, to avoid loss of mane. Wishes was a show horse, in the small riding horse classes. Lumps of hair missing was not a good look.

As Ella pulled the turquoise blue lycra in place it took her back to being eight years old. Her dad talking to his groom, Sarah, on the subject.

"Marmite. Keeps the little buggers away. Bot flies, gnats, horseflies, they hate the smell."

She smiled to herself in a rare memory of her dad. Pictured him adding a spoon into each feed every day during summer. It must have worked. She couldn't recall seeing any of the Arabs covered in a swarm of black buzzy things.

The horses may have been sent to their pastures as cool and fly free as possible. But getting them there and cleaning their stables ready for their return was hot work. By the middle of the afternoon

Ella had gone through several cans of lemonade on top of numerous coffees. She doused a hose over her twice to cool down and to stop the incessant twitch of skin as another bug landed. Sometimes, she snuck around the back of the big hay barn. An opportunity to have a sneaky cigarette and a break.

Despite it being Saturday, when assisted liveries did the horses for themselves, the day was manic. Several full livery plus requests in the book. A holiday, at a wedding, or some summer event. Somewhere less sweaty than the yard in full sun that's for sure, she thought.

With only Mike and Tay on hand in the morning, it was nearly five in the evening before all the horses were back in. After dinner they would require a skip and an overnight haynet.

Ella declared that she needed to go to the supermarket to buy a few things. Pick up sun tan lotion for one. Her skin had taken on a pink hue and she didn't want to burn. Ed nodded. He was covered in dry sweat and caked in a layer of dust. His objective being a shower and a cool beer.

As soon as she drove out of the yard, she turned right, towards the village. Although she now continued past the supermarket. Took the bend in the road to the right. Finally, she arrived at the front entrance to the Wingfield Estate.

Two great pillars made from red brick stood either side of wide metal gates that opened as the car approached. On each pillar perched a granite peacock.

The drive wound its way through parkland filled with mature trees of several varieties in full leaf. Narrowed as she reached a cotoneaster hedge that ran several hundred metres along the right of the track.

Eventually she arrived into a large circular courtyard at the front of the manor. Laid in a pattern of red brick, faded over time, some parts now the palest of pink. A semi-circle of granite planters filled with a colourful array of pot plants sat either side of the manor.

The purples, yellows, oranges and reds were almost an assault on the eye, vivid hues set against the backdrop of a cloudless blue sky.

Ella was here to visit Piers. She decided to take him up on the pop-in-for-coffee anytime offer he had made at the pub. The day the Strangles news occurred. Whilst happy the horses had all been ok, it had been the best news. A revelation even. One she opened last night.

She'd worked it all as the hours ticked by, played through various options until she had a fixed plan of action. Strategy was everything. She even had a Plan B and a Plan C if she didn't pull A out the bag first time.

She walked up the set of steps guarded by three columns of red brick pillar. At the top stood two immense oak doors that reminded her of some creepy Halloween film, Night of a Thousand Mummies, Vampires at Midnight or something equally spooky. Half expected them to creak open with the groan of a thousand souls.

Instead, Piers appeared. He seemed openly pleased to see her, greeted her enthusiastically with a kiss on each cheek. Rather too enthusiastically, she thought, as his mouth veered closer to her lips than her cheeks. He put an arm around her shoulders, ushered her into the large hall.

Ella looked about at the sweeping semi-circular wooden staircases on either side, that led up to an open landing. Oak panels lined the bannister, carved like slats. Behind them, she noticed several doorways. Sweet. Lots of potential.

They walked across the chequered floor to the corner behind the stairway to the right. Piers opened a door that led into his main living room.

"Smelling good Piers." She flattered him. The first step in any assault.

The man was clean shaved. His hair could best be described as sparse, perhaps thinning would be polite. But the mottled scalp was clearly visible through the wispy white strands that he had so carefully combed over the top. Held in place with wax, an attempt at a wispy quiff.

Dressed in a smart pair of beige chinos under a white short-sleeved shirt adorned with the polo insignia. What else, she thought. Signs of his life as a polo player were everywhere.

From the life-sized painting of Piers sitting atop a horse, puck slung over his arm, that hung between the stairs, to the coffee table. A collection of books on the subject spread out over the top.

The high ceilings and cream walls in the lounge made it appear twice its size. A magnificent arched door in the back wall looked like it opened onto a large patio.

Ella saw it looked out across a garden some might call a park. The borders full of colour. Glorious hues of orange, purple, red and white carpeted each side of the lawn. A spectacular splash of colour that would not be out of place at the Chelsea Flower show, she decided.

Ella crossed to stand at the French windows. Looked out to where the garden ended. There, what seemed to be a small bungalow sat, an arch of pink roses at its front, a white picket fence surrounded it. To the side, a gate lead to the fields beyond.

Piers stood next to her.

"It's all rather stunning isn't it. It took years to get the mix of colours right. Ah, I presume you're looking at the summerhouse?" he gushed.

"My wife and I used to use it as an escape. Sometimes for guests that wanted a little, ahem, well, privacy shall we say." He coughed at the implication.

"A love shack Piers?" She turned to look at him teasingly. He stared ahead for a moment as if reliving a memory, before turning back to her. He broke into a wide smile, a twinkle appeared in his eyes.

"Well, yes. I suppose that's a rather apt name for it, young lady."

He guided her to the sofas. She sank into a worn but comfy old green Chesterfield. Scanned the room, taking stock of the antiques, the art and the white marble fireplace. This is the lifestyle, she concluded.

He rang a little bell "to ask Mrs C to bring in tea and biscuits," he explained.

"Ooh, I'd rather have coffee please." Ella hated tea. Even less that shit green stuff Lilly drank. She'd tried it out of curiosity that morning. Nearly gagged.

Ella got to the point quickly. Explained how Lilly was away for the weekend, staying with a friend in London. But of course, he must know this already. He nodded. Obviously fond of the girl. She would be careful what she implied.

She continued. Informed him that she and Ed were now employed to help Lilly. In fact, this weekend they were staying at the house to dog sit Ruby.

Piers seemed pleased. He told her how he'd been concerned things had mounted up. Lilly was so busy with the trials, then with all that sorry Strangles worry. On and on about Lilly and how bloody wonderful she was. Little Miss Perfect.

Ella wanted to like Lilly. Had no reason not to. Other than the fact she was turning out to be the most liked person in the Universe.

Ella further embellished her role. Bigged herself up. How she had dealt with this issue herself. Emphasis on herself. She had organised the clean-up. Ensured a strict daily routine. Yes, yes, of course, only too happy to help out. Helped in her spare time with Ed on the DIY unit. Getting it ready for the new input of assisted liveries.

She kept it light. Nothing for him to question. Humble brags to kick start.

Mrs C bustled in, wiped her apron with her hands. She appeared surprised as she noticed Ella lounge comfortably on the corner of the sofa. She gave Piers a questioning look as he sat upright on the single seat next to her.

Ella offered the old lady her warmest smile. She'd met the housemaid once before, when Lilly had brought her up here to introduce them. Her of the blue rinse and bustle.

"Would you mind if we had a pot of coffee?" Piers asked. Mrs C nodded, disappeared off.

In the next few minutes Ella had him agree that yes, maybe Lilly was a tad too ambitious.

"Thank goodness she has you, my dear." He leaned over to pat her knee.

"She speaks so highly of you, and that young lad of yours, Ted, is it?"

"That's so sweet of her. And it's Ed, she smiled brightly back at him, patted his hand in return.

Ella stayed careful not to overemphasise anything. Well aware Lilly being high on his list of favourite people. How many times had she heard how amazing that woman was these last few weeks? It was tiresome. Be patient, she reminded herself. Use the chip and chip method to slay it.

With a clink of china, the old lady arrived with a tray laden with cups and pots and a bowl of biscuits.

"Thank you soooo much for making me coffee, I'm afraid I'm an addict." Ella gushed.

Her doleful eyes were returned with ones that pierced hers, the sharpness burning into her inner sanctum. Ha. She'd get a shock if she could read minds? she scoffed.

"Helen isn't it? No problem at all, my dear. Now Piers, do you wish for me to pour?"

"It's Ella," she replied.

But Mrs C had already turned to Piers, dismissed her as unimportant. Ghosted by an oldie. She'd regret that. Another casualty to add to her list as she struck out for the prize. Why did people do that? It tore at her heart, made her doubt her existence. When this happened, it took all her resolve to remain calm, to not cry out.

"No, no, I'll play mother thank you," Piers insisted. At which Mrs C turned. Another look that sliced the nerve endings of her deepest insecurity, insignificance.

"Why do you call your housemaid Mrs C yet she calls you Piers? Shouldn't it be the reverse?" she asked curiously.

He chuckled as he moved forward to pick up a cup.

"Clara has been in our employ way too many years for her to a mere housemaid, my dear. It's an old joke that has become habit in our old age," he replied pleasantly.

"She has been my lifeline after losing Janette. She lost her husband just two years before Janette got sick. My wife helped her, guaranteed her a job for life with us. So, when Janette was bedridden with cancer, not a day went by when Mrs C didn't care for her. Right to the very end, Clara remained at her bedside. Now, I don't know where I'd be without her. She keeps me in order."

Ella smiled her sweetest smile. As if I am even remotely interested, she thought to herself.

"She sounds like a truly devoted lady," she agreed instead, struggled to suppress a yawn.

"Though, she's a bit mean with the red meat," he confessed.

"Since the ruddy doctor spoke with her on his last visit about my high blood pressure, told her to limit fatty foods. Ever since, I discover my plate consists of vegetables and turkey. Whereas that's all good and proper on Christmas day, I find the meat a tad too dry. Sometimes I yearn for a juicy sirloin in pepper sauce or a chunk of pork pie in my ploughman's," he confided.

Puleeese, spare me the low down, she was tempted to say.

Ella picked up her coffee cup, took a sip. A clatter erupted from the hallway.

Instantly, Piers jumped up, ran to the door.

"Mrs C, whatever happened?" he gasped. Ella walked to the open door. The woman lay slumped on her hands and knees by the entrance to the lounge.

"My apologies for the interruption. I saw a mug stain by the phone. As I went to wipe the surface, I tripped, knocked this blessed stool over. Anyway, at least it's clean now," she exclaimed. Piers helped her back on her feet. She saw Ella and waved the duster as evidence.

Nosy bitch, Ella muttered under her breath. She'd have to play it cautious if that one held a glass to the wall. Like she didn't know all the tricks to eavesdrop! Ella was not about to be stopped by an old biddy in need of retirement.

Ella spent nearly an hour charming Piers with her witty tales of life as a Devon deckchair attendant. Not that she ever had been one, but the idea entered her head when he asked about her youth.

Often, she made up stuff to cover reality. He was in tears of laughter with her stories as a beach babe. She thrust her boobs up, slapped her backside, rustled her hair. The old man turned purple as he chortled in delight.

After what seemed like sufficient time, she glanced at her watch in mock surprise. Declared that she must be going home. She had made a good start.

She dreaded the moment she would have to come clean with Ed. But she was sure he'd agree if she gave him the full treatment. She'd cook him dinner, put on her sexiest underwear, stockings even.

Ella wondered how easy Piers would be if she did the same for him. As she kissed him on the cheek at the front door, she decided he would be a pushover.

Ed was angrier than expected. She knew he was super honest. This wouldn't sit well with him.

"Ella, fuck it, you just can't do that," he protested.

"But it's a chance to make a difference," she implored.

"A difference to what? I'm happy as I am. I have you, somewhere to live, a job I enjoy amongst some great people. Lilly has been nothing but good to us."

"I want more than to live in a small flat scraping by on our wages working long hours. I want to be the one that gives the orders, not take them," she insisted.

"What don't you get? Ruin Lilly, you ruin our chances. Can't you see everyone likes her? You think you can waltz in; swish your blonde hair and they will forget her?" Ed snapped back.

Ed was not convinced and had flat refused to continue the conversation. He wouldn't even look at her, despite her pleas. He'd stormed out of the house with Ruby, returned after more than an hour, switched on the telly, sat hands folded in front, his eyes zoned out.

Never had he been so angry. However, later in bed the stockings worked. She was passionate, provocative and very, very naughty. With the promise of more to come if he accepted her plan, he finally relented a little. Though she had to promise to only go for the DIY yard, not the entire property. Yes, yes, yes, she assured him, kissed his face all over.

He was too deeply in love with her, he'd do anything to make her happy. Especially if she gave him this treatment more often.

What Ella failed to mention was the additional level of plan A. One Ed would be less than happy with, but one she intended to implement in order to succeed. It had almost worked the last time; she had a real chance.

Her own interests must come first. She could not continue to scratch a living for the rest of her days.

Eventually she fell asleep in the early hours, dreamt fitfully, her conscience not quite in the clear.

CHAPTER NINETEEN

Lilly returned home ready to take on the world.

She found Ed down at the smaller yard. In blue paint splattered overalls, on a stool facing a stable door. With concentration he painted it in vanilla cream, the colour she picked to offset the wood.

A softer touch to the previous brilliant white. Or rather coffee splashed, manure stained and green dribble-marked white.

Had it been only two years since she'd cleaned all this? she wondered.

Ed seemed pleased with how enthusiastic she was about his work. But as she walked back up the track, she considered his initial reaction when he saw her, as if he'd been spooked.

He'd dropped the brush, his face frozen before he'd broken into his usual charming smile. Maybe he'd been deep in a daydream, she decided.

The niggle was dismissed as she spotted Alison walking towards The Colonel's stable with an armful of compacted straw ready to freshen up his bed.

Lilly helped her heap it all into a pile in the middle, then used a pitchfork to spread it out, ensuring the banks were neatly aligned.

Lilly chatted about her weekend, replacing Jay for Jackie, a luxury flat for a reasonable hotel. Alison swept stray bits away from the door.

All had gone well, Alison confirmed, no disasters this weekend. She looked as if she were about to add something, shook her head.

"I can't think what it was now, must have been a lie," she laughed.

"Well, if you remember, I'll be out and about a bit longer," Lilly told her.

She found Ella sat just outside the kitchen area having a coffee and a cigarette. This was the only place smoking was permitted.

Whilst she'd rather ban it completely, she compromised with the smokers. Willow sat next to Ella, alongside Jeremy Chapman, the Major's son. Three flumes of smoke clouded the air about their heads as they spoke, like a set of chimney stacks.

Jeremy wore a shock of bright blond hair that fell over his forehead like the mane of his grey mare, Tilly. Injured badly in his teens, his skullcap saved his life. Whereas, his handsome features wore a scar across the jaw which had shattered.

Lilly knew his mother indulged him to compensate for the trauma. It left him spoilt, bored and at times arrogant. She took his offhand manner as his coping mechanism, conscious of the permanent disfigurement he now wore.

Piers had told her that the Major, another polo pitch pal, would continue to top up his son's finances so that he never had to work. A healthy investment in ore thirty-odd years ago had set the family up financially for life after the mine in Brazil had literally hit gold.

Lilly encouraged Jeremy to mix on the yard. She smiled to herself as she watched him deep in conversation with Willow.

Just twenty, true to her name, a willow the wisp of a girl. She sported a freckled pixie face and shaggy strawberry coloured locks, often full of shavings.

They were discussing her style of mucking out. She giggled as he picked random bits of bedding from her head.

Ella viewed the pair as she dragged on her cigarette, settled back in her chair, a mug of coffee in the other hand. As she saw Lilly, she breathed out smoke rings.

"Hey, how did it go? Tell me all about your friend, was she pleased to see you?" full of questions as Lilly pulled up a chair and sat with them.

Jeremy and Willow joined in, eager to hear. She felt herself redden slightly as she lied about the whole wonderful weekend.

After an initial acceptance of how it had been so wonderful, she turned to quiz Ella. Had Ruby been well behaved? As the girl spoke once again there was the strange sensation of something not quite right. Ella was friendly enough, chatty enough.

Except that Lilly knew deception, and this woman hit the red button on the word LIE.

For now, she dismissed it, rose from her seat, told them all she had to crack on. People to see, places to be, blah blah blah. After a few steps, she turned back.

"Before I forget. This Friday, a BBQ after work? I know I've not been around much on the yard recently. It's an opportunity for us all to congregate, let our hair down, have a joke or two?" she suggested.

"I'll put a note up on Facebook. Everyone brings something. I'll do the sauces, salad and jacket potatoes to start the food chain rolling."

"Rock on, I'll bring the sausages" Kerry called out from the stable nearest the chairs as the others all agreed.

The smokers disbanded, returned to work. Even Jeremy, who insisted he help Willow fill the thirty odd haynets ready for later.

As the grooms prepared to leave for the day, Rico arrived back from the show with more good news with the success of horses and riders from their show trip.

Not so good was his news when alone in the kitchen with Lilly. He explained what had happened in brief. Lilly cupped her hand over her mouth when he got to the part where Sam appeared in nothing but a knee-length red coat.

"How is that poor woman? She must be gutted. First her husband, now her lover. Rico, how could you?" She was horrified that he'd been so careless.

"She took it well, it's all cool, Lilly. Actually, I was surprised how well in fact. I had visions of a knife in my heart, especially as you were not there to rescue me."

He continued, "There is no need for you to have concerns. I made it clear always to her. We enjoyed good sex, no commitment. You know I've been seeing others, maybe she did too, no doubt got her PI out on me." He gave a snort.

"So, you get to keep your private parts intact for now," she commented. "I'll have a chat with her anyway, make sure you haven't scarred her for life," she admonished him.

There was nothing to do. Both adults, both had consented. Yes, she might be a control freak, but this was not her business. At least he hadn't been caught in her hay barn again.

"But Paul Greenwood, really? Rico! He's one of my favourite clients. Are you to take him for a ride?"

Rico looked sheepish; his eyes turned to his boots as he shuffled uneasily.

"Honest Lilly? I am in confusion. A craziness in my head and my heart pumps fast. Like…" he let the last part of the sentence hang in the air.

"OMG, no?" Lilly understood where this was going.

"Maybe. I won't rush in, but maybe."

"We need to do dinner, all four of us."

He hugged her, held her close for several moments.

"Rico?" She croaked, her face stuck under his armpit.

"Hmm"

"Go home. You stink of horse, sweat and sex."

He released her, held her at arm's length.

"So, you're not mad at me?"

"I will be if you sleep with anymore of my yard." She slapped his backside. "Now go home, take a shower."

The week sped past with an ever-increasing workload. A press release had stirred up the media at the announcement of the major sponsor.

She was interviewed by Horse and Hound for their magazine. Joe appeared in Farmers Weekly about his role managing the farm fields. Even the local paper had been up to talk to a few people for a feature.

Out of the spotlight she confirmed more entries, met with the Committee, approved the polo shirt design for the crew, booked a band, ordered a loud speaker system. She even managed to ride a few horses.

Lilly was glad for the chance to unwind at the end of it with a party. Certain she'd missed so much on the yard, she looked forward to it.

More and more people appeared as Friday afternoon progressed. Rico lit the BBQ at six, burgers and bangers were incinerated, whilst Lilly busied herself buttering baps and putting cheese on the jacket potatoes.

Then the beer came out. Crates had steadily stacked up as the party developed. The more they drank the sillier the conversation.

Then the wheelbarrows appeared. Never a complete yard party until the wheelbarrow races. Though race not in the true sense of the word.

By then everyone was too tipsy to take it seriously. Instead, the runner could barely run for laughter, those in the barrow fell out. Unable to keep a straight line they knocked into each other, or jumped from one wheelbarrow to the other.

Lilly didn't notice anyone make it to the finish line, marked by a jumping pole.

The celebrations lasted into the evening. Their horses looked out, in between snatching wisps of hay, munched slowly as their humans discussed the time at a show…., or the moment that….. The stories became wilder and more elaborate by the beer.

Lilly remained sober. Watched with interest in who pulled up a chair closer to another. If someone sauntered off to the toilet, how another would wait five minutes then 'go for a smoke'.

Sam, her children still in California, had joined the throng. After an initial chat with Lilly in the kitchen in which she admitted, in tears, it had been a shock, she now sat next to Paul. He took care to include her as he regaled the group with crazy tales of life on the journalistic road.

"So, there I was," he began. Took a sip from his beer bottle, looked around for maximum effect. "Tucked up in bed, in my jams. Quite content with a bit of Queer Eye on the telly for company, when I get a call from Chris. He's the editor of Quest magazine I was working with."

"Where was this?" Rico asked, leant back on his chair, feet up on a spare one, a can of coke in hand.

"Oh, Kentucky, darling. I'd been sent to cover the race meeting. One of the jockeys was making a return after losing his leg in a car crash. He was to wear a metal leg designed for him, that could bend in the saddle but be strong enough to keep him balanced. Light as a feather, made of carbon, latest thing.

So, the angle was both the comeback kid and the bionic leg with new technology." Paul explained, his hands dancing about his arms as they wiggled emphatically in his exuberant way.

"Anyways, as I was saying. There I was in my *Kentucky* hotel room, watching a bit of the boys doing their makeover, when Chris calls me. He'd been out walking with the local TV journo and her dog. I'd met them both earlier in the day, made a fuss of the animal.

Well, the bloody thing had only slipped its lead and run off. The dog obvs, not the journo. They reckoned I might have some luck. Said I was a natural with animals. I know, right? What help would I be in the dark, in a strange neighbourhood?" he shrugged theatrically, then continued.

"I rushed out, still in my jimmy jams, good quality of course, and clean on. But heavens, I hadn't done my face. No eyebrows!" he declared with a look of horror, hands going to his cheeks. The very same neatly shaped dark eyebrows now raised high, his mouth pursed in feigned shock.

"Oh yeah, that's why I didn't recognise you when…" Sam blurted out then stopped. A flush appeared, as she shook her hair to enable the curls to envelop the faux pas.

"When you arrived first thing this morning," she added quickly.

Rico looked over to Lilly, made a funny face. Thankfully, people were too busy laughing at the story to notice.

As the evening wore on Lilly did spot how Bob, who had supplied a crate full of red vodka shots, watched Sam with interest. He slurred his words, more than a little worse for wear, unusual for him.

In his forties, he was a successful drink magnate. Started out selling imported wine from the South of France he picked up himself in a clapped-out old van. Today, one of the top UK merchants. He'd told her previously how he liked a drink but chose not to over indulge to avoid clichés.

Lilly could see that not only did he hit that cliché, he was also hitting on Sam. His chair sidled every closer to her. Drunk and at the leery stage. Sam discreetly attempted to move her chair further towards Paul.

By now gone eleven, she persuaded Bob that she would drop him home. Lilly had Rico help her ease him into her little car, then left the yard party as it carried on. She didn't want to risk tensions breaking due to high alcohol consumption level.

Bob had been easily led to the car, chattering away in his intoxicated slur. How much he loved his horse, Cav. How pretty Sam was. He'd not noticed before now how big her boobs were. Did Lilly notice how big? Was there a spare beer in the car?

Bob lived less than twenty minutes' drive away in a new block of exclusive flats that stood on the outskirts of the village. Still close enough to the shops, but surrounded by countryside views.

His apartment was two floors up. A concierge was on night duty and helped her get him into one of the elevators as he swayed precariously.

"Come on Lilly, what shay you we go get hammered, I know a cool little club closhe by," he suggested.

For real? Wasn't he already totally smashed? She needed to lay him down on his bed, not take him partying.

On the outside, the apartment block looked like it was all floor to ceiling glass windows. She imagined nothing but luxury inside.

The only glimpse she got was as she used his key to open the door into the hallway. It was full of cardboard boxes lined up along the floor. At this point he insisted that he was fine, he would be totally fine.

"Promise me you'll drink a glass of water first? Get some sleep. I'll sort Cav in the morning for you, no charge. A return for the vodka shots," she told him.

"Yes, yes, yesh, I kin insure you, Lilly, the prettiesht yard bosh I know. By the way, you have great boobies too. I shill be wine."

She shook her head at him with a dry smile. He would be horrified when he sobered up and realised what he'd just said.

He staggered in, waved her goodnight, closed the door. She had no alternative but to hope he would indeed sleep it off and have nothing more than a serious hangover when he woke. On the safe side, she left her number with the concierge on night duty. Just in case Bob decided to take a trip to the club.

On her return the party had descended further into horse humour as she heard Kerry almost spitting her words out through peals of laughter.

"Then he said to me, sit deeper, move with the rhythm and stick your chest out."

"Wait, wait, I've got one." Gemma, a top dressage rider, usually a little aloof, shouted.

"Rico only told me to open my thighs more and give him his head," she squealed.

Two people fell off their chairs backwards and Rico tilted his head with a grin at the double entendre.

"Oh guys, it's that time is it? The out of context things horse riders might say." Lilly grinned as she took a seat.

"Ok, joke time. What's the hardest thing about learning to ride a horse?" she asked.

"The ground," Kerry yelped.

It was enjoyable to watch everyone let off steam. Last year it had been a regular fixture, nights like this. She vowed to not let it go so long before the next.

At midnight people started to drift away. Lifts offered to those worse for wear, rounds of coffee appeared in some vain attempt to sober up.

Ed began to clear bottles and cans, helping Lilly get the yard tidied. It didn't take long, a couple of tubs for bottles and cans, a black bin bag for food waste. Ella remained seated, sipped on her coffee.

She had pretended to get up to help, but Lilly waved her back down.

"Stay as you are. You're off duty Ella. Please, relax," she'd insisted.

Ella didn't hesitate. She was happy to ponder the little story she'd heard from Tommy. He'd been a walkover, unsuspected her quizzing. She'd enjoyed the evening, but for other reasons other than being part of the gang. She was ultimately a loner, unable to reach out to other women. Especially those that appeared to have everything in life she wanted.

Lilly gave them both a grateful hug before they drove off. Told them she'd struck gold meeting them. Missed the way Ed eyed Ella at that compliment.

A final walk around the yard, satisfied nothing was left out, Lilly locked the gate, turned off the lights and went to bed, happier than she had been for weeks.

CHAPTER TWENTY

"Ella, I'm not sure if I can continue your sham scheme. Why are we even doing this again?" Ed questioned her on their return to the flat they shared. It sat above the newsagents in the village of Lower Alton. A short drive from the yard, a half-hour walk at the most.

She'd enjoyed the party, it was true. She too had remained sober, watched everyone, especially Lilly. So casual, so easy going with everybody, like she'd been born to it. Which she hadn't. Ella had. She should be the one in control, not Lilly. Why was life such a bitch? Why had Amyr's hoof connected with her dad's head?

She bit at her boyfriend.

"Because I want more, ok. To buy my own place. A yard with twenty odd acres to keep my own horses, to make my own fortune. I've seen her accounts, remember? I reckon I can clean up here. Five years tops, I'll have enough for the deposit on a decent property," she snapped.

He looked at her in shock, shook his head slowly.

"I. What's that saying? There's no i in team. If I'm involved in the deception, how come you speak as if you're doing this for yourself? Didn't we agree, DIY only? You're taking the piss now."

"My bad. Babe, you know I can't do this without you," she now purred. She realised she'd said too much. Excluding him would not serve a purpose. Yet.

"You are going to destroy her, you know that?" he warned.

"Shrapnel. She'll live. That's life, that's shitting life Ed, and I'm fed up of being the poor girl that once had it. I'm really fed up," she threw back at him. Angry at her boyfriend for his defence of Lilly.

"Fed up with me? As that sure sounds like I'm part of your damn problem." Irritation flared in his eyes.

Ella turned her face to his, batted her eyelashes and pouted. A change of tactic was required. Allowing her voice to waver a little, she gasped in indignation.

"Never fed up with you. You're all that's good in my life, and I could never cope without you by my side."

It seemed to work. Subdued, Ed slumped back in his chair and said little else as they prepared for bed. Still, she'd give him another night of it, pull out all the tricks. She didn't want him to fail her before September.

She figured that if the trials were a success, she'd drop the bomb, wave Lilly goodbye and claim the kudos. She'd add an endurance event into next year's schedule. Maybe persuade mother to give her the old customer book.

If she could keep it all on track her dream may finally come true.

Step one in place.

Step two. Well, she worked hard on Piers on this stage to persuade him to agree to the DIY yard switch.

Ella had been making trips up to the manor regularly. She picked up a couple of pork pies or a slab of Stilton cheese for lunch, let Piers indulge his belly, unbeknown to that nosy old cow. If not lunch, she'd drop by after work to have a 'snifter' with him as he termed it. She had learnt that he enjoyed a drop of whisky around six in the evening.

Ella would sip on a gin and tonic whilst encouraging him to talk about his youth, laughed enthusiastically at all his tales. Each visit, she unbuttoned her blouse one button further than necessary before going in. Shook her hair out from the pony tail as she sat, the straight tresses falling around her like a splayed broom.

She teased him with a touch on his arm, let her fingers stroke his flesh just a little, enough for him to gaze at her with longing.

When he asked how she was getting on, she'd sigh dramatically. Shake her head, a hand sweeping back her long hair over one shoulder. Reply with an 'Ok, I guess.'

This would be further explored by Piers. She insisted she'd rather not talk about it. Or, it had been a long day. Alternatively, she found it challenging faced with the problems higher up.

She refused to expand on any of this, held back to ensure Piers would spend days mulling over why she looked so sad. To question what might be happening on the yard to make Ella feel she'd taken on the world's troubles.

Once she had poked the fire enough, she was ready to implement step two.

The following Thursday, Ella was on bath duty. What seemed like dozens of horses, actually six, required their makeover ready for a show the following day.

She asked the others if they could swop, but they all said no. It wasn't on their roster and no, they had their own work.

Fuck it. Why had she not checked the forecast when she'd agreed to her tasks? It was hotter than a day at the beach in Tenerife and no sea to cool down in.

A couple of the owners chipped in to help, but they did nothing but nag. Really? How did anyone expect you to maintain pace in such heat?

Twice she'd tipped a bucket of cold water over her head, doused herself in the coolness. It had offered mere minutes of relief.

At the first opportunity, she roped in Willow to take over. She told the girl she felt a bit faint, needed five minutes to get herself a coffee and sit down. Or was it fifteen? Anyway, she deserved a break; she was a lowly groom, not a frickin' slave.

Lilly had been out around four to see how the horses were shaping up and to help with pre-plait work for the morning. Advised on what rug to put on, which hoods, found bandages to wrap legs in order to try to keep them clean.

No doubt they'd lie in their own poo overnight, anyway. Guarantee a back quarter or neck would be caked in it for the morning.

Ella followed her about, chatted avidly about the horses, the people, anything to keep Lilly unfocused. She didn't want her to see the bridles still waiting to be cleaned.

Also on her task list that day. Seriously? How hard did this woman push her team? Surely they all felt the same? Yet they never seemed to complain, they even said how much they admired the woman. Admired? Must be Stockholm disease, she concluded.

Ella filled the kitchen sink full of mugs, cleaned up the sugar strewn over the sideboard mixed with coffee granules and milk spills. Most from her as she was the one that drank so much. She didn't need Miss Pretty Fucking Perfect to be drilling her about tidiness.

By the time her shift ended she was hot, sweaty, dirty and her nerves jangled. Her clothes streaked in the muck she had removed from the horses.

Not to mention their boy bits. Sheath cleaning five geldings in one day was like an afternoon on a porn set. She had used a whole pack of baby wipes and a bottle of winky wash on that one job.

Dust, soap and smegma stuck to her clothes. Sweat stuck to her hair that now resembled mouldy hay in look and smell.

It was definitely time to hit go for the next segment of Project Takeover.

Driving the long way round to the front entrance of the estate, she was surprised to see Joe Pickford. The farmer stood by the gate, a bag on the ground and a selection of tools.

You couldn't miss that hulk, she reflected as she slammed on the brakes. Not before he had seen her. Shit. She knew Joe and Lilly were friends, who wasn't, helped her with the cross-country route over the farmland. A pang of guilty alarm spread through her.

She leaned out of her window, wore her brightest smile.

"Evening Joe, all ok?" she asked with concern etched in her voice.

"Yeah. Got to fix a bit of the gatepost for Mr Wingfield Brown, some moron hit overnight," he replied a tad grumpy.

"Oh my, doesn't he have someone other than his farmer to do that?" she exclaimed, as she let out a slow breath to calm her nerve.

"Aye, I expect he does. Though, I spotted the damage this morning, thought I'd spare him the bother and do it myself. Won't take me long. What brings you here?" he asked, curiosity forming on his face.

Shit. Quick, think. Ella glanced at the passenger seat, saw a notepad next to her handbag. Boom. She picked it up and waved it in the air.

"Lilly is so tied up with preps for tomorrow's show, I volunteered to drop this to the boss. Notes for her event she promised him," she lied.

Joe paused, then nodded and bid her good day, turned to rummage in his bag.

She hoped he bought into the lie, didn't mention anything to Lilly. Why would he? she reasoned, she'd made it clear she was helping. Agitated, she smacked the steering wheel.

Another bloody Lilly devotee. If not for Finchy, she might just be in some fairytale Disney film where the next scene saw Lilly singing with fucking bluebirds. Well, soon it wouldn't matter, Ella was about to poison the apple either way.

A few minutes later she was on the patio outside the arched lounge doors. Piers fussed about with a tray of drinks and nibbles.

The cool of his pale blue pair of trousers, the white short-sleeved shirt, contrasted to her filthy green polo top and shorts.

That she smelt of horse dust and sweat was one thing, to turn up in jods covered in the crap from her day was another. The cut-off jeans emphasised her coltish legs which he admired openly.

Still a handsome man in an old guy way, she reckoned thirty years ago he must have been quite the pin up. The portrait above the large fireplace suggested it too. Sat upon his polo horse, Desiree, it was a painting he commissioned Susan Crawford to do in the late fifties. She knew this as he had pointed it out three times now.

She sagged exhausted into the raffia bucket chair, stretched her legs in front of her and sighed. Piers passed her the tumbler of gin and tonic with a slice of lime. Sat opposite, his elbows rested on his legs, a finger pressed into each cheek as she studied her.

"It's been a bad day?" he remarked matter-of-factly.

Ella said nothing for a few moments. Took a gulp of her drink, carefully placed it on the table next to her. Offered a defeated shrug.

"Oh Piers, I don't want to speak out. But after today, in all this heat, well, I admit, I feel trampled." She whispered in a forlorn voice.

She revealed how Lilly expected so much. The extra work required to bring the top horses into condition. Baths, tack clean, load the lorry, travel to the shows. The relentless demands Lilly insisted on.

All in addition to the daily trashed beds, grooming, sweeping, riding. All duties, well, she had not expected quite so much when she agreed to the deal. A deal she had been so grateful to accept of course.

As if that wasn't enough, she'd been left to cover for Lilly so she could take a weekend off. Ella claimed exhaustion in these extras. It had been a challenging few weeks, for sure.

Take today, for example. She had just spent the entirety in direct sunlight so that client's horses looked perfect for the show weekend.

"Look at me!" She wailed for dramatic impact. She glanced down at her dirty top, grabbed at her hair, bedraggled and dirty.

Piers peered at the dirty top. He could see the tops of her breasts, small tanned mounds that heaved as she breathed deeply.

"I will admit in being surprised. Lilly is always so kind. How can this be?" he reasoned.

Ella sat up, drew her legs under her chair in a swift movement.

"Oh no, I'm sure it's not her fault. No, she has been so terribly busy, you see. When she's on the yard, she's on the phone, or dragged away to meet with someone. I've just been kinda left to cope, and it's been tough. I'm the newbie, so I seem to have mopped up all the extra work. I shouldn't complain, I'm just worn out," she declared.

Piers took off the straw boater he wore, scratched his head, swept back the hair from his brow. Placed the hat back with a pat.

"Well, what can be done to help her out and lessen your load?" he offered.

Ping. You have reached your destination. The apple is about to be dipped.

"Piers, you're asking me? Ok, well, if it were me and all that…." She drifted off, stared out over the lawn.

"Go on, what do you think?" he encouraged her, pulling his chair closer to rest his hand on her shoulder.

"Well…" she paused. A well-rehearsed speech, ready to act out.

"You recall Ed and me were tasked to fix up the DIY yard to make way for livery? I've helped Ed work on it in my spare time." Another lie. She'd not been anywhere near the place. It helped the old man focus on her workload.

"Yes, yes, one of Lilly's projects this summer to add value to the yard." Piers nodded.

"I was wondering. You know, rather than Lilly having to be involved, she's clearly stretched enough. Well, what if you let Ed and I take it on? We could manage it as a separate yard? It would free up Lilly's time to focus on the incredible event that's coming up in only a few short weeks.

Piers shook his head, took his hand from her shoulder.

"It might seem like a good idea to you, but my hands are tied. That yard is part of her contract with the Estate. I can't get involved, even if I wanted."

She held her breath tightly within her, unable to keep the stiffness out of her voice. Her smile was charged with meaning.

"I'm sorry. I thought you were the top banana, with ultimate power over all decisions?"

Piers looked shocked at the comment, sat back in his chair and fiddled with a stray piece of cord that was loose on the corner.

She had overstepped herself. She continued urgently, "What I mean is, you are top banana, can't you amend the contract? A favour to Lilly, before she crashes and burns?"

At the idea of helping Lilly, he softened. He was not as easy as she had hoped. Between legal contracts and his deep affection for Snow White, she spent a good hour or so to convince him otherwise.

Piers finally succumbed. He'd contact his lawyers to amend the contract 'for a trial period' under the due cause. Due cause condition being that it gave Lilly time to oversee her event, then offer a settling back period. If she failed to prove herself capable, the DIY yard defaulted permanently.

Job sorted, in the bag, bobs your uncle. Ella announced that she best be getting home to sleep.

Just before they went back into the manor, she twisted round, pulled him into her, kissed him on his lips.

"Thank you, Piers, for being so understanding. I can't tell you how much I appreciate it." She murmured with a tantalisingly gentle voice.

"Well, you could try that again dear?" he suggested with a chuckle.

To his surprise, she did. She encircled her arms about his neck, kissed him deeply at length, her tongue finding its way through his teeth, overpowering his mouth. As she drew back, she gave an audible sigh.

"Is that thank you enough?" she breathed.

He was about to put both hands around her waist and draw her back in when he heard a door open, stepped back quickly. Mrs C appeared through the open doors, gave them both a harsh look.

"Ah, Ella, *again*, are you on your way out?" she asked in a unfriendly tone, a scowl of disgust.

Ella smiled and nodded, squeezing Piers' hand as she moved away, out of sight of the housekeeper.

"And like I said, so grateful for the help you're giving Lilly. She deserves a break. But please don't say I suggested it, you know how much I admire her," she added as she walked past the old lady.

"Good evening Mrs C." She flicked her a hostile glance in return.

"Piers, what was all that about?" she heard as she shut the front door.

Wouldn't you like to know old crone, she mocked as she walked down the steps.

She hummed all the way home. She had felt his loin ignite, sensed a fire burning inside for her. She'd send flames roaring through his body soon enough. Victory might be hers.

Her plan a major triumph, the kiss, a spur-of-the-moment thing just to see what it tasted like. Too old for her long term, but he was a charmer. She had even started to rather enjoy time with him.

Was kissing a rich old man better than kissing a poor young one? Much the same she decided. Though the rich old one relished it more.

In contrast to Ed, he had more to offer her in gratitude. Way more. She hummed to her favourite song.

"Her life ain't always gonna be this way, hmmm hmmm hmmm, in her dreams she rides wild horses."

Announcing the news to Ed was emotional. His face a portrait of unease. And she'd only mentioned the yard. The rest, that kiss, the potential future, she kept to herself. Let it simmer in her head, play out a few scenarios.

Ed flatly refused to take the DIY section without consultation. Without Lilly's involvement in the process, he felt they were being dishonest to the point of treachery.

It had taken resolve not to shout and scream. With a degree of manipulation, she convinced him to accept that she was right. In her hands he was putty on the potter's wheel, spun, moulded and shaped to her will.

As she drifted off to sleep in the early hours she realised, with a fair degree of sadness, that Ed was nearing the end of his usefulness. Her lust for a life of riches consumed her. Step three would see fireworks.

CHAPTER TWENTY-ONE

June and July had been difficult months, but when was it not with horses? Unpredictable, prone to illness or accident, able to create damage and destruction. And that was just the owners.

Lilly drove up to the manor to report on the developments. They sat on the terrace talking comfortably. Advertising for the event now well into its stride.

She showed him the flyers, advised on the huge response for entries. All four categories near capacity. A junior event for under sixteens, two for amateurs and one for professionals. Twelve top internationals signed up, paid, booked their place.

On demand, Lilly had added a small show jumping arena for a series of heights classes. Even secured the use of Ross Peake, one of the top dressage riders in the country, to judge on the Friday for the categories. He would also cover the Saturday morning to grade people on a pay as you enter basis.

Ross was a friend of Brent's, instrumental in persuading him. This allowed Brent to enter Kabishka without doing the jumping element.

For twenty-five pounds, Ross would watch the rider perform from one of three tests of their choice. Their score hidden until the end with tips on improvements.

Everything was on schedule. The Council team had helped her with exhibitors and market stalls, which now totalled thirty-seven. Food sellers had called to offer support, and the website was alive with comment and promise of attendance from members of the public.

"You really are pulling it out of the bag, aren't you," he acknowledged. "First rate, it's going to be a storming success, I am sure of that. Not only top sponsors, but top judges. I'm most impressed."

He paused; a shadow passed over his face. He kept his mouth closed in a thin straight line, his hands clasped and unclasped with a nervous distraction. Lilly worried he had received bad news.

"However…" he hesitated, his voice cracked and hoarse. He coughed, took a sip of tea, then ploughed on.

"I am concerned you may be taking on a bit too much. You look beat up dear, like you haven't slept for weeks. How is the yard doing after all the recent events? Terrible business, that Strangles. Then a worm problem on the DIY? Good job that got sorted out. Although, it must be an extra strain on your time?"

Lilly sat back as if hit with a sledgehammer. When did she go into detail about the DIY issue to him? She searched for a memory but had none. Someone else must have blabbed. But who? It could be anyone. Several of her top clients were linked to Piers through family connections. Gossip was gossip. She knew Piers loved tittle tattle, a juicy tit bit to chat about.

Lilly grasped for words, recovered quickly. "Not at all, Piers. Everything is under control. Spreadsheets for each project, daily zoom meetings, and plenty of time on the ground with my team. As I said before, I am not behind on anything."

"I'm sure you're not, but I worry about you, dear. Why not just commit to the big one, the three-day trials? You have my total back-up for it to succeed, tip-top on board with you. Bring in help on the yard. You know, give someone else the daily work. I can't remember when you took a break for nigh on two years now."

Lilly shot him a hard look. Where was this coming from, and where was it headed? Did she really look so beat up? Accepted, she was a bit frazzled, not slept well last night.

But the mirror had not indicated she was about to keel over when she'd glanced at herself before leaving the house.

"Seldom do I interfere but I really want you to make the best of this opportunity. Which is why I've decided that the DIY yard should become a separate body from the top yard. Take the heat off you." He pushed his hair over his head two or three times.

"Piers, what are you talking about? The DIY yard is separate, that's why I'm joining it up. To create less hassle!" she replied, with a growing sense of unease.

"I'm sorry Lilly, like I said, I've made my decision. I'm going to ask Ted to take it over. He's worked so hard already, hasn't he? Cleaned and fixed it up, it would be an opportunity for him and a solution for you, don't you agree?"

Lilly fought a powerful wave of impatience at the suggestion. Sat back, took a moment to compose herself.

"No Piers, I don't agree it's a good idea at all for Ed. Where the hell has this come from? Have I angered you in some way?"

He looked pained, his face contorted with emotion, eyes fixed, watery, as he blinked rapidly.

"No of course not, no no, quite the opposite," he spluttered.

"Just that I think it's a good idea, what with the trials so close now. I'd rather you concentrate, give it your total attention. In fact, why not let Ella run the top yard? She could even oversee things between now and the end of September. I've heard she's a bit of a star on the court, so to speak."

Lilly's mouth went to speak, but nothing came out. She felt it open, like a goldfish for air. Stunned.

"Has she been talking to you or something? Because there is no individual that shines out as a star. On the court or on my yard. My grooms work bloody hard all the time and they all do a great job. Why this sudden concern?" Once she found air to speak, she was furious.

Piers was white as a sheet. He trembled as he picked up his cup to take a sip as he spluttered.

"I appreciate you may be a little surprised. I just think logically, it's a sensible move. I admire you, the business you have created, you know I do. Tell you what, we run with it for now as I suggest, then review three months down the line? Allow yourself a month's break after the trials, come back refreshed. Let Ted deal with DIY, make Ella the Yard Manager. Both oversee the day to day and you commit one hundred percent to the Wingfield Trials?"

Lilly's rage boiled over.

"A little surprised, a little surprised?" she repeated, her voice several pitches higher.

"That's the understatement of the month. How the hell will Ed bring in the right people? He doesn't know anyone. And how will he vet them? Are you ready for the unknown to wonder about your property? Oh, and don't think for one minute I will share field access with him. As for Ella, I already have my team rostered right up until the end of September. No one is about to mess with my grooms, thank you very much."

"Fields? No problem, there's five acres across the road that he can use," Piers retorted.

"You have got to be frickin' kidding me, Piers, really? Those five acres I've been asking about for the last eighteen months? The same ones you wanted left for wildlife as part of a conservation project? Nice, thanks."

The more he spoke, the more he revealed his alter ego. She remembered someone once said that no one gets to the top without being ruthless.

"May I also remind you, Piers, that I do have a contract with you. I suspect that you are in breach," she added.

"Lilly, I think it's my right to say what can and can't happen on my land." Piers told her sternly. Clearly, he was in the most goatish of moods.

"Not when I have a bloody contract that says I have rights too. What the hell is wrong? Why all this, out of the blue, no warning, and totally unnecessary?"

Piers winced. He pushed his hair back over his head several more times. Appeared to waiver, then turned back.

Lilly felt deflated, the wind taken from her. Tears stung her eyes. She needed to get out of here.

"I really don't have time to fight you right now. Let Ed take the sodding DIY yard and be it on your head. But Ella is not going to run my yard. Alison is head groom, she can cover for me."

Lilly shuffled up the papers, squashed them into her folder as she fought to remain collected. Shoved the lot into her bag, jumped up, then turned to him with sadness.

"Upset and pretty bloody surprised. I always thought you were more than this. A gentleman, not some rogue overlord from the eighteenth century."

With that she walked to her car, head high, blinking back the waterfall that fell, a sob erupted from her mouth.

As her car roared off, he sloped silently upstairs to make a phone call out of earshot of Mrs C. He was sure she must have heard that unsavoury exchange.

"Oh Ella, I've upset her so badly, but it's done," he whispered. He felt broken hearted to have caused such pain in a woman he admired, whose company he enjoyed.

"Good. It was the right thing, Piers darling. As I said, it's for the best all round."

"You are certain she needs this help, aren't you? I feel such a cad, especially as I couldn't explain why."

"Of course, I'm certain. She will thank you later. I could do the same, thank you later. In a more, shall we say, enjoyable way?" she purred down the line.

"What did you have in mind, my dear?" a new sensation tickled his insides as he thought of the kiss from the other week.

"I'll show you," she replied.

She hung up, then sent through a selfie she'd taken in her bedroom the night before. A picture of her laid out on the bed, wearing nothing but a seductive smile.

That will raise his blood pressure a few notches, she smiled to herself. She picked up a wheelbarrow to begin the task of trashed beds. She hummed happily as she pushed lumps of manure under the bank of shavings. Why not let someone else do the hard work once she changed the rosters later?

CHAPTER TWENTY-TWO

Lilly drove halfway down the farm track. Parked up under a large chestnut tree, its branches swept low, covering her from sight. It allowed her to sob out the frustration and hurt.

To have part of her livelihood swept from under her feet and given to Ed to take over and cash in. She had not seen that one coming. All her plans up in the air until she had time to kick back.

She decided not to call Jay, which had been her first instinct. He would get involved and she could do without the fallout from that so close to the event.

No, she'd sit down and talk openly with Ed. Reason with him. If she were to agree to this three-month trial, she'd at least ask that he work with her on who filled the stables.

She shuddered at the likes of Terry or Jane returning, the disruption, strangers wondering onto her yard.

She'd read too many stories from other livery yard owners of horses being attacked, tack stolen, one even had five horses die in an arson incident. She would limit the access to her sandschool too. Until she found time to speak to lawyers, there was little else for it.

However, giving Ella a more senior role in the main yard, no way. On earth. Ever. Alison and Kerry had been with her since she started. She trusted them, relied on them, was friends with them.

If she agreed, accepted her mind lay on ensuring the reputation of Wingfield Industries, he must allow her to make decisions to guarantee her reputation with the same courtesy.

Lilly concluded to put something in writing. Face him again tomorrow. This was not a whitewash. Whilst she didn't have an issue with Ella, she didn't think she could trust her either.

The mark on her bedroom door, the displaced folder under her bed. Someone had worked the lock and searched her room. There were only two people with access to her home in the last few weeks.

Though she said nothing, she observed. The shadow of irritation that darkened Ella's face momentarily when Lilly called her out on uncleaned tack had not gone unnoticed.

Clearly Piers had a rattle about something if he'd been in touch with his lawyers. She wondered if he picked up on gossip and made two and two equal eleven.

Her phone beeped, a reminder for a meeting she was now late for. In addition, fifteen texts to be read and three voicemails.

Without wasting time on the why's and what the fucks, she must crack on. She would talk it through with the pair of them, explain how Piers was unable to honour whatever it was he'd promised to them. Suggest they may not want to really get tangled up in legal shit.

It was without question that Piers must have chatted to Ed on one of his yard visits. The ones when he felt lonely and in need of a little spark of chatter, a pat on the nose of a horse. Often, she saw him stop a client from their day to talk about the good old days when he was a young fit polo machine.

Wonky Wingers he'd been called, because he would twist his body over his saddle, lean low, putt the ball half way across the field.

He entertained some, annoyed others, and was ignored by many. But she never asked him to leave the yard. It stopped him being isolated in his large empty house. A bit of banter, the smell of the horses and the bustle that went with it all perked his spirits.

Stories she had listened to a hundred times over. Ones he could ram up his rear right now.

Driving back, she parked up sharply, slammed the door, took a deep breath. She'd seek out her current head groom and see what she made of it all.

In confidence, she relayed to Alison the general conversation. Alison's steady, sensible approach to life made her a trusted and loyal employee to Lilly. Her boyish cropped brown hair kept short to avoid a sweaty nape and lanky hair after a day on the yard in the heat of summer, or the cold of winter, her face pretty enough to retain her femininity.

Mucking out stables and wearing a riding hat for hours a day was equivalent to several workouts. It left an impact on the state of each groom by five o'clock.

Alison bristled. As she spoke in her soft Irish accent, a shadow of irritation darkened her face.

"That explains it. Ed has driven us mad all morning. Up and down to the DIY yard with all sorts of paper, tools, fencing, singing away like some bloody boy band lead. And Ella, we thought was so lovely? I found out last week she's been talking to owners on the QT. One voiced his concern to me; said she's been putting it about you made her cover for you that weekend. Did the early morning feeds, cared for Ruby, for no pay?"

"What the actual fuck is wrong with her?" Lilly retorted.

"Yeah, I know right. Turns out she's been spilling it about how you spend all your time on grand ideas that will never work out. Ever since they helped you at the start, she claims you've ordered her about."

"Wow, what have I done to deserve that? I seem to have missed something." Lilly looked ahead, blinked back the urge to cry again.

"Oh, there's more. Piers, he's been down too. Funny thing, he seems to hang round her like a lovesick puppy. We've placed bets on whether she would or not. Bit of goss for you to make you feel better. After Piers left on Saturday, she and Ed had words. And when I say words, I mean a hum dooly of a shouting match. Ella got in the car and drove off like she was on a Formula One track. Today it's like nothing happened. Now, he's some chirpy Captain blood America with better things to do than fix the faulty light switch in Cammie's stable."

"Really? I've read her all wrong, clearly. I wonder if it was her that put the suggestion in his head?" Lilly sniffed, wiped her eyes, pulled herself back together.

"I really do miss loads not being here all day," she declared.

Alison raised her eyebrows with a laugh.

"It all happens here for sure. Never a day without dirt. Talking of which, I also think Chris is now seeing Helen after she finally forgave him for that slap. I've noticed them disappear into the hay barn together a couple of times now.

"That hay barn. If it could talk it would reveal a hotbed of intrigue and indiscretions," Lilly laughed, grateful for the break in mood.

She walked up to the sandschool to watch Rico teach, let the last few weeks of crisis after crisis wash over her. She was still standing. Only a few weeks to go. She wouldn't bring Jay into the crisis, it would tear him apart. She could handle it. Hang in there until the trials were over.

Rico wound up the lesson, then approached Lilly, gave her a hug. Nodded towards the track that went between the fields. They began to walk. A few horses ambled towards the fence, the stopped to rub a nose or two, allowed their fingers to be nibbled, produced a treat for them to munch, swishing their tails and stamping a hoof to flick off a fly.

As they reached the end of the track, she asked him if he'd picked up on any talk, but for once he said he was gossip free.

"Ok, you are not going to believe this, but I think I'm loved up," he announced, half choking on the words. "Dust," he claimed as he punched his chest.

"I hope you are not about to tell me not only did you bed Paul in my lorry, but now you have found a new body to lust over?" she hooked his arm in hers, walked back down in time to his step.

"No, none of the above. I tell you; I feel different about Paul. Almost like… well, you know. He is always so happy; his life is quite incredible and he's the nicest person. Plus, he's pretty dishy, is he not?"

"Dishy, who says that these days?" she howled.

"Ah, I heard the word when I was learning English, I rather like it, no?" he chuckled.

"Dishy." She looked down, shaking her head at the word.

That evening she face timed Jay, chatting whilst she threw some veg into a wok and boiled the kettle for noodles. Stir-fry was her staple diet, easy to fix up after a long day. Her concession was a bottle of white wine that had sat chilling in her fridge for the last month.

She glossed over the boring bits, remained sealed on the argument with Piers.

She did tell him about Rico and Paul, and how she'd had to take Bob the drinks guy back to his flat after he had drunk all his stock. And, yes, absolutely she looked at her ring every night before she went to sleep. Kissed it even.

Everything would be ok because of her love for this man, she reminded herself.

CHAPTER TWENTY-THREE

Lilly acted quickly. Rather than fight Piers, she'd confront the Ed and Ella. Offer a compromise that would keep it until such time it could be dealt with. In a way that Piers would least expect.

She brought Rico up to speed, discussed her plan with him. Immediately he had insisted she sack them both, slap a lawsuit on the old man for his interference. She reasoned that, for now, her enemies were best kept in the open. Better the devil you know.

"And no change in our attitude to them, we play it calm. Once I've spoken with both, she will be as mad as a mustang caught in a lasso. Let me handle it. September Rico, we wait til then. It will give them the shock of their lives when it comes."

Rico remained mad, but he knew she was right. And what a shock! He hoped he would be there to see their faces.

"As you would say, Vamos. Come on, I have stuff to do and you have a Poppy to school," she hugged him with a bright smile and renewed vigour.

Lilly found Ed in the kitchen area of the DIY yard, fitting a fridge into place. The entire area looked like new. Thanks to the money she had sunk into it, she thought with a stab of anger.

Calm exterior, don't give away a fig, she told herself as she disguised her emotions behind a veneer of cool politeness. Accepted the glass of water as they both sat at the table. Lilly admitted it puzzled her, but would agree, on a temporary basis, that he could take control of the DIY, but not to expect it to be long term.

He seemed nervous, apologetic almost, kept thanking her, agreed without hesitation to work with her. Lilly pointed out that as she had paid for the work, she expected a return, which he accepted.

"Three months, Ed, that's my compromise. If you manage it well, maybe we can discuss a deal on a percentage basis."

Lilly knew that would never happen but Ed seemed eager to settle on her terms. Sheepish even. As per any agreement, a contract was printed ready for him to sign. To offset her associated costs, she demanded thirty percent of gross takings.

He signed hastily, scanned through the one-page document on her insistence.

Next, with resolve, she searched out Ella. Not hard. By the tearoom, sat, coffee and a cigarette in hands.

Lilly took her into the house to keep from being overheard. Ella sauntered along with an air of confidence and self-importance. Sat at the kitchen table, with the nerve to reach over to look at the papers by the laptop.

Lilly snapped them up, moved them to the kettle, then turned, hands behind gripping the edge of the worktop.

"It doesn't seem like a minute ago you two were my rescuers when Strangles was a possibility on this yard," she began.

Ella sat motionless, staring out of the window. As if she were there purely to accept whatever Lilly had to say and get out. Fixed like a waxwork at Madame Tussaud's.

"I'll cut to the chase. It has been suggested to me you be given a position as Manager to oversee the yard whilst I focus on the event. I'll make it clear. Someone who has been a groom here for a matter of weeks is never going to jump over the likes of Alison or Kerry. Both have been with me since it all started. I think the words used to refer to you being 'a bit of a star'. Have to admit, I've asked a few people. No one can offer quite the same glowing descriptive," Lilly added a touch of sarcasm.

Ella felt her hackles go up, continued to stare away. She determined not to react as Lilly continued.

"Therefore, the answer is not a rat's chance. I don't care what you may have been led to believe, but I am in charge here. I make the decisions and if you're not happy you can always return to the pub," she suggested.

Despite the anger heating up her face, Ella refrained from responding. Her sapphire eyes narrowed, now almost black. Instead, she looked at Lilly, an arrogant smirk played about her lips.

"You finished?" she asked. Stood, swished her hair and with a 'humph' strutted out, the front door slammed as she left.

Lilly rang Piers to announce her decision, told him it was non-negotiable. If he raised an objection, she'd call a halt to the trials and announce the reason. She even mentioned Jed Owen in the mix.

She hoped the threat may be enough to tide her over until after the trials when the truth would out.

He'd spluttered down the phone, announced that she'd regret not seeing reason. But she'd already hung up.

Time was ticking, and she would not stand back and agree to petty demands when she knew she had a handle on it all.

Now, she needed to clear her head. Lilly grabbed her riding boots and headed to the stables to tack up Cochise. She enjoyed the opportunity to canter through the downs on a western saddle.

The calm pace of the appaloosa gelding eased her mind and replenished her soul. There was nothing like a horse to take away the cares and complaints. The movement under her soothed like a child rocked in a cradle.

Patting Cochise on his shoulder, she spurred him on as the track rose towards the heathland. The wide-open moor with views of fields, ferns spread out all around, a dusting of purple heather and yellow ragwort cutting through the green.

As they started to canter, a rabbit or a hare bolted out of the gorse. Most horses would have spooked, jumped sideways or spun around, knocked the rider off balance. Cochise was one of the most laid-back horses she'd ever ridden. His canter altered for a split second, before he carried on as if nothing had happened.

Now she reached the ash tree, a branch hung low over the path. Ducking slightly through the leaves, she lengthened the rein, squeezed her legs, urged him into a gallop.

It was her pointer, where she knew the land reached out straight and clean, the animal burrows either side easy to see and avoid. Cochise responded, legs pounding along, dust kicking up in all directions from the dry track.

By the time she returned an hour later, she was invigorated, happy, layered in grey ground and feeing ready to kick ass. No hour of life was wasted that is spent in the saddle.

Rico wasted no hour of his life either once Lilly had trotted off. He quickly rescheduled his commitments, reassured people he'd make the time up.

So many wanted practice sessions to be ready for September. Some had never been involved in anything as big and nerves were kicking in.

He drove off in his jeep to stop in a layby and make a few calls. Next, he rang Paul and asked for his help. The conversation Rico had with the woman in Somerset had sent an icy chill down his throat.

Other calls confirmed his fear. Ella's beauty was surface deep. Inside, she was rotten to the core.

CHAPTER TWENTY-FOUR

By Friday Lilly felt like she had regained control of the situation.

A small concession being dressed and on her laptop by five a.m. The extra hour before feeds was useful to catch up on emails and messages. Responding to them all before six therapeutic even.

Already she'd had a reply from Karl to ask what she was doing working so early. Good. Let the Committee see she was on the ball. It would feed back to Starch face and now even more importantly, Piers.

She studied both the event website and the Facebook page, noted the additional pages added from yesterday, the changes she'd asked for.

Dozens of questions, some of which Matt from the Council team had emailed her that were equestrian related.

She responded to him with the answers, relieved to avoid the general ones.

Like the lady who asked if she could bring her cat to the show on a lead? Was the honey organic? Would there be children's entertainment? Who knew where the bees sought their nectar, and surely a cat on a lead was entertainment enough for any child?

She rushed breakfast as she'd promised Joe a walk about to view the new bit of course recently finished. She wanted to ensure he was happy with it all. To point out where he'd need to take away fencing, put up fencing, move cattle, any shrub clearance. He'd been so supportive and she was keen to avoid disruption as much as possible.

Caught midway to her car by Sean delayed her by an hour. He wanted to ask her advice about Rupert, one of their coloureds, who was displaying signs of laminitis.

She suggested soaking his front legs in buckets of hot water for ten minutes, then ten in cold, twice a day. Roo should remain stabled for the next few days to be safe.

Lilly felt sure the horse had stretched the fetlock, but Sean looked happier that he could do something. And that he didn't need to pay Katie to offer the same advice as he received from Lilly for free.

Lilly was full of apologies as she saw concern on Joe's face stood in the field earmarked for public access.

"You ok there? I've heard some weird tale that the old man gave your yard away?" he asked, direct as ever.

"I would laugh out loud, but let's just say I'm firmly in control," she offered, fudging the reply. Changed the subject by asking him about his Southdown sheep. His rare breed collection was a delight. She particularly loved the sweet smiling face of the little teddy bear look-a-likes that wondered the pasture adjacent to her fields in the spring.

"Grand. The babies are growing fast. You'll have to pop by before the trials, for a visit. I've also got my plum puddings in training for their audience," he added with a touch of pride.

"Plum puddings?" she looked puzzled.

"The Oxford pigs. You know, my sandy ones, you admired them last time you were down at the farm when Harriet gave you the eggs?"

A gang of little black spotted piglets came to mind in a flash of comprehension and she gave a little giggle.

"I most definitely remember those guys, I wanted one as a house pet."

"Aye and she damn near gave you one too. By the way, nice to see you still using the tried and tested off-road shortcut." He looked at where she had driven, along the five-acre field, over the bridge and up the farm track.

"Should I not be?" she asked.

"Oh, absolutely. Just that I surprised that blonde girl, your groom She was using the main entrance to the estate the other day."

Lilly was puzzled.

"Sorry, Joe, I'm not following at all."

"The one with long straight white blonde hair, Elsa, Anya or something? I met her as she drove through the front gate the other day. Said she was dropping off some notes for you," he explained.

Ella. Notes?

"I have no idea what notes they might be," she confessed.

"Well, I thought it odd she came through via the front, must have taken her an extra fifteen minutes or more," he pointed out.

She shook her head, unable to recall asking her to take papers. Why would she? Lilly went up once a week, or rang if important. A warning wailed in her head. Little ends began to knit themselves together.

"I can't remember, but maybe it was on her way home?" she responded, but remain confused.

They both walked over to the new part of the course at the edge of the farm boundary bordering the woods. Her original plan had been to use the woods, but they were so overgrown not even the local hunt took a scent rag to them in winter.

Full of low branches, overgrown paths and brambles, she deemed it too risky for horse and rider. Lilly didn't want unnecessary falls or injuries to mar what she hoped to be an amazing opportunity to ride around such beautiful grounds.

"Did she have anyone with her in the car?" she paused as her brain connected with a sum equals theory.

"Who?" Joe asked, then remembered, "nope, she was on her own." Now he was intrigued. "Why?"

"Nothing, just something and nothing I guess," she pondered as they approached one of the jumps.

The mist was clearing as to where Piers had got his half-baked idea from.

Joe agreed to take down a part of the fencing to provide access through into the next field. A Trakehner fence had already been put in situ.

Competitors loved and hated this type of fence. A fairly innoxious log around three feet off the ground, a ditch underneath gave it the appearance of being higher. The idea behind this being to spook the more timid of horses, though it mostly put the yahooza up the rider.

Following this a zig zag brush fence, all three sides different heights to allow the rider to choose which they wanted to take on. This was the fence with the brush removed from over greedy sheep. Lilly would put that back in the day before.

From there a right turn, then a short gallop to the far end of the field where a natural bank became a drop fence into the next field. An eight-foot-long log knocked into place; the drop shored up by a sturdy wooden bracket.

For this jump the rider had to slow down to prevent the horse launching itself before it noticed the three-foot drop. Too slow, the horse might refuse, or catch itself.

Piers agreed they could use part of the lake that had been the perfect spot for parties held on a warm summer evening.

Strings of fairy lights once strung along the edge, lighting up a semi-circular grass lawn for dances. A hired band, a caterer, a hundred guests, this area had flourished with laughter and frivolity.

She'd sat through a whole pile of photo album memories to know about this back story.

It had been a challenge to pass it for use in the cross-country. The British Riding regs stated no more than fourteen inches deep, and in parts it was more than that. She sought expert advice which resulted in part of the lake being fenced off, the deep area in the middle.

Now she looked over at the drop fence into the water, circumventing the water level posts to a jump shaped like a rowing boat, oars on each side. To the right, out of the lake via a brush fence.

Joe came with her as they walked around the water. They'd wade in with wellies the day before to check for potential hazards lurking under the surface.

Back to grassland again where he'd enclosed an area to gallop onwards towards the next fence, a tiger cage in three sizes. A long box that looked like a crate, no tiger.

Their walk took a good hour and a half, but she was pleased with how it was going. The final fence was to be a horseshoe log with 'Wingfield Estate Trials' written around its arc, with wings on each side for fun.

Another field had been set aside for the finish point that Joe had planned to rotivate at the end of September ready for winter planting.

With lots of people walking over it and horses kicking up a storm, it would be churned into mud. He had joked it would give him less work by the end of it. In one corner, the media would have their main mobile units and scaffolding.

Lilly thanked Joe for his time and drove back to the yard, chuffed with how it all looked. The first fence was still in construction and not due to be set up until the day before the event, as a surprise for Piers. It was a replica of the main entrance. The pillars to look like the red brick, one with a horse rearing and the other with the peacock. The fence, two solid gates in faux grey brick, the black hinges either side painted on with the gold crest of the Wingfield Brown family in the middle.

In the current climate she'd like to throw the lot over his head following his recent behaviour. The polystyrene fence with his head poking through may be worth a gamble.

The first thing she noticed as she walked back from parking her car was Ella. Sat with a mug in one hand, cigarette in the other, talking to Simon, one of her liveries. He spent most of his time overseas speaking at conferences.

Ella was enjoying the flirtation, swishing that Princess hair around her shoulders. She crossed her legs so that her boot touched his, giggled like a teenager.

With a sigh Lilly walked towards them with a grim expression. She greeted Simon, who had jumped to his feet when he spotted her, proffered a kiss on each cheek. She nodded at Ella.

"Simon, lovely to see you. How have you been?" Lilly asked as she pulled up a chair.

"Are you here long enough to enjoy my three-day trials?"

Ella glared, but she blanked her out.

"Yes, absobloodylutely. In fact, I've cleared my diary for the occasion. Lilly, it sounds incredible. Ella's been telling me how much it's taken you away from the yard, all those extra jobs you have to get it up and running. Lucky for you she's here to help. Maybe you can take a break afterwards? You're very welcome to use my Barbados shack if you want? October's a great time to be over there, much quieter, before winter kicks off."

Lilly tried hard to keep the smile on her face, frozen in total disbelief. What the hell was the bitch doing to her? Hadn't she made it crystal clear the job was not on the table?

"Delighted you can be part of it, Simon. I'll be keeping an eye out for Toffee tearing up the turf, you'll both love it. The whole process has been a learning curve for me, the unexpected snags that arise. Nothing that I can't stamp out. Barbados? Does it sit on the beach?"

"Right on the shorefront, yes, with a balcony to sit out and enjoy the view."

"What can I say? That sounds cool, I may take you up on the offer." Lilly thanked him, glanced at Ella. She hoped she had made it clear of her insignificance in life. She checked her watch, stood back up.

"Right, would stop, can't stop, love you, bye. I have to check on Tootsie. He's on box rest after pulling a tendon at a show last weekend. I promised Lucy I'd keep my eye on him, check the heat has gone."

Lilly turned to Ella, too comfortable in her chair.

"Ella, when you're ready, can you make sure the hay nets are done? I can see most of them are still lying outside the boxes, waiting. They should be hanging back up by now."

Ella winced. Good. In front of Simon, that would sting. Lilly had never been a bitch before, but she'd never employed one before either.

"Literally just next on the list, I don't need a reminder." Ella stubbed her cigarette into the ground and walked off.

"Ella, sorry babe, but you know I have a thing about that," she called in her sweetest voice. Pointed at the crushed stub.

"Fire hazard number one in any yard, my biggest fear." Lilly turned to Simon for confirmation.

He nodded a little unsure. A clear chill in the air.

Ella glared at Lilly, the mask slipping as she leant down to snatch up the stub. Lilly caught the flare of anger in her eyes, the twitch of her mouth. She went in for the jugular.

"And I'm told you were up at the manor the other night, dropped some notes to Piers for me. You know, I still can't remember what notes, but thanks for taking the time."

Ella stopped, as if rooted to the spot. Colour left her as she was caught on the hoof.

"Oh yeah. That day. Don't ask me what they were about, not for me to pry into your affairs. You were in a rush, asked me to do it for you. I left them with that old woman who helps up there." Ella caught her breath as she climbed back out of her hole.

"You mean sweet Mrs C?" Lilly screwed up her face, still trying to remember. Nope. Nothing came back to her. It would have been super urgent for her to ask Ella for the favour. Plus, Piers never mentioned receiving them. Odd. Very odd. What could she have been doing up there? Unless…. Click click whirred the cogs.

"Yeah, that's that sweet," came the sarcastic reply.

Ella was pissed. Sat happily doing her usual, flirting with the rich guys. Got to keep her options open after all.

She'd already worked out how much each must be worth. Simon charged minimum fifty thousand pounds a time for his after-dinner talk. POA it said on his website but she'd googled it. Upwards of a hundred grand a day contract to a large company. One hundred grand a day!

He'd just told her how he'd completed a survey for a pharmaceutical company in the US that took him twenty-five days. Fuck, a quarter of a million quid in a month. If he was doing that, he must be worth millions.

She'd also discovered that Bob's drink company was valued just short of twenty million. Boring beautiful Brent the accountant earned around ten percent of that in Christmas bonuses alone. Manny remained closed. Charming but dead to her flattery. She'd resorted to google again, to learn the family were only in the top five hundred richest people of the UK!

How the fuck did Lilly snag such wealthy clients? She could guess. Because everyone loved her, she was so fucking amazing. Well, Lovable Lilly was about to have her parade rained on. Not long now.

That Lilly had made her look incompetent and lazy infuriated her further. Fair enough, that cigarette stub admittedly sloppy. Ever mindful of what a fire would do, it was the last thing she wished for. Horses being her one true love.

But to point out the hay nets? Cheap shot. She stomped off to find Rahima and vent her anger on her.

Rahima was an easy target to be rude too. Dressed in those stupid robes, she cowered like a dormouse, withering away at each outburst. She knew Lilly adored the girl and it made it all the sweeter to reduce her to tears.

The girl had tried to explain to Ella about respect for her religion and how she loved horses nearly as much as her God. Lilly had spoken with senior members of their mosque and her parents, all had agreed Rahima's attire of jods and a casual shirt under her hijab. No one previously blinked an eyelid. Why now?

The more the girl remained impassive, ignoring the slurs, the more Ella dug. When she ran the show, this one sat at the top of the list to fire.

CHAPTER TWENTY-FIVE

Bob reappeared a couple of weeks later, embarrassed about his performance at the BBQ.

He told Lilly the incident had spurred him to check in to a rehabilitation clinic to clean up his act. A broken heart had led to the booze, and he spiralled out of control.

"I cannot apologise enough for my lewd suggestions that evening after you'd hauled my sorry ass up to the flat," he began.

"It sounds like you had issues that led you there. Don't worry, you've paid for it in the extra I'll bill you to exercise your horse!" she laughed.

"Make sure to add ten percent on top to cover my inappropriate language," he insisted.

Lilly waved her hand and shook her head. She'd heard worse on the circuit. She was glad Bob recognised a problem and dealt with it.

Other than morning feeds and a dash to the car to avoid being caught in conversation, Lilly now stayed clear of the yard. After handing over to Alison, she discovered it was a huge relief.

She missed the hum of show preparations, the banter with her team. But she did not miss being caught in a stable by a client that rambled on for half an hour.

Whether they should put a martingale on their horse or change the bit. Whether to use biotin supplement. Sometimes just to tell her about a funny thing that happened at their workplace.

Many of the owners perked her up, had stories she actually enjoyed. It was the others that sought her out to gripe she was glad to avoid.

To be able to concentrate for more than fifteen minutes without disturbance was novel and rather enjoyable. It also gave her more time at the end of the day to keep up with Jay.
Despite their promise of more regular contact, he was neck deep in preparations for the move.

The company had a private jet he seemed to live out of as he darted about Europe to meet with clients. Each required a one to one to explain the changes, none of them lived in the UK.

Lilly kept the talk away from yard changes, chose instead to chat about a holiday. Time to themselves. They discussed the Barbados beach shack. Simon was delighted to confirm availability. Though on seeing photos, a shack it was anything but.

She refused to raise the subject of the American, the one she continued to keep an eye on. The one that seemed thirsty for likes, so many photos of her in so few clothes on her open facebook page and Instagram account.

The chase for the hot British guy remained a theme and Lilly kept track quietly, tying up the timeline with his whereabouts. Ninety per cent of her believed in him, but there was that ten per cent that idled in her thoughts.

The DIY yard was now full of assisted livery, though not all as she'd have liked. Alison had turned people away a few times, trying to use the sandschool without checking.

Taylor said that within the week people were muttering about the degree of care given to their horse. It remained a thorn in her side she would pluck out soon enough. For now, she was satisfied the heat was on Ed. He had signed the damn contract.

Towards the end of August Rico found her at her desk. She was mid conversation about wings. He put the kettle on and picked up her mug, made drinks then settled himself on the opposite side of her. Waited for her to wrap up the call.

She picked up the tea with a smile of gratitude and a question on her face.

"Everything ok?"

"All good, just to catch you up on yard gossip. You look like you could do with a little light relief," he remarked.

"Fuck yes," she sighed. "Enlighten me with your news."

Lilly had just discussed the delivery of the pillars and gate design to honour Piers. She had been tempted to tell them to keep it.

He leant in close to her face with a wide grin.

"I'm off the hook."

"You're certainly off the peg, but give me more than that."

"Sam." He announced as he sat back in his chair with satisfaction. "Sam and Bob are an item."

"Bob the drink Bob?" she yelped, interest peaked.

"Bob the sober Bob, with the drink company. Yes, Lilly, which other Bob is there? Sam told me just now. They've been seeing each other for a few weeks, since his stint in rehab. She says its early days, but she's happy."

Lilly clapped her hands together.

"Brilliant. Maybe we should all do dinner, after 15 September", she beamed.

A rare treat of good news rather than disturbance on both yards. The day could not come soon enough when she would kick a certain pair out the gate.

Alison met with Lilly Monday morning and Friday evening to run through the yard book. Each time she came with a further grumble about Ella's attitude. Whilst some clients praised the woman, others complained about finding manure in the banks, tack still dirty from the last ride, little niggly things that should be part of the daily work.

Ella had developed a grudge against the youngsters. Even though Alison called her out, Rahima remained a target. By late August both Willow and her were ready to leave.

Ed, on the other hand, had withdrawn into himself, refused to help on the main yard. Lilly spoke with him about the racist slur. Pointed out that the girl was entitled to her religious belief and dress code, that it didn't bother anyone else. Employed for her ability.

Unlike his girlfriend, she added. Lilly exampled Ella's ability to pick and choose her tasks. How she would waltz off on some errand when it was her name on the poo picking roster.

Or how she'd feel too faint to bathe client horses in the twenty-eight-degree blaze of summer sun. Anything to get out of the actual physical work.

Yet she was quite able to chat to clients about supplements whilst sitting with a cigarette in hand.

Ed looked embarrassed as Lilly talked to him about the lack of rapport with the team. He agreed he'd speak with Ella, but by the end of August she was working the hours she chose.

Lilly had no choice but to issue her with a warning. If it continued, she would be dismissed.

The judgement, the back stabs, it made Ella more determined to make the jump. She would have the last laugh. They'd be sorry they were all so dismissive.

The Friday before the big weekend, Lilly rounded everyone up for a BBQ to thank them for all the patience, assistance and hard work.

Ella had not stayed, which didn't seem to disappoint anyone other than her boyfriend.

They drank too much, resulting in a game of Chase me Charlie, without the horse. Lilly fell over the pole at eighty centimetres, blamed it on laughter. Manny was declared the winner, as he was the only one still able to jump with any capability.

It felt like the old days. Maybe once September fifteen had been and gone, her engagement announced, they could get those old days back. She'd even laughed with Ed, despite the temptation to ignore him. Somehow, it was if he wasn't in control of decisions. He seemed to be enjoying himself, more open than he had been in a while. Released from a cage.

Meanwhile, as the party was kicking off, Ella prepared herself for her own night out.

She hummed as she prepared a bath in scented oils, lay in the warm water planning each second of the evening ahead.

Wrapped up in a large white fluffy towel, pulled out the bag she'd hidden under the bed. She sprayed bronzed shimmer across her body, wiped a little onto her cheekbones.

Next, the black lace body bought from an online lingerie shop. Checked herself in the mirror as she posed seductively, head back, mouth parted, hands on hips. Boom! she owned it!

The black dress hugged her body as she wriggled into it. A plunging neckline and so short it barely skimmed her backside. Clipping her hair up in a couple of hair grips, tendrils left to fall as if random. No jewellery. She wanted to highlight the lack of bling.

A final dab of lipstick, strappy heels to add a few inches to her already long legs, done. A last look in the mirror. The mission would be a walk in the park.

Ella checked her phone, saw several messages from Ed and four missed calls. The messages all asked her to join him at the yard; the party was such fun. Maybe for him, she contended. Did she need to spell it out for him? Enlighten him of the obvious? Her appearance would have killed fun in one blow. She didn't care; she had fun of her own to work on.

After all these years with no daddy to spoil her rotten, the Princess was on her way to receive a crown.

Staring at the phone for a moment, deciding not to reply, instead tucking it at the back of her bedside drawer. After deleting a few images and a contact number.

She paused as she reached the door. A moment of weakness peaked her conscience. Thought of the man who had been her rock through so much, never scolded her for all the things she'd done in her attempt to be someone. He really was far too nice for her. Should she even be thinking of doing this?

After all she'd done so far, she shook her head to rid the image of Ed. As soon as he found out he'd hate her, anyway. No, her destiny awaited elsewhere.

Not long after Ella left the flat, she was being greeted at the door of the manor.

Piers acted like an excited puppy as soon as he saw her. His eyes bulged. His hands touched her shoulder, her back, her leg, as they sat next to each other.

She'd picked up a Chinese takeaway on her way after he'd mentioned how he would love to try one.

Now he tucked in with relish. Enthused at the taste of the sweet and sour balls. How the special fried rice was just perfect. How grateful to her that she had gone to this trouble.

He excused himself once the food was eaten. Returned with a small black velvet box, he pressed into her hand, closing her fingers over it.

"It belonged to my wife. But the sapphires are the blue of your eyes, I'd like you to have it," he gushed.

With a heart that thudded with excitement, she opened the box. Inside she found a gold chain attached to a long gold square, inset with five large sapphires.

She had turned her head up with a shining smile. With her right hand she reached up to bring his head down. Her tongue snaked between his teeth as she kissed him passionately. A gasp erupted from deep within him.

Ella stood, entwined her arms about his neck, allowed him to explore her body with his hands. Piers paused to catch his breath. His eyes shone full of passion and intent as she whispered in his ear to show her his bedroom.

Once by his bed she slipped off her dress. His face as he stood looking at her in nothing but a wisp of delicate black lace was a revelation. His ability as a lover was too.

She had not expected to enjoy sex with an older man, but he impressed her. Sure, the body lacked the taut rippling muscles, the thrust or the stamina of Ed. But he made up for it with knowledge. Piers was eager, flattering and quick.

The night ended as planned. In the early hours of dawn, she left him quietly snoring, curled up on his pillow, to stand naked on the balcony looking over the garden. The early shards of morning light appeared jagged in the dark sky,

She breathed in the fresh scent, a deep inhalation of air, her body intoxicated by the moment, her mind filled with images of the future.

Could she pull off a commitment, maybe a large diamond ring? Announce it just as Lilly took the final bow? With an engagement, she'd be able to make Lilly's life a misery. Make her wish she'd been nicer. Given Ella that Yard Manager role after all. Been more of a friend.

Oh yes. She would delight in causing trouble. It would be her turn to enjoy being the centre of attention, the one everyone wanted to talk to. She'd bury that bitch in the muck heap, and out of her life.

Peering back into the room where Piers slept, he lay under sheets askew from their night of passion.

If only he didn't pant so much towards the end. She'd have to get his fitness up or the heaving and noise would drive her mad.

Still, it was only until they were married, then she could do what she liked, have who she liked. Once she was Mrs Wingfield Brown, mistress of the manor, she'd demand a seat on the Board.

Imagine the opportunities in charge of the entire business? Her mind raced away with the possibilities.

She stepped right to the edge of the balcony, leant against the railings. Stretched, took in another deep lungful of air. Arms reached high above her head, fingers pushed up to the sky, chin in the air, hair cascaded to her thighs as she pushed her knees into the bars to steady her.

The plan was coming together perfectly. Soon she'd have it all. Mrs bloody Wingfield Brown.

She failed to notice the slight sway of bushes to the left. Failed to hear the soft click of a phone camera. Because at the moment a foot crunched on a twig, Piers had risen, wondered onto the terraced to wrap his arms about her. Kissed the back of her hair lightly as she leaned back into him with a grin the Cheshire cat would be jealous of.

Rico checked the images. Took a couple more to make sure. His body ached from crouching amongst the rhododendrons for so long, but his hunch had paid off.

Paul's investigation had worried him for days. He'd kept a tab on the girl. Whenever she drove off, he followed. Seen her turn in through the large brick pillars with confidence. Lilly's problems with Piers started to make sense. His own intuition, master as he was in secretive liaisons, had turned up trumps.

How he would use this information was something he'd chat over with Paul.

He didn't want to upset Lilly the week before her dream event. To ruin the months of hard work. Her moment in the spotlight, so deserved. Still, he needed to find out what Ella was up to. Now it had become obvious. She must be stopped.

The Spaniard slipped away in the shadows of the dawn, returned to his jeep and drove home.

CHAPTER TWENTY-SIX

Saturday was show jumping day. A forty-minute journey to the grounds. In the lorry were Camelot, Viking and Knights Templar alongside the smaller Seren.

Both Charlie and Sophie were jumping today. With Rico's tuition and encouragement, Sophie got brave and agreed to do a sixty-centimetre class. Lilly said she would attend; the day out would do her good and clear her mind in readiness for the week of her life.

Paul would meet them there and take Viking in the one metre class. Rico was also going to try him out in the one twenty. The horse had been on great form all season and worth a shot.

It was the local county show with thousands of people and a large VIP area to smooze the captured audience in. Rowena arranged that Lilly text her time and venue within the grounds to allow her to toddle over and see her horse in the affiliated class. One of the top events, a big prize and plenty of publicity guaranteed.

Amber usually drove herself to shows, but as the others were going, she tagged Knights Templar in. The six-horse lorry guzzled juice and could easily run up a hundred-pound bill in diesel for the day.

Whoever owned a horse inside paid a share at the end of the month. Plus, a fee for preparation of the horse and whoever rode it. Shows took a big chunk of extra time in the life of the yard, but it's what they all lived for.

The thrill of turnout, the buzz of the day and a bigger thrill with a red, maybe even a sash, to stick on the lorry console to display success.

Last night's party rambled on until gone ten, though Lilly turned in long before that. She skyped Jay, remained upbeat, full of the stories of the week. More so as they approached their future, the new life they were about to embark on. Finally, to be together.

He was in London, getting settled in his new offices. As usual, swamped with client meetings.

With regret he couldn't make Friday. The morning was tied up in a Board meeting and the boss had arranged a dinner with a tennis star keen to invest his winnings. This being a potential first UK client, it was really important.

She accepted his apologies, but felt sad he'd miss the launch. Still, he would drive up after the meal, be around for the cross-country segment.

He told her how excited he was at the prospect of watching from the VIP tent that overlooked the lake. She blew him a kiss and with a yawn bid him goodnight. Reminded herself that no matter what, he loved her. And that Tania was on a yacht in Croatia. Stalking was easy when the girl laid out her life on social media.

Today's show was fast and furious. With the clang of poles being knocked down, the calls of the crowd and the excitement in the voice of the commentator, he lived each twist, turn and roll of every pole a horse took, rallied the spectators into raptures of applause as each completed the track.

Viking continued his best season with a clear in both classes. Seren jumped the sixty centimetres with Sophie. She flapped like a windmill to kick him on over the small fences.

He regarded them with disdain and knocked half of them down with a casual half trot, half leap. Rico watched it all. His hand covered his face, a gap in his fingers as he peered through. He dashed to the exit to grab the pony and speak to the girl, already in tears.

"Do the next class, he'll have more respect for the larger fences. You can manage it, Sophie," he urged her.

Sobbing to the point of hyperventilating, she shook her head.

"Do it Sophie, you will be fine, I promise," he encouraged her.

Sam arrived, and Sophie leapt off the pony to sob into her shoulder. Bob looked over to Rico with a shrug of his shoulders.

"This is all new to me, mate," he said.

Gamely, with a sniff, the girl remounted and took her turn in the eighty class. As Rico predicted, the pony found the course more exciting and cleared everything at a steady canter. She didn't win, but a yellow rosette put a smile back on her face.

Lilly had begged the ride on Cammie from Rico. She'd had little, actually none at all, opportunity to jump all season. Rowena, surprised at the request, admitted she was intrigued to watch. Several from the yard appeared on the ringside too.

No pressure, she muttered to Rico as they waited at the gate for the steward to announce her.

"Just be thankful Manny is in St Tropez or you'd have the possé of Missies up here too," he grinned.

Camelot was a breeze in comparison to some animals she'd lugged about the ring trying to focus them on each fence. This horse was eager and as agile as a pony in his twists and turns.

To whoops of delight, she took half a second off the best time to win, punching the air as the grey gave a large buck in excitement, cantering around the ring with his neck arched, farting loudly as he swished his tail.

One more time, Rowena tripped across the grass in her wedges and tight skirt to stand by her horse and hold the trophy whilst the cameraman snapped away.

She beamed up at Lilly, admiration in her face. Lilly winked back at her, relieved she hadn't embarrassed herself by falling off at the buck.

Rowena insisted that Lilly take the prize money. Eighteen hundred pounds. A healthy unexpected bonus. Lilly offered a share to Rico as she had pinched his ride, but he shook his head, holding his hand out to her in refusal.

"Set it aside and do not spend it on the yard," he told her.

She pictured Barbados and decided she'd buy herself a designer bikini or two, a pair of expensive sunglasses. Try to look the part in an exclusive Caribbean beach villa.

On their return, another party kicked off as people celebrated a successful day.

Bob drove off to pick up a selection of Indian food and Sam helped Lilly set up a couple of tables outside. They chatted as Lilly rooted about at the back of a kitchen cupboard for disposable plates and cutlery.

Sam shared the news that she had decided to divorce her husband. Bob encouraged her to stand on her own two feet, no longer in the shadow of a man who didn't deserve her.

Lilly could feel herself well up as she hugged her. What a year for the woman.

"You know, whatever happens now with Bob, I no longer felt worthless, weak or incapable. The warrior had been unleashed," she giggled.

"I need a pint of that," Lilly marvelled.

Ella was conspicuous in her absence and Ed texted Lilly to declare exhaustion. The others were in high spirits and ready for the next day.

Sunday was set to be the start of chaos.

JoJo would jet in to meet them for a practice event. The mare could jump, it was the precision of leg extensions she needed to improve on.

Rico pushed her hard all summer on extended trot, transitions and hold in pirouette. The flying leg changes Poppy had on the button. Rico was confident Jojo would enjoy the outing.

Seren was going again to do gymkhana events with a bouncing, ecstatic Sophie. Charlie wasn't interested in anything other than jumping. He chose to stay home.

JoJo and Poppy looked like a couple of models on display. She came dressed entirely in her own designs. A diamante line sparkled around her riding hat and down her dressage whip. She received the highest marks she had ever scored, eighty-six percent.

Piers came to watch, eager to take her away for some lunch in the VIP area. He was cordial to Lilly but chose not to invite her along.

"But I must have my instructor with me after such success," JoJo protested.

"I'm sure she is too busy. Anyway, I'd like to have my goddaughter to myself," he'd insisted, a little too sharply.

Jojo looked surprised, turned to Lilly with a quizzical look.

Lilly hastily insisted she needed to check plaits. Go enjoy yourself, she'd encouraged them both. She would catch up later.

The incident had bemused her, the strange way Piers had looked, almost embarrassed. Like he harboured a secret.

Previously, an invite would have been natural. An expectation even, for her to join his table. Today the shutters were up. Lilly shook her head as she returned to the lorry.

Too many people acting too weirdly at the moment. She couldn't wait to get it cleared up come Monday week. A complete scrub down would be required in more than one area.

It was close to midnight when Lilly finally got to bed. Far later than her usual time. After such a hectic three days, there had been much to sort out before she turned in.

She'd told Alison and Kerry to go home once they'd unloaded the horses. Young Mike had insisted he stay, helped her rug up, put in hay nets and top water up.

Rico took the tack out of the lorry and left it in a corner of the tack room ready for cleaning the following day. Into a large water bucket went the numerous bandages they'd gone through over the last two days.

Poo and shavings cleared out of the lorry; the floor hosed down. He was finished just as Paul arrived in the Skoda.

A final yard check, horses chewing on their hay. All calm for another night.

Too exhausted to do more, she climbed into bed, drew the duvet around her and fell into a deep dreamless sleep.

CHAPTER TWENTY-SEVEN

Only two days away from the big day and the atmosphere totally buzzed. Marquees were going up. The stage for the band in place, as were the show jumps in the lower sandschool.

Rosettes, trophies and prize money envelopes all stacked neatly in a couple of crates in the spare room. Social media posts being liked by hundreds.

Tomorrow Lilly would walk the cross-country course, then brief the judges, the volunteer stewards, the car park attendants and her own team. All of which she rostered around their day jobs.

Nearly the entire yard had entered in some class or other and it had been a marathon preparing a spreadsheet just for that.

Some clients preferred to get their horses ready themselves. Others required the services of a groom. A few wanted their horse ridden for them and purchased tickets to watch. In between all this, horses had to be mucked out, waters changed, feed and hay nets prepared.

Alison brought along her daughter to help. Taylor almost lived at the yard in her excitement. She found a handful of students from the nearby equestrian college that Lilly agreed to pay. It allowed her to cover much of the daily yard tasks and take the heat off her own team.

Lilly's early start proved useful and by seven she was back in the house to dig out the dressage letters to start placing in the top sandschool. As she picked up the box, the doorbell went. Thinking it may be one of her grooms, she rushed down the stairs; the box held in front of her.

She opened the door, peered around the cardboard to see who was there.

Ed. Dishevelled, unshaven, red eyed, shoulders slumped. Dejected. He looked like he'd battled with the devil and lost.

"What the heck?" she asked with surprise.

Ed walked in, closed the door behind him, headed for the kitchen. He slumped on a chair, his head face down on the table, hands over the back of his head. Lilly heard the sobs and realised something serious had happened.

About to reach for the kettle, she looked at him again. Changed her mind. A cup of tea was unlikely to help in this instance. Instead, she took out two glasses and an untouched bottle of Jack Daniels she kept in the cupboard behind the tins.

The emergency bottle for when it all got too much. For her, that moment hadn't yet happened. Maybe it was about to. Either way, she poured him a couple of fingers worth and a thimble portion for herself.

"Want to tell me?" she asked, nudging the glass into his arm.

"I'm so sorry, Lilly, I'm so sorry." He sobbed, lifting his head to take a gulp of the liqueur.

"Fair enough. Want to tell me what you are sorry for?"

"I never meant for this to happen, I really didn't. It's all such a mess now." He looked up at her, his face drained of the summer tan, his cheeks sunken in and his eyes hollow. A shadow of the cheerful and handsome face.

She noticed he still wore the same clothes from the day before. The yellow polo shirt stained with ketchup down the front. At least she assumed it was ketchup and not blood.

That was it, he'd got in a fight. He smelt like a stable after a mare had spent forty-eight hours inside. The potent aroma was enough for her to open both windows.

"You best tell me what the hell it is that is wrong as I haven't got all day to sit here and guess," she coaxed.

"I don't know where to start, Lilly. I just can't believe she's actually done it this time."

"At the beginning might be good." Lilly glanced at the box of numbers, listed to be in place by eight. Mounting irritation built as she tired of the snippets and sobs he gasped out between gulps. With so much still to do, this had better be important.

"The start? Well, that was three years ago when I first set eyes on her. I should never have believed I could change her." Ed took another gulp of the liquor, swallowed it down as if to give him strength to continue.

"Ella always wanted the good life back she lost the day her dad died. He owned a stud farm, bred Arabs. Sold them all over the world. She had everything, the best of the best."

"Do I need her back story. Is this going to take long?" Lilly replied with sarcasm.

Ed seemed to be unaware of the tone, so deep in his own pool of pity.

"When we met, she worked on a livery yard in Devon, close to home. She was lonely. Her mum a drunk. Ella was a bit wild in her teenage years and got into trouble, left school with no qualifications. She told me that one day she would have a yard of her own. I wanted it for her too."

He slumped back in the chair, his face still devoid of life, his eyes glazed in a stupor of disbelief.

"We moved to a place just outside of London. More money, more opportunity to learn. It was there we almost fell apart." He stopped, transfixed by his own admission.

A crawling sensation tingled in her neck and worked its way up her head. A yard of her own. A bit of a star.

Ed continued to recount in pockets between sobs. How she'd run off with the owner of the private livery, returned to him when the guy moved on to the next model. She promised him never again.

"She was so sorry and so sad I took her back. Fucking idiot." He scolded himself.

"So, she came here and ring a ding ding." Lilly whispered almost to herself. Ed paled and nodded.

"She suggested we make problems for you so that you'd leave. I persuaded her to limit us to the DIY yard." He choked as he admitted his guilt in the deception.

"Thanks to the information she found when you jimmied the lock to my bedroom?" Lilly laughed out loud in disbelief.

He looked stunned, embarrassed, his face crumpled and tear stained.

"You knew? Fuck, Lilly. I told her she shouldn't. I begged her to stop, but she did it anyway. I tried to cover up so you wouldn't notice."

"Yet you conspired with her to take the bottom yard, anyway?" Lilly stabbed.

"I never asked for it. She said she had sorted it with Piers. Told me I had no option but to agree. I went along because I love her. Loved her."

Lilly drank the thimble worth of warm, soft bourbon. Looked at the glass.

"Fuck it," picked up the bottle and took a long swig.

The day it all got too much appeared to be today. The bitch! But how in blazing hell had she persuaded Piers to change the contract? Joe's words came to her head. The notes.

"She's been going up there to see him, hasn't she?" she snapped. "Piers, she's been up to persuade him to change the contract?"

Ed's head rocked up and down like a puppet, his mouth open, his eyes glazed over.

"She's been up there almost daily after work. She said she chats with him. Suggests how hard you work her. Spun a few stories of how you are struggling. A load of crap about how you expect her to cover your duties and more. Gives him the puppy dog eyes is what she's told me. I've found out she's showed him a lot more than just her eyes." Tears now ran openly down his face. His shoulders shuddered. He reached into the back of his jeans pocket and produced a brown envelope. Plopped it on the table for Lilly.

Inside were four photos. All of Ella naked on the upstairs terrace at the front of the manor as she stretched in the early morning light. The last one showed Piers with his arms around her waist, also naked, a huge grin on his face.

It wasn't rocket science. Lilly didn't need to add up the numbers to make ten.

"Have you shown her? Does she know you know?"

"Yes. I had no idea, I'm so sorry Lilly."

"Fucking hell Ed, this is heavy. I must admit, I'm disgusted the pair of you could even think of doing this to me. I opened my home to you as friends, gave you both work. All the while you plotted behind my back. Pretty fucked up, don't you think?"

Lilly felt like a boulder had fallen on her, her body crushed by its weight. She shook as she tried to move a hand to reach the bottle. She took another swig to steady herself. Picked up a photo and waved it at him.

"Where do you fit in with this now?" she hissed.

"Collateral damage. I've been calling her ever since the night of the party when I got home to find her gone. Searched the flat, found her phone in the bedside table turned off. The photos arrived Monday morning. I called the manor, got her on the line. She admitted it. Even told me he's in love with her, that she has him dangled on a string, ready to give her anything she wants. And she wants the lot, Lilly. She's after the heart. Wingfield dot com. Not just you, but the estate and the business.

Lilly gasped with shock.

"Piers has actually said he's in love with Ella?"

Ed nodded sadly.

"But yesterday she rang in sick, you didn't say a word?" Lilly remembered, gave him a hard stare of accusation.

"She rang you?"

"Yes. She sounded off. To be honest, I didn't take much notice. She gave me more problems than the thirty odd horses on my yard and their owners put together. Especially after all the shit over contracts." She shot him another furious look.

"What was the plan, huh, what did you two think you could do to me?" she asked him. She had no sympathy for this sheep.

"Oh God, this is so hard. I really am so very sorry, Lilly." He bowed his head in shame, finished the drink and continued.

"Ella said that it would be announced you were stepping down at the end of the show. That she would replace you. A clause in your contract she would void. She never mentioned anything more."

To Lilly it felt like daggers stabbing her at every revelation. Real pain tore at her chest and she sagged like a rag doll.

How could someone be so nasty, so manipulative and cold? And he played a part of this deception for weeks. No one should love another so much they'd be prepared to destroy lives.

Though the last few months finally fitted into place.

She knew there must have been a reason Piers had been so niggly. Still, even that plan backfired on them all. Taylor reported Ed had taken on four liveries without her knowledge.

Each spent no time up there, which had left Ed working flat out to keep the yard in order. Nor did he receive payment from them. No wonder he'd made the lame excuse over the money he owed her.

She wanted to scream, but Ed was back sobbing into the table top. Love clearly does stupid stuff to you.

"Look, I appreciate you have had the bottle to come and tell me to my face and show me the photos. I'm can't say I'm sorry, you're as guilty as she. Before we continue, there isn't anything else you need to get off your chest is there?" Lilly appraised him square in the face.

He shook his head and confirmed there was no more.

Lilly wrestled with herself for a moment before taking the lead. She reached over and grabbed his wrist, made him look at her, directly into her eyes. Puffy and bedraggled, he was a sore sight.

"Don't think for one minute that I am about to let anyone take my livelihood. Nor ruin an event I've worked my butt off for," she told him severely.

"What neither of you would know is that your stupid little idea could never work. That life will continue for me." Her voice rose from its usual soft tone as she fought back her emotions. She took a deep breath, told herself to calm down.

"FYI, your girlfriend is about to get the shock of her life." She slammed her fists on the table, made Ruby jump.

Ed shot her an anguished look. His swallow almost audible, a nervous gargle spilt from his throat, swamped with overpowering misery.

Lilly told him to sort out the DIY yard then go home. He was to pack her things into boxes and get some sleep.

She searched her sugar pot for the emergency supply of tablets she kept. She'd been prescribed them when she first started at the yard and was finding her feet.

As he left, she closed the door and slumped with her back against it, her eyes closed, fought back the tears that now squeezed out.

All this fucking work and now she had a trophy hunter on the loose! Well, not exactly loose, shacked up with Piers. Of all people.

Why had such a clever man lost all sense and reason? He was but a money magnet, no more. All the signs had been there.

Only the weekend before last he'd been short with her, the refusal to invite her to lunch with Jojo. Very clear now.

Lilly thought about it as she stayed sat by the door, her arms wrapped around her knees as she bent her body up into herself. Her mind whirred over the last months since the pair arrived on scene.

This could end with one call. In an instant. She looked down at her phone, saw the flow of messages from the last hour. Decided the call would wait.

Ruby had snuck beside her, so she gave the little dog a hug. Tasting the moist salt on her owner's cheeks, she licked them away.

CHAPTER TWENTY-EIGHT

Ella stretched. Luxuriated in the richness of the bedding. Opened her eyes to gaze about the room with a contented smile.

It was tastefully decorated. From the elegant chandelier in the centre of the tray ceiling, to the gilded side tables on whose dark mahogany tops stood antique Victorian lamps.

Touching the headboard with her fingertips, a camel backed gold tufted affair, she felt the porcelain mould that adorned the centre top, a spray of blue flowers.

The room smelt fresh, scented with perfume from the pillows. What a contrast to the small flat above the post office she'd shared with Ed. That smelt of sweat and horse, along with the dank of mould from condensation around the windows that stuck shut from over painting.

Next to her lay Piers. A curl of satisfaction played on his lips as he breathed deeply. His white hair lay about his pillow like tendrils of cobwebs haphazardly.

She would have to make some changes. Probably rip out the blue shag pile carpet. Replace it with a dusky pink. Renew the heavy drapes for a light, fresh curtain.

It was important to remove all signs of a previous woman's touch. To stamp her own style onto this room, and all the others.

Ella had seven whole glorious bedrooms and their ensuites to play dress up with. Not to mention downstairs.

As she often did, she pictured the beautiful home in which she had lived as a child. The English country décor of oak and colour.

The way her mother would lighten a room with a bright throw over an old woven chair. Or the smell of leather and books in her father's study where she'd watch, fascinated as he entered blood lines meticulously into his stud book. Always explaining to her how important it was to keep the breed pure.

Now she could use those books again. Build up her own pedigree of the breed she loved more than any other.

Smiling, she wondered what her mother would think now. Imagined the catty comments. Never as close to her as dad. By the age of fifteen, she rebelled. Since she'd left home at eighteen, they hardly spoke.

The next move being to make Piers understand her dream linked them together. In her plans she would keep the livery, the well-heeled ones, for now at any rate. Become influential in her own right as a trainer.

Once she was in, she would acquire a few mares, artificially inseminate them with a top endurance stallion. She might even travel to Saudi, check out the quality of the studs there.

Plans that circulated about her head for years. Always waiting. Watching for the opportunity. Now so close, she could almost touch if she reached her arm out high.

She stretched one out towards the ceiling as her dreams swept her away.

Oh, the pleasure in seeing that irritating housekeeper despatched. She made him offer up a reason to send her away Tuesday morning.

Ella wanted to ensure the old bat didn't go running to his son, or worse, Lilly. She refused to get out of bed before it was done. After all, she'd not had a lie in for years. With an enormous TV set into the wall opposite and a set of remote headphones, she stayed put, watching the Country Horse channel.

A pang of sadness engulfed her as Ed's face popped up in her mind. He had been the light in her dark, the smile on her scowl, always wanting to make her happy.

Still. He'd get over her, meet someone who loved him back. He deserved better than her.

Ella purchased a pay as you go phone on Saturday. Used to send Lilly a text Wednesday morning. Some bullshit story about nipping over to Somerset to see a friend. Gotten food poisoning.

She hoped that Ed would keep quiet about the argument they'd had. When he'd told her about a bunch of photos of her.

Who the fuck had taken them? She didn't pretend it wasn't her in the pictures. No point in denial. He knew what she looked like naked. But she had been sad to hear the sobs as she told him it was over.

She dismissed all thoughts of what lay before as she concentrated on what now lay ahead.

Piers attended to her every desire, in exchange for her body. Except that she was a bit put out at his eagerness for more. Actually, more than a bit.

She shrugged off his advances as he woke. Jumped out of bed to take a shower. Insisted that too much lovemaking might give him a dicky ticker. He seemed to be only thinking of his dick and not his ticker, but she pleasured him. Made all the right noises. Enough to keep him enthralled, to make up for the times she denied him. She'd had no idea how horny a sixty-five-year-old could be.

Over the next couple of days Ella was cautious. Kept clear as people began to arrive. Either to drop objects off or ask Piers to drive down and check the placement of the seating around the lake. Check where the cameras were being placed and so it went on.

Lilly rang him several times a day to keep him posted, and he made a few zoom calls with the Board.

She'd busy herself in the kitchen. Made them cheese and pickle sandwiches for lunch, pie and chips for dinner. Her culinary skills were not the best.

Usually she'd pick up a takeaway, or shove a ready meal in the microwave. If actual cookery ever took place, it had been Ed who did it.

Piers didn't seem to mind. He told her how he enjoyed the delight of eating food from the forbidden list without someone to tell him otherwise.

Ella closed her eyes again, settled back down under the soft duvet. Carried on dreaming about a bright future.

As Ella established herself as the Lady of the Manor, Rico was with a woman. Paul had spoken to her during his investigations. Ones that sent sirens raining about Rico's head like the bells of Notre Dame.

He'd driven down south on Monday after a lesson with Simon, who had said no to a reschedule. A minor setback of a few hours, but he'd enjoyed a stroll along the seashore with his lover in the setting sun.

It took Rico back to when he was a boy growing up in Andalusia. The trips to the sea with his family when they'd walk along glorious open sand dunes that overlooked the Mediterranean Sea. In the distance, the craggy rock of Gibraltar.

He was minded to take a trip back with Paul. Show him where it all started. In the hope that the slate was clean in the village of his birth. That there was no wanted poster out for him.

The smell of the salt air, the sound of the gulls, music he had stopped hearing a long time ago. When horses came into his life. He'd travelled all over Europe before moving to the UK.

But it seemed like years since he had taken his socks off and waded through the water. Now he enjoyed the sensation in his feet as they sank into the soft sand on the shore line.

Waited for the sea to draw itself back, then cascade forward again. The foam splashed up his leg with a joy that almost allowed him to forget why they were there.

Paul, ever exuberant, playfully pushed him further in until the tops of his rolled-up jeans were soaked. They held onto each other as they laughed with the happiness of two children. Strolled back to the hotel that overlooked the far corner of the bay, holding hands.

They talked about Viking, the upcoming three-day event, its likely success. Anything to avoid the following afternoon's confrontation.

The afternoon that found them both sat in a café three down from their hotel. It too overlooked the beach. They perched near a window, open to allow the warm air to permeate inside. Both with a mug of coffee, waiting for the woman to show up. She'd agreed to meet them at four o'clock and it was now five.

"Do you think she's had second thoughts?" Rico asked nervously, his eyes darting about the room in the hope someone would appear through the door. With only nine tables of which three had families, a baby in a high chair, face covered in ice cream, it was clear she wasn't already there.

"She was very anxious, but she was willing to speak to us. Relax, I'm sure she'll be here soon," Paul assured him.

"I hope so, I need to figure out what I'm to do to help." Rico tapped his fingers on the pale wooden table with agitation.

As he spoke a woman entered, wearing navy blue slacks, canvas slip-on shoes and an open-necked cream cotton shirt. A gold chain hung around her neck that held two gold rings. Large dark sunglasses covered most of her face, her white hair tied in a bun, still streaked with a touch of light blonde.

She noticed them both instantly and walked over with a stride of hesitation. Her right hand clenched her shoulder bag, the other dangled by her side.

An enormous diamond caught the sunlight, almost dazzled Rico as the sparks of white shot about as she walked, playing off the glass of the many paintings that covered the white walls.

Rico and Paul scraped back their chairs, stood quickly, offered hands to shake as she approached.

"Mrs Bailey, I'm so glad you could make it, can I get you a coffee, tea, something stronger?"

CHAPTER TWENTY-NINE

Lilly had to keep going. There was too much at stake to detract from the plan.

She sipped on a cool peach green tea, startled at how easily Ella managed to manipulate everyone. What happened on the yard was easily forgotten. But sleeping with Piers? Moving in with him? That was a whole different grooming kit.

How to extract him from the gold digger without creating friction or humiliating him required some thought.

A steely resolve overtook her as she finished her drink, straightened her back and took a long breath.

In her favour, Ella had no idea Lilly held the ace up her sleeve, and extracted she would be.

But for today the show must go on. It was the last day to prepare the yard, walk the course and tick every checkbox on her list before the morning.

On Thursday the yard would be full of liveries prepping horses and practicing for the dressage element on the Friday. Added to that, she needed to speak to press, brief the marshals, meet the judges.

Shit! Meet the judges! Two were due to stay with Piers.

With a groan she realised she'd have to see Piers tonight. Awkward, but she needed to know they still had accommodation. She'd take Ed up with her, if he could keep his fists to himself. Maybe he might talk sense into Ella and remove her quietly.

Walking out with a breezy smile on her face, she greeted her team who had already taken horses to pasture.

Alison and Kerry were walking back with headcollars and lead ropes slung over their shoulders as they chatted. They waved as they spotted her.

A wheelbarrow stood outside a stable door filled with flying manure and straw from Tay and Mike working inside. Rahima walked towards the tap with buckets to wash and refill. Willow was adjusting the girth for Jeremy who sat on his horse, Timmy, ready for his lesson.

She paused for a moment to survey the scene. Breathed in a deep gulp of yard life. A warm sense of feel good spread through her body and re-energised her. If only she could freeze this moment in time, she considered.

"Hey guys, got a minute for a quick recap of today?" she called out instead, a packet of hobnobs held high.

"Hell yes, if we're opening biscuits over coffee" Kerry laughed, skipping towards the team room to switch the kettle on.

"Where's the Ice Queen today, by the way?" she asked, looking over her shoulder at Lilly.

"Food poisoned in Somerset according to her message." Lilly grimaced, waiting for the comebacks.

"Overdosed on cider, more like. Is she coming back?"

"Not sure, but the good news is I'm here, ready to help, once we've had a biscuit or three. I've turbo charged my pitchfork and I'm ready to scoop poop." Lilly flexed her arms to demonstrate her muscles.

Alison was peering at Lilly through narrowed eyes. When they were headed towards the stables she leaned over.

"All good?"

Lilly gave her a small shake of the head.

"Nope, but I've got it together. If you see Ed, my advice is don't ask," she smiled at ruefully as Alison looked puzzled. "I'll tell you later."

It was good to get physical, allow her energy to focus on the straw beds. Lilly enjoyed the satisfaction that came with clearing the overnight mess.

The mucky mares, the box walkers, the bed eaters, each stable carefully cleaned and left with a symmetrical bank, level bed and a bucket of fresh water in the corner.

With a sweep of the yard for stray bedding, wisps of discarded hay and hoof shaped lumps of shaving dispersed as the horse walked out that morning she was done. Clean yard, clean horses.

She left Rahima to continue with the water bucket rounds, collecting them all for a quick brush before refill. Checked she was still good for the interview later.

It disturbed Lilly how Ella had been so nasty to the young girl. With collaboration from the family and senior figures in the Muslim community, Horse & Hound were to feature her in an article on stable life. It would focus on her job as a groom but allow inclusion of her Muslim belief and the normality of working in a Hijab.

Calls continued all morning. Lilly glad she'd bought the second set of cordless earphones. Both pairs died by the time she stopped for a lunch break and put them back on charge.

She perched at her kitchen table, crossed through jobs done, added requests from the calls and messages she'd received.

Lilly tried to call Rico again. He was due to sit with her to run through his training sessions booked all day Thursday. It went to answer. Again. When had she last seen him? Must have been Sunday afternoon. Odd.

Lilly tried Paul's number, but it too went to answer. She left a message on both phones. Are you guys ok? Can't get hold. Call me urgently please.

Before her meeting at three with the British Eventing steward and Joe, Lilly had feeds to prepare. At least whilst she was in the feed room, she could cover a few more calls. Hoped that Rico might find time in his new world of love to ring her back and reassure her he too hadn't done a moonlight flit.

As she filled scoops of hi-fi a thrill passed through her despite the daunting prospect of tonight's encounter. Months of planning about to come alive. This would be her show if she had to remove Ella by her hair herself.

Mrs Bailey was a mature version of Ella, Rico concluded. Tall and willowy. The same sapphire eyes that stared directly at him as she lifted her glasses to rest on the top of her head. Deep-set, blue eye shadow, black eyeliner and long black eyelashes.

He assumed she must be in her late fifties. An air of sophistication dampened by the sadness. A once beautiful face etched with misery in the lines that circled her mouth, the deep shadows under her made-up eyes. No amount of clever contour could disguise the wretchedness he saw.

Rico tried hard not to gawk, conscious that he studied people he met who intrigued him. What had happened to make Ella so bitter, so resentful? What drove her to wish Lilly's life a misery?

Mrs Bailey glanced at her Rolex with a sniff.

"Good, it's after five. I'll have a G&T please, slice of lime, no ice. And call me Sarah."

As Paul headed off to the bar, Rico offered her a seat.

"So, what's the little bitch done now?" she turned to him with a piercing stare.

Smash straight in. She didn't mince words. Might Ella's issues have started at home? In the eyes of her mother, she was not the beloved child.

"I believe Paul spoke to you briefly on the phone. You indicated it was no surprise to hear she was ruffling feathers?" he replied as delicately as possible.

"None whatsoever. She's been a difficult child since her father died. Full of bitterness, it all got taken from her. When we owned the stud, she wanted for nothing. After the accident, I had to move away from that world. Came here to Devon to live. In truth, I barely found the strength to get out of bed in the morning, let alone care for a child." Sarah picked out a tissue from her handbag and sniffed into it loudly. Dabbed her eyes.

"It's true then. You were the Bailey's of the Arab horse world?" he exclaimed as Paul returned, putting three glasses down.

"Thought we could all use a gin about now," he suggested.

Rico shot him a grateful look. Under the exuberance of Tigger lay a smart, perceptive person. One that melted chunks of ice around his heart faster than a blow torch.

Sarah nodded. Took a large gulp of her drink.

"Once upon a time, a long, long time ago," she remarked dryly.

He narrowed his eyes. Thought for a moment before speaking. How best to be tactful but honest.

"I'm so sorry for your loss..." he began, but she waved the tissue at him with an irritated sharpness.

"Ok, I will get to the point. My best friend runs a livery yard on a large estate owned by a rich widower. You may have heard of Wingfield Aggregates?" Rico paused. Sarah shook her head.

"I can guess the rest though. My illustrious daughter has moved in with him and you're worried she'll kick your mate out?"

Rico and Paul looked at each other, then back at the woman as she took another long drink of her gin.

Sarah stared out of the window for a moment.

"About it, in a nutshell." Rico agreed.

"Paul, you already discovered this isn't the first time, or you'd not have got the lead back to me?"

"I did. From what I learnt she's tried twice already. Uses her boyfriend to help her, then dumps him. When it went wrong, he took her back."

"She has that boy round her little finger. Dangles him like a Yoyo. Though, she can switch that sugar coating on a real treat," the woman confirmed.

"Until she snaps out of her quest for what isn't hers. Wakes up to the real world, I won't give power to her demons. As long as she rages, I keep the truth from her," she divulged.

"You've lost me," Rico replied. He looked over to Paul, full of confusion and slight agitation. He had to sort this out so he could help his best friend. Time was not on his side.

"Oh, come on boys, get with it. We didn't go poor overnight just because my husband died. There're millions sat in a trust fund with her name on it. As a Director I have control of distribution. She won't get a penny until she accepts herself. At that point she'd be able to buy her own stud farm. Live like the Princess she thinks she is. With no need to take from someone else."

Both men now sat in stunned silence.

"Does she know?" Rico finally choked out.

Sarah snorted into her glass.

"Of course not. I tried to tell her once, but she was off her head on weed. She used to smoke a lot in her teenage years, hung out with some no hoper bike gang. Stud through her nose. Hair the colour of cut grass one day, blue the next, even blood red on occasion. She'd fall into the house at all hours. Puke up over her bedsheets, then leave me to clear up her mess. Can you imagine that, with a trust fund account?" She shivered to herself.

Of course. Why had he not asked himself that very question? Where had the money gone? The stallion that killed her dad would have been worth a six-figure sum in stud fees alone.

"Can you help us, speak to her maybe?" he asked.

Sarah Bailey sat back in her chair, her long lean legs crossed, glass poised in hand as she studied him.

"I don't think my involvement will do much to help your friend. You see, the last time I saw Arabella she told me to stay the fuck out of her life. Since then, I have. I wait for the day she wakes up. Neither her dad nor I were born rich. We worked bloody hard for what we achieved. She needs to understand and value her inheritance. So no, my speaking to her won't make the slightest difference. Sorry, boys." Sarah sat with an air of defeat and acceptance.

Rico paled, crushed by the wall he'd reached.

As she said goodbye, she paused. "If you see her, tell her to call me. And to think about what happened to Amyr. That's the best I can offer," she shrugged.

The pair sat outside, once more overlooking the bay, this time Rico didn't feel the pull of the sand in his toes. More the sand in the timer.

"At least we know where it came from. We could warn Lilly?" Paul suggested.

Rico stared out at the sea, as if each crash of a wave would bring the answer he sought.

With a sigh he looked at Paul. "Just one thing left to do now, I'll make the call."

CHAPTER THIRTY

Lilly escaped from the yard at five thirty. The activity had ramped up several notches as people milled about. Some went for a hack to take the edge off their horse.

Others spent time practising their quarter marks. Many sat with tack on their knees and bridle parts all about.

The smell of saddle soap, hoof oil, mane and tail spray and shampoo filled the air. The whirr of a washing machine full of numnahs and bandages competed with the whickers of horses and the scraping of horseshoes.

All being pampered as if Hollywood stars about to walk the red carpet at the Oscars.

Already she had been half an hour longer than she'd wanted.

A question, for the thousandth time, about the cross-country. Many were doing it for the first time and the nerves had started to kick in.

It was one thing jumping a fence in the show ring, when a pole could fall from its cups. But these were solid fences. It took a bold human and a bolder horse to leap these. Mags was not feeling the boldness.

"You'll be fine, honestly. All have been safety checked this afternoon. At any time during the course, you can always pick the smaller option," Lilly offered reassurance.

Chrissie wanted general advice on taking the fences.

"Stay between the flags." Lilly responded as she edged ever closer to her house.

She was in. Quick, shut the door. A sigh of relief. As she bent to pat Ruby, her mobile vibrated in her pocket.

The screen showed it wasn't Rico or Paul. Disappointed and now a little concerned. It was not like Rico to go AWOL on her. If she hadn't received a call by the time she returned from the manor, she'd have to call the police.

Lilly dismissed the nag of concern. Dug about the kitchen table full of tabards and forms to find her laptop underneath.

Two hours later she heard a loud knock. She'd not noticed that sunlight had faded, giving way to a warm evening with a deep gold in the sky.

Ed stood at the doorway. Shoulders drooped, his hair still covered with hay, he looked older than Piers. Though at least he wore a clean top, she noted.

In silence they drove up the farm track. The car lurched over potholes; dust clouds billowed around them as she kept the pedal down.

She was distracted by an unfamiliar urge to punch someone or something. Having put it to the back of her mind, she was headed to face an uncomfortable scene. She could handle Piers. But Ella was going to have her claws drawn and sharpened.

Piers answered the door himself. Peeped out through the narrow slit as he held it ajar a few inches.

"Piers, are you on front door duty now? Where's Mrs C?" she asked casually.

"Mrs C?" he appeared flustered. "Ah yes, Mrs C had to rush off, a relative taken sick."

"Oh, how terrible for her. And such a shame, she'll miss the trials then?" Lilly replied with sadness in her voice. She doubted this to be true but reserved that thought.

"Yes, yes, well, ahem, most unexpected, but there it is." He nodded vigorously as if to verify the statement.

He peered through her to Ed, who stood close behind her. So close she could feel the rays of hatred permeating her back.

"Ted?" Piers took a sharp intake of breath. "Lilly, is it important? I'm a bit busy at the moment?"

"Well, can we come in for a start?" she asked. Stepped up further, pushed the door a little wider.

"Um, well, I'm about to have dinner," he stalled. Tried to close the gap again.

From behind him Lilly glanced a mane of platinum. A long fingered bony hand moved Piers away. Ella appeared in the crack to smile sweetly at Lilly.

"Lilly, Ed. Lovely of you both to drop by and all that, but do fuck off." Her tone was ice cold. Menace fired up in her eyes as she glowered at them.

About to close the door, Ed stepped forward and placed a foot in the doorway. His face inches from hers, his left hand moved swiftly upwards. Lilly gasped involuntarily. Would he hit her?

"I don't think so, babe," he hissed between clenched teeth. He used the palm of his hand to hold open the door. With a strong shove, he forced her to step backwards.

He marched in with Lilly close behind. Ella quickly moved to stand next to Piers, slightly behind. She looked at Lilly with a steady, lofty gaze of one who felt born to privilege and entitlement. Lilly stared back, tried to figure out what was going on inside that crazy head.

Piers stood defensively, chest puffed out, a stern expression on his face. His hand clasped Ella's firmly.

"What is it you have to say? Say it and be on your way," he boomed with a confidence that came from a lifetime of being in charge. Irritation flared at the unwanted intrusion into his home.

Ed held his nerve. With a deep inhale of breath, he stood straight. His muscular six three frame dwarfed Piers, caused the older man to sag a little. Nerves made the corners of his mouth twitch.

"She doesn't love you, she never will." Ed shouted; his finger pointed at Ella. His face contorted, overwhelmed with anger, contempt and disappointment. The words almost spat from his mouth.

Lilly put her hand on his shoulder in an attempt to calm him down. What she didn't need was a fist fight to break out. He flicked her away, stepped towards Ella.

"If I'd known you were going to screw the old man, I'd never have done what you asked of me."

Ella shrank behind Piers, as if hit by the force of the anguish.

Ed's fury turned to Piers as he continued to point.

"Has she told you? She's plotted and schemed since the day she met Lilly in the pub. No matter how much I asked her to stop. Soon, she'll spit you out like the rest of us, once she's sucked you dry," he wailed as his emotions ran unchecked.

Ella remained composed, whispered into Piers' ear.

"Poppycock!" he snorted. "Listen here, both of you, I have nothing further to say on the matter. Plots and plans, what utter nonsense."

He looked at Lilly, agitated by the disturbance. His hand swept through the scraps of hair several times.

"Lilly, you surprise me. Jealousy is so unbecoming. I guess your ambition took over your previous good nature. Just as soon as this weekend is done and dusted, changes are on the way. I want nothing to stand between Ella and I being happy together on my estate as long as I have breath."

Lilly gasped out loud. Before she had time to respond, shadows cast over the group from the doorway.

"I think you're overlooking something rather important, father." A deep, husky voice announced from the steps.

CHAPTER THIRTY-ONE

"Julian?" Piers looked over as his son appeared. Surprised, but with a smile of relief flooding his nervous face. A renewed flush on his cheeks.

"Rico? Paul? Jojo?" Lilly looked as the others appeared behind. Now she was confused. Though she could tick off the lost property call to the police.

"Well, we have a right old party going on," Ed said with bitter sarcasm. "Excuse me for not bringing the cucumber sandwiches and cheesy puffs."

Ignoring Ed, Julian walked in past the others. His arm went around his father's shoulder as he spoke quietly.

"Father, we should move to the lounge, get more comfortable than stood in the hall. I hear there's been a few issues I wasn't informed about until last night. We need to chat through, then I have important news of my own. News that's overdue." Julian scanned the small crowd gathered, winked at Lilly. With a wave of his left hand for them all to follow, he led his father through.

"Rico, what's going on? I've been trying to get hold of you all day." Lilly hissed as they filed in.

He touched his nose with a secretive smile.

"I was on a secret mission," he assured her with a pat on her back.

Piers puffed himself up with increased confidence now that his son and goddaughter were in the room. He sat next to Jojo, a smile played on his lips as he anticipated the shift back to his corner.

"Right, father. Let's begin, shall we?" his son asked, as he walked across and opened the windows to the patio. Came back to stand with his back to the fireplace, in charge of the room.

With expectation on his face, Piers regarded his son. His happiness twisted as he saw the anger ablaze in his eyes. The same colour and shape as his mother's. Twisted around to find Ella, to be reassured. He half stood to reach for her.

"Sit down father. Stay where you are, next to Jojo," Julian requested sharply.

Lilly was rooted in her own chair. This was definitely not what she had expected. Rico sat next to her, his grip firm about her waist as Julian took control.

"I received a call this morning from Rico," the newcomer began.

Rico refused to look at Lilly.

"It left me no option. I have had to drop an important meeting to come here." His voice started to quaver.

Rico's face was impassive. Paul and Jojo slunk in a corner keeping a low profile. She could read nothing from any of them.

"This weekend was meant to have been special. Not just an incredible horse event, but an announcement I've longed to make. A secret I've kept from you. From nearly everyone in fact. Though, father, you've trumped me with your own firework display."

Lilly legs began to shake, her head a little dizzy. Rico glanced over to Julian to get his attention, who nodded back reassuringly.

"An announcement? Good news? But then, why are you so angry with me?" Piers asked.

His son silenced him with a hand and looked over to Ella with a scowl.

"Angry? It doesn't even touch the sides in description to your recent behaviour." Julian faced Ella as if he had a bad taste in his mouth.

"You will be devastated to learn that there is no deep pot of gold for you to dip your greedy little hands in."

Ella returned his scorn with haughty impatience. Furious at the intrusion into her house. At the same time puzzled at the venom targeted at her. What was she missing?

He turned back to look at his father with a sigh.

"Father, don't you recall? You are President in title alone. An honorary position befitting one who has done so much. I own the estate, the bank accounts, the business, all of it. I have control of everything Wingfield does. The annuity you receive is agreed by the Board each year."

"I don't see why my having Ella here makes any difference to any of that?" Piers demanded. "What I do with that money is my own business. I may have signed it over to you, but it's family money, Julian. I have a right to live here. Lifetime enjoyment."

"Totally. And you living here doing your thing with the monthly allowance you receive is a pleasure to me. I hope you remain doing so for many years to come. But here's the problem. I'm engaged to marry, and will be living here too."

Piers looked at Jojo and beamed. Overcome with emotion, he jumped up, slapped his son's back and grabbed his hand to pump heartily.

"I knew it, I knew it! You've been friends for so long now. Why, you must have been all of about four or five when you first met on the polo grounds. Jojo, ma chere, I'll be delighted to have you as a daughter in law. You kept this so quiet, you naughty children." He wiggled a finger at them both. The cruel words his son had spat out moments before forgotten.

Jojo looked at Julian, then at Piers, then over to Lilly. Then she roared with laughter. Great peals of mirth, her body creased in two as she held her stomach.

"Piers, ca c'est la betise, madness. I think you have it all wrong. I could never marry your son. It be as if I marry my brother! Oh, mon dieu, I am not the one you should be congratulating."

The room went quiet other than the continued chuckle from Jojo.

Ella spoke. She'd sat imperiously on an ornately carved wooden chair tucked into the wall by the large window. It elevated her, as if sat on a throne.

"Can we get on, I'm bored already. So, Julian is getting married, but not to Jojo. Who cares? We'll play happy families, take the gatekeeper cottage, er, should I call you son? Oh, and your dad needs a pay rise. I am not prepared to live off a pittance."

They all looked across at her. Ed with hatred burning from his eyes at the betrayal. Julian, a quirky smile. He really was as hot as Kerry had said, too bad he was taken she thought momentarily.

Jojo, laughing as if all of this was fucking totes. Paul didn't seem to know where to look. Rico smug, gazing at Lilly.

Piers, those faithful puppy dog eyes goggling at her, as if she were his entire life. Well, short term at least she mused.

Ella looked hardest at Lilly. A disturbing stillness had fallen about her. Why was she so bloody pure and perfect sitting there? Maybe it hadn't clicked yet that after this weekend she'd be out on her backside.

Piers was the first to break the silence.

"Please, Julian, can you speak in plain English. I'm so mixed up; I need a drink. Ella, my darling, get me a drink, will you? Brandy, make it a large one," he begged of her.

Julian moved across the rug from the fireplace, over to where Rico now stood, exchanged places. Julian placed his arm around Lilly protectively.

The moment the pair looked at each other the penny dropped. Ella's body lurched, a sickness in her stomach as she understood.

"No, father, not Jojo. The reason I'm so angry is that you have upset Lilly. My fiancée."

CHAPTER THIRTY-TWO

The silence was broken by a choking sound coming from the ornate seat as Ella reeled.

"What on earth are you talking about, dear boy? How can you be engaged to someone you hardly know?"

"That you knew of, papa. Actually, we first met at a ball Easter before last. Lucky for me I was sat right next to her. We've been seeing each other whenever we have had the chance."

"But……" Piers shrank in stature at each disclosure, confusion on his face as he gaped around him.

"We've kept it secret at Lilly's insistence. I've been trying to shout it from the rooftops for months. But the bloody stubborn woman was set on wanting to prove she is a capable, independent businesswoman. As if I'm bothered about such things, but apparently, she is. We were going to announce it to you at the finish. Lilly didn't want people to think I'd influenced the success."

Ella's jaw was on the floor.

"No money and no influence?" She looked about the room in despair.

"Zilch money of his own. Influence? Well, he offers valuable wisdom and he can make a magnificent speech at meetings. By the way, I see that you have managed to grab one of my mother's necklaces."

Julian rose to approach Ella, his hand held out. She put a hand over the pendant protectively, glowering at him. He stood over her, one hand on his hip, the other remained palm out, his face calm but with intent.

With an indignant snort, she undid the chain at the back of her neck and threw it into the outstretched hand. Instantly it closed over, snapping shut her chance of a new life.

She stood, nervously looking about for the nearest exit.

"But you said this was for real, you loved me?" Piers stammered.

Ella looked at him, towards Lilly, then at Ed. What a fucking hash up. Months of planning fucked up in an instant. The rich old man was just an old man. Without money or estate of his own, worthless. Lilly had secretly bagged the number one. Unbelievable. Fucking unbelievable. Now what was she to do?

She looked back at Piers, who stared at her adoringly. She cringed at the sight of him, his old face suddenly appearing so wrinkled and wizened. Ella slowly shook her head.

Piers looked back round. His gaze landed on Lilly.

"My son is right; it looks like I've been taken for a fool." He bowed his head and sighed; his whole body shrank into the corner of his Chesterfield.

Julian turned to Lilly.

"Get the pair of them out of here for me, love. I'll take him into the kitchen and make a cup of tea. Once they're gone, come through, we'll sort it out. Hey, it'll be all right." He tried to reassure both his father and his fiancé with a quick flash of a smile.

Lilly beckoned Ed and Ella to the hall, opened the door wide.

"He was your London trip, wasn't he?" Ella asked.

Lilly nodded.

Ed took the crestfallen Ella out. She had automatically accepted his hand, walking in a daze. Ed tried to smile at Lilly.

"I can see it in your eyes, you're going to take her back. Forgive everything she's put you through. You do know she'll be your downfall?" she told him sadly.

He shrugged his shoulders at her.

"She's all I've ever wanted. She'll need me, now it's fallen through. I'm all she has left," he sighed.

As they walked down the steps towards Ed's car, she overheard Ella's words.

"Ed, this was not what it looked like, I've only ever loved you…."

About to close the door, Rico passed Lilly at haste, strode to the car.

"You nearly destroyed my best friend, who is worth a thousand of you. So you know, I met your mum, who told me everything. She sent you a message, can't say I remember what it was though," he hissed through the window.

"Mum?" Ella gawped, still numb with shock at the last half hour.

"Go figure. You bothered me from the get go. Turns out you're quite the bitch. I am sorry about your dad, but it's no excuse. Get off your high horse and go see her."

With that, he marched back into the house.

Closing the door, he found the kitchen where the others now sat around the large oak table laden with mugs of tea and plates of biscuits.

"Where is Mrs C and how can we get her back? We need to give her the good news before anyone else finds out." Julian asked his father, who was taking a sip from his cup, looking forlorn and bedraggled.

"I sent her away. She didn't really want to go. I'm so sorry, I've caused an awful lot of bother," he groaned.

Lilly took a deep breath. She was shocked but not surprised.

"I should have let Julian tell you a long time ago. It's me that's been selfish. If Julian is in agreement, I'd like to forgive and forget. Though we must get Mrs C back to have a party. What do you think?"

Julian looked at his dad, who nervously watched his son's face for a sign. Julian allowed his face to soften, a hint of a smile, as his face glowed.

"You see, father? This is why I love Lilly so much. Now, get that tea down you. Then go and get changed. We're off out for dinner. The whole bloody lot of us. You, me, my sister, my fiancée and the two guys who saved the show."

CHAPTER THIRTY-THREE

The event was a huge success. Over one hundred competitors entered, many arrived on the Thursday to set up their lorries and settle their horses into the temporary stabling.

During the three days a ground breaking seventeen thousand visitors walked through the gates. A shopping village was filled with shops, food stalls, drinks and exhibitors, a stand for a variety of bands to entertain people and a tented area for the rare breeds to be displayed.

Saturday's cross-country delighted watchers with a few 'early baths' in the lake, crowds gasping as the horses flew over the final fence as if they too had wings.

Paul split his time between taking Viking through his paces and sending copy. Every local paper in the area, the big equestrian magazines, all bought articles and images to use.

Even Paris Matin, the French paper where Jojo's family lived rushed into print her win in the amateur over eighteen class.

Rowena revelled in the number of photos she managed to find herself in. Whether she be presenting prizes, or just posing for the camera in her new autumn Dior look. She joked she might even have to build an extension to the house to have a room to hang them in. A snug would be perfect.

On the Monday she had pulled Lilly aside to confide excitedly that she had met a man at the rare breed exhibits. He was so charming, even invited her to dinner. In her excitement she'd forgotten his name, Jed or Jake. But he owned a golf club and had the most dazzling smile. Lilly had nearly burst out laughing.

"You laughing at me for being so ditzy I can't remember? I got so flustered I must admit," Rowena admitted.

"I'm laughing that my biggest sponsor has gone under your radar but managed to get a date from you anyway," Lilly smiled.

On reflection, Jed Owen would be a good match. Both will be rushing out for a new outfit but it was good to know someone had seen through the façade.

With Sam's persistence Bob made it to the event sober. He declared himself a changed man. His confession to Lilly being that at one point he'd have sucked the alcohol from his deodorant stick if he'd found himself out of booze.

Although, the news of Lilly's betrothal was the biggest topic of conversation.

"Julian!" Kerry had said, shaking her head. "How many times must I have said how hot he was, and there were you, knowing just how."

'Scorchio', Lilly winked.

Mrs C came back as soon as Julian called her. No one was happier than she at the news. She clucked over Lilly at the breakfast table like a mother hen.

"Oh, if only Janette could have met you," she must have told Lilly a dozen times. She even insisted she take Lilly to visit the grave to announce the news to the headstone. A bit weird. Lilly had suggested she would go in a couple of weeks.

After everyone had departed, Julian remained to talk to his father. Lilly and Julian would live with him in the manor. Both understood how easily he had been manipulated; both had underestimated his loneliness.

Lilly announced she would oversee the yard, but gave the Yard Manager job to Alison along with the little house she'd called home for 2 years.

Ruby enjoyed the run of her new home and the occasional scraps she persuaded Mrs C to part with in the kitchen. The puppy dog eyes worked every time, followed by a roll on her back for a tickle.

As Rico sat watching the TV one evening, Paul passed him a glass of wine and sat on the sofa next to him having cleared their dinner plates away. He studied him intently, to the point Rico hit pause on the remote, turned and reached out to touch his partner's face, stroking his lip with his finger.

"What? You have that look you want to question me?" he asked.

Paul kissed the finger, taking his hand and placing it between his own.

"You need to open that letter," he said gently.

Rico froze. He knew which one Paul meant, the official one A4 one from a solicitor. He hated official stuff. It had sat unopened on the side since it arrived at the start of September.

"Rico. It'll be important."

With a sigh he pulled his hand away and stood, walking away then returning seconds later with it. Taking a deep breath, he broke the seal.

ACKNOWLEDGEMENTS

First thanks must be to my husband and children, for their love and support.

Carole and Sue, for being my reviewers, Delphine for her professional guidance and Ken for the cover design that completes the package.

Most of all thanks to you, for buying and reading my work.

Enjoy, please leave me a review and come back soon – there's more to come!

AUTHOR BIO

Annie has wanted to write a book since she could hold a crayon, but something else always got there first. Job, husband, children, animals (especially horses, they take up your entire spare time - and money!).

She finally completed her first book when the kids were old enough to muck out horses by themselves. Teenager en Provence is a relocation memoir of her family's journey to the South of France when she was still at school.

Now living in Hampshire, Annie continues to write, paint and groom her children's horses.

You can find Annie on facebook, instagram and at AnnieLeVoguer.com for updates.

WINGFIELD EQUESTRIAN SERIES

Book 2 to be released in 2021

Rico's life is thrown into chaos when he receives unexpected news.

As the full implication of the lifestyle change hits home, he is torn between his natural tendency to destroy relationships and the deepening love he has for someone special.
Will his wild spirit take hold or will he realise actions have consequences in time to create happiness and hope?

One thing's for sure, none of this can happen without a horse. Or several.